IN
ANY
LIFETIME

OTHER TITLES BY MARC GUGGENHEIM

Overwatch

Arrow: Fatal Legacies

IN ANY LIFETIME

A
NOVEL

MARC GUGGENHEIM

LAKE UNION
PUBLISHING

Text copyright © 2024 by LegalScribe Entertainment, Inc.
All rights reserved.

Published by Lake Union Publishing, Seattle

www.apub.com

Amazon, the Amazon logo, and Lake Union Publishing are trademarks of Amazon.com, Inc., or its affiliates.

ISBN-13: 9781662518034 (paperback)
ISBN-13: 9781662518027 (digital)

Cover design by Adrienne Krogh
Cover image: © Tony Watson / Arcangel; © Mike Ver Sprill, © Songquan Deng / Shutterstock

Printed in the United States of America

For Lily and Sara.
I love you too much.

In a universe of infinite possibilities, the only constant is love.
—Henri Thibault, PhD

TWO YEARS AGO

In the quiet moments since his world was shattered, Jonas Cullen would reflect that fate had a sense of humor, which wasn't exactly a quality he associated with a supernatural power—nor, for that matter, was an appreciation of irony. But both were applicable in ways that alternated between comedic and tragic. In the midnight hours, when sleep refused to come, he'd think back on that night, which started off as the best of his life—filled with milestones he had aspired to only in dreams—yet ended as the worst, the stuff of nightmares.

He had stood backstage at Aula Magna, the largest auditorium at Sweden's Stockholm University, cracking his knuckles against his rising anxiety. His wife, Amanda, had never managed to cure him of the fixation, but he found the habit oddly calming, the bones of his hands giving way with a series of satisfying pops, like kernels of corn or plastic packaging bubbles, as he imagined his stress evaporating into the air.

The Aula Magna was built deep into the ground, which served to hide its massive size. Outside, visible beyond its glass facade, old oaks rose from the ground like giants, their limbs burdened with tufts of snow. The night sky was black silk festooned with diamonds.

The building had been designed by Ralph Erskine, a British architect who had lived in Sweden for most of his life. The Aula Magna wasn't the first project that Erskine had undertaken for Stockholm University, but it was the last one completed before his death. Jonas felt that that piece of trivia lent the building an air of pathos. So appropriate, he thought, that a great man's final achievement should serve as the site to mark the achievements of other men and women.

The speech that Jonas had labored over to acknowledge his own accomplishment pressed against him: four single-spaced pages, triple folded to fit inside the pocket of his tuxedo jacket. He told himself he didn't need them. He could almost recite the entire thing from memory. His subject was a topic to which he had devoted the previous three years of his life. To expound on it, he reassured himself, was like describing walking or breathing or seeing. And yet his heart punched at the confines of his chest, and his hands felt clammy, and his stomach cursed the glass of champagne he had been convinced to drink at the party held in his honor less than three hours earlier.

For the umpteenth time, Jonas reminded himself that he was comfortable speaking in public. The life of a college professor required at least one lecture a day. But this was no ordinary lecture, and those in attendance weren't his students. This was the most important speech he would ever give in his life.

Consequently, his tuxedo felt three sizes too small, as confining as a straitjacket. The starched collar grated against his throat. His tie felt like a noose. Even the patent leather shoes were punishing him for anxiously shifting his weight from one foot to the other and back again. Jonas found himself running out of ways to calm his nerves and wished for another glass of champagne—or two—despite the protestations of his gut.

He cracked his knuckles again, working one hand with the other, kneading it like dough.

"Stop that. You'll give yourself arthritis."

He turned to see Amanda approaching. She looked resplendent in her evening gown, the creation of some designer Jonas couldn't name even upon pain of death. His wife had no interest in high fashion, but they had both been amused by the offer of free couture. The gown—which was truly a work of art—could be mistaken for the reason she appeared so radiant tonight, but Jonas knew better. There was something different about her that would have come across even if she'd been wearing a baggy sweat suit. She had a glow that was independent of her wardrobe. At thirty-four, Amanda Cullen could hardly be considered old, but this evening she seemed as though—while Jonas had been swilling champagne—she had sipped from the fountain of youth. Her eyes had a sparkle about them. She seemed brightened. Renewed.

"That's a myth," Jonas rebutted, not for the first time. "No *science* to it at all."

Amanda beamed. They were both riding the night's special high. "I'm going to be right out there. Front row, center. If you get nervous . . ."

"Oh, I'm already there," Jonas said.

"*If* you get nervous," she reiterated, "just focus on me. Talk to me. You've never had a problem doing that before."

"No, I haven't," Jonas said. The love he felt for her was almost overwhelming. He felt himself bathing in it, soaking it in. He wanted to take her in his arms, to find words to capture the feelings that swelled his heart. He had just started to tell her how much he loved her when a bumptious official intruded.

The man, white and in his sixties, with a tuxedo of his own and salt-and-pepper hair in full retreat, spoke with a thick Swiss accent, his fingers tightly interlaced in front of him. "We're just about ready to start, Dr. Cullen. How are you feeling?"

"Probably best not to ask," Jonas deadpanned. He felt a wave of nausea well up inside him.

"He's going to do great," Amanda reassured him, her hand gently caressing his back.

Jonas remained unconvinced.

The official excused himself with servile politeness, and Jonas wondered how it was that his life had taken such a surreal turn. His only ambition had been to ask questions of the universe, to probe the contours of existence. Every child pondered why the sky was blue, or what created the universe, or how animals got their names. Jonas was simply one of the small subset of such children who ultimately made those questions their calling. And the questions were themselves the answer, the reason for *his* existence. They had nothing to do with awards or accolades or spectacle. Jonas didn't ask these questions so he could lecture to an audience of almost two thousand people. He asked these questions and sought the answers because he had no choice. Receiving an award for it was like being honored for learning how to walk or tie his shoes.

He felt Amanda's eyes on him, watching him the same way he occasionally caught himself watching her, trying to breathe her whole being into him, to consume her soul through his gaze, an expression of astonished bewilderment that asked how he could ever be so lucky to share his life with this other person.

"How are *you* feeling?" he asked, though he could not remember seeing her more content. Trying to identify what was different about her tonight was like trying to catch smoke.

"I feel like tonight is a very special night," Amanda answered, pulling a small box from her purse. It was white and tied with a red ribbon. She handed it to him.

Jonas turned the box over in his fingers. "What's this?"

Amanda leaned over and stared at the box in mock fascination. "Hmm. It appears to be a gift of some kind."

Jonas chuckled. He hated the cliché that scientists lacked certain human graces, but he had to admit that some clichés rang true. He stripped the ribbon off the box and opened it. Inside was a thin stick. Two pieces of plastic glued together. One blue, one white. A faded cobalt cross peeked out from the tiny window cut into the blue side.

He felt his breath leave him as his mind raced to catch up. The plastic rod felt firm between his fingers. He wasn't dreaming. *This was real.* He stared at his wife in gobsmacked disbelief. He struggled for words. His heart raced and swelled in his chest. He looked down again at the pale-blue intersection of lines and felt his whole world change. "I—I—" Words refused to come. "The doctors said," he croaked, "that you—" He breathed hard. He didn't know whether to laugh or cry or scream. He was overwhelmed with the desire to do all three with no regard for who might take notice.

"I know," Amanda said. Her eyes gleamed, or maybe it was just the light hitting the thin film of tears welling in them.

Either way, Jonas had never known his wife to be so radiant or happy. "I—I didn't even know this was possible," he said, staring in disbelief and awe at the tiny pregnancy test. "How?"

"And here I thought you were a scientist," Amanda teased with a puckish grin.

Jonas marveled at the little device in his hand. "Even a scientist can recognize a miracle." *She had gifted him a miracle.*

"This wasn't easy, you know."

Jonas did. They had tried for years without success.

But Amanda shook her head slightly. That wasn't the difficulty she was referring to. "You have no idea how hard it is to compete with a Nobel Prize."

"I think you found a way," he said, still cradling the little plastic stick in his fingers.

The official pulled Jonas aside. "They're about to announce you, Dr. Cullen." But Jonas's eyes didn't leave the tiny stick. It looked like a piece of a toy. How could he possibly turn away from such a wonder?

Behind the curtain, another Nobel official was addressing the crowd. Her voice was amplified by the Aula Magna's natural acoustics. "Good evening," she boomed. "Thank you all for coming. As you know, the Nobel Foundation statutes require laureates to deliver a lecture on a subject connected with the work for which their prize was awarded . . ." She reeled off Jonas's academic qualifications and professional achievements, but Jonas wasn't listening. He felt a surreal sensation, a reminder that he was living out a dream. "Tonight, it is my privilege to introduce this year's recipient of the Nobel Prize in Physics for his mathematical theorem confirming the existence of parallel universes—otherwise known as the 'Many Worlds Proof'—Dr. Jonas Cullen."

The amphitheater thundered with applause. Jonas's anxiety returned in a rush. Amanda must have noticed because she reassured him: "You're going to be fantastic."

"I love you too much," he told her.

"I love you more," she replied.

"Dr. Cullen," the official continued, "will go into detail about the work that has garnered him this honor, and I'm eager for him to astonish you, as he has astonished the world. But the not-so-simple principle underlying his work is this: our universe is just one among countless others."

"Ten bucks says she mentions Frost." Amanda winked.

"The American poet Robert Frost—"

"Told you." Amanda grinned.

"—famously wrote: 'Two roads diverged in a yellow wood, and sorry I could not travel both and be one traveler . . .' There are those who contend that this poem is an allusion to multiple realities, the universe diverging into multiple paths. Dr. Cullen has used quantum theory to prove the existence of such a 'multiverse.' And that is why he is this year's recipient of the Nobel Prize in Physics."

The ensuing applause trembled the building. Jonas squeezed the pregnancy test in his hand and considered it the true honor of the evening.

"I'm going to go take my seat," Amanda said, leaving him with a kiss that he considered all too brief under the circumstances.

He forced himself to take a deep breath. And then another. The audience continued to applaud as they waited for him to take the stage. He pushed aside the curtain, strode out, and was momentarily blinded by the spotlight, which enveloped the audience beyond the first row in darkness. The Nobel official who had introduced him clasped his hand and gave him a peck on the cheek. When he took his place at the podium, he found a second copy of his speech dutifully waiting for him.

Jonas squinted against the brightness and peered out toward the front row, where Amanda was sitting in the center seat, as promised.

Her smile was bright enough to compete with the spotlight. Pride radiated off her. Jonas felt the pregnancy test in his grip and experienced the little jolt that came from two people with a secret. They shared a knowing look. An instant of private rapture. The happiest moment of their lives.

Neither had any idea this would be her last night on earth.

NOW

Every night he has the same dream, and each time it sounds like a symphony. The squeal of three tires trying in vain to find purchase on slick asphalt emits a wail evocative of brass horns. The limousine's metallic hide scraping along the guardrail of Stockholm's Centralbron overpass makes for a perverse violin. Each *ka-thunk, ka-thunk, ka-thunk* of the punctured tire—as regular as a heartbeat—is a powerful strike against a timpani's head. The chorus of honking cars as the limo leaps from the overpass rivals any horn section. All these instruments conspire in unison to craft a stomach-churning composition.

But there's nothing musical about what always comes after. The impact of the plummeting limousine sounds like nothing less than the end of the world.

It jolts him awake, as it does every night, and spares him the sight of Amanda, dangling upside down, hanging like a slaughtered fawn, her limp form straining against the nylon seat belt, her mouth agape, crimson blood leaking from one corner. Amanda's face is etched with confusion, as though astonished by what's happened. Astounded but lacking the spark of life.

His eyes snap open before he has to face the terrible image. This is how he awakes every morning, his sheets cast aside in fitful, restless slumber, soaked through with sweat. Every morning. For two years.

This particular morning, he awakes in a room in NH Genève Aéroport, an unassuming hotel just a five-minute drive from Geneva

Airport. The overhead wail of the airplanes taking off and landing competes with the bleat of his iPhone's alarm, set for 5:00 a.m. Dawn's first light spits through the open blinds of the modest room, illuminating his solitude.

He staggers to the bathroom and catches himself in the mirror. He doesn't recognize the man he sees as Jonas Cullen, PhD and Nobel laureate. Gone is any patina of youthfulness. Instead of a man in his late thirties, a fortysomething stranger stares back at him. Unshaven. Unkempt. Eyes that once held the spark of brilliance now bloodshot and weary.

Without bothering to flush or wash his hands, Jonas pads out to the chair where he laid out his clothing the night before. A simple shirt. A pair of slacks. A sweater. All custom made. All woven from cotton and other natural fibers. Even the soles of his leather shoes are made from caucho, a natural rubber. Each article of clothing—save for his socks and underwear—is dyed black. Nothing is artificial. Not a stitch is manufactured. This is important.

Once dressed, he moves over to the room's small desk. Atop it is an aluminum briefcase with a combination lock. Jonas wheels the dials to Amanda's birthday, pops it open, and lifts the briefcase's lid to reveal a cluster of circuitry. He constructed the device only after arriving in Switzerland, assembling it from parts purchased from electronics and hobby stores. It would have been impossible to smuggle the technology through airport security. Its appearance is indistinguishable from that of a bomb. It would take three doctorates to divine its true purpose.

In the center of the technical mélange is a Raspberry Pi, a credit card–size computer. Jonas snakes a USB cable from it and plugs the other end into the HDMI port on the hotel room's flat-screen, converting it into a makeshift monitor. A keyboard connects via Bluetooth, and Jonas goes to work, encoding a final set of calculations, which he confirms against the formulae inscribed on his inner left arm.

The tattoo is less than a month old. Its edges still betray a hint of inflammation, angry red skin, a wound not yet fully healed. The formulae are complex equations that cascade down the length of his forearm. Letters. Numbers. Greek symbols. Parentheses and braces. All with a timeless beauty and flow, like text on an ancient sandstone tablet.

The tattoo artist laughed when Jonas showed her what he wanted. She had thought it was a joke, some elaborate prank on the part of her employer or perhaps a coworker. A bit of whimsy to liven up the day. But Jonas had assured her that he was serious, that he needed the work completed in a single painful session, and that it needed to be precise.

He hopes the tattoo won't be necessary. If he's successful, he'll have no further need of it. But there are still millions of ways that things could go wrong. *No, that's not right,* he corrects himself. There are an *infinite* number of ways.

The television flashes green, indicating that the encoding is complete. Jonas reaches inside the briefcase, into the menagerie of circuit boards and microchips, and finds the ring of tungsten at its center. It is featureless but for a small groove where it forms an electrical connection with the rest of his invention. Removing it, he considers the small object, a simple band of dull gray metal. Beneath a layer of aluminum so thin as to be translucent, a small white light throbs like a vein.

Jonas slips the ring on the finger where he used to wear his wedding band. It radiates a subtle warmth, generated by a tiny lithium battery inside, against his skin.

A photograph hangs taped inside the briefcase's lid. Amanda. Radiant, standing in Manhattan's Central Park. A day that can only be described as perfect. She holds a Frisbee, fluorescent-pink plastic suffused with sunlight. A diamond engagement ring is taped to the underside, its sparkle outshone only by the sparkle in her eyes. Her smile is luminous, all teeth and naked exuberance.

This is his favorite photo of her. He knows each detail like he knows his own name. The second piercing in her left ear, devoid of a stud. The faint stain of yellow on her T-shirt from the hot dog they'd shared earlier that day. The hint of a dimple in her right cheek. The collie prancing in the background, its playful form slightly out of focus. He could draw the entire image from memory but still drinks the picture in, knowing that this is the last time he'll ever see it.

A knocking at the door—three precise raps—returns him to the present. He glances at his iPhone: 5:45 a.m. Right on the tick.

Jonas opens the door to find Macon standing outside, all six feet, three inches of him. He wears a dark gray commando sweater, black jeans, and black leather boots. No jewelry to break up the utilitarian ensemble. He has a face like leather, wrinkled and hardened by too much time in the hottest places around the globe. Tiny strands of gray fleck a goatee groomed with military precision. His eyes remind Jonas of two black holes, drawing in everything and emitting nothing. Eyes that have seen the worst the world has to offer.

"It's go time," Macon says with as much emotion as one might use to report the weather. Jonas just nods. He moves to leave, but with the barest hint of effort, Macon blocks his path. "No pay, no play."

Jonas stops short. He completely forgot. Retreating into the room and moving toward the closet, he realizes that he's more scared than he'd let himself admit. What he's about to attempt could very well result in his arrest, injury, or death.

On the floor of the closet is a navy blue gym bag. Jonas lifts it, feeling its heft. He turns around, surprised that Macon is standing right behind him. Pushing that breach of etiquette aside, Jonas hands him the bag.

Macon unzips it, and Jonas watches him mentally tally the stacks of euros bound with currency straps. "A lotta money." Then, a hint of suspicion. An incredulity honed by a lifetime of dealing with the less scrupulous members of humanity. "Didn't think you academic types pulled down much bank," he says. He makes "academic types" sound like a curse.

"My wife had a life insurance policy."

This answer evidently satisfies Macon, because he produces a Glock 19 from beneath his jacket, expertly trombones the action, and holds it out to Jonas.

"I specified no fatalities, Mr. Macon." Jonas had been firm on this point, but now the words come across as slightly ridiculous, as if Jonas were as accustomed to hiring mercenaries as he is ordering a pizza.

"Well, Doc," Macon patiently explains, "there's what we plan for, and there's what actually happens."

Jonas thinks on that for a second. He takes the gun.

The Glock digs uncomfortably into the small of Jonas's back where he has secreted it as instructed. Although he hopes he won't have to use it, he now knows how, after two weeks of intensive instruction by Macon and his team. For fourteen days, they drilled and rehearsed and trained. For fourteen days, Jonas pretended he was someone else to learn what he needed to do. Like quantum physics, the field to which he'd devoted his life, the training had its own rules and, within that structure, a kind of beauty. Jonas has always been good at following instructions, taking comfort in the bright lines drawn between "do" and "don't." Between "correct" and "incorrect." But the line he's straddling now—between "right" and "wrong"—is blurred and indistinct, a suggestion more than a rule.

He strides with Macon across the tarmac at Aéroport de Genève. Spinning up ahead of them, its shape backlit by the morning sun, is a Eurocopter AS365 Dauphin. Although its carbon fiber rotor blades are revolving a good four feet above his head, Macon gestures for Jonas to duck as they climb aboard.

Three men wait inside. They wear bulletproof vests and balaclavas, each man professionally inspecting semiautomatic rifles that Jonas can't identify. The sounds produced by their ministrations—the snapping in of bullets, the slamming home of cartridges, the racking and reracking of actions—fills the cabin with a percussive staccato that reminds Jonas of an orchestra tuning up.

"Somebody hook the doc up with his Kevlar," Macon grunts.

In short order, a heavy bulletproof vest is thrown Jonas's way. For an instant, he debates whether to put it on. He'll only have to remove it later, and that could end up costing him precious seconds. On the other hand, he doesn't know what kind of resistance they'll encounter. *There's what we plan for,* Macon had observed, *and there's what actually happens.*

Jonas tries to put on the vest but struggles with its complex system of folding plates and Velcro fasteners. The other men smirk and titter, finding humor in Jonas's inexpertness.

"Help you out?" Macon asks, more impatient than amused. Without waiting for an answer, he manhandles Jonas, spinning him around and slapping the Kevlar into place.

One of the mercenaries throws Macon a wary glance. "Hope you got us paid first." The other men laugh. Macon just points Jonas toward his seat and dons a Kevlar vest of his own.

As Jonas straps himself in, he feels the mercenaries studying him. Assessing. Judging. Considering whether his inexperience will get one or more of them killed today.

The fuselage vibrates as the rotors begin to pick up speed, and the helicopter lurches upward. As it climbs, Jonas cracks his knuckles. He feels a coldness form in his chest as his heart begins to gallop. He considers the ring on his hand. Sunlight streams in from the helicopter's windows, glancing off its matte silver finish. Its white light pulses, as reliable as a promise. *Everything will be all right. Everything will work out.*

He takes a deep breath. But it will take more than that to calm him. The Control Centre building is five minutes away.

The Dauphin's rotor wash sways the stalks of corn growing on the fringes of the Conseil European Pour La Recherche Nucléaire laboratory, more commonly referred to as CERN. The facility has two entrances, one on the Swiss side of the border and its twin to the northwest, on the

French side. The helicopter is making for France, where the Centre de Contrôle du CERN—CERN's Control Centre building—sits amid a two-square-mile cluster of low-slung buildings, each as unremarkable as the next. From the sky, one of the most advanced and sophisticated scientific complexes in the world resembles an office park.

Although the security is nowhere near commensurate with a place that houses the globe's largest science experiment, the gate at Route Dirac is formidable enough that Macon had recommended the helicopter. Why figure out a way around the guard and gate when they can merely go *over* both? The plan also has the added virtue of circumventing border patrol.

A snowcapped mountain range looms in the distance as the helicopter descends. Jonas watches the mercenaries, their eyes—visible through the holes of their ebony balaclavas—filled with steel and resolve. Jonas dons a balaclava of his own. In failure, it will be best if his face isn't caught on any security cameras. Then he pulls on the padded black gloves he'll need for the elevator shaft later.

"Just like we drilled, all right?" Macon says. "Move fast. Stay sharp. Keep up." *Henry V*'s Saint Crispin's Day speech it's not. Jonas just bobs his head.

The helicopter touches down outside the Control Centre. Within seconds of its skids hitting the asphalt, they're spilling out, just as they drilled. The helicopter remains behind, its rotors still spinning, to spirit Macon and his men away before the Police Nationale can arrive.

If all goes according to plan, Jonas won't be leaving with them.

One of the mercenaries carries a small battering ram, the kind favored by SWAT units and their equivalents all around the world, but it proves unnecessary as the building's double doors are unlocked. The ram is quickly discarded—dead weight that will only slow them down—as the men lead Jonas inside.

The lobby could be mistaken for a doctor's or dentist's. Linoleum flooring. Wood appliqué everywhere. To the right is a unisex restroom. Next to the door hangs a poster of the Compact Muon Solenoid, known

15

as the CMS. The receptionist's desk stands unmanned, the building empty. Dawn is barely an hour old.

Expecting no resistance but prepared for any, the mercenaries push left, a pair of sliding glass doors parting to allow them access. Jonas follows them into the control room, a huge space with blue-gray flooring. Twelve flat-screens hang around the circumference of the room. Beneath them are filing cabinets topped with empty champagne bottles, each one representing some team achievement. No one is working at this early hour. Jonas inwardly sighs in relief.

The room's computers are arrayed on four "islands" throughout the space, each curved like a magnet. Jonas moves to the one labeled "LHC," the Large Hadron Collider. The largest and most powerful particle collider in the world. His fingers dance across the keyboard like a concert pianist's. The monitor directly overhead comes to life. Colorful data and computer graphics spill across the flat-screens, confirming that Jonas has successfully brought the LHC online.

Satisfied, he moves to a huge metal box nestled between a passel of computer screens. It looks like a prop from a 1960s science fiction movie, a beige box covered with rows of yellow and red and green buttons. Keys dangle from a series of locks. Jonas turns one and is rewarded with a blinking green light. He's just opened up access to the collider itself. He turns to Macon and gives a thumbs-up.

Macon turns to his men. "Next phase."

Jonas leads Macon and the mercenaries out to a small hallway that terminates at a set of elevator doors. Macon wedges them open, revealing a column of thick cables. One mercenary keeps watch while another—Perez, Jonas thinks his name is—disappears inside the dark elevator shaft.

Macon gestures to Jonas. *You're up.*

Jonas approaches the elevator's maw. Of all the steps in the plan, this one frightens him most, but he sees no alternative. The LHC is twenty-seven stories down, and a proper elevator ride would cost minutes that Jonas doesn't have. He takes hold of one of the cables with both of his padded gloves and steps into the shaft.

Gravity throws him down. Jonas tightens his grip on the cable. The gloves, coated in nylon and Teflon, do their work, slowing his descent enough so that he's like a firefighter going down a pole. The cables shimmy, making a deep, echoing twang. The sound of Macon and the other mercenaries' descents echo from above. Jonas turns and sees that Perez has already opened the elevator doors. They are now over 260 feet underground. The height of a small building. As Jonas steps out of the elevator shaft, he's greeted with the persistent hum of the three hundred industrial fans that work around the clock to keep billions of dollars' worth of technology cool enough to operate.

Macon lands. "Let's move." He's already stepping past Jonas and Perez, deeper into the facility. Jonas has been here three times before and knows the layout best, but Macon has spent weeks studying blueprints and schematics. By this point, he may know this part of the LHC better than the dozens of scientists and support staff who work at the facility.

As a group, they plunge farther into the subterranean space. Computing equipment in blue casings lines the walls of the corridor. It took CERN seven years to tunnel out nearly fifty-five million gallons of soil and rock, and the engineers dug so deep into the earth that they wound up excavating an ancient Roman villa.

"Watch your step," Jonas warns.

The narrow corridor is a warren of jutting conduits and low-hanging piping, and it takes the men a minute to make it into the LHC tunnel, the seventeen-mile subterranean loop that straddles the French-Swiss border. Jonas takes the lead, moving fast. He's close. After two years, he's so close. The mercenaries keep pace with his urgency. Jonas knows that Macon is mentally calculating how long their luck will hold out. Whether a worker or, worse, a security guard will arrive for duty early. Whether they've tripped some hidden alarm. Whether something transpires that their thorough planning doesn't account for.

The Compact Muon Solenoid is anything but compact. Rather, it's the size of a four-story apartment building. Its endcap alone is fifty feet wide, conjuring the giant eye of a massive robot. It holds seventy-six thousand lead-tungstate crystals, but the most important component—the reason Jonas is here—is the large circular ring that constitutes the world's most powerful superconducting solenoid magnet.

Ladders and stairways abound. At the top of one flight is a set of controls of such complexity that they look like they could operate a fleet of Space Shuttles. Jonas has barely gripped the stairway railing when the metal in front of him sparks. The sound of multiple gunshots echo from below in the cavernous space.

He's out of luck. And time.

"Move your ass, Doc," Macon barks as he and his men exchange gunfire with an enemy Jonas can't see.

Jonas throws himself up the stairs, two at a time, shedding his Kevlar vest and balaclava on his way up to the instrumentation panel. As he climbs, he steals a glance below. A small war has broken out, which means either the police have arrived much faster than anticipated or CERN's security team is better equipped than Jonas knew. In any case, this is why he hired a group of trained mercenaries. But he pushes the thought aside. He has work to do.

Reaching the CMS's controls, Jonas begins flipping switches and turning dials. He pulls up his sleeve to consult his tattoo, a formality—given that he remembers every element of it—but a necessary one. *Leave nothing to chance.* He enters a complex series of instructions into the keyboard mounted against the CMS and is rewarded with an earth-shaking thrum from the huge machinery surrounding him. Energies intended to reveal the secrets of the universe begin powering up.

Jonas chances another glance at the firefight below. Perez and a second mercenary are both down, bleeding onto the concrete, their bulletproof vests having proved impotent against shots to the head.

A zipping sound above him steals his attention, and he sees three men fast-roping down. Their fatigues mark them as Armée de Terre, the French Army. Jonas blinks. *What's the military doing here? Were they nearby? Maybe on maneuvers? Or were they stationed here? Did they know we were coming?*

But there's no time for such questions. The soldiers are nearly on top of Jonas and the remaining mercenaries. The Armée de Terre are equipped with M4 carbine assault rifles but wouldn't risk harming the sensitive technology Jonas is operating. His proximity to it is probably the only reason he is still alive, he reasons. He continues to work.

Suddenly, footfalls behind him. Rubber on steel, pounding hard. Jonas peels his attention away from the terminal. Behind him, Macon is bounding up the stairs, his Glock belching fire. *Chak. Chak. Chak.* Three precise shots, and a trio of French soldiers drops at Jonas's feet, seconds away from arresting him. Or worse.

"Hurry," Macon says. His voice carries no urgency, only iron.

Jonas returns his attention to the instrumentation. A panel of glowing lights confirms it's time for the next phase. He's about to say as much to Macon when the mercenary's head snaps back, trailing crimson like a comet. Blood sprays over the terminal's buttons and dials and across Jonas's face. He feels a pang. Macon was the furthest thing from a friend, but Jonas had gotten to know him well enough to feel his passing.

Macon's impact on the steel floor is the equivalent of a starting gun. Jonas takes off. More gunfire dogs his heels. Bullets blur past him like murder hornets. He continues to sprint as fast as he can off the platform and onto a catwalk. Bullets spark and ricochet around him. Whatever compunction the French Army had about damaging equipment worth billions of dollars has apparently been set aside.

As he runs, Jonas produces the Glock he'd been given. But despite the fact that he's being shot at, he tosses the gun away. He can't take it where he's headed. A clanking noise resounds as the gun pinballs down the chasm.

Jonas vaults a railing and free-falls before landing on a sister catwalk stretching six feet below. He maneuvers across it toward a component of the CMS called the barrel electromagnetic calorimeter. It's aptly named, looking for all the world like the mouth of a massive cannon. Overhead, the Hadronic calorimeter, a towering ring of brass and steel, emits a rising groan.

It's almost time.

Jonas peers down at his ring. Its white light pulsates. It's ready. He's ready. In seconds, the CMS will be ready. Metal vibrates beneath his feet. The entire cavern quivers with enough power to hurl protons and electrons at velocities close to the speed of light. Depending on the experiment, these particles explode into a target or each other, and their collisions create new particles—*entirely new forms of matter*—recreating the conditions just after the big bang. Such acts of universal creation are the province of gods.

Then, a voice echoes through the metal and concrete canyon. *"Halt! Arrêtez!"* Jonas wheels to see a French soldier, eighteen years old if he's a day. The kid is white-knuckling his M4, his face pale as he makes his way down the catwalk, closing in. *"Éloignez-vous de la machine. Descendez par terre."* He sounds as afraid as Jonas feels. The barrel of a machine gun ratchets up and down in his trembling hands.

Jonas grips the railing with one hand. The catwalk now shakes with the force of the machinery he's put in motion. The light on his ring pulses. He's standing dead center in front of the Calorimeter Barrel. He scrutinizes the formulae inked into his arm. Not for the first time, he questions whether his calculations are correct.

The soldier chances another step forward.

"Step away," Jonas admonishes him. "I've released the safeties on the machinery. Do you understand? If you stay here, I can't guarantee your safety."

"Descends par terre," the soldier repeats.

"I'm really very sorry," Jonas says with sincerity. All around him, miles of machinery grow louder, building to a thundering crescendo.

It's time.

Jonas closes his eyes.

And waits.

And waits.

Nothing happens.

Impossibly, incredibly, nothing happens.

Jonas opens his eyes.

He barely has time to ask himself what he could have gotten wrong, which calculation was off, which variable unaccounted for, when the soldier is on top of him. Jonas opens his mouth to speak—and say what, he has no idea—when the butt of the man's rifle hits him square in the face.

The world goes black.

FIVE YEARS AGO

Perfect sunshine beamed down through the trees, their branches drawing little spangles of light in the air and casting shadows on the South Lawns. The skyline of Manhattan raked the perfect blue overhead, surrounding it like the fingers of a giant who nestled the campus of Columbia University in its massive palm. Faculty laced the lawn, shuttling to classes or back to their offices. Graduate and undergraduate students ran and walked and flirted, while others leaned against trees or sat at outdoor tables. The air smelled of spring, a cocktail of jacarandas in bloom and winter in retreat.

Finished with his classes for the day, Jonas walked with his fellow professor, Victor Kovacevic. Victor was more than a mere colleague. Jonas would have described him as a friend. Victor, six years older, would have described himself as Jonas's mentor. Both were accurate.

At six feet, four inches, Victor's frame was gangly, and his clothes—on this day, a pair of jeans and a dress shirt with the sleeves rolled up—had a tendency to drape off him like cobwebs. He wore a thin goatee, which Jonas suspected was dyed, despite the fact that Victor was only in his early forties. He wore glasses with Transitions lenses that were dark gray in the sun.

As they traversed the campus back to their faculty offices, Jonas handed Victor a sheaf of papers covered in a mélange of equations and formulae, written in a mosaic of mostly pencil and blue and black ink.

Red marks made the occasional appearance, dotting the pages like a teacher's corrections on an exam.

"Would you take a look at this for me?" Jonas asked. "I'm curious to know what you think."

Victor grimaced at the untidy stack. Jonas was the only faculty member he knew who still worked longhand instead of on computer or tablet. Victor acted as if he found the practice to be an amusing eccentricity, but Jonas had never been sure. Despite knowing the man for over ten years, Victor Kovacevic remained to Jonas an inscrutable, sphinxlike figure. To the extent that Victor exuded any emotional qualities, they had the tendency to be limited to amusement and vexation, though it was often hard for Jonas, or anyone else, to distinguish between the two.

"What's this?" Victor asked as he leafed through the pages. But the question itself was mendacious. A physicist of Victor's brilliance could decipher Jonas's calculations at a glance.

"It's early stages, but I think I'm close to a methodology for solving the problem of quantum decoherence . . ."

"Drifting a little out of your lane, aren't you?" In the arena of passive-aggressive put-downs, Victor Kovacevic had no equal. In this instance, though, he wasn't entirely wrong. While physics was Jonas's discipline, he had rarely ventured into the realms of theoretical or quantum physics that were Victor's domain.

"I happened to enjoy a flash of inspiration." Jonas shrugged with as much humility as he could muster, a hedge against Victor's ever-fragile ego. "Maybe it's something, maybe nothing. *Probably* nothing. But I remember how you said your 'many worlds' proof broke down over quantum decoherence and—"

Victor cut him off. "And you thought you'd apply salt to the wound?" he asked, flashing a taste of the anger that had cowed countless students, teaching assistants, and the occasional faculty member over the years.

"I thought I'd *help*."

Victor had tried for years to develop a means of proving the existence of multiple universes, or parallel realities. He had worked with intense focus and brilliant creativity, the perfect combination of inspiration and perspiration that Thomas Edison had famously spoken of. Jonas was convinced that Victor was working his way to a Nobel Prize, although even that achievement would be too small to encapsulate the magnitude of an actual mathematical proof of the existence of parallel worlds.

But one day, as quick as a thundercrack and for reasons Jonas could barely grasp, Victor declared the project a failure. In a fit of characteristic pique, he destroyed all his notes and research. An attempt at glimpsing a vast multitude of realities ended in scorched earth.

"I stopped working on this three years ago," he reminded Jonas.

"I know—"

"After *fourteen* years." Victor's voice was cold, clipped. Jonas watched as his jaw tightened and the muscles in his neck tensed.

"I know—"

"Fourteen years, and you think you've got it solved in—what was it?—a 'flash of inspiration'?" Victor made no effort to hide his skepticism and let disdain drip from every syllable, waving Jonas's papers around as though to cast them into the wind.

"Victor—" Jonas started, trying to adopt a diplomatic tone.

"Inspiration, I suppose, that eluded me," Victor interjected, his tone indicting.

"I was just trying to help a friend," Jonas said, laboring to keep even a hint of defensiveness from his voice. "I thought, if you see something of value in here, maybe we could collaborate." He indicated his work, which Victor was still clutching.

"So I'm a charity case now, is that it?" Victor's voice was like ice.

Jonas shot Victor a chiding look. "C'mon, man, don't give me that." He pointed again to his notes. "This is just a fresh perspective from a colleague."

"And I appreciate it," Victor replied, but his words lacked sincerity, the performance of an actor reading a line from a script he found inauthentic. Then, he softened. "I wasted more than a decade on parallel-worlds theory," he said, making no effort to hide the pain of that endeavor. "Don't make my mistake." He whipped the sheaf of papers back into Jonas's hand and continued on with neither a goodbye nor an apology.

Jonas watched him recede into a sea of coeds and administrative buildings. He looked down to consider his work and tried to reevaluate it in light of Victor's ill-fated project. Was it hubris to think he might have succeeded where Victor had failed? Quantum physics wasn't in Jonas's wheelhouse, as Victor had been only too quick to point out. The truth, though, was that Jonas really felt like he was making progress. Quantum decoherence—the loss of a definite phase relation between a quantum state and its environment—led to a wave function collapse, among other things. Studying his calculations, Jonas once again felt a swell of excitement, like a hunter who has caught the scent of his prey. The work wasn't finished, not even close, but Jonas could see the path forward. His mind imagined a set of gears and tumblers, a visualization of all the problems still left to solve, but he could see the beginning of a way that the gears might mesh, the tumblers fall into place, a virtuous cascade of breakthroughs that could, one day, open the lock that had so vexed his friend.

Then the papers scattered, and he felt a dull pain in his hands. As the sheets swayed in the wind, dispersing like a flock of birds, a fluorescent object fell at Jonas's feet. A Frisbee.

"Ohmygod!" came a female voice. The voice's owner quickly followed and immediately set to work collecting the wayward papers. "I'm so sorry!"

Jonas stared at the woman, in her early thirties from the look of her, and he felt his life change. She wore flip-flops and shorts and a pale-blue T-shirt with the name of some band Jonas had never heard of (Ash Dispersal Pattern). Her brown hair was pulled back in a high ponytail, exposing her blue-gray eyes. Jonas saw a small tattoo on her inner right wrist: an Ouroboros, a snake eating its own tail, curled into a sideways figure eight, the symbol for infinity.

"I'm horrendous," she said as she retrieved the last sheet and returned the reconstituted stack to him. "I hope I didn't ruin anything."

Jonas was suddenly conscious of the gaping silence between them. He was at ease when talking to women, but flirting was an art as elusive to him as playing the piano. "It's fine. Thanks." He instantly chided himself. He had three PhDs, and that was the best he could do? One word per doctorate? Pathetic.

The Frisbee caught his eye. It rested on the grass and practically shined with potential. He stooped to pick it up and, returning it, managed to say, "I'm Jonas." Five words. He was on a roll.

"Amanda." She waved her chin toward his papers. "I'm sorry about mixing up your math papers there . . ."

"It's quantum physics," Jonas replied, instantly wishing he could reel the words—*so stupid!*—back in.

But for some reason—by some miracle—Amanda seemed to find Jonas's unease charming. She flashed a smile that illuminated his entire world. He could spend the rest of his life basking in the warmth of that smile.

"Again, sorry." She waved and began to move off.

Jonas watched her retreat. His brilliant mind was screaming at him not to let her get away. "What's your field?" he managed to croak, desperate to say something, anything at all. Three more words, none of them particularly interesting or original, but at least he managed to keep the desperation from his voice, he hoped.

"Actually, I don't go here." Amanda gave the Frisbee a little wave. "Just playing with a friend."

She started to turn away, and again Jonas's mind grasped for a way to keep her engaged, to spend just another few seconds with her. "Could I call you sometime?" turned out to be the best he could come up with. He was instantly mortified by his lack of game, as his students liked to say, but in a world of dating apps and anonymous hookups and one-night stands, it came across as unexpectedly endearing.

"You could if you had my number," Amanda replied, seeming genuinely interested.

"Yes. That was kind of my way of asking you for it," Jonas confessed.

Whimsy passed over her face, and Jonas could have sworn he detected an actual twinkle in her eye. "I don't need to give it to you," she said. "You can figure it out on your own."

"I don't know your last name."

"This is true."

"And you said you don't go to Columbia."

"Also true."

Jonas blinked. "Well," he ventured, "there are one point six million people in Manhattan."

"It's kinda cute how you just happened to know that number from memory. Also, you don't know if I live in one of the outer boroughs, or Long Island, or even"—she faked a horrified gasp—"New Jersey."

"Exactly."

"C'mon," she said, "it shouldn't be too hard for a rocket scientist."

"Quantum physicist," he corrected. He was smiling. Maybe flirting wasn't so difficult after all. "My point being, detective work isn't exactly my field of expertise."

"Something tells me you won't have a problem."

Gripping the Frisbee, Amanda bounded off across the quad. Jonas watched her go, drinking in every detail of her form, her gait, the way her ponytail bounced with each exuberant step, its sheen catching the afternoon light. He carved each detail into his memory. It wasn't every day that one's life changed forever.

NOW

The room is an oppressive gray. Gray walls. Gray floor. Fluorescent lights hang from the gray ceiling, casting a sickly gloom. Even the sparse furniture, two steel chairs and a table bolted to the floor, are the color of gunmetal. The only exit is a single door—gray, of course—with a window cut into it. Thick panes of milky glass sandwich steel mesh between them.

He sits at the table as he has been instructed. The guard was kind enough to remove his handcuffs, but his wrists are still bruised and the skin still raw where the metal bracelets had been cinched tight. His head throbs where the rifle butt struck him. There's no mirror or reflective surface of any kind in here to confirm his suspicion that his face is badly bruised.

He's been relieved of his ring, the only object left on his person after he'd discarded the Glock. He imagines the French police had some questions about that when they accepted custody of him from the military. He had no wallet, no form of identification whatsoever. Just a ring and an unusual tattoo. The police took pictures of it when they processed him.

He thinks of Macon, the image of the mercenary's head exploding. The way it jerked back sharply, as if in spasm. The blood flecking Jonas's face. He still feels it on him, caked dry and itchy. He wonders if the entire team of mercenaries suffered a similar fate. If there are any survivors, he reasons, they'll be interrogated before it's his turn to be questioned.

He has no idea how long he's been here. No clock on the wall. No watch on his wrist. He left his phone back in the hotel, with no expectation of returning. He cracks his knuckles, but the ritual doesn't quell his disquiet. He doesn't fear prosecution, or even imprisonment. The thought of either feels alien, unreal. The idea of being branded as a criminal is academic, an intellectual abstraction. Ironic, even. Of the multitude of ways his plan could have gone awry, he never considered his present circumstances as a possibility. He had forecasted any number of setbacks, curated a complete menagerie of failures. Most scenarios had involved his own death—being obliterated by the primordial energies he had unleashed or ending up underwater or fused to a solid object. It never occurred to him that his attempt simply wouldn't work. The oversight now feels like an act of vanity, a blindness born of ego. Of all the forms of failure he had imagined, Jonas had never contemplated *actual* failure.

Now his life is over. He has nothing left to live for. And what life he has will be consigned to a room even smaller than the one he's in right now.

After an eternity, there's a jangle of keys, and the thick metal door creaks open. A young man in his thirties enters, navy blue uniform, gold badge on his chest, sidearm on his hip, file in his hand. Without preamble he sits down at the table opposite Jonas. "I am Inspector Gillard."

"Jonas. Dr. Jonas Cullen."

"I know who you are, Doctor." The inspector lays the file open in front of him on the table. Despite his youth, he speaks with a calm reflective of long experience. "Of the four men you were with, three are dead." He pauses for effect. "The fourth told me all about you." Another pause. "He had some very interesting things to say."

Jonas knows he only has one card to play here. He had decided it was the first thing he'd say if given the opportunity. "I want to speak with my embassy."

"He said," Gillard continues, as if Jonas had said nothing, "you paid them a quarter of a million euros so you could break into CERN to conduct—and this is *his* word—an 'experiment.'" Gillard makes no effort to keep the incredulity from his voice.

Jonas remains stone faced, offering as little as possible.

"Quite an interesting approach," Gillard observes. "I was curious why you didn't simply make a formal request to CERN—a physicist of your renown—but then I was informed that you'd made *six* petitions in the past two years." Gillard pushes the file toward the center of the table like a poker player cashing out. "All of which were declined."

Once again, Jonas says nothing. When your life is over, he has discovered, you have all the time in the world.

"Well," Gillard continues, "you certainly managed to come up with an unconventional solution to your problem. One can't help but ask," he adds delicately, "if this is somehow related to your wife's passing."

Jonas reacts, surprised that Gillard would know about Amanda. For some reason that he now knows was unfounded, he hadn't expected the French authorities to know about Amanda's death.

This must be evident from Jonas's expression, because Gillard raises an incredulous eyebrow. "Do you imagine I wouldn't at least google you before walking in here?"

A fair point. Jonas finds himself liking Gillard, despite the situation, which places them in a naturally adversarial relationship. Initially, he had no intention of explaining himself, but now he sees no reason not to be forthcoming. "I was trying to get to her."

"Excuse me?"

"It wasn't an experiment," Jonas insists. "I was trying to get to her. To Amanda. To be with her."

Gillard blanches. Jonas watches him shift uncomfortably in his seat. He knows what the inspector must be thinking: the man thought he was interrogating a renowned scientist but is now starting to consider the possibility that Jonas has some kind of mental illness. Gillard speaks slowly, choosing his words with some delicacy. "Dr. Cullen . . ." He pauses, searching for the right phrase. "Your wife is dead."

Jonas remains patient. He knows this is a difficult concept for anyone to grasp. "She's dead in *this* world. But there are others. A near-infinite number." Gillard still seems confused, so he adds, "I was trying to get to one—a parallel universe—where she survives. A reality where she's still alive."

Gillard's reaction is barely perceptible. Jonas can see it's taking all the man's effort to hide his distrust and skepticism. "All right, Doctor," Gillard says. "We're in contact with your embassy. As you can imagine, this incident presents a number of diplomatic complexities." An understatement. The inspector is droning on—"You'll be transferred to a holding cell, pending your arraignment . . ."—when Jonas first sees it.

Gillard's military watch. Numbers orbit the center: 1, 2, 4, 3, 5, 6 . . . counting up to 12.

The sight jolts Jonas like a subway's third rail.

The 4 and 3 . . . are transposed.

Jonas shakes his head. Blinks. The 4 and 3 remain swapped. He reminds himself that he was struck in the head with a rifle. He's concussed. He's not thinking strai—

But wait.

Gillard's file, still open on the table. From Jonas's vantage, the papers are upside down, but he can make out strange symbols where familiar vowels like "A" and "I" should be. Hope sparks. He tamps it down, preventing his mind from racing like it wants to, forbidding it from grasping at that tiny spit of hope. Such anomalies are replete with possible explanations, particularly in a foreign country.

"Doctor?" Gillard asks, sensing that he no longer has Jonas's attention.

In the end, the answer is right in front of him: a French flag pin on Gillard's left breast. The flag is the familiar "Tricolore," a vertical banding of three colors. Blue. White. But *green* has replaced red. Jonas supposes this could be some eccentricity of design, but the instances are starting to multiply, defying coincidence.

Jonas grabs the folder, flipping it closed to reveal the French flag emblazoned on its cover. The same flag. Blue and white and *green*.

Somewhere, Gillard is protesting the manhandling of his official file, but Jonas can't hear him. His mind is racing too fast now. He checks his hand and confirms the absence of his ring. He fights off a swell of panic. His eyes ricochet between the swapped numbers on Gillard's watch, the altered flag on his uniform, and the strange letters in the file. Together, they form a mosaic of possibility, circumstantial evidence of what, just a few minutes ago, Jonas thought was impossible.

He dives over the table. He moves fast, knowing that surprise is the only chance he has. His body skids across the table's metallic surface, sending the file folder pinwheeling away. Inertia throws him into the inspector, and gravity sends both men crashing toward the concrete floor. Gillard is thrashing, trying to throw Jonas off him and yelling in French. Jonas doesn't listen. He grasps at the holster around Gillard's waist, fingers snatching forth to unsnap the leather thumb break. In response, Gillard's struggling becomes twice as fierce. The butt of his hand rockets up, striking Jonas's nose, aggravating the earlier injury and making him see stars. Jonas recoils, staggering to his feet. With one hand, he smears away the blood gushing from his nose into his mouth.

His other hand holds Gillard's gun.

It feels solid in Jonas's grip, like the Glock he trained with. Whatever the make, its operation is similar enough that Jonas can thumb its safety off. Gillard flashes surprise when he hears the click. If he'd hoped that Jonas wouldn't know his way around a firearm, that consolation evaporates.

"Dr. Cullen," he says with surprising calm, given the circumstances. "Don't do this."

Jonas ignores the directive, pulling Gillard to his feet. His rapid heartbeat counts the seconds, and he knows he's running out of minutes. In fact, it's astonishingly lucky that he's not dead—or worse—yet.

"Get up," Jonas orders. "I don't have a lot of time."

"Doctor, calm down—"

"I'm the picture of calm," Jonas says. He manhandles Gillard to the door, digging the barrel of the gun into the man's back. He tells Gillard to open the holding cell. The gun is very persuasive. As the door opens, Jonas wraps one arm in front of Gillard, pressing the gun to the inspector's temple with the other. They fall out of the room, entwined like lovers caught in some perverse dance.

The police and support staff in the hallway react immediately to the sight of one of their own taken hostage. Guns are drawn. Commands are barked in English and French. But Jonas hisses in Gillard's ear. "When I was brought in, I had a ring on my left hand. Where is it?"

"We can work this out," Gillard says, using the magic phrase taught in hostage-negotiation courses. He evidently isn't aware that this is not a negotiation.

"I need that ring."

A Klaxon starts to wail in the distance.

"I can get it for you," Gillard says, still trying to bargain. "But you need to be reasonable. You're an intelligent man. You have to know that you're suffering some kind of breakdown."

"The ring has no sentimental value. The Large Hadron Collider untethered me from my reality, and I slipped into yours."

"At least we can agree you're untethered from reality," Gillard observes.

But Gillard doesn't understand. How could he?

Then, a miracle. A nearby door, with a placard identifying it as SÉQUESTRE DES PREUVES. Jonas again knows hope. He nudges Gillard toward the door, the surrounding cops parting in front of them.

"Open it," Jonas instructs.

"You're going to get yourself hurt, Doctor . . ."

"Get me in. Do it now." His voice is starting to rise. He feels tingling in his extremities but can't tell whether it's adrenaline or a sign that he's running out of time. He senses the police closing in, so he reminds

Gillard of the gun by pushing it against his head. "Tell them to put their guns down and back away."

With apparent reluctance, Gillard utters through gritted teeth, "*Si vous avez un coup de feu, prenez-le.*"

"Tell them to put their weapons down," Jonas reiterates. He's shouting now, partially out of stress and partially to compete with the bleat of the Klaxon.

"I just told them."

"And I'd believe you," Jonas retorts, "if I didn't speak French." With that, he pistol-whips Gillard, and the inspector collapses at Jonas's feet, hopefully close enough that the other police won't chance shooting their comrade. He's bought himself seconds, but he wastes them on a futile attempt to open the door. It's locked. Behind him, the police officers advance, guns poised. Doing his best to ignore them, he brings Gillard's gun down and fires a quick shot, the first in his life with live ammunition, blowing the lock apart. He swings the door open and closes it quickly behind him.

Jonas scans the room, a warren of file cabinets and shelves and lockers. He drops the gun and, fueled by adrenaline, drags one of the larger cabinets in front of the door. The police throw their combined weight against this bulwark, but the file cabinet holds its ground, a silent sentinel.

He's pulling drawers and knocking items off shelves, thrashing desperately like a drowning man grasping for a rope, when reality begins to change around him. At first, he could mistake the phenomenon as a trick of the light or the by-product of all the adrenaline singing in his veins. Like heat rippling off a stretch of asphalt, the world begins to blur, losing shape and form. Jonas strains to focus but only manages to trade his warped, diffused vision for a swiftly shifting one. The walls, painted a utilitarian gray, shift to an olive green, then off-white. File cabinets grow shorter, then taller. The shelving changes orientation. The pattern on the floor beneath him changes color, the linoleum tiles shifting and swapping and flipping. The file cabinet skids an inch deeper into the room. The police on the other side of the door are making progress.

Jonas feels the clock ticking down. Around him, the room flickers. He glimpses new universes—new interiors, new landscapes—flashing around him like images through a zoetrope. Night. Rain. Snow. A sunrise. A city. A forest. With each flash, the evidence room seems farther and farther away.

Jonas tells himself he should surrender, let the cosmic forces he unleashed sweep him away through an infinite number of parallel realities. He's about to give up, to let go, praying that if there's any justice in the universe—*in the multiverse*—then somehow, some way, he'll be reunited with Amanda.

When he sees it, he thinks he's hallucinating. It doesn't seem real. *Can't* be real. And yet . . . there it is. Black text on a white field.

His name.

CULLEN, JONAS

A sticker affixed to a bag of thick, milky plastic. Jonas surges toward it with violent urgency. The world around him shifts and slips and changes, like radio stations snapping in and out of frequency, giving him glimpses of other universes.

His fingers grasp the bag. It's on top of a pile of similar evidence bags, right out in the open. Some distant part of him chastises himself for not realizing it sooner: the evidence was waiting to be filed, so of course it wouldn't yet be in one of the cabinets. The bag is as light as air. His fingers fumble for its singular content, his ring, its white light still throbbing. He fishes it out of the bag. His hands tremble, pulsing with adrenaline. All around him, reality slips, compounding his disorientation. He wills himself to focus, to steady his hands.

Please God, just let me complete the simple act of slipping this ring onto my finger.

The Almighty, apparently, isn't taking requests at this particular moment because the floor disappears out from beneath Jonas's feet, and a furtive glance confirms that it's not just the floor. The entire room, the entire building, blinks out of existence, and in an instant, Jonas is in free fall, alone, plunging through an oil-painting sunset.

The ring pinballs between his fingers. Every second that ticks past is another where he could lose his grip on it entirely.

Around him, the sunset shifts to an acrid gray sky. The horizon rises to meet him in a jagged apocalyptic vision. He plunges toward the upturned wing of a downed airplane, jutting up from the ground like a pike. He's seconds away from being impaled upon it, when . . .

The wing is gone. Replaced by a city whose buildings are integrated with vines and other varieties of verdant growth. A perfect, seamless blend of cityscape and landscape. Breathtaking.

Another reality-slip, and the city winks away. The ground now speeding toward him is covered with an immaculate garden the size of a small town. It's encased by a translucent dome several stories high. Explosions, blossoming like fireworks overhead, reflect in its glass surface.

Then a cluster of skyscrapers rises from the earth, clawing at the sky and blotting out the sun. They missile toward Jonas, the ring still fumbling in his hands, refusing to cooperate, as he asks for one more miracle . . .

The ring slips onto his finger with such simplicity that Jonas is given cause to ask himself why it had been such a chore in the first place. In an eyeblink, the buildings shooting up at him flash away. Gravity retains its hold on him, though, and he continues to fall.

Until a car smashes into him.

No, that's not right, he tells himself. He considers his positioning and comes to the conclusion that *he* smashed into the car. From above. Its roof has crumpled beneath his weight, the windshield blown out in jagged pebbles.

He's on his back, he realizes. Everything hurts. Every nerve sings in agony, but at least they confirm that he's alive. He stares up and recognizes his surroundings. He's in Pregnin, a small town near CERN, a little over a mile and a half from the Swiss border. He's been here before, albeit in another reality, and knows the buildings, the architecture. He knows in his bones that he's still in France, but the houses and structures are suffused with a Japanese aesthetic.

He feels warm. Astonishment wells in his gut. *Elation.*

He's done it. He has become the first human to travel between universes, to traverse realities. The enormity of this achievement hits with the force of a blow. His Many Worlds Proof, a work so momentous that it garnered him a Nobel Prize, feels suddenly insignificant by comparison. Proving the existence of parallel worlds was the academic equivalent of summitting Everest. But to *travel* to one . . . that's landing on the moon.

Questions and uncertainties stampede through his mind. *Is Amanda here? Which reality has he ended up in? Is Amanda here? Is this the right universe? Is Amanda here?*

Sounds begin to leak into his awareness. He hears urgent French, an overlapping of voices. People emerging from their homes to see what's happened.

"*Cet homme, il est tombé du ciel.*" *This man, he fell out of the sky.*

He hears excited chatter and the sound of people running toward him. He shifts, trying to right himself atop the crumpled steel, and is rewarded by a pain unlike any he's ever felt before. It shoots forward, spreading out from behind his eyes to overwhelm his whole body until he topples from the car, landing hard on asphalt. Tiny pieces of safety glass dig into his face until he passes out.

FIVE YEARS AGO

Jonas walked through SoHo—an artsy enclave waging a losing battle against gentrification—past the condos and clothing stores, the street vendors and restaurants. He consulted his phone, its GPS guiding him. The air tasted of pollen. The sun felt warm. It was spring, and the whole world felt new.

As he walked, he felt his pulse rise. For three days, his thoughts had dined on recollections of Amanda. How the sun had danced in her eyes. The little dimples formed by the upward tilt of the corners of her mouth. The way he felt when he replayed their brief encounter over and over, drawing out new details, exulting in its ephemera.

Of course he was attracted to her. He had perfect recall of her T-shirt draping over her breasts, the tone of her legs. How supple her skin was. Beautiful in every conventional sense. But all that felt ancillary, borderline irrelevant. What attracted him was her energy, her spirit. He saw in her a kindness that he was immediately drawn to, an effect he felt compelled to investigate. She was a diamond he could envision examining from every conceivable angle, each facet rewarding him with a new color.

Jonas had had his share of relationships and assignations, but whatever aesthetic qualities he may have possessed were always blunted by his "boring," "academic" occupation. Possessing multiple doctorates in quantum physics wasn't exactly a turn-on. Yes, he met the occasional undergrad who found the student/professor dynamic alluring, but Jonas steadfastly resisted such attachments. They felt lurid, as if he would be taking illegitimate advantage of his power. What he craved was more substantial. He didn't want or need a relationship or a long-term commitment—not that he would have resisted either—so much as hunger for a *connection*, the magnetic pull of another human being.

The phone vibrated in his hand, alerting him that he was mere steps from his destination. The gallery was modest, no different from every third storefront in SoHo. Galleries, apparently, were the bulwark against the encroaching tide of condominiums that threatened to engulf the entire neighborhood. This one had oak floors and wrought iron pillars. Large canvases hung from the exposed ceiling on thick steel cables. Tiny laminated cards announced their titles, artists, and media. Jonas examined the menagerie, playing a little game in his head, seeing if he could identify which works were Amanda's.

He felt drawn to a series of canvases, each one either four feet by four feet or six feet by six feet, massive squares covered in watercolor and gouache. Each depicted the New York City skyline from a different vantage, high and wide and expansive, daring to depict Manhattan the way God sees it. But a single painting stood out from the rest, depicting a vantage from Downtown—specifically, the rooftop of One World Trade Center—gazing from the southern tip of the island north toward a looming Manhattan. It was like being perched on a giant's toe and staring upward. The painting was titled *Pinnacle*.

Jonas found the image breathtaking, portraying the city he knew so well in a way he had never seen or even imagined. *Pinnacle* and its siblings were photo-real but offered vistas that seemed beyond human sight. It made no sense, and Jonas had no rational explanation, but he knew in an instant that Amanda's hands had wrought these incredible images. He confirmed the suspicion with a glance at the tag beneath each painting and fell even deeper in love.

As he stared at one of the paintings, drinking in all the details, marveling at the artistry, a dealer approached—a guy no more than twenty, with an earring and a hipster's wardrobe, no doubt some art major working his way through college.

"Awesome, right?" the dealer asked.

"Awesome," Jonas agreed. "Can you help me? I'm looking for Amanda Monroe."

"This is her," the dealer said, gesturing to the painting Jonas had been admiring.

"And they're stunning," Jonas answered truthfully. "But I'm looking for Amanda the, y'know, person."

"She's in today," the dealer responded. "Do you want to talk with her about purchasing one of her paintings? Not that you should feel like you have to limit yourself to just one."

Jonas shrugged off the joke and reached into his messenger bag, a slab of leather he'd had since his undergraduate days, and pulled from it a Frisbee he'd bought at Walgreens for eleven dollars and fifty-one cents, plus tax. "Just give her this," he remarked with a smirk.

The dealer took the Frisbee with an air of confusion and trepidation, disappearing into the rear of the gallery. As Jonas waited, he returned his attention to Amanda's paintings. He studied the images, taking in every brushstroke. He had never considered himself a connoisseur of art, far from it, but for some reason, these works spoke to him. The skill was self-evident. Amanda had managed to capture vistas that appeared as real as photos yet as ephemeral as dreams.

"Okay," came a voice behind him. "How?"

He turned. Amanda stood in front of him, her hip slightly cocked, daring him to impress her. She wore a pastel sundress and leather boots that rose past her calves. Her eyes danced, less surprised than amused.

Jonas offered up a modest shrug. "Your tattoo," he said. "The skin around it is a little red," he observed, "so I assumed it must be new. I did some googling and got a list of tattoo parlors." Her eyes blazed back at him intently. "I called and asked if they had a recent customer—female, of course—who got an Ouroboros tattooed on her inner right wrist."

Amanda stared back at him in disbelief. "There have to be . . . there have to be over fifty tattoo shops in Manhattan," she exhaled.

"Seventy-three, actually. And an additional nineteen in the outer boroughs."

Jonas stared back at her with a mixture of defiance and pride. He watched her expression change, revealing an interest he hadn't detected earlier. Like she was seeing him for the first time. The look on her face was the same one Jonas had seen staring back at him in the mirror since he'd met her. The look of someone utterly smitten.

He eyed her with a hint of satisfaction. "Will you give me your number *now?*"

NOW

Jonas shoots up and is rewarded with a throbbing in his skull. Settling back down, he realizes he's lying on a bed. He inspects his surroundings, expecting to see his hotel room in NH Genève Aéroport. But the room is painted white. No wallpaper. No mass-produced paintings of the Swiss countryside on the walls. The floor is covered with linoleum instead of industrial carpet the color of vomit. A thin white sheet covers him instead of the oddly patterned quilt he expects. A tube snakes into his arm, trailing back toward what he assumes is an IV stand. The room is antiseptic in both smell and decor.

He's in a hospital.

A new worry strikes him like lightning. He throws off the sheet to find his hand. It's there. The ring. It's still there. He exhales his relief.

Relaxing back into the bed, he takes a quick inventory of his circumstances. He's alive. He's in an alternate, parallel reality. Another universe. And he's remained in it for as long as he's been unconscious. The odds of all this are almost too infinitesimal to contemplate. He has become the first person to traverse the multiverse, and he managed not to die in the process.

Jonas is still contemplating the enormity of this when the doctor enters. He appears to be in his late sixties, has a kind face, and wears a white lab coat over olive green medical scrubs. A stethoscope is draped over his neck.

"*Bonjour, vous êtes un homme très chanceux,*" he says.

Jonas notices the name embroidered on the man's lab coat: **GUYER**. "*Où suis-je?*" Jonas asks.

"Covance Hospital," comes the answer.

"*Suis-je toujours en France?*"

The doctor shakes his head. "*Non, vous êtes en Suisse.*"

Jonas nods his understanding. He's back in Switzerland. An ambulance must have responded to his arrival and taken him to the closest hospital, even though it was in an entirely different country.

"*Nous sommes l'hôpital le plus grand,*" Guyer continues, "*proche de l'endroit où vous avez été trouvé.*"

"*Parlez-vous anglais?*" Jonas's head is throbbing too aggressively to be constantly translating.

"Of course," Guyer answers. "Are you American? You speak French with an American accent."

Jonas entertains a buoyant thought. In his home reality, Jonas was a kind of celebrity, the first person to prove the existence of parallel worlds. In addition to the Nobel Committee, Jonas captured the attention of social media and talk show hosts. His notoriety had spread to Europe, so if this doctor doesn't recognize him, it's reasonable to hope that Jonas has no counterpart in this universe. At least, not one who developed a Many Worlds Proof. No Nobel Prize, no speech at the Aula Magna. His limousine never slipped the bonds of earth and came crashing down like Icarus.

If an Amanda resides in this universe, it's likely that she's still alive. Jonas's final prayer—his last request ever, he vows—is that she is. Hope brightens once again. He sits up, eager to escape the bed. The doctor watches, concerned, as Jonas rips the IV from his arm and tries to vault to his feet. But then, without warning, pain grips his body, reminding him why he's in a hospital in the first place.

"Yeah, I don't think that's a very good idea," Guyer deadpans.

"I need to get out of here."

"Apparently. But I don't think that's wise. And evidently, neither does your body. You've been out for two days, and you've suffered a severe concussion. You should rest."

"I need to leave. I need to find someone."

Dr. Guyer just shakes his head. "I've called for a psychiatric consult."

"I don't blame you, but—"

"It's just unusual," Guyer interrupts, "to find a man atop a crushed automobile. No wallet. No form of identification. My colleagues suggest you're a skydiver, but I've never seen a skydiver without a parachute." He gauges Jonas with a stare. "I would assume a suicide attempt, but there were no buildings tall enough in the area to serve that purpose. So if you were trying to commit suicide, I regret to inform you that you're not particularly good at it."

"I wasn't trying to kill myself." Jonas tries to stand again, but an ice pick stabs at him from behind his eyes.

"The psychologist I've reached out to is a friend of mine. She majored in physics for a time before going into medicine. I thought she'd find your tattoo of interest." Guyer's chin bobs in the direction of the formulae on Jonas's arm.

Teeth gritted against the pain, Jonas attempts to stand again. He moves slower this time and accomplishes the feat of toddling on watery legs. "I don't want to speak with a psychologist." He casts about for his clothes. "I just want to leave."

"I think you and I both know that you're in no condition to go anywhere."

Ignoring that, Jonas considers the room. It's empty, apart from some medical equipment, a chair, and a flat-screen mounted on the wall. "Where are my clothes?"

"You have a concussion—"

"Where are my clothes?"

"You really should get back in bed."

Jonas would very much like to. His head feels light, and each breath brings a new volley of agony. Nevertheless, he surges toward the doctor.

He doesn't want to get violent, but he feels out of control, consumed by an overwhelming hunger to get out of this hospital. Once he's out, he can think. He can orient himself. He can figure out his next move. He can see if she's here, and if she is, *he can find her.* That's all he cares about. Out of an infinite multitude, that's the only reality that exists for him.

∞

Covance Hospital is a thirty-five-minute drive from Eva Stamper's office on a good day. On a bad day, when the narrow roads are clogged with traffic, it's nearly an hour. Today is a bad day. And so Eva is in a mood. The hospital has a phalanx of psychiatrists and psychologists on staff, and even more on call. Paul Guyer must know that he's taking advantage of their friendship by asking for her.

"An attempted suicide, I believe," he had told her over the phone.

"So?" Eva rejoined. "You have people for that sort of thing. Good people."

"I know, but . . ." And then his voice trailed off.

"But what?" Eva had asked, almost immediately chiding herself for taking the bait.

"There's something different about this one."

"Different how?"

"He has a tattoo on his inner forearm, to start." Eva remembers rolling her eyes. "I've never seen anything like it."

"What type of tattoo?" she asked, knowing that with every question, she was inserting herself deeper into a situation she wanted no part of. No, that wasn't it exactly. It was that she had no time. She had patients enough of her own without taking on one of Paul's pet projects.

"It looks like a formula of some kind," he had explained. "An equation, I guess you could say. I don't know. It doesn't resemble anything I saw in medical school. But it's odd."

"That's not a good enough reason to cancel on my patients and come down there in the middle of the day."

"It's barely ten in the morning."

"You know what I mean, Paul."

Although Paul is thirty years her senior, they'd always enjoyed a close relationship that skulked just up to the line of romance. One drunken evening, months after her husband's passing, Eva had made a clumsy attempt at crossing that bright line, but Paul was kind and respectful as he gently rebuffed her. In another life, another universe, they might be lovers. The fact isn't lost on either of them, and it makes for an unexpectedly strong bond. "The truth is, Eva," he had said on the phone with a hint of mischief, "you're looking at this the wrong way."

Then it had been Eva's turn to smirk. "And how's that?"

"I could be the one doing *you* the favor. You could get a paper out of this," he dangled.

"You say that every time, you shit," she shot back lovingly. "And never once has it ended up being true." Then they both enjoyed a good laugh.

And so she finds herself at Covance. Paul has arranged visitor parking for her. She navigates the corridors from memory and has to acknowledge that she's been here too many times, seen too many of Paul's patients "as a favor," and not for the first time, she questions why Paul feels the need to call on her in this way. Or why she lets him.

But when she enters the patient's room, everything changes. She feels like the victim of a prank. The world doesn't make sense.

"What is this?" she asks.

Paul shoots her a quizzical look as Eva studies the patient. He's a man in his thirties, somewhat on the thin side. His black hair is cut short, almost military length. He wears black jeans, and she can see the tattoo Paul mentioned as the man pulls on a black T-shirt. Her attention ping-pongs between the tattoo and the man's face. She tries to make sense of what she's seeing, but her best attempts bring her back to the suspicion that Paul is having some fun at her expense. He must have hired an actor, some kind of impersonator. Still, she can't fathom why Paul would prank her like this. It's too random. Too specific.

"What's going on here?" Eva finally asks.

"What are you talking about?" Paul replies. He seems just as confused as she is. If it's a performance, it's a good one.

Eva returns her attention to the man, feeling him watching her. She points to him and asserts with as much conviction as she can muster, "This man is dead."

"What?"

"Do you know who he is?" she presses, gesturing in the patient's direction.

"H—he told me his name is Jonas," Paul stammers.

The name is eerie confirmation of the evidence before her eyes. "Yes," she whispers, her throat dry. "His name is Jonas Cullen." The man startles, his face registering shock at being recognized. "Two years ago, he and his wife were killed in a car accident."

Paul blanches. The man claiming to be Jonas Cullen appears staggered, almost doubled over with what seems like grief.

"She's not here," he whispers, his voice cracking with a hollowness she finds heartbreaking. "She's not here," the man says again, with greater conviction but no less dolor.

"What are you talking about?" Paul asks him. "Who is 'she'? Who are you?"

Eva watches the man, this Cullen look-alike, as he drops into a chair. She knows the emptiness in his eyes. It's the same emptiness that was in hers when she waited to hear whether her husband had been killed—a strange amalgam of lost hope and the bitter realization that hope was futile in the first place. "Can I have a minute alone with him, Paul?"

Once Paul leaves the room, Eva searches the recesses of her mind for traces of those years she spent studying physics. Equations in the stranger's tattoo tug on her memory. She tries to piece together what she knows. Jonas Cullen isn't dead. He's right in front of her, as real as anything she's ever known. But his wife is dead, and he appears to be . . . surprised at that? Eva plays with these disparate thoughts. It's like a puzzle, but one where the pieces don't fit . . .

"How do you know who I am?" he says. His voice rises barely above a whisper.

Eva shrugs. "I read about the accident on Google News last week."

"Last week? Not two years ago?"

"Last week. Tragedies have a way of"—she strains for the right words—"of making an impression on me. Your wife was pregnant, wasn't she?"

The man droops in the chair, nodding as though the effort to do so exhausts him. He seems utterly lost, his eyes devoid of life. Eva's seen eyes like that before, in hundreds of hopeless patients: despairing.

She expects him to start crying, but he doesn't. She has the sense that all his tears have been spent. "The formulae on your arm," she ventures. "I've seen some of them somewhere before. At university. That's a Schrödinger equation, isn't it?"

She's rewarded with a hint of recognition. "That's right," he says, slowly emerging from his fog. "What do you remember from your university days?" The words come out with the croak of effort.

Eva bends to study the formulae, trying to disregard the letters and symbols she doesn't understand, working to excavate the Schrödinger equation from both the tattoo and her memory. She can feel the man watching her think. She senses that she's stumbling toward the truth, a marathoner straining in the final inches to cross the finish line.

"It's a linear partial differential equation," she breathes. "It describes the state function of a quantum-mechanical system." Her thoughts begin to gather momentum and form, like a snowball rolling downhill, picking up mass and speed. "The reason you're here, and your wife isn't . . ." She stops, not yet ready to say it out loud.

"For someone convinced that she's meeting a man from a parallel universe," Jonas deadpans, "you're rather calm."

"Do I look calm?" she asks, knowing the answer.

He stands from the chair. "I'm sorry to have unnerved you. Thank you for coming to see me, but I'm afraid Dr. Guyer wasted your time. I have to get out of here."

He moves for the door, but she stops him. "And go where?"

Jonas turns toward her. Eva stiffens her back. She has no idea why it's important to her that this person, this apparent miracle, not walk out of her life. She feels a sense of fate. Of destiny. She knows she can't—shouldn't, at least—let this man from another world get away. "I don't need to be a psychologist to know you need help."

"I don't have a mental illness," Jonas assures her.

"I'm not talking about that kind of help. I'm talking about help with . . . with whatever your situation is."

A bitter chuckle escapes his lips, like ice cracking. "You don't know what my situation is."

"Then tell me. Tell me, and I'll help. Do you believe in destiny, Dr. Cullen?" She watches him ponder the question.

"No. I don't."

"Well, maybe you will. Because a psychologist with a working knowledge of physics has just been placed in your path. I don't believe that's either accident or coincidence." Her eyes lock on his. "And I think it's only a matter of time until you don't believe it's accident or coincidence either."

Eva watches him ponder that. She knows many, many smart people, but she doesn't think she's ever met a bona fide genius until now.

"Is there a place to drink around here?" Jonas asks.

Eva's surprised. "You . . . want to go to a bar?"

He offers up a shrug. "You're right, I could use some help." He pauses. "And I bet you could use a drink."

$$\infty$$

She takes Jonas to a quiet pub that's a five-minute walk from the hospital. Every bone in his body croons a chorus of pain from the same broken hymnal, but it's good to be out in the open air. Even though his stretch in police confinement proved mercifully short, freedom is a cool drink on a scorching day. On the way, she tells him her name: Dr. Eva (pronounced "Ava") Stamper. She is, he cannot fail to notice, stunning. Almost six feet tall, she wears a tan blouse and a dark gray pencil skirt. The simple outfit complements her ocher skin and striking black hair, which frames her piercing green eyes.

As they walk, Jonas notes that this portion of Switzerland has the same Japanese-influenced architecture he'd witnessed back in France. They pass a newsstand, and he is compelled to stop and examine its offerings, his first exposure to the news of an alternate reality. He doesn't recognize any of the celebrities on the covers of the glossy magazines. An English newspaper's headline proclaims, "US PRESIDENT CHANG ISSUES STERN WARNING TO RUSSIA." The article is accompanied by a photograph of a Chinese man in his sixties whom Jonas doesn't recognize.

He can sense Eva studying him, taking in his astonishment. She watches as he takes inventory of all the different ways this world is different—and yet not so different—from the one he knows. He expects her to pepper him with questions, but she waits until they've both had a chance to get a drink.

The pub is called Pub des Vergers. In English, the name translates to "Bar of Orchids," which strikes Jonas as a very strange name for a bar. Bottles of beer and liquor stand at attention against a red brick wall, up lit by violet lights. Jonas finds them a table while Eva orders two local beers.

Eva sips hers and laments, "Maybe I should have ordered a stronger drink. Given what I think you're going to tell me." She sets her bottle down. "Where should we begin?"

"What do you know about the Many Worlds Theory?" Jonas asks.

"Only what I learned in Introduction to Quantum Mechanics." She smirks. "Got an A, though."

"I'll bet you did," Jonas says, impressed. A puckish intelligence winks back at him, the same inner glow he first saw in his wife. The warm dazzle he fell so deeply in love with.

He asks Eva for a coin. After digging in her purse, she hands him a two-euro piece. Jonas turns it over in his hands. His intention is to explain multiverse theory to Eva as he did with Amanda. On their first date. The first time their hands touched. The moment comes alive in his memory, and his eyes tingle with the threat of tears.

"Are you all right?" Eva asks.

"Fine," Jonas croaks, shaking away the memory. He flips the coin, its patina glinting in the light of the pub as it tumbles back into his hand. "Heads or tails?"

"Tails," she shrugs. Jonas reveals the coin in his palm. *Heads.* Eva grimaces. "Too bad for me."

"Not exactly. You see, the Many Worlds Theory holds that there is now a universe—a parallel universe or, if you prefer, an 'alternate reality'—where the coin came up tails."

Eva furrows her brow. "That's never made much sense to me. What you're describing would lead to an incalculable number of realities. If the universe favors efficiency, it doesn't make sense that a new one is created every time someone flips a coin."

"You're right. The coin flip is just a convenient illustration I use with laypeople."

She rears back. "Laypeople? You wound me, sir," she says in mock offense.

"But you happen to be absolutely right," Jonas continues. "The multiverse *does* prefer efficiency, which it achieves by limiting branch points—instances where circumstances could go right or left and, therefore, birth a new universe—by constraining the number of times that it happens."

"How?" she asks.

"By *favoring* certain outcomes. Which limits the total number of realities in the multiverse from the impossibly infinite to manageably so."

"And how do you know that?"

He tells her about his Many Worlds Proof. The Nobel Prize. The night in Stockholm. The accident. He doesn't know how he manages to get it all out and not have his voice tremble.

"I'm so sorry," she says. There's more than sincerity in her voice. Jonas senses experience. Eva has trod this unfortunate emotional territory.

"I devised a means to travel between realities," he says. "My hope is to find one where Amanda is still alive."

"Your *hope*? I would think there would be . . . well, I would think there would be a lot. I mean, in a universe of infinite universes."

"Yes. But you're forgetting something."

Eva brightens. "The universe favors . . ."

"Certain outcomes, yes."

Eva takes a pull from her drink, evidently thinking hard on all that Jonas has unloaded on her. "What happens," she ventures, "if you find a world where your wife is alive . . . but so are you?"

"I don't know," he admits. "I think it's unlikely, given the universal bias I mentioned."

"But what if?" she insists.

"Then . . ." Jonas's voice trails off. "I guess that would fall under the category of a 'quality problem.'"

"It would certainly make for the world's most interesting love triangle."

"Maybe I'll write a book about it," he jokes. "Get a Pulitzer to go with my Nobel."

Eva is still working to absorb all this, wrestling with whether to accept what he's told her and what she's observed on his forearm or to hold fast to common sense. "I can't even begin to fathom the energy expenditure required to jump realities."

"Of course you can," he offers. "Consider where we are."

"Switzerland."

"*Meyrin*, Switzerland," he specifies.

"The Large Hadron Collider," she realizes aloud, the words tumbling out in a whisper.

He points at her—*exactly*—before saying, "My body is now suffused with quantum energy. The process essentially unanchored me from my reality, allowing me to slip into yours."

Her beer bottle empty, Eva—saucer eyed—reaches forward to drain Jonas's. "If that's true"—Jonas can see her mind grasping—"then why aren't you continuing to . . . 'slip,' to use your word? What keeps you in *this* reality?" But she doesn't wait for Jonas to answer as her understanding gains momentum. "In fact, what's to keep you from slipping realities forever?"

"This." Jonas holds up his hand, showing her his ring. "I call it my 'tether.' It's the only piece of nonorganic matter that can make the trip with me."

"Nonorganic?"

"Anything synthetic," Jonas confirms. "I even had to have my fillings taken out and replaced with silver."

"But *why*?" she asks.

"Remember, we're dealing with *radiation*, essentially. Quantum radiation, yes, but *still*. Different types of matter absorb and retain radiation differently. When I first started out, all my computer models were . . ." He searches for the word.

"Totally wack?" Eva offers.

"To use the technical term." This time, they both share a smile. A moment. "In any case, the model results changed when I only factored in organic materials."

"Except for your 'tether.'"

Jonas points to it, resting on his finger. "It's different from everything else because it's *regulating* the radiation in question. As long as I'm wearing it, I'm rooted in whichever universe I'm standing in."

"And if you take it off?"

Jonas flutters his hand upward, fingers wagging. "I move through universes like a feather on the wind."

"And, what, you *land* when you put it back on?"

"Actually, it takes a universe or two to settle."

"Settle?"

"Like a roulette wheel slowly coming to a complete stop."

Eva furrows her brow. Taking all this in. Turning it over in her mind, examining the whole impossible, incredible situation from all available angles.

"You're taking this all very well," Jonas observes.

Eva barely acknowledges the compliment, still thinking, still probing. "What about your clothes? Paul didn't mention you showing up naked."

Jonas plucks at his shirt. "All-natural fibers and materials. Even my shoes."

"So you're not carrying any money," she notes.

"Good point. You're going to have to pay for our drinks." They share another flash of connection even in the face of a conversation that seems, at best, on the outer edge of sanity.

"So, your tattoo . . ."

Jonas rolls up his sleeve, turning out his forearm. "The collider needed to be calibrated very precisely."

"I'd imagine."

"I couldn't chance leaving all this to memory, and I needed a way to bring my notes, my calculations, with me. I considered keeping them on cotton parchment, writing with something like squid ink, but *that* would mean risking losing the formulae, so I employed the obvious solution."

Eva's gaze flits across the tattoo. Once again, her eyes spark at the Schrödinger equation at the center of the calculations, the cornerstone of the Many Worlds Theory. "If the Jonas Cullen of . . . of *my* universe wasn't a Nobel-winning scientist, I don't think I'd believe any of this."

Jonas smiles inwardly, taking some small measure of pride in being a Nobel winner in at least two universes. "What did I win for?" he can't help but ask.

Eva winces, searching her memory. "Something about the control of particles in entangled states?" she grasps. "But forget about that a second."

"Forget about winning a Nobel Prize? Sure. No problem."

"I'm serious," she insists. "*This* is serious. I have to ask . . ." She pauses, measuring her next words. "I just . . . I don't understand why you'd go through all that trouble. I mean, you were risking your *life* to travel to a reality where you and your wife are both dead."

Jonas breathes out a sigh. "You strike me as much smarter than that, Dr. Stamper."

"You're lost." The conclusion escapes her in a breath. The conspicuous answer, present all along.

Jonas runs a finger along his tattoo, across the arcane mélange of letters and numbers and symbols, feeling like they have betrayed him. "I thought I'd correctly determined how the LHC needed to be calibrated in order to arrive at the universe where Amanda's still alive."

"And how does that work, exactly?"

"It's highly technical," he demurs.

"Really?" she says sarcastically. "That's almost hard to imagine."

Jonas leans forward and parts his hands. *Okay. I'll play.* "I altered the Large Hadron Collider so that it would leak out a small amount of quantum radiation. Radiation is nothing more than the emission of energy in the form of waves. Waves have *frequencies*. Change the frequency, and you alter the quality of the radiation. Alter the quality of the radiation, and you change the *effect* it has on the cells of the human body. In this case, mine."

Eva shakes her head. "I'm afraid you lost me."

"I *did* warn you," he chides playfully.

"Yes, you did." He catches her staring at him. There's no mistaking the look on her face as attraction, but Jonas compels himself not to dwell on it.

"Bottom line, I intended to use the quantum radiation to untether myself from my home reality, but in a very specific way. Think of it like letting go of a helium balloon with the intention that it floats up through a skylight."

"And this theoretical 'skylight' leads to a reality where your wife is still alive."

Jonas feels a pang of disappointment. "I thought I'd located a reality where Amanda was still alive and I wasn't. Clearly, something was lacking in my calculations, because I originally ended up in a reality where she was already dead."

Eva seems confused. "Originally?"

He tells her about his arrest, his encounter with Gillard. During the interrogation, Gillard had mentioned Amanda's "passing." At the time, Jonas didn't know he'd reality-slipped, so he thought Gillard was referring to *his* Amanda, but with the realization that Gillard was from a parallel universe came the conclusion that the Amanda in Gillard's reality was dead as well.

Jonas recounts the confiscation of his tether and how its loss led him to arrive in this universe. He explains that when he reality-slips, he *doesn't* move in space or time: if he's standing on the third floor of a building that disappears because he swaps universes, he's liable to plummet to his death—unless, say, a car breaks his fall. Hence his arrival at Dr. Guyer's hospital.

"So now what?" Eva asks. "What will you do next?"

"I don't know," he says, trying not to sound hopeless.

Almost a minute passes. In the silence, the sounds of the bar fill the breach: the indistinct chatter of dozens of overlapping conversations, the chime of glasses being set down on tables, a pop song struggling in vain to be heard over it all. Jonas returns his attention to Eva, and in her eyes he sees a familiar emotion, one he's seen countless times since Amanda passed away.

It's pity.

∞

It's not pity.

Eva stares at Jonas with empathy and the understanding of a fellow traveler on the road of loss. She's further down that path than he is and recognizes in him a despair akin to hers, which has scarred over with the passage of time. But for Jonas, the loss of Amanda is still fresh. To hear him talk about it is to take in the extent of his grief. However, rather than see it as pathetic, Eva finds it alluring. His sorrow is as pure as his love. Who *wouldn't* find such devotion attractive? Who wouldn't want to be coveted the way Jonas covets Amanda?

"I'm sorry if I seem . . . pathetic," Jonas says.

"You're not pathetic," she says from her depths. "It's never pathetic to love someone, and it's certainly not pathetic to mourn them." She laces her fingers together and brings them to her mouth, contemplating. "And what you're doing . . . looking for her, risking *everything* to be with her again . . . it's heroic."

She watches as Jonas warms to that idea. Sees him sit up just a little straighter, his flagging resolve recharged by her endorsement. A smile spreads on his face. She's surprised to find it attractive but instantly sheds the thought. Jonas either has a mental illness, hails from an entirely different universe, or—potentially—both. Still, that smile . . .

Evening has fallen by the time Jonas and Eva exit the pub. The air is crisp and smells like smoldering wood. The buildings' nighttime illumination only enhances the odd hybrid of European and Japanese architectural styles. Jonas resists the almost overwhelming temptation to ask Eva to summarize the entire history of this alternate world. There will be time enough for that, he reasons. He'll be able to dive as far down that rabbit hole as he pleases. But he knows he can't stay in this universe. It no longer has who he's looking for . . .

"Can I ask you another question?" Eva says, stirring him from this reverie.

"I couldn't fathom setting a limit, after everything I've told you."

"Well, this one's kind of delicate."

"Sounds like the kind of question a psychologist should be asking." Jonas leans back in his chair. Spreads his hands. *Hit me.*

"If I understand the Many Worlds Theory correctly, there's a universe where you and your wife are both alive, where perhaps the accident never even happened."

"What's your question?"

She gives him a tremulous glance. In the end, she doesn't ask a question. "There's already a world," she asserts, "where you're happy."

"I don't know what that world looks like." His voice cracks with emotion. To will himself not to cry, he gazes out at the street, at the flotsam and jetsam of an entire city—representative of an entire world—full of people whose lives have unfolded in an infinite number of ways that differ from those in his home reality. His mind swims with the enormity of it. What had been theoretical for years is now real and tangible, almost beyond his ability to fully comprehend.

"So," Eva says skeptically, "you're just going to jump around universes until you find her?"

"I can't," Jonas answers. "Eventually, I'll expend the energy I got from the collider. And that's assuming I don't reality-slip into a wheat thresher or some such first." He feels stress rising, hope descending, as he considers the dangers of his mission. "I ended up in the reality I intended, but it was the wrong one. My math was off somehow, in some way. I need to figure that out first, or I'll just get lost again."

"If that's why you decided to trust me," she says, "I have to remind you that parallel-universe theory wasn't my field."

Jonas cocks his head and gives her a mischievous smirk. "But didn't you get an A in quantum mechanics?"

That draws an amused look. And Jonas senses a connection, an invisible electricity between them, the type of valence that could form the foundation of a lifelong friendship. The last time he felt such magnetism was five years ago.

FIVE YEARS AGO

The name of the restaurant was unimportant, a neighborhood place in Tribeca that would be out of business within eighteen months. Still, Jonas would never forget it was called Jackson's. The decor was exposed brick and piping. Apparently the designer's only artistic vision was to strip away every wall and inch of ceiling, then populate the space with chairs and tables sourced from *Architectural Digest* and art inspired by postcards from the gift shop at the Museum of Modern Art.

He had been so nervous that before their date, he ran out to a liquor store two blocks from his apartment and bought a bottle of whatever whiskey the man at the register had recommended. He poured it into a glass he had filled with ice and took a generous swallow. The whiskey burned the back of his mouth, shot fire into his chest, and rendered him no less anxious. He stared at the bottle and questioned if it contained any alcohol at all.

But in hindsight, Jonas didn't need an alcoholic sedative. Just seeing Amanda again was like unwrapping a present. She was light. She was sunshine. Radiant warmth in human form. And she was here. Real. Spending time—time she could spend in an infinite number of ways—with him. His whole life had been devoted to the academic. The theoretical. But *she* was real.

And she seemed to like him. Jonas had always seen the gulf between art and science as unbreachable, two sides of two very different coins. Never would he have imagined that paintings and quantum mechanics would find a connection, but Amanda had seen it instantly. Their work, she said, required them each to identify patterns and connections. They both labored to conjure reality—the appearance of it at least—from the speculative. His work and her art (as *she* practiced it) were even bounded by the same inalterable physics. Light. Perspective. The limits of human observation. They were both in the business of understanding and interpreting the marvels of creation.

"What are you working on right now?" she asked.

"Nothing all that interesting," Jonas promised. "How about you?"

"I'm scouting locations, looking for the next rooftop I'll paint from, the next 'vantage point,' I like to say, because it sounds more impressive," she added with a touch of self-effacing whimsy. "So what about you?"

"I'm working on a mathematical proof of the existence of parallel universes." The second the words left his mouth, he regretted them. They sounded ridiculous, esoteric. He drained his wineglass.

"Parallel universes?"

"Have you heard of them?"

She shrugged. "Everyone's heard of them, I guess. I mean, everyone's seen the movies. At least one of them, right? I think . . . parallel universes are one of those things everyone's heard of but never really understands."

"That's an accurate way of putting it," he said.

"But it's not real. I mean, it's just theory." She wrinkled her face with disapproval. "I'm sorry. It sounds like I'm shitting on your work, and that's absolutely the last thing I want to do." She paled, catching herself. "I mean—"

Jonas held his hand up. "It's okay. You're right. You're absolutely right. It's weird and even a little silly. I mean, what's the difference between science and science fiction, right?"

"I think you're supposed to tell me."

Jonas tipped his head. *Fair point.* "Do you have any money in your pockets or your purse?"

"Wow. And the check hasn't even come yet."

Jonas canted his head. *Good one.* "Do you have any coins? Preferably a quarter?"

"Are you going to do a magic trick?" she asked playfully.

"You'll see," he teased. "Do you have a coin?"

She reached for her purse and dug around in it until she'd success-fully excavated a quarter. She offered it up, but Jonas shook his head. "No. You keep it." She stared back at him quizzically. "Just flip it. Flip it, and catch it in your hand. But don't look."

"Seriously?"

"Humor me."

"Okay," she said, and did as instructed. They both watched the coin pinwheel for a second before she caught it in one hand and slapped it on the back of the other.

Jonas reached out to clasp her hands in his. When his skin con-nected with hers, he felt a jolt of electricity. She made no move to retract her hands as he stared back at her. "Now," he said, his eyes locked on hers, "the quarter came up either heads or tails, right?" Amanda nodded. "And now," he said, "there are *two* universes. One heads, one tails." Her hands were still clutched in his.

"How many undergrads have you tried this on?" There was whimsy in the question.

"This is just a variation on Schrödinger's cat. It's an illustration of the apparent paradox of quantum superposition."

"Quantum superposition?" She spoke with the slowness of some-one saying the words for the first time.

"Yes. It means that until you open your hands, the coin is *both* heads *and* tails."

"At the same time?"

"At the same time. But when you open your hands . . ." He peeled away his fingers and pulled off one of her hands to reveal the quarter. George Washington's profile lay on the back of her hand. ". . . you reveal one universe. But you've created *another*. A *different* universe. One where the quarter came up tails."

"Seriously, if you haven't pulled this with at least one of your students, that's just a tragic waste."

"Maybe I've just been waiting for the right student."

Amanda wagged her index finger in his direction. "Oh, that's good. That's really good."

They shared a laugh and leaned back in their chairs. Jonas felt himself relaxing and knew it wasn't the whiskey or the cabernet. Talking to Amanda was as easy as breathing. And, as with breathing, he felt unable to stop. He wanted to learn everything about her. How did she become an artist? Why? What were her dreams? How did she see the world? What place could he have in hers?

Eventually the appetizers came, and then their meal, and then dessert. They enjoyed another drink. Jonas didn't want the evening to end, and he sensed she didn't either. He offered to walk her home to a three-bedroom walk-up in Chelsea that Amanda shared with a poet and another artist. His hands were clammy as they arrived at her stoop and stood in a pool of white cast by a nearby streetlight. A pregnant moment hung, and Jonas tried to divine whether she wanted him to kiss her. Her eyes were tethered to his, and the space they shared hummed with a kind of magnetism.

Amanda's lips were parted slightly, and the air between them was combustible. Jonas leaned in, and his lips found hers. She tasted like strawberries. As his hands rounded her back, he felt her tongue slide to meet his. She felt small and firm in his arms. Her hands draped across his neck before sliding back to cradle his face. As gentle as a breeze, she pulled back, her hands still on his cheeks. Their mouths made an almost imperceptible *pop* when they parted.

"Thank you for a great evening," she said. "And for dinner. And for walking me home."

Jonas grasped for a response, but words eluded him. How could he find the words for all he was feeling? He thought of asking Amanda's roommate, the poet, but instead, he commanded his mouth to curl into a smile that he hoped could express his emotions in that moment.

Amanda gave a little half chuckle to indicate that she found his inability to speak charming. He saw that expression on her face again, the one that teased that she was smarter than him, at least in matters of the heart, that suggested she was thinking five to ten moves ahead but found herself attracted to him all the same. He knew right then and there that he could spend the rest of his life looking at her.

Ultimately, she withdrew into her building. Jonas stayed on the sidewalk until she disappeared inside and for at least a minute after that. He walked home carried by a lightness he'd never known before.

He texted her the next morning. He didn't care what the rules of dating required. This was different, he told himself. This wasn't dating. This was courtship, as ridiculously old fashioned as that idea was. He couldn't wait. He wanted to see her again. She'd either feel the same or she wouldn't. Either way, the decision wouldn't depend on the timing or manner of how Jonas asked for a second date.

They made plans for the next Friday.

He'd wanted to plan a more memorable evening out than the standard drinks or dinner or movie or some combination thereof. He tortured himself with ideas that he rejected as stupid, desperate, or unromantic. He ran a few past Victor, who had managed to find some-one to marry, despite all reason. Jonas queried colleagues and interro-gated grad students and teaching assistants only to be embarrassed and annoyed at himself when it dawned on him that presidential inaugura-tions were given less thought.

Eventually, he settled on the Hayden Planetarium at the American Museum of Natural History, despite a chorus of internal protestations that Amanda would consider it corny or lame or—the cardinal sin of romance—desperate. And maybe it would have been any or all of those things, but Jonas had pulled a favor, and they would have the Hayden Sphere's Space Theater all to themselves.

"Where's the rest of the crowd?" Amanda asked as Jonas walked her inside. She was wearing another sundress, and he watched as she tucked an errant strand of hair behind her left ear.

"Well, as it turns out, if one of the docents is a former student, you can arrange something special to impress a girl."

On cue, the room's customized Zeiss Star Projector revolved and pivoted in the center of the theater as the houselights slowly dimmed. Amanda let out a warm laugh. "Nice." She grinned.

"I did *not* expect that to time out as well as it did," Jonas said, chuckling a little to himself.

Above their heads, the projector beamed a high-resolution video of the night sky. It had the feel of magic.

Amanda craned her neck up to take in the show. "Why are you showing me this?" Her voice carried a tone of awe.

"Third grade," Jonas shrugged. "Mrs. Weingarten's class."

Above, the night sky projection morphed into a view of the Milky Way. Nebulae danced overhead. Jonas took it all in, marveling in the memory of the first time his whole life changed and the thrill of sharing that with the person who embodied the second.

"In the face of all this . . . wonder," he told her, "I felt small. But not insignificant. In fact, it was the opposite. I was inspired. Where did this all come from? Why? Who created it? And who created whoever created it? I was flooded with questions, each one more recursive than the last. My head began to swim." His eyes blazed, reverent. "And I was hooked."

He felt her staring at him. A bolt of self-consciousness surged. He'd taken it too far, been too corny, revealed too much. It was only their second date. What was he thinking? He felt the blood draining from his face. His stomach turned over.

"So am I," she said.

"What?"

"Hooked."

Jonas strained to understand what she meant, what was happening. Her entire affect had changed in a breath. She was more . . . earthy.

Dangerous. There was an expression on her face that he was incapable of recognizing as lust. "Do we have this place to ourselves?" she asked.

Jonas looked around. He knew nothing, understood nothing. "Yes."

"The person who turned on the thing . . ."

"The Star Projector," he clarified. Amanda met him with skepticism. "Really, that's what it's called."

"A bit on the nose, isn't it?"

Jonas shrugged his admission. His head was swimming, caught between dread and panic. "I think the people who design planetariums don't value subtlety," he may have said. He wasn't sure.

"But the person who turned it on," Amanda probed, "they can't see us?"

"No, they just press a button and leave. Why?"

She answered him with a kiss. And then with more. Her hands drifted down his body and took hold of him. Realization grabbed him as well, and he returned her ardor. They peeled off each other's clothes and lowered themselves to the floor. Above them, the majesty of the cosmos wheeled and turned, oblivious to their passion.

NOW

The connection between Jonas and the woman is evident, Victor Kovacevic notes, even from across the Rue Virginio-Malnati. Cars and trucks and buses whip past, occasionally obscuring the pair. He doesn't need to see more, though. He's found the needle he has been searching for in an infinite number of haystacks. He sees the woman giggle at whatever Jonas has said, and he feels that pang of envy, as familiar to him as the sound of his own voice.

Victor reaches down to manipulate his bracelet. Capacitance sensors in the housing register his touch, and he starts to feel the cosmic energies at work. He resists an urge to close his eyes. He wants to see it happen, to watch this universe fold in on itself as he slips the bonds of one reality and deposits himself in another. The sight reminds him of a reflection rippling on the surface of a pond while fireworks blossom and spark overhead. And when the phenomenon is over, when his body no longer feels like it's plugged into a wall socket, he sees that he's back in his Manhattan apartment.

Normally, floor-to-ceiling windows offer breathtaking views of the Upper East Side, but Victor has kept the curtains drawn for months. Walls that once held original works of art, a collection amassed at great expense, are now bare. The hardwood floor is discolored where his Steinway Grand once stood. But those were all personal effects, discarded like a snake's shed skin. The apartment is no longer a home. It hasn't been since his wife left.

In the void left by art and furniture and sentimental items stands a parade of whiteboards, each covered with exotic equations. They flank a massive device wrought of exotic metals, which reminds Victor of the eye of a giant robot. Cables as thick as human arms curve from it and run along the floor. Enough power flows through them to service ten city blocks. Getting the necessary waivers from Con Edison required an army of lawyers and millions of dollars.

The doorbell startles him. Apart from the occasional food delivery, he hasn't had a visitor in months. He shucks the coat he wore against the chill of an evening in Switzerland and pads to the door, opening it without bothering with the peephole.

Columbia Dean Dorothy Stanton stands there. He should have known. He should have expected his boss to visit weeks ago.

"Hello, Victor." She's five foot three, in her late seventies, and Victor would swear she's lost an inch since he saw her last. Her skin reminds him of a dried-up apple.

"Dorothy," he says, willing warmth into his voice. "How are you?" He hopes he's smiling.

"Can I come in?"

Victor takes more time to consider the question than he should. Eventually, he remembers his manners and waves her inside. "Can I offer you a drink?" he volunteers out of some moribund sense of propriety. She doesn't answer. He watches her take in the apartment. He knows how it appears, an eight-million-dollar Manhattan penthouse on the Upper West Side reduced to a scientific laboratory. He knows she thinks it's perverse.

"Your TAs came to me," she ventures. Victor can tell she's choosing her words with care. "En banc. They say they've been covering your lectures."

"That's what teaching assistants are for, isn't it?" He's trying to grin, but the image it conjures in his mind is grotesque.

"They say they've been covering for you for the past three months."

"I've been consumed with a recent project."

Dorothy's head bobs toward the massive device, the elephant in the room. "I can see that," she says, her tone bone dry. She turns to him with that look he's learned to despise, that look he's seen in too many faces, in too many sad expressions. That look he has to clench his fist against, lest he lose his temper. *Pity.* "I heard about Phaedra. I'm very sorry, Victor."

Victor swallows his rage. Like anything, it's become easier with practice. "I know the hour's late, but I'm really quite busy, so . . ."

"I'm worried about you, Victor." For once, she sounds sincere. "Everyone at the university is, in fact."

"I'm perfectly fine," he asserts, believing it.

"I don't think that's true," she says in a way that suggests she hates to say it. But Victor knows better. He knows how they all see him, how they all judge him, despise him.

"I might be too focused on work at present," he says, a suspect under interrogation repeating a rehearsed cover story. "But really, I'm fine."

"This isn't the home of a man who's fine, Victor," Dorothy says, apparently having decided to drop any pretense.

Victor wills his temper to remain in check. He tells himself he's simply here to play a part. "It's the home of a newly single man who's thrown himself into his work. Work that fulfills him."

"I think you need some time off," she says, sounding like she's been practicing the line in her head. "To take care of yourself. Deal with the divorce and whatever else is . . . ailing you."

"I told you. I'm fine." The words come out more clipped than he cares for.

The moment yawns, and Victor can see Dorothy is working herself up to bad news.

"The board voted for your suspension tonight," she finally says. "One year. Half pay."

A year's suspension is an ivory-tower death sentence. Victor commands his voice to remain level. "Without a hearing? That feels extreme," he says, as if all they did was move his parking space.

"It was all I could do to save your job." Her tone conveys a genuine sympathy. That's what angers him most of all.

"Well, thank you for that." He spits out the platitude, devoid of even a glimmer of sincerity. Dorothy begins to talk again, but he cuts her off. "Get out, please." She tries again, uttering some crap about a therapist that one of the faculty recommends, but it's just static. He endures as much as he can manage before thundering, "Get out!" Even he is surprised by the might of his rage. The light fixtures tremble in the wake of his outburst. He calms himself, breathing deep, and quiets. "Please." The word escapes his lips like a prayer.

He moves to his device and begins making adjustments. His ministrations are reminiscent of a lover's, seeking refuge in the work. He's so singularly focused on what he's doing, he barely hears the door shut behind her.

Eva lives in Switzerland. Her apartment is in a diminutive building sandwiched by two skyscrapers. After Jonas's first week there, when it becomes clear that no solution to his problem is imminent, he offers to get a place of his own. He doesn't want to intrude on her life any more than he already has, but she reminds him that he has no job and no money. In fact, he doesn't even possess any form of identification. She has opened her home to a man who doesn't officially exist.

Each night, Jonas converts the living room couch into his bed. By day, the makeshift bedroom becomes an equally makeshift laboratory, filled with rolling whiteboards he's purchased on Amazon with her credit card. He works diligently, often for hours, covering and erasing and re-covering the whiteboards with color coded equations sketched out with dry-erase markers. He buys a refurbished MacBook Pro and coaxes every ounce of processing power out of it. He promises to pay Eva back for all his expenditures, but they both know that once he leaves, he won't be coming back.

Weeks pass into months. One morning, Eva walks into the living room clutching her bathrobe around her with one hand and a mug of scalding coffee in the other. "You didn't sleep?" she asks, eyeing the couch, which hasn't yet made its nightly transformation into a bed.

"Lost track of time." Jonas moves to the whiteboard, erasing an equation with the heel of his hand and replacing it with a different calculation.

"Your wife's a lucky woman," Eva observes. Is it a trace of envy Jonas hears in her voice?

"Being dead, she might disagree," he notes.

"What I mean is, any woman would be lucky to have a man willing to search the world for her. Your wife has a man willing to search an *infinite number* of worlds."

Still at the whiteboard, Jonas stops writing. He's only gotten this far by denying the enormity of his task. He could do without the reminder.

"Have you ever heard of Henri Thibault?" Eva asks.

"Of course," Jonas says, finally turning from the whiteboard. "His paper on Bohmian mechanics served as one of the foundations for my Many Worlds Proof."

"Have you thought about asking him for help?"

"I certainly would, if he hadn't died eight years ago." He hopes he doesn't sound patronizing.

Eva arches an eyebrow. "You strike me as much smarter than that, Dr. Cullen," she says, playfully parroting the words he'd used with her back when they'd first met.

The epiphany hits Jonas right in the center of his chest. "Thibault is alive in this reality."

"He's a very difficult man to get an appointment with. Fortunately, one of my patients knows someone who knows someone who was willing to make a few calls for me." She pauses, as though about to reveal a secret. "Do you want to meet someone even smarter than you?"

∞

By the end of the day, Jonas and Eva are standing in the middle of École Polytechnique Fédérale de Lausanne's sprawling modern campus. Students and faculty shoot across the quad, its concrete peppered by patches of fake grass meant to convey the image of protons in flight.

Jonas studies the man sitting on the bench in front of him, peering intently at the glow of Jonas's MacBook. Apart from the consequential quality of being alive, this universe's Henri Thibault, PhD, is no different from the one Jonas knew back in his own reality. This Thibault favors the same wire-rimmed glasses and tweed sport coats, appears older than his years, and coughs with the rigor of an ex-smoker. Jonas considers telling Thibault that his doppelgänger died of lung cancer and thinks better of it.

It feels to Jonas as though it's taking a dozen lifetimes for Thibault to render a verdict on his work. Hoping to prompt some response, *any* response, he tries humor. "I'm relieved you're not calling for the men in the white coats."

If Thibault considers this amusing, he doesn't show it. His focus never leaves the computer's screen as he remarks, "You and your wife died two years ago, Dr. Cullen. I read your obituary. And yet, here you are, standing opposite me, talking to me. If I were to call for a psychiatrist, believe me, it'd be for myself."

"Both of you can relax," Eva says. "I'm a practicing psychologist, I'm a *licensed and published* psychologist, and I'm here to tell you I don't find either one of you to be the least bit nuts." Then, apparently as impatient as Jonas is, she adds, "What do you make of Jonas's equations?"

"I could spend the rest of my career studying them and barely scratch the surface," Thibault says. He pulls himself from the screen to marvel at Jonas. "Your work is the stuff of Einstein and Heisenberg. Of Podolsky and Rosen. Theoretical physicists spend their entire careers hunting—*praying*—to identify a paradigm shift like you have here."

That paradigm shift, as Jonas had explained to Eva, had been that the scope of the multiverse *isn't* limitless. The universe favors certain outcomes, and minor differences aren't enough to prompt the birth of a new reality. "With the multiverse reduced to a series of calculations," Thibault exults, "the mathematics changes to one of *probabilities*. And if the universe is predisposed to *some* realities, it becomes possible to calculate the *likelihood* of those realities."

"I'm afraid you've lost me," Eva admits.

"Think of a beach," Thibault says. "With an uncountable number of grains of sand, rocks, pebbles, seashells. To catalog it all would be impossible. But Jonas has figured out a way to calculate, to *predict*, how many grains of sand, how many rocks, et cetera."

Eva grasps the point. "And he's looking for the grains of sand where his wife is still alive."

"That's correct." Thibault stands with a resignation that fills Jonas with creeping dread. The affect of an oncologist armed with a damning MRI scan. "But I think you already know what I'm going to tell you."

Jonas does. "The reason," he says, "that I'm having such difficulty calculating the reality where Amanda survives the accident . . ." His voice trails off. The act of giving voice to his lack of hope fatigues him beyond his capacity to speak.

Thibault picks up the train of Jonas's thought. "Out of a nearly infinite number of probabilities, there's only one where your wife is still alive."

If hope were a living thing, this is a death sentence. One that Jonas had rendered weeks ago but lacked the courage to face.

Eva shakes her head, confused. "Wait. Just *wait*." The two men watch her think, wrapping her brain around the impossible. "You're saying that out of the entire multiverse, Amanda dies in every single one."

Thibault is the first to answer. "I'm saying, Dr. Stamper, that while there may very well be an infinite number of worlds, they all tend toward the same qualities. They all have gravity, for example. Oxygen. People. The multiverse is replete with these tendencies, these 'laws,' for lack of a better term. In the case of objects, we call them 'physics.' But in the case of people, we call them . . ."

"Fate," Eva breathes, her tone full of epiphany.

"Fate," Jonas echoes. "Or destiny." Fate and destiny aren't phenomena that scientists care to traffic in, any more than faith and religion, but he's found them to be as real as time, as immutable as gravity. "It's Amanda's destiny to die in that accident," he finally acknowledges. The words catch in his throat. In his mind's eye, he watches his wife die for the millionth time.

"I'm very sorry," Thibault says.

"You said . . ." Jonas lurches, his mind flailing. His thoughts are plummeting, thrashing about, desperate for any handhold. "You said that according to my calculations, there *is* a reality where Amanda is alive. 'One reality,' you said." His eyes plead with Thibault for this to be true.

The older professor's head bobs slowly, almost imperceptibly. Jonas can see the man's prodigious brain working. Game, as his students used to say, recognizes game. "Through my university," Thibault says, "I have access to a supercomputer that should aid considerably in making the calculations required to pinpoint it under your rubric."

It's all Jonas can do not to drop to his knees in gratitude. "You would do that for me?"

"Publishing wouldn't be without its challenges," Thibault muses, indulging in massive understatement. He winks like a coconspirator. "But I've been craving another Nobel." He hefts the laptop with some reverence. "All kidding aside, the work you've done here, Dr. Cullen, is beyond what even a room full of Nobels could acknowledge."

Terms are negotiated. Thibault will need a week at least. He's free to publish whatever he wants, wherever he wants, and to use Jonas's name and all his calculations. But even as Thibault negotiates, Jonas's mind is somewhere else. He feels an emotion so alien to him he didn't even feel it at CERN. For the first time in two years, he feels hope.

∞

Night falls, and Jonas remains ebullient as Eva drives her secondhand FIAT down the Seidenstrasse, a modest two-lane highway. She doesn't speak. After nearly a half hour on the road, the silence has grown loud.

"Penny for your thoughts?" he ventures. "Do they have that idiom in your universe?" Maybe he can lighten the mood with humor.

"I don't really want to talk about it," she says.

Jonas doubts anyone has ever said that and meant it. "Are you okay?" he asks.

"I said I don't feel like talking." The lights of a nearby city comet past.

"I know. You seem upset about something."

"That's one way to put it."

"Or you could put it another way," he tries. "You could talk about whatever it is that's bothering you."

"Right," she says with a hint of sarcasm, "because when I said that I didn't feel like talking, what I *really* meant was that I wanted to talk."

"You're right. I'm sorry to push."

They drive on. In the quiet of the car, each little sound seems magnified. The tires bumping over the seams in the highway. The purring of the engine. The snapping of Jonas's knuckles as he cracks them in a vain effort to fight his discomfort.

Finally, Eva breaches the silence. "You made it sound," she begins, her tone clipped, "like you were doing something noble—even heroic— just trying to get back to your wife."

Jonas is confused. "I am," he reassures her. "That's all I'm trying to do."

"Thibault said the universe favors certain outcomes." She says it like an accusation.

"Actually, *I* said it. I told you that weeks ago, and Thibault merely confirmed it." He shakes his head, at a loss. "What's going on?"

Eva's hands grip the steering wheel tight. "You told Thibault . . . back at the university, you said that your wife . . . I'm sorry to put it so bluntly, but you said it's your wife's fate to die in that accident." Jonas

77

watches her frown in disapproval. But not at him. At herself. He can see she doesn't want to be this person.

"That's right. And so?"

"So," she says, biting off each word, "you're screwing around with the fundamental laws of the universe."

"Actually, I'm screwing around with the fundamental laws of the *multiverse*." Another attempt at lightening the mood.

It doesn't work. "Don't make light of this," she snarls. Then, calmer, "My Introduction to Physics professor liked to say, 'Einstein described the workings of the universe as being like a finely tuned watch.'"

"Yes. Einstein said that. I'm sorry, but what's your point?"

"That watches are *fragile*." Eva takes a deep breath. Her exhale is ragged. Primal. She takes her eyes off the road to drill them into his. "You think you're the only person to have lost something or someone? The only person who wishes things were different? That the dice roll of their lives came up as another number?" She doesn't raise her voice, but it trembles with rage. She returns her eyes to the highway with a faraway stare, accessing a distant and painful memory. "I was married too. An American army ranger. He was stationed here before deploying to Afghanistan. Paktia Province. His unit received intel on a 'potential' Taliban stronghold." She chokes back tears. She swallows bile. "There was nothing 'potential' about it."

Eva's grief, so palpable that Jonas can almost touch it, fills the small car. He forms condolences in his mind, but they all sound hollow and wrong. A lone tear tracks down Eva's face. She swats it away.

"I'm sorry," he says. "I didn't know. I'm sorry I didn't ask."

"Why do *you* get a second chance when the rest of us don't? What makes you so special?" There's a bitterness to her words that Jonas didn't think she was capable of. A reminder that, in the end, everyone shares the same human shortcomings, the same pain.

"You know I'm not special," he says with care but also sincerity. "If your husband meant as much to you as Amanda does to me, you have to know why I have to do this."

"I do. Of course I do."

"But?"

The question goes unanswered. Silence hangs between them. The next few minutes are filled with the droning of the car's engine and the rush of traffic.

Finally, Jonas reminds her, "You said you'd help me."

"This *is* me helping you," Eva rebuts. "The fifth and last stage of grief is acceptance. Your wife is dead. You need to accept that." She turns to him again to make her point firm. "You can't swim against the tide of the universe."

The words hit like blows, pummeling Jonas with the truth. With reality. "I don't believe that," he whispers.

"Don't. Or won't?"

"*Can't,*" he answers. He's never set foot in a confessional, but he speaks with the urgency of the penitent and the resolve of the faithful. "I can't let her go. I can't . . . accept that in an infinite number of worlds, there's not even one where Amanda and I can be together."

Not for the first time, Jonas watches pity pass across Eva's face. "But you have to accept it."

"Why?" He honestly doesn't know.

"Because you're fighting the universe."

"I know," he admits. "But so what?"

"So the universe is going to fight back."

The words prove prescient as the driver's side of the car suddenly caves in, crunching glass and rending steel. The impact sends Jonas flashing back to another road in Switzerland not all that different from the one he's on right now. History has a way of repeating itself, so the saying goes, and there must be a reason for the axiom. What if there is an infinite dance of events, fated to unfold in the same movements, over and over and over into infinity?

He sees Eva clutching the wheel, wrestling it for control of the car. Wind shoots in from what had been the driver's side window. Jonas peers through the jagged aperture and sees the cause of the collision—an eighteen-wheeler as big as a small house running alongside them.

His mind races, grasping for an explanation. The driver is drunk. Or fell asleep at the wheel. Or is simply negligent. But all these possibilities are dashed when the truck escapes from its lane again, missiling back toward the FIAT, once more digging its mass into the car's crumpled side.

Jonas hears Eva scream, her wail carrying both terror and confusion. On some level, they both know the truism that one time is an accident, twice is deliberate.

This is an *attack*.

Eva deftly tries to keep the car on the road. She floors the accelerator, coaxing as much speed as she can from the FIAT's modest engine, and Jonas suspects that they both have the same instinct: they won't survive another collision. Their only chance is to race off the elevated highway to more level ground with enough space to get away.

The truck is drifting back—positioning itself for another assault—when Jonas sees the driver. Amazingly, impossibly, Jonas knows him. The driver's face is unmistakable. It belongs to a dead man.

The driver is Macon.

Jonas's first thought is that he's hallucinating. Macon here—in this specific time and place, acting with malicious intent—has to be a mirage conjured by adrenaline. But while Jonas might deny his lying eyes, there's no mistaking the reptilian coldness in the driver's. Whoever this universe's Macon is, and for whatever reason, the man clearly intends to kill him.

Jonas watches Macon's face contort with malice as he aims the truck at the FIAT. He barely notices the gunmetal-gray bracelet on Macon's wrist before the truck hurls into Eva's car again, a battle at sixty miles per hour between a David and a Goliath. But this time, David has no slingshot.

Eva is screaming. Or maybe that's just the sound of tortured metal as the truck sandwiches the FIAT against the guardrail. Steel wails as the Seidenstrasse begins to stretch over Lac Léman. The truck recedes once more, and then slams into them again. The guardrail crumples, and the FIAT is airborne.

Instinct and sad experience impel Jonas into action. Snapping off his seat belt, he envelops Eva. A million times, he has relived the accident with Amanda, and a million times he has embraced her as he wishes he had on that fateful night. Tonight, he swallows Eva in his arms the way he wishes he'd done his wife, hoping it will mean the difference between life and death.

Closing his eyes, he tenses, knowing from experience what happens next. Impact. Violent and abrupt. The sound of the world ending. Old Testament brutality and tumult.

The FIAT slams into concrete. *No, not concrete.* The waters of Lac Léman. The car begins sinking instantly, plunging into the inky darkness. Water gallops in through the mangled driver's side. It smashes against Eva like a fist. And with each ounce that cascades in, the car's descent quickens.

It's the smallest of miracles that Jonas had the instinct to unbuckle himself. If they survive this, that will be the reason. Holding his breath, his fingers fumble with Eva's seat belt, but the water makes both skin and metal as slick as ice, and his hands struggle to find purchase. Eva's eyes go wide with shock and fear as she discovers she's unable to keep her mouth closed, to resist the primal urge to breathe. Her mouth births tiny bubbles of carbon dioxide. They float gracefully from her lips. The last thing she'll ever see . . .

Jonas feels his fingers give way beneath his efforts. His heart leaps at the realization that it's the seat belt surrendering. Eva is free. Jonas allows himself to feel relieved until he sees the cloud of crimson rising from Eva's midsection. Panicked, his lungs burning, he looks down and sees an angry metal shard protruding from the driver's side door, impaling Eva's abdomen.

His body goes cold. This isn't how Amanda died, but it's close enough to torture his soul. Maybe it's the urgency of Eva's predicament, or just oxygen deprivation, but conscious thought leaves him. All he knows, all he cares about, is extricating her, and he feels this with terrible urgency.

The next few seconds blur. Untangling Eva from the seat belt, wrestling her from its nylon grasp. Pulling her from the metal's jagged grip. The horror as the murky water turns red. The impotent attempts at opening the door, and the realization that the weight of Lac Léman won't yield to it. Jonas pulls himself, and then Eva, through the broken window, glassy shards scraping at them like rows of gnashing teeth.

Seconds later, Jonas is exploding out of the water—miraculously—with Eva in his arms. He manages to beach them on the shore. The ground is hard, unyielding, and terribly cold, but Jonas greets it as a gift. He pushes Eva onto her back and readies himself to perform CPR, though he knows only what he learned from a junior high class and God knows how many movies.

He alternates between chest compressions and blowing life into her lungs. As he retracts his lips from hers, he tastes copper. Which means internal bleeding. He's losing her. He redoubles his efforts, leaning down, the butt of his hand pressed to her sternum. "C'mon," he whispers. "C'mon . . ."

He moves back to her head, pinching her nose with one hand and keeping her mouth open with the other, ready to deliver another series of breaths, when she coughs violently. Fresh water flecked with blood geysers up unexpectedly as her eyes fly open, disoriented and scared and confused.

Jonas's mind flashes to the image of Macon behind the wheel of the truck. *What was he doing? And why?* It couldn't possibly be a coincidence, could it? "Just—try not to talk, Eva. Just breathe. Just breathe."

As Eva does her best to comply, Jonas considers her abdomen. The wound beneath her rib cage glistens, spurting blood with each beat of her panicked heart. His hands work to stanch the bleeding, but he feels Eva's warmth flowing between his fingers.

"Jonas," she says, each syllable a labor. "I feel cold."

He starts ripping away at his shirt, tearing strips for a makeshift bandage, when he hears the sirens. 'They're growing louder. Closer. He packs Eva's wound with the remains of his shirt, but the fabric quickly goes damp with her blood.

"You have to go," Eva says.

"I'm not leaving you." If Jonas knows anything, he knows this.

"*I'm* leaving," she whispers.

"We'll get you to a doctor."

"Too late, I think." She shudders. An involuntary spasm, as if she's about to fall asleep. Sirens echo in the distance. "You can't let them arrest you," she says.

"They won't."

"They *might*." She draws a jagged breath. "You're at the scene of an accident. And if they take you into custody . . . they'll take your tether." She clenches her teeth, willing herself to get out the undeniable conclusion. *"You have to go."*

She's barely uttered the words before everything is bathed in red light.

"Geh runter!" Jonas hears. *"Geh weg von ihr!"*

Next, footfalls. The sound of men vaulting a guardrail. The jangle of equipment and the clatter of guns.

"Don't be sad," Eva says. Contentment on her face. "It's okay. There are other realities where I'm alive."

Emotion overwhelms him. Sadness. But also guilt. The knowledge that Macon must have been after *him*. That she's dying only because he came into her life. "Thank you," he says, fighting back tears. "For everything."

But she's gone. He fears she never heard a word. A tide of grief washes over him. Not as visceral as when Amanda died, but no less profound.

"Geh runter! Geh runter!"

Swiss police surround him. Guns aimed. Voices raised. Eva was right: this is now a crime scene, and everyone present is a suspect. Jonas allows for the possibility that the police in this reality are particularly prone to outsize reactions.

"Beweg dich nicht!"

He doesn't react to them. He doesn't turn away from Eva. He's thinking. Presented with an impossible choice. Eva was right: if he's taken into custody, they might confiscate his tether. He calculates his likelihood of getting lucky—either by persuading them to let him keep the tether or reclaiming it before he reality-slips without his ring—as extraordinarily low. But to leave this universe would mean leaving its Thibault and the man's promise of identifying the reality where Amanda is still alive.

"Beweg dich nicht!" They're addressing him like a suspect. Jonas ratchets down his odds of retaining the tether in police custody, comparing them with the odds of divining Amanda's location without Thibault's help.

He slowly removes his ring from his finger.

This time, he isn't panicked. This time, his heart isn't pounding out of his chest. This time, his breathing isn't halting. Once again, police are descending upon him, barking orders in foreign tongues, but this time, he is calm. His eyes are wide, his vision clear.

It's the only way to witness a miracle.

How else to describe what he's seeing? What no man or woman in history has ever seen? The folding in of the universe itself. Movement across the multiverse like a stone skipping across a pond or like moving along a radio dial, new stations sliding into and out of focus.

Most unexpected is his perception that he's standing perfectly still. Instead, it's the world—*worlds*—around him that is changing. He remains statue still as his environs alter and morph. To his astonishment, the beat of his heart, as tangible as a fist, keeps a steady meter. With each pulse, the worlds around him change.

Pulse. The Swiss police are gone, and the waters of Lac Léman burn with ethereal emerald flames.

Pulse. Bombs fall all around him. Explosions blossom, bursts of fire hurling up dirt with terrifying ferocity.

Pulse. The bombing is over as quickly as though someone threw a switch. And although Jonas knows there's no connection between the previous fusillade and now, his blood is chilled by the sight of the distant skyline festooned with swastikas.

Pulse. Lac Léman abruptly disappears, and Jonas is standing in the middle of an arcing twenty-lane highway as strange cars, futuristic but possessing a 1960s aesthetic, bullet past, each one missing him by inches, seeming to grow closer with each pass.

Jonas shifts on his feet, afraid that any movement will draw him into a path of one of the vehicles whipping past. But then some animalistic instinct alerts him that he's standing directly in the path of an oncoming car. He confirms this with a glance over his shoulder. One of the many cars bears down on him, but his feet are rooted in terror.

Some innate part of him is screaming a directive now. Jonas's mind reaches deep to grasp whatever it is, but the thought is slippery, elusive. Fortunately, the idea is stubborn, an infant wailing ever louder, determined to be heard. Demanding that he feel the metal in his right hand, wedged between his thumb and index finger.

His tether.

FIVE YEARS AGO

At the time of its construction, the skyscraper at 432 Park Avenue in Manhattan was the tallest residential building in the Western Hemisphere, the fifth tallest building in the United States, and the twenty-eighth tallest in the world.

Amanda relayed all these statistics to Jonas during their elevator ride to the roof. *The tower is 1,396 feet tall. It holds 125 condominiums, including a private restaurant for residents.* She reeled off pieces of trivia, machine-gunning ephemera in impressive detail, all from memory. Every aspect of the building was important to her, and he found the depth of her passion intoxicating.

Jonas felt the air hit his face as they stepped out onto what he assumed was the roof. For an artist, Amanda was surprisingly good at blindfolding someone. He could perceive no light and distinguish no shadows at the edges of his vision as she led him by the hand across the roof.

This was, technically, their third date. But they'd already made love seven times and spent countless hours on the phone, FaceTime, and text. They were already as inseparable as limbs. There were times when the urge to tell her that he loved her was overwhelming, but some corner of his mind implored him to resist. *It's too soon,* the voice warned. Whatever their connection and despite their attraction, both of which were profound, Jonas couldn't assume that Amanda felt exactly as he did exactly when he did. *That would be foolish,* he told himself. Better to take things slow. There was no urgency, save for the restless beat of his heart and the feeling of longing he had during every minute he spent apart from her.

"You know," he deadpanned as she guided him across the rooftop, "I grew up on Long Island. I've lived in Manhattan since I was a college freshman. I've seen the city more than a few thousand times." In his mind, he calculated how far across the roof they had walked. They had to be close to the roofline, and he was struck by a mild panic.

Then he felt her hand on his shoulder, guiding him, and with the other, she encouraged him to take a step up. And then another. And another. Jonas felt a slight wobble under him and reasoned that he must be climbing a stepladder. As it teetered under him, he felt untethered, despite Amanda's steadying grip, the stepladder fragile beneath his weight.

"You haven't seen the city the way I see it," Amanda said.

And removed the blindfold.

Jonas teetered off the corner of the rooftop's balustrade. He felt his body shudder in reaction, a jolt of natural panic, but Amanda held him firm. The threat of vertigo hit him before subsiding, replaced by a warm feeling of calm and then a sense of beauty. He twitched and began to wobble slightly, adrenaline electrifying his chest, but Amanda's grip was a soothing balm, a lifeline.

His eyes widened, and he saw the city as the pigeons did: an endless horizon of glass and steel, rods and shafts of silver and gray erupting from the ground beneath a canopy of blue roped with white. He felt as if he were standing *inside* one of Amanda's paintings.

"How did you convince me to do this?" he whispered, already knowing the answer.

"You trust me."

Jonas chanced a glimpse downward. A concrete canyon spun below him, and vertigo made a return appearance. "That's what they'll write on my tombstone. 'He trusted her.' *After* they squeegee me off the pavement." He was joking, but not. He was terrified, but not. He was, he told himself, merely taking refuge in humor against the strange concoction of astonishment and terror he was feeling. It was, he would consider after, very much akin to being in love.

"You want to get down?"

Jonas smirked. "Eventually. Safely. The *slow* way."

"Well, you showed me what *you* find magical. This seemed only fair."

Jonas chanced raising an index finger in front of him. "For the record, no one ever died in a planetarium."

"I'm pretty sure that's not true." She held Jonas with one hand while reaching up to nudge his chin slightly to the sky. "Look," she said, her voice filling with awe. "Every car. Every window. Every street corner teeming with life. As many lives as the stars at the Hayden. As many as in the evening sky." She spoke with the reverence of a rabbi or priest. "But each star *here* holds someone's hopes and dreams. Each one, its own tiny universe."

Jonas peered out, his vision heightened by the reality that the clutch of a single tiny hand was really all that stood between him and death. From this vantage, the city was a labyrinth of color, a sculpture of right angles and vertical lines. He was seeing it as she did, and it was wondrous.

"I try to capture it on canvas," she said, her voice laced with humility. "Not the image. The *feeling*. Life. All those people. All those dreams. All those *universes*." He heard her gasp for breath, as caught up in the moment as he was, humbled by the majesty before them both. "I've never managed it. Not really. Not yet. But one day. One day . . ."

"I've seen your work," he said. "I think you have."

"You're sweet. But I haven't painted anything that captures . . . *all of it*." She paused, hit by some epiphany. "You found me in this multitude," she breathed. The awe he heard in her voice matched what he felt in his heart.

Jonas turned, and their eyes locked. "I'll *always* find you," he said. "In any multitude. In any *lifetime*." The promise felt like a vow.

Her body pulsed toward his, and their lips found each other's, their arms entwining. The altitude and the precarious footing afforded by the stepladder were forgotten. They were over a quarter of a mile in the sky, wrapped in nothing but the open air. She no longer held him. They held each other.

"I love you," he said, and he didn't care if it was too much or too fast. It was, and would always be, the truth. "I love you too much."

"I love you more," she beamed back.

They kissed again. The city teemed beneath them as they flew.

NOW

Manhattan's arteries are clogged with cars and trucks. Tourists and finance warriors on public bikes rocket by—no helmets—over special lanes designated for the purpose. The sounds of jackhammers and construction echo. Steam pours from an uncountable number of orifices. Scaffolding covers a full third of the city.

Victor pays attention to none of it. He walks to clear his head, not surrender it to the overdose of sights and smells and sounds that is New York City. Hedge fund managers on cell phones and pantsuited women in white sneakers impede his progress. The flotsam and jetsam of the capital of the world.

As he rounds a corner, nearing home, he sees Phaedra. Waiting at the building's entrance, wearing a simple blouse and skirt and an exasperated expression. She's still as beautiful as she was the day they met. "You told the doorman not to let me up?" she demands.

"You don't live here anymore," he answers, working to keep resentment from his tone. He throws in an innocent shrug to sell it, but the effort is halfhearted.

"Dorothy Stanton called me. She's concerned about you."

"Then maybe she shouldn't have fired me," Victor retorts.

"*Suspended* you," Phaedra corrects. "Out of concern for your well-being."

"And I suppose I'm enjoying that same concern from you right now?" This time, he doesn't try to conceal his bitterness.

Well traveled in Victor's darker moods, Phaedra doesn't take the bait. "Dorothy says you've turned our home into a monument to your obsession with Jonas Cullen."

"It's no longer 'our' home. And I'm *not* obsessed." They both know he's lying.

"Really? Then what destroyed our marriage?" The question hangs, laden with remorse and shared history.

Eventually, Victor says, "I don't know what destroyed our marriage, Phaedra. I suppose you could say its demise was an example of quantum entanglement, where cause and effect existed simultaneously."

An experimental physicist in her own right—and a former student of Victor's—Phaedra understands the analogy, even though she doesn't agree with it. "You traded our marriage for your vendetta. If I didn't support you—"

"You didn't," Victor bites.

"Because I didn't *understand* you. I didn't understand why you should be so envious of someone else. Someone who was your *friend*. I didn't understand why you had him fired, why you kept him from getting published."

"He stole my work," comes the simple reply.

"He built upon your work," she clarifies. "Isn't building on the work of others what scientific inquiry—if not all human achievement—is about?"

Victor lets out a long fatigued sigh. How many times must they have the same argument? "He used my work as the foundation for his without even *asking* me first." That he doesn't raise his voice is a triumph.

"And you couldn't forgive him that *one* transgression?" Phaedra asks. "He was your best friend."

"Exactly."

She stares back at him, incredulous.

"I've been in academia long enough to expect slings and arrows from fellow colleagues and professional rivals," Victor elaborates. "But to be betrayed by a friend . . ." He shakes his head with disgust. "I might not have dealt with it in the most . . . positive way, I admit that. And I regret it." His remorse seems genuine. "But the betrayal just hurt too much."

He watches Phaedra process this. For a heartbeat, he allows himself to indulge in the idea that he's come off as reasonable, sympathetic enough to begin repairing his relationship with her. His only mistake was not getting her to see where he was coming from sooner, why he was so pained and vindictive.

"I'm sorry," she says, confirming his aspiration. She seems sincerely apologetic. "I'm sorry you can't see it."

Victor feels a twinge of worry. "Can't see what?"

"That no one betrayed you, Victor," she says, exhaling the thought like a sigh. "Jonas *invited* you to work with him, and you told him to pound sand."

Now Victor gives full license to his animus. "Invited me to participate in my own work. Yes. Very kind. I can't believe I was so wrong about him." The words are drenched in sarcasm, his tongue snapping out each syllable.

"Get help, Victor," she says, more in surrender than in earnest. "The university has good people for this sort of—"

"Thank you," he growls. "I appreciate the concern."

He turns on a heel and heads into what was once *their* apartment building. Phaedra watches him go, trailing resentment and vitriol.

It's the last time she'll ever see him.

NOW

The first thing Jonas notices when he opens his eyes is that he's not dead. The highway is gone, replaced by the same shoreline as when he departed Eva's reality. He looks to the skyline. It's still recognizable as Geneva, but the Japanese architectural accents are gone, as though erased by an artist's brushstrokes. In their place are trees and leaves and fields of grass. It's as if the buildings were constructed by an architect and a gardener working in tandem, a perfect blend of cityscape and nature.

It only takes a clutch of seconds for him to shake off the awe of an entirely new world. He's a man of singular focus. The reality he has randomly traveled to is of interest only insofar as it contains the possibility, albeit gossamer thin, that Amanda is still alive in this universe.

He hikes up the slope that leads back to the Seidenstrasse, or whatever it's called in this brave new world. As in his home universe and the one he just departed, cars and trucks whip past. He sets off along the shoulder, clutching his torn shirt closed against the gathering chill, the thumb of his free hand aimed toward the passing traffic. A wry thought intrudes: *In this world, is an outstretched thumb a signal for hitchhiking?*

It is. A car slides up to meet him, its electric engine emitting a faint soothing hum. A gull-wing door rises, and as Jonas climbs in, he notices that the rear of the car's body tapers back to a single wheel.

The driver, a woman in her twenties, doesn't speak English, but Jonas's French is enough to communicate his destination, the offshoot of Geneva where Eva lives. At least, where Eva *lived*, an entire universe away. The car—a "tryke," he'd later learn—lets him off five blocks from where Eva's apartment should be. He walks the rest of the way. When he arrives, the two skyscrapers that had bookended Eva's apartment building in another universe are still standing. But here, they buttress nothing but air, the ground dedicated to a public garden.

∞

Jonas walks. There's no point in hitchhiking. Hitchhiking is for people who have someplace to go. But he is lost. Not in Geneva—he knows the city as well as any local—but in the multiverse. Without conscious thought, he walks east before noticing that he's navigating toward the closest university, the Université de Genève.

He sleeps atop the heating vent of the university library like a homeless person. In the literal sense, it's strikingly true. Several universes removed from his own, Jonas is as homeless as anyone has ever been.

Eventually, the morning light rakes across him, slapping him awake. He walks laps around the campus for the three hours until the library opens.

Once inside, he locates the public computers. The sight of a man who appears as though he slept in his clothes draws more than a few curious stares, but Jonas ignores them and sets to work. He starts by opening Google, but a "404" code informs him that *http://google.com* doesn't exist. This prompts a laugh. Who could fathom a reality without Google? Eventually he finds this reality's preferred search engine. In this universe, Apple has apparently added internet search to the breadth of its domain.

He starts by typing Eva's name into the search field. The query yields no results. Henri Thibault is next. Jonas's heart leaps with hope as the screen cascades with mentions. He scans the information spit out by the search: Grammar school teacher. Science fair. Fan fiction. Comic book collection. Two children. Jonas darkens. Thibault's life took a very different turn in this reality.

He types his own name next. The search returns websites that tell an encapsulated story of his life. Specifics are in short supply, but the major details are encouraging: PhD in physics, PhD in quantum mechanics, PhD in quantum field theory, professor at Columbia University. At least, until two years ago. Then the trail goes cold. He clicks on his Columbia University profile and gets an uneasy feeling, which is confirmed when he reads the bio.

He died two years ago.

With rising urgency, he delves deeper, eventually surfacing his own obituary. It's a discordant reaction, but his spirits rise at seeing the account of his death. What he reads causes him to exhale with volcanic force as the lungful of air he wasn't even aware he'd been holding escapes him in a ragged breath. Not for the first time, other library patrons cast suspicious, uncomfortable glances in his direction. He doesn't care. He just reads the same eight words over and over.

Doctor Cullen is survived by his wife, Amanda.

His heart sings with a lightness he hasn't felt in two long years. His head grows fuzzy, and he thinks he might pass out from relief and joy.

She's alive. She's here, and she's alive.

It's beyond improbable. It's impossible. Like finding a specific single grain of sand along a beach. And yet . . .

Maybe the universe has granted him a mercy. Maybe his calculations were not as far off as he'd assumed. Maybe his arrival in Gillard's universe was an anomaly, a quantum hiccup of some kind. Maybe his reality-slipping ended exactly where he had always intended to be. He turns to the screen again for confirmation. Doctor Cullen is survived by his wife, Amanda. Its meaning doesn't change, no matter how many times he reads it. Incredibly, he's arrived in the one reality Thibault had promised where the car accident claimed him instead of her.

He types with breathless urgency, and another search confirms that Amanda still lives in their apartment in Manhattan. The same apartment. It's almost beyond imagining.

His mind gallops. His first impulse is to call her, to hear her voice, to assure her that he's still alive and will explain everything once they're finally together. But then better instincts take over. He doesn't want to frighten her. A call from a dead man? No. She's likely to think it some kind of scam. Better their reunion be in person. Suddenly, there's no rush. Suddenly, he has—*they have*—all the time in the world.

He feels lightheaded but not just with euphoria. He's hyperventilating. He works to steady himself and slow his breathing. *We have all the time in the world.* The most important thing is that he's found her.

He grips the desk, breathing deep and deliberately. He has to get to her. He has to get halfway across the globe with no money, no passport, no form of identification whatsoever. Again it occurs to him that calling her would be easier. She could fly to him. Wouldn't that be easier? But then a new thought strikes him with a force that feels almost physical. He grimaces at the simplicity of the solution and types:

recovery of stolen credit card

∞

It takes Jonas less than ninety minutes to hitchhike from the university to Aéroport de Genève, where the American Express office is situated atop a row of escalators, sandwiched between an OMEGA store and a Ralph Lauren. The Amex representative behind the counter is a pleasant woman who Jonas calculates can't be older than twenty-seven. This is fortunate, he tells himself. With age comes cynicism, and he's going to need a little credulity to pull off what he has planned.

He tells her his prepared sob story about how he was the victim of a pickpocket, how he had kept his US passport, credit cards, driver's license, and cash in the same travel wallet. "So stupid," he berates himself, adding with a hapless shrug, "but Switzerland has the reputation of being one of the safest countries on earth."

The young woman is sympathetic. "This sort of thing happens all the time," she assures him. "More often than people think." She hands Jonas a form with a litany of security questions. He answers every one, his entire scheme hinging on the hope that the details he recalls—his social security number, his home address in Manhattan, his mother's maiden name, the make of his first car, and other ephemera—remain consistent in this reality. As he fills out the form, he makes small talk with the representative, doing his best to endear himself to her, to build a personal connection should he need to take advantage of one.

After he hands over the completed form, the representative disappears into a back room for what feels like an eternity. He passes the time thinking about what he'll do if his ploy doesn't work. It's an interesting challenge, he reflects, bringing forth the identity and financial resurrection of a dead man. But if it seems as though he's trying to con American Express, to steal a deceased identity, he's going to have to get out of here quickly.

When the representative emerges, she appears stricken. Jonas's heart sinks, and a new concern billows forward. What if she suspects him of attempting to defraud her? What if she called the police? He can't allow himself to be taken into custody, nor can he leave this universe. Landing here was winning the cosmic lottery. No one does that twice. He can't leave, and he can't permit the circumstances that would compel him to.

He forces a friendly smile to reaffirm that he's a good guy just having a bad day and to cover a glance behind him to confirm that the door to the Amex office is open, should he need to effect a quick escape. He resists the urge to ask if there's a problem. *Don't admit the premise,* he admonishes himself. *This could be nothing. Just your paranoia.*

But it's not. There is, in fact, a problem.

"Mr. Cullen, I'm afraid there's something unusual with your account."

Jonas forces an air of easygoing detachment. "Unusual how?"

"According to our records," the woman starts, almost apologetic, "you're dead."

He works hard to pretend this development is unexpected, smiling broadly but not, he hopes, too broadly. "Funny, I don't feel dead," he quips. *Disarm with humor.*

"Good point." She seems genuinely sympathetic to his plight. "And you match the photo we have on file for you, but the account was closed two years ago."

Jonas is prepared for this but tries to come off like he's just had the thought. "Y'know, it's funny . . . I just read—I don't know when, maybe a month or two ago—I read an article in *Wired* magazine about how hackers are altering public records like that. Y'know, make someone appear to be dead. I guess it makes identity theft easier somehow." He punctuates the idea with a naive shrug, ignorant of the dark ways of cybercrime. It's time to cash in on the connection he hopefully made with the lady earlier. "Is there—I don't know—a manager you can talk to or something? This is all such a nightmare."

Sympathetic, she says she'll see what she can do and disappears again into the back room. The call she's making is to one of only two possibilities: her boss or the airport police. Jonas can't see her behind the divide, can't read her body language or facial expressions. Can't know whether to stay and hope or run and escape. His hands leave a film of perspiration on the Formica countertop.

Over his shoulder, he spots two uniformed police officers moving toward the office. He wills himself to remain calm, only to note that his fists are clenched and his legs feel rubbery. He fights an urge to vomit.

"Okay." The voice comes out of nowhere, shafts of sunlight through gray storm clouds. The representative approaches the counter holding a green card, another form, and a pen. "We got it all squared away. It helps that you're here and, you know, *alive.*"

"Very much so." He tries to keep the relief and exultation out of his voice, but the attempt comes off comically. The woman titters slightly as she places the items down on the counter. The green card is, as Jonas had hoped, a brand new American Express card. The letters **J-O-N-A-S-C-U-L-L-E-N** bubble up in black over the field of green and white. The pen is for him to sign the form acknowledging receipt. He initials and signs where instructed. Relief washes over him.

∞

After getting a cash advance from an ATM using his new Amex card, Jonas hails a taxi. Within ninety minutes, he's waiting in line outside the United States diplomatic mission to Switzerland.

Fortunately, he doesn't have to wait long. The consular officer he happens to get is a man in his fifties with salt-and-pepper hair and absolutely no warmth or sense of humor. Whatever charms Jonas was able to work on the Amex representative, this man is impervious to them. Nevertheless, Jonas launches into his rehearsed remarks: "Pickpocket." "So stupid." "Switzerland has the reputation of being one of the safest countries on earth." But this time his recitation includes the added novelty of "I'm just lucky I kept this in a separate pocket." And he holds up his newly minted credit card as if it's an Olympic medal.

Once again, he deploys the line about the *Wired* article and computer hackers committing virtual murder. "Yeah, I think I read that one too," the consular officer says, and Jonas considers the possibility that maybe it wasn't an invention after all. In any case, after a new photograph is taken and a three-hour wait, he is once again officially alive and an American citizen.

Leaving the embassy, he discovers that taxis are in short supply, so he elects to take public transportation back to the airport, and soon enough he's handing his new passport and credit card to a kindly attendant at Swissair. He splurges for a first-class seat. It's not every day one flies home to a deceased spouse.

His direct flight to New York doesn't take off for another two hours, and he spends them using his newly obtained line of credit on a shaving kit, an iPad, and a meal at McDonald's. He cleans himself up in the restroom and fills the iPad with as much information on Amanda's life as he can pull off the airport's glacial public Wi-Fi. He considers purchasing a change of clothes but decides that would be tempting fate. He keeps his reality-slipping wardrobe on.

After settling into his seat on Swissair flight 4587, he fires up the iPad and plunges into the life his wife has lived without him. He does this without envy or concern that she's found someone else. He has no insecurity about the speed with which Amanda may have processed his loss. She's alive in this reality, and that is all that matters. He takes in every detail the internet reveals, reading about a new gallery showing, indulging in an interview in *The Art Newspaper* and another in *Vulture*. He reads with the fervor of an obsessed fan. Each factoid and piece of trivia confirms she's still alive, and the feelings fill him with light.

She's alive. He repeats this to himself over and over—an incantation—playing with the idea in his head, examining it.

She's alive.

The mantra is a warm blanket, soothing and reaffirming. The calm eventually opens the door to a fatigue that comes slamming in. The lethargy pulls down on him, making a triumphant return after being held at bay through force of will for the past two years. Jonas stops fighting to remain awake.

She's alive.

His mouth is fixed in a contented smile when sleep takes him.

FIVE YEARS AGO

Two months into their relationship, Jonas knew they would marry. But he never raised the subject, and neither did she. He felt no urgency to propose. For one thing, it had only been two months. All he cared about was that they were content. Amanda seemed as happy as he was. The synchronicity they enjoyed seemed like the stuff of bad movies or trashy novels, yet it was all the sweeter for that. They exchanged "I love yous" with the frequency of "thank yous."

One night, they found themselves at a bar in the financial district. It was an upscale place with throbbing music, staccato lights, and onyx floors—the kind of establishment with mixologists instead of bartenders. The clientele mostly worked on Wall Street, letting off steam after days spent trading options or stocks or hedge fund positions. Work hard, play hard.

Jonas threaded through a sea of brokers and bankers, each of them seeming to conspire to knock into him and jostle the drinks he precariously ferried over to the two-top where Amanda was waiting. He handed over her cocktail before sitting down with his cabernet sauvignon.

Amanda lifted her drink and stared at it. Light caught the edge of the martini glass and made the rim sparkle. She talked, but Jonas couldn't hear her over the music. The bar had a karaoke stage, and some twentysomething market analyst was mangling a Taylor Swift song.

"What?" Jonas asked, leaning forward.

Amanda raised her drink again. She pointed to it with her free hand and raised her voice above the Taylor Swift wannabe's warbling. "What is this?"

Jonas considered the drink and answered confidently, "It's purple." Amanda cocked an ear. "The bartender recommended it," he explained. "He told me what it was, but to be honest, all I understood was 'elderberry' and 'infusion.'" Amanda chanced a sip. Her reaction was inscrutable. "How is it?"

"You're right. It's purple."

"Here, take mine." He swapped out his drink for hers, tried the purple concoction, and found it to be pungently floral, like drinking a spa.

Amanda glanced in the direction of the karaoke stage. The analyst was nearing the bridge. "I put us in the queue."

"What queue?"

"For karaoke. You know 'It Had to Be You,' right?"

"*Everyone* knows Sinatra. But I don't sing."

"You took me to a *karaoke* bar . . . ," she said, incredulous.

Jonas lifted the martini glass. "For a drink," he said, laughter in his voice. "This place is close to our dinner reservation."

Amanda cocked her head and wrinkled her face in a wry expression. "You lecture to dozens of students a day. You can't handle singing in public?"

"No," he blurted out. "I mean yes. I mean—" Amanda stared back, reveling in his predicament. "I mean that—what I mean is, I don't sing. Like, at all."

Amanda's eyebrows rose, suspended by disbelief. "Who doesn't sing?"

Jonas slowly raised his hand like a kid in school.

Amanda eyed him with mock pity. "I'm guessing you don't dance either."

He shrugged. "Guilty as charged."

"Who doesn't dance?" Before Jonas could raise his hand again, she added, "I mean *why* wouldn't anyone dance?"

"The better question is, why would they? I mean, when you think about it, it's a little silly." The insecurity he'd felt in the run-up to their first date rushed back to him in a torrent. "Is this a deal-breaker for you?"

Amanda folded her arms defiantly over her chest and pouted. "I don't know. I've never met anyone who thought singing or dancing was silly." She pronounced "silly" as if it were two separate words.

"When you think about it," Jonas said in his defense, "the conveyance of ideas via melodious chanting or rhythmic movement serves no useful biologic, intellectual, or societal function."

Amanda threw her hair back and gave a dramatic, exasperated roll of her eyes. "God, you're such a scientist." But the way she said it seemed more compliment than criticism. "And you're wrong."

"I'm not."

"First, any time you've found yourself tapping your foot to a song is evidence that there is an innate connection between the human body and rhythm." Jonas opened his mouth to protest, but she silenced him with a finger. "Second, dance relieves stress. It conveys ideas. Some cultures—*many* cultures— tell stories through dance. But most importantly, it's one of humanity's ways of making one attractive to those of similar sexual orientation."

"The relief of stress and the conveyance of ideas don't relate to any humanistic imperatives, which was the point I was *really* trying to make."

"Agree to disagree."

Jonas tilted his head. *Fair enough.* "And your theory doesn't withstand scrutiny because you're attracted to me despite the fact I don't sing."

"Or dance," she added with feigned disappointment. "Please don't remind me." She thought for a moment. "Wait. If you don't like music, how do you know 'It Had to Be You'?"

"I never said I didn't like music. I just don't sing."

"Or *dance.*"

"Or dance," he repeated. "But Sinatra is inescapable."

On the karaoke stage, the mutilation of Taylor Swift ended, and the analyst wobbled off. A flat-screen mounted on the wall flashed AMANDA & JONAS. She pointed at the monitor. *Last chance . . .*

"You don't have to go up there alone," Jonas said.

"Apparently I do."

"I mean, you don't have to go up at all. We could go to dinner."

Defiant, she said, "No thank you. I've had a sip of a purple drink. I'm ready for a little *silly*." Once again, she stretched the word out for mocking effect.

He watched her move toward the stage with a confident, defiant stride. She grabbed the wireless microphone and threw Jonas a wink as the song began to pipe through the speakers. Violins glided in. Amanda brought the microphone to her lips and dove in to what Jonas had to admit was a remarkable rendition of the Sinatra classic.

Why do I do just as you say? Why must I just give you your way?

The crowd roared its approval. A halogen spotlight backlit her, outlining her form as it swayed in sync with the music.

Why do I sigh, why don't I try to forget?

Throughout the entire song, her eyes never left his. Each note, each lyric, was a new promise not only to share her life with him but also to elevate his. She was daring him to be more than who he was. To live life at a brighter luminance.

It must have been that something lovers call fate . . .

It *felt like* fate. When they were together, there was no time. No past. No future. There was only now.

NOW

A hand pushes against Jonas's shoulder, and he awakens with a start. A flight attendant stands over him, the expression on her face partly warmth and partly regret. She speaks to him in English with a thick German accent. "I'm very sorry, sir. But the gentleman in the galley asked me to wake you. He said you'd want me to."

"Galley?" Confusion pushes through the fog of sleep.

The flight attendant gestures forward toward the first-class galley.

"There must be some mistake," Jonas says. "I don't know anyone on this flight."

"The gentleman told me you might say that," the attendant responds. "He told me to tell you he's a friend from work." Jonas must still look confused, so she adds, "Columbia University?"

Jonas rubs his eyes in the vain hope that doing so will bring clarity. It doesn't, but . . . maybe there is someone he knows aboard. It's a small world, after all. In any universe. The thought that he's deceased in this reality doesn't occur to him.

"Thank you," he says, undoes his seat belt, and spills out onto the aisle. His slumber was deep and profound and refuses to relinquish its grip on him. He pads forward to the first-class galley.

It's impossible for the man he sees in front of him to be on this plane. The world may be small, but it's not microscopic. This man's presence cannot be a matter of mere coincidence.

The man standing in front of him is Victor Kovacevic.

Victor leers at Jonas, savoring this reunion. He's older than he was when Jonas last saw him, aged beyond the mere passage of years. He wears an oily grimace, which advertises that he's been looking forward to this.

"You probably have a lot of questions," he says.

Jonas says nothing. He just stands there. The plane canters slightly. Cups and mugs and bottles clink and chime in the galley.

"Let's start with the most pressing," Victor says. "No, this isn't 'my' reality any more than it is yours. I'm a fellow traveler, just like you."

Jonas remains quiet. His mind races, a million thoughts competing for primacy.

"Second question," Victor continues. "How could I reality-slip with such precision? To know exactly where you'd be? Onto a plane moving at six hundred miles per hour?" He dangles the question like a lure, fishing for a reaction.

And still, Jonas says nothing. It's all he can do not to scream. Not to beat this man—this cocky, self-righteous, overbearing man—with his fists. A wine bottle in a plastic holster jangles nearby, volunteering to be used as a potential weapon. Jonas envisions the bottle breaking off at the neck, cabernet splattering everywhere as he shatters it against Victor's head.

A flight attendant enters to retrieve the bottle, startling Jonas. "Are you all right, sir?" she asks.

"Fine. Thank you." His tongue is sandpaper. The words come out a whisper.

"Can I get you gentlemen anything?"

"No, thank you," Victor answers. "We're just stretching our legs." He sweeps a hand in Jonas's direction. "Getting reacquainted."

The flight attendant exits with the wine. Victor watches her go. "Where were we? Oh, that's right," he says, feigning recollection. "We were discussing how it was possible that I could reality-slip myself here."

Pleased with himself, he raises a wrist. On it is a band of steel. A single ivory light pulses beneath its surface. Jonas recognizes the design. *It's a tether bracelet.*

"You stole my work," Victor explains. "I *improved on* yours."

Epiphany strikes Jonas with the force of a slap. In the space of a heartbeat, everything is clear.

"Macon," he breathes. "*You* sent him." The image of Macon flashes in his mind's eye, a dead man behind the wheel of the truck, his expression contorted with malevolence. "Somehow . . . you sent him. Or . . . a version of him. A doppelgänger from this reality, or another."

Victor strokes his goatee as though in contemplation. "It struck me as . . . poetic. Hiring the same mercenary you had. The only difference being that I have a multiverse of Macons at my disposal. One dies, I simply hire another. And another. And another."

"How did you know?"

"About Macon, or what you've been up to?"

"Any of it."

Victor parts his hands, still smiling. "You hired a team of mercenaries to break into CERN. Suffice it to say, the event made a news site or two. Of course, no one had any idea what you were after or why you disappeared, where you went. To them, it's all one big mystery. But I found your intentions to be plainly conspicuous."

"Why?" Jonas's mind lurches, straining to fathom why Victor would hire Macon to kill Eva, to kill anyone. Whatever Jonas's and Victor's issues over the past four years, their conflict never rose to the level of murder. "I don't understand, Victor. Why would you—you had Macon *murder* someone. Why?"

"The truth is, I have no desire to see you dead, Jonas. As surprising as that may be to both of us. Macon's instructions were only to stop you. He just happened to be"—Victor studies the ceiling—"a bit too enthusiastic."

"Enthusiastic," Jonas repeats through clenched teeth. He tastes bile. "A woman *died*, Victor. Macon killed her." He hears his voice rising as his finger ratchets out to assault Victor's chest. "Because of *you*."

With surprising speed and even more surprising force, Victor swats Jonas's hand away and slams him against the galley compartments. Plates and glasses rattle. In the confined space, the sound seems deafening, but no flight attendant comes to inspect what's going on, leaving Victor free to yank up Jonas's sleeve, exposing his tattoo.

"This," Victor says, the word stabbing the air. "This is *my* work. Fourteen years."

Their noses are inches apart. Close enough to kiss. Close enough for Jonas to smell the liquor on Victor's breath.

"Fourteen years," Victor repeats through gritted teeth, loud enough to draw the notice of another flight attendant. The man enters the galley, and Victor freezes him with a stare.

Still, the attendant manages to croak out, "Sir, your voice is carrying . . ."

"My apologies." The words come out clipped. Evidently reading Victor's tone, the flight attendant spins on a heel and escapes.

With privacy restored, Jonas rips his arm from Victor's grip and allows his own temper to flare. "The board cleared me of plagiarism. The Nobel Committee gave me the medal with absolutely no doubt I had exclusive authorship."

Mentioning the Royal Swedish Academy of Sciences only fuels Victor's rage. "You wouldn't have succeeded—not even *started*—but for my work. Admit it."

"Victor—"

"*Admit it.*" Victor jabs his finger in Jonas's face and snarls, "You wouldn't even have *thought* to try to prove the existence of other realities if *I* hadn't tried to first."

"Fine. Yes," Jonas confesses. *What's the harm?* "You're right." If Victor is intent on acting like a rabid dog, then the least Jonas can do is throw him a bone.

It's not enough. "Do you know what it's like?" Victor asks, his tone dripping with venom. "To work on something for fourteen years, only to watch someone else *steal* that work out from under you?"

"I didn't steal anything—" Jonas protests. It's an old argument, but the fact that Victor's ire has calcified into an impulse to murder is new and bloodcurdling.

"It *destroys* you," Victor says, answering his own question. "It eats away at the core of you. At your soul." His voice cracks. "I couldn't work. I couldn't . . . draw any inspiration."

Jonas is whipsawed by Victor's abrupt shift from volcanic rage to self-pity. He stares back, as confused as he is terrified. Victor continues, his voice hollow. "Phaedra left me." With a shrug, he confesses that he could hardly blame her.

"I know, Victor. I'm sorry," Jonas says, meaning it.

"I'm not angry. I was a husk of the man she fell in love with," Victor admits with clinical dispassion. "But then . . . karma. I never really believed in it until two years ago."

Epiphany—shock and horror in equal measure—punches Jonas. Victor is talking about Amanda. He's talking about the accident. That this man—this horrible, petty troll—should invoke Amanda's death is a perversion of irreducible proportions.

"When Amanda died," Victor continues, "it felt like . . . like the scales had balanced. We'd each lost our loves."

"Phaedra is still alive, Victor." Jonas seethes, his body trembling with rage.

"Things were set right. But you—you just couldn't leave well enough alone."

"Could *you*?"

"This is about balance, karma. That's why I don't want to see you dead. I just want you to stop."

"I can't, Victor. You know I can't. And you know why."

Victor shakes his head, his lips curling to a snarl. His nostrils redden and flair. "Just answer me something. One thing. I'm curious.

Everyone . . . all of us . . . we all have to live with loss, to get over it. *Learn to get over it.* But not you." This last part is offered with an almost scientific fascination. "What makes you different? What makes you so very goddamn special?"

Jonas is at a loss. How can he make sense to a man who's taken leave of his senses? "Victor," he says, spreading his hands wide, "I'm just doing what you would do if you were in my situation."

Victor shakes his head with a violence that reminds Jonas of a child's tantrum. "No. No, you don't get to do this. You don't get to use my work—*my work*—to unbalance the universe."

"No." Jonas shakes his head. "That's what *you're* trying to do."

But it's like he isn't even speaking. Victor keeps talking, each syllable launching a volley of spittle. "I won't let you. I won't. I'll stop you. *I'll stop you.*"

"Victor—"

"Final warning," Victor says, his finger jabbing at the air. "Stay away from Amanda. Accept the judgment of the universe." He simmers for a few seconds. "Or so help me God, Jonas, I won't be held responsible for what happens next."

Jonas bolts forward, either to rail at Victor, or hit him, or both—he doesn't know—but the space where Victor stands begins to fold in on itself. For an instant, the small confines of the galley wink with light. And then nothing.

Which is when Jonas starts to shake.

With unsettling urgency, he grasps for a glass and the closest bottle of liquor. He pours a drink and gulps it down. It burns the back of his throat but does nothing against the terror rising within him.

Victor sent the man who killed Eva.

Victor is trying to stop me.

He pours another glass. A flight attendant enters and brews a fresh pot of coffee. She's talking to him but might as well be on another planet. The entire universe has been reduced to Jonas and the liquor in his hand.

Victor doesn't want me to reunite with Amanda.

It's beyond comprehension. It's irrational. Victor's affect, Jonas recalls, wasn't that of a rational human being.

Victor is so envious that he wants to stop me from being with my wife.

Fortunately the liquor starts to take hold. Victor may have taken leave of his senses, but Jonas doesn't have to. Victor tried to destroy his life once already and failed. This will be no different. At the end of the day, there's nothing Victor can do to prevent Jonas from being with Amanda. If death itself didn't stop him, Victor Kovacevic certainly can't.

At least, that's what Jonas tries to convince himself.

Jonas spends the rest of the flight in a stupor enabled by first class's endless flow of liquor. He downs each drink in equal turns unnerved and enraged. *Victor.* The man's self-righteousness and jealousy has metastasized to the point where it extinguished a human life. Jonas vibrates with fury and orders another drink. He's so consumed with emotion that it never occurs to him to consider how Victor managed to locate Jonas twice, in two different universes.

His stomach drops, but it's just the plane settling in for its final descent. A flight attendant's voice, flecked with a German accent, comes across the loudspeaker. "We're approaching Newark's Hillary Clinton Airport. In preparation for landing, please return your tray tables and seat backs to their upright and locked positions . . ."

Out the window, the once-familiar skyline of Jonas's home seems altered, unexpectedly unfamiliar. A new skyline transects the city, buildings of bleeding edge design rising from the older, shorter buildings that surround it. It reminds Jonas of a healed-over scar. The thought brings a chill.

On the ground, the customs officer, a heavyset man in his forties with three-day stubble, studies Jonas's new passport for an unsettling length of time.

"Is there a problem?" Jonas asks despite his best instincts, hoping the question is inflected with the certainty that there couldn't possibly be a problem.

"It's just funny," the officer says. "But there was a Jonas Cullen who died. A Nobel Prize winner. Read an article about him recently."

Jonas spreads his hands in a gesture of innocence. "Well, clearly I'm alive, so . . ."

"The thing is," the officer muses, not taking his eye off Jonas's laminated passport photo, "you look *just* like him." The man reaches for his phone. "Here, lemme show you . . ."

Jonas fights panic as the man googles. "Y'know, I'm actually in a bit of a rush," he says apologetically, offering a hapless shrug.

The customs officer casts a suspicious eye in Jonas's direction. The phone glows faintly in the man's hand. Jonas holds his breath. Fortunately, the officer notices the line of weary travelers snaking behind Jonas and determines that he doesn't have the time for this either. The sound of Jonas exhaling in relief is covered by the officer pounding his passport with a stamp.

"Anyway, the resemblance is dead on," the man says, returning the passport.

"I'll be sure to tell my wife. I bet she'll get a kick out of it."

The taxi fights its way through Manhattan. Jonas doubts there is any universe where the city isn't clogged with traffic, and he considers whether walking might not be faster. The taxi lurches. Every inch is a victory, and Jonas reminds himself it's not the traffic but his excitement that makes his progress into Midtown seem glacial. He consoles himself with the litany of things he can't wait for. The feel of Amanda in his arms. The sound of her voice. The scent of her hair. For two years he's clung to these memories, but they've been receding, slowly slipping away.

Even the image of her face has faded, though he has stared for hours at that photograph of her in Central Park, with the diamond ring nestled inside a Frisbee, eclipsed by the more indelible, tragic portrait of her hanging upside down, the blood racing up her face and pooling under her eye like a tear.

Jonas slams his eyes closed and violently wills the image away. *This will all be over soon.*

Five blocks away, he surrenders to his impatience and thrusts a fistful of bills through the plastic divide that separates him from the driver. He spills out onto the street and starts walking. It's a beautiful spring day. The city smells fresh, like it has thrown off the shackles of winter and is stretching out its limbs. Heat bounces off the sidewalk. Light spills down through chasms of steel and glass.

With two blocks to go, he starts running. He threads through tourists. He hurdles a dog leash. He throws himself through a crosswalk and dodges traffic, ignoring the irate honks the maneuver draws. His sprint attracts confused and curious stares. He avoids a painful collision with a worker pushing a hand truck.

He doesn't even know what day of the week it is. Amanda might not be home. But logistics and reason and all sense have left him, swallowed by the overwhelming need to get to the home they'd once shared. *She'll be there.* He has faith. No, that's not right. Faith is belief in the absence of knowledge. *She'll be there.* He knows this. *She'll be waiting.*

And then . . . he's there. He bounds up the steps of the modest brownstone. The front door is locked. His finger flies over the building directory until he finds **CULLEN**. He stabs the corresponding button. Over and over. No answer. His impatience melts into desperation.

Then, behind him, labored breaths. The crinkle of paper. The clinking of glass. Jonas spins, expectant, but it's not Amanda. It's—*What was her name?*—Mrs. Gomez, her sixty-eight-year-old body winded from carrying too many groceries. She glances up, peering over the edges of her shopping bags, to see Jonas. Out of habit, he waves.

Her groceries drop.

Produce slaps the sidewalk. A bottle shatters, spraying tomato sauce. Oranges and tomatoes roll away.

Mrs. Gomez stares at Jonas. Slack jawed. Blanching. Her chest is still heaving but no longer from exertion. Her jagged breaths border on hyperventilation.

"*Dios mío,*" she whispers.

"Mrs. Gomez—"

Jonas chances a step toward her, but she begins to tremble. "*Estás muerto. Estás muerto,*" she repeats, her lower lip quivering. "*No es posible...*"

Her mouth, already agape, opens farther, and Jonas knows she's going to let loose a scream. And a scream will cause a commotion. A commotion will draw a crowd. And a crowd will attract police attention. He can't risk dealing with the police. Not when he's so close, standing on the literal doorstep.

He surges forward, nearly falling down the stairs, an arm outstretched, palm jutting, fingers splayed. "Please," he implores, "don't scream."

She doesn't. She just stands before him, ashen, her feet rooted among the vegetables and broken bottles and packaged baked goods.

Jonas plasters on as reassuring an expression as he can conjure. He speaks slowly and calmly. "It's me, Mrs. Gomez. It's Jonas. I know that is confusing, but it's really me. You're not looking at a ghost. I promise."

"Mr. Jonas," she exhales, her shoulders slackening with relief. "They said that you died." She genuflects urgently.

"It's a very long story. Suffice it to say, reports of my death have been greatly exaggerated." This is greeted with a blank stare. Jonas stoops to begin collecting the wayward groceries. "Here. Let me help you with these. I'm sorry if I frightened you." He sorts items into the shopping bags. Salvageable items in one. Shards of broken glass in the other. "Do you know if Amanda's home?"

Mrs. Gomez just shakes her head, apparently struggling to regain the power of speech.

Jonas is placing a head of cabbage and a container of instant coffee into the "salvageable" bag when he spots Amanda amid the bustle of Riverside Drive. She's on the opposite side of the street, obscured behind a curtain of commuters and cars, but it's her.

Instantly abandoning the groceries, he springs to his feet and throws himself into traffic. Time slows and the world shrinks to a seventy-square-foot patch of asphalt covered with Jonas and protesting traffic. Tires squeal. Brakes whine. Car horns bleat in protest. A taxi driver unleashes a swarm of epithets. A bike messenger extends his middle finger as he whips past Jonas, close enough to blow his hair back.

Then, he sees her.

She doesn't look surprised. If he didn't know any better, he would say she had been expecting him. And why not? Five years earlier, he promised an alternate version of her that he would find her. If the multiverse is replete with points in time that are universal—*fated*—then this Amanda's Jonas must also have vowed to find her in any lifetime. It makes sense to Jonas that she would hold him to that oath.

They collide in the middle of the street and throw their arms around each other, holding on for dear life. Neither speaks. There will be time enough for words later. There will be questions and answers and more questions. They'll talk through the night and into the morning. She'll thank him for finding her. He'll thank her for waiting. They'll plan the rest of their lives.

When he finally takes her head in his hands and finds her lips with his, their kiss is desperate. Hungry. Jonas feels slickness on her face and sees that she's crying. Tears of joy and relief cascade down her cheeks. He moves to wipe one away, and it's only when she does the same that he notices that he's crying too.

And he goes pale. Jonas's connection to Amanda shatters. His whole body goes cold.

Macon is standing on the sidewalk.

"What's wrong?" Amanda asks plaintively.

117

Jonas shakes his head. How can he explain? He peeks over Amanda's shoulder again and sees that Macon's still visible behind her. The man's remorseless stare drills into Jonas, nothing in his eyes but cold professionalism.

Careful not to alarm Amanda, Jonas takes her hand. "C'mon," he says, "let's get out of the middle of the street." As they make their way back toward the brownstone, Jonas maneuvers himself slightly behind Amanda, placing his body between her and Macon.

"What's wrong?" she asks again.

"Nothing." He doesn't have the presence of mind to come up with a more convincing lie. As they step back up onto the sidewalk, the thought of getting inside, taking refuge in their home, is all-consuming. He'll call the police. The customs officer mentioned that he's a Nobel laureate here. A minor celebrity. He should be able to get protection for them both. All he needs to do is get them inside . . .

But Mrs. Gomez is intercepting them now, her arms again full with her bags. Tears are falling down her face, her groceries bouncing in her arms with her excitement, as she turns toward Amanda. "*Es un milagro,* Mrs. Amanda," she exclaims. "*Un milagro.*"

"I know, Mrs. Gomez," Amanda says. "I don't know how to explain it."

"We should get inside," Jonas urges, finally dropping all pretense of calm.

"Why? What's going on?"

"I'll explain once we're inside. It's okay. Everything's going to be okay." He takes her hand again and—

Somewhere, a car backfires. Jonas startles. In front of him, Amanda's worry morphs into confusion. "Jonas?"

Her face remains baffled even as her legs give way, and she crashes to the pavement like Mrs. Gomez's groceries. Jonas has no idea what's happening, but then he's on his knees, pulling Amanda to his chest. Mrs. Gomez is screaming in Spanish. Jonas's hands feel damp and slick, and when he turns one over to examine it, the wetness is red.

Jonas can't breathe. In a panic, he jerks his head back over his shoulder and glimpses Macon behind the passing traffic, still on the other side of the street.

"Jonas?" It's Amanda. Still looking up at him with a child's puzzlement.

"It's going to be okay," he reassures her, because that's what one does.

"I warned you," comes another voice.

Jonas turns his head in its direction. Behind him—on the sidewalk, standing just a few feet away with a gun in his hand—is Victor.

"I gave you fair warning," Victor says. "You've got to allow me that much."

"Jonas?" Amanda again.

"I'm here. I'm here." A wail of sirens seeps into Jonas's limited perception. *Hope.* "Help is coming."

Out of the corner of his eye, he catches the wink of light that accompanies Victor's escape from this reality.

There are gasps and exclamations, various reactions to the incredible phenomenon of Victor's disappearance into thin air, but they sound to Jonas like they're coming from a million miles away.

"How . . . ," Amanda is saying. "How did you find me?"

"I love you." It's both an assertion and an explanation.

With trembling fingers she reaches to touch his cheek. "I should have known . . ." Every word is a labor. Each one launching tiny droplets of blood, which spatter her chin. ". . . that you'd keep your promise."

swirling around them. But she invests them with a commitment that makes them emanate from the depths of her soul.

"I love you too much," she says.

Jonas's lips tremble, his mouth trying to form the words of the response—*I love you more*—but he can't. There's a wrongness to Amanda right now. It stabs at his heart, torturing him with the irony that he can still feel. That he's still capable of experiencing grief. That loss and despair can still find him. It's her eyes. They're . . . glassy. Vacant.

Desperate, he shakes her. "Amanda?" But she's limp in his arms. "Please. Please don't go," he pleads, knowing she's already gone. "Don't go. Don't go." Then, beseeching, this time to the God who delivered him to this moment. "Not again. Please. Not again."

The world goes blurry with the flood of tears obscuring his vision. Someone is pulling him to his feet. His legs are rubber. He pushes away the cloud of grief and sees two paramedics working to revive Amanda. But the sight of her body, rag-dolling in sync with their ministrations, sickens him. Her head lolls to the side and back as they work in vain to stanch her bleeding and start her heart. But Amanda's dead, and any manipulation of her body, short of burying it, is perverse.

The hands that pulled him to his feet are strong. A man's hands. Jonas fights against them, struggling. He wants to be down on the concrete with Amanda. He needs to be with her. He strains and writhes against the man's grip. Inconsolable.

"Calm down, pal," the man is saying. He has an accent dipped in Brooklyn. He wears a blue uniform. Short sleeves for the spring. A shield on his chest. A police officer. "Let these guys do their jobs." He relinquishes his hold on Jonas as more police descend on the scene to hold back the tide of onlookers. Jonas begins to drift backward down the sidewalk, away from the paramedics. But the cop with the Brooklyn accent follows him. "I've gotta ask you some questions," he says authoritatively, narrowing the gap between them.

NOW

Jonas hadn't cried when he came to beneath the Centralbron, awakening to see Amanda hanging lifeless next to him. He hadn't cried when the police confirmed the worst, that his wife was gone. He hadn't cried at the funeral or at the reception afterward. He hadn't cried after the friends and former colleagues and well-wishers had all departed, and the apartment he had once shared with Amanda felt as lonely as a grave. His grief had been profound, and it expressed itself in a multitude of ways but never as crying.

But Jonas is crying now. Quiet, plaintive tears. They escape unbidden. He's not even aware of them as they carve lines down his face. In his darkest hours, he had consoled himself with the faith that he'd lost everything there was to lose, that nothing remained inside him to be broken. He now knows he was wrong, as that last surviving piece of himself—that lonely, unbroken quadrant of his soul—fractures.

"I tried," he whispers, unsure whether he's speaking to Amanda or himself. "I tried so hard."

This was my last chance. The thought strikes him center mass. When Amanda died the first time, a small corner of his consciousness was already hard at work on finding a way back to her. That ephemeral strand of hope had sustained him through a despair so deep that it appeared bottomless, that his descent would be forever.

Her lips move, and after a second or two, words manage to escape. They're barely audible against the approaching sirens and the tumult

Answering questions is the last thing Jonas wants to do. He quickens his step, walking backward for a couple of feet before turning around. He's walking fast now, but the cop keeps pace.

"C'mon," he says, "you know how this works. I gotta detain you."

"What?"

"This is a crime scene now. All witnesses gotta be brought in for questioning. C'mon, it's been this way ever since 10/16."

Ten-sixteen. Jonas had forgotten he's in an entirely different reality from the one he knows. He sees the officer's hand wander down to the handcuffs on his belt.

"I've gotta take you in for questioning back at the station," he says. "It's mandatory. I've got no discretion here."

A second passes in which Jonas considers letting the officer take him into custody. Let the police arrest him. Let them confiscate his tether, and he can spend the rest of his life passing between universes, like a specter soullessly wandering the earth, unable to find its final rest.

The cop's meaty fingers reach for his arm when Jonas bolts. He has no idea why. Some instinct propels him to run.

He darts into the street. His arms and legs pump, propelling him forward. His escape is unexpected, and the element of surprise gives him a head start measuring in seconds. He darts into traffic and threads through cars positioned like linebackers. Behind him, the cop is giving chase.

A traffic light must have changed, because now the cars are hurling toward Jonas. A chorus of angry horns Dopplers past as Jonas flies against the steady vehicular flow. One car swipes him, the impact of its side-view mirror nearly spinning him around, but he keeps his balance and continues on. He feels the policeman behind him. The cop's breathing is labored, but he's fast.

Jonas jumps a curb and races down a perpendicular street. The cop is yelling now, imploring the crowd to "Get outta the way!" and "Make a hole!" The bystanders barely react. The reputation New Yorkers have for jaded apathy is well earned, no matter the universe.

Jonas is leaping into a congested intersection when a voice from some distant precinct of his brain asks what his plan is. He has no idea. Maybe the cop will get winded and give up. Maybe he'll trip or get taken out by one of the dozens of cars charging at them both. This is a game of seconds, and whoever ends up with one more than the other will win.

And that's when the city bus lurches up on him.

Its horn blares a warning, but it's too late. It might as well be a building flying at him. Jonas has the impulse to throw himself to the pavement, ducking beneath the bus as it surges over him, but a quick, instinctual calculation warns him that he's too close. The bus will smash through him before he can hit the ground. All these thoughts laser through his mind in milliseconds as he's swallowed in the shadow cast by the oncoming bus.

Amanda . . . I'm coming.

The cop tackles him with enough force that the impact almost knocks out Jonas's teeth. He feels the man's weight carrying them both out of the path of the bus, whose tires clip the sole of Jonas's left shoe as the sidewalk crashes upward toward him.

His skull bounces off the concrete. He hears a ringing, and tiny projectiles comet around in a starburst pattern, obscuring his vision. He wills himself not to pass out.

The officer is pulling at his arms. It feels like he may dislocate them. "Sonofabitch," the cop repeats, over and over. It's unclear whether he's cursing or addressing Jonas. He expertly pins Jonas's wrists behind his back with one hand, while the other retrieves the handcuffs. Their jangling reminds Jonas, strangely, of bells ringing. "Struggle and I'll break your arms," the cop promises. Jonas has no reason to doubt him.

And then he remembers that he doesn't have to wait for that to happen. He doesn't have to be here at all. The fact that he still has his tether was obscured by his grief and his efforts to outrace the officer. His fingers scratch at the ring, but they're too slick with Amanda's blood. As he struggles, the cop slaps one handcuff on his wrist, tight enough to close off circulation, tight enough to hurt, to punish Jonas for the temerity of running. Jonas fights against it all, but the tether continues to avoid his grasp.

Click. The second handcuff is applied. Jonas grits his teeth, continuing to strain. He's losing feeling in the fingers of both hands as they writhe against each other like two fighting squid. Above him, the cop shifts his weight, readying himself to haul Jonas to his feet, but then Jonas's fingers seize on the tether—a good grip, finally—and pull it from his finger, clutching it tight in his other hand.

Jonas doesn't know what the cop will think of what happens next. He has no idea how the officer will explain it to himself or his superiors. Surely, he will interrogate the gathering crowd and implore, "Did you see that? Did you *see* that?" But Jonas doesn't care. The now-familiar tingling sensation courses through him once again. Light blazes. Space folds. The handcuffs, some cash, a freshly minted United States passport, and an American Express card fall to the sidewalk, and Jonas blinks from the world.

Maybe it's the fact that Jonas is lying on the ground. Maybe it's that his heart is now broken beyond repair. Maybe it's that his body is still processing the quantum radiation with which he's flooded his cells. Whatever the explanation, the experience of reality-slipping feels different from before. This time, he feels a miasma of physical pain, a thin coating of agony over pins and needles in his extremities.

The concrete sinks beneath his body, as though the sidewalk is absorbing him. But that's not it, he realizes. The concrete has been replaced by a thick carpet of grass. The blades tickle his face. The scent of pine fills the air. Jonas staggers to his feet and sees that the entire city is gone, its concrete canyons replaced by undulating fields of grass as far as he can see. It's beautiful. The sky is a violent crimson, a red deeper than any dawn or sunset.

He's slammed down again. The city has returned, along with its omnipresent pavement. The fall exacerbates the concussion Jonas is sure he's received, and he's assaulted again by another volley of what knocked him over in the first place: water. Torrents of it charge past him, the city's buildings acting like massive sluice gates. The rush rag-dolls him again, the water sending him hurling toward a towering office building. A wall of steel and glass rises to meet him, and once again, Jonas thinks this is the end.

But a reality-slip swaps the building for only slightly more forgiving ground. He lands hard. Once again, New York's concrete proves a harsh mistress. He fights disorientation as universes cycle past. Each reality-slip is the pull of a trigger in a cosmic game of Russian roulette, and it's a daisy chain of good fortune that he hasn't been worse than injured thus far. He has won a few seconds of calm and spends them on returning the tether to his finger. The cascade of alternate realities slows, and Jonas looks down at his hand, where the tether's white pulse is as soothing as a mother's touch.

He breathes deep and is rewarded with the smell of shit. The air is also thick with the smell of burnt rubber and electricity. The ground is hard beneath him. Gravel digs into his buttocks. A newspaper wafts past. He sees other refuse—a bottle, a purse, a boot—scattered about him in the darkness. One piece of trash is an empty coffee cup. He has traveled through multiple realities, entirely different universes, to find the Starbucks logo staring back at him.

A rat skitters past, causing Jonas to startle. Wherever he is, it's not the kind of place he wants to stay for long. But he's so broken, in both body and spirit, that he can't summon the energy or the will to stand, much less walk. The blood in his head mounts a fresh assault with every heartbeat. A pain in his side punishes him with every breath. So even though it's dark, even though he's surrounded by trash and vermin and the smell of burning rubberized shit, he doesn't even consider moving. The hard ground and harder wall that presses into his back, cold and unyielding, feel like the downiest comfort he's ever experienced.

As his breathing slows and his pulse descends to a manageable gallop, the twin assassins of loss and hopelessness steal their way back into his thoughts. Emotion bubbles up from his depths. Grief clutches him and squeezes. His eyes begin to well with tears.

And that's when he hears the screaming.

No, that's not right. It isn't a human scream but a marriage of high and low pitches, part whistling and part thrumming. And growing closer.

The ground beneath him tremors. The gravel does a little dance. He sees three ribbons of steel transecting the ground. A subtle light bleeds in, revealing to Jonas where he is.

He's in a tunnel. And judging from the encroaching light and the approaching "scream," it's a *subway tunnel.*

He shoots to his feet. Grief steps aside so that fear can have a turn with him. He spins away from the approaching light and sees nothing but a long stretch of darkness in front of him. The rumble announcing the subway train's approach feels like an earthquake.

Jonas is now enticed by the thought of death. He has felt this temptation before, the desire to surrender everything, to escape the grief and despair and pain, to sleep at last. The advancing subway train offers an end to the horrible Amanda-less existence he's endured for over two years now.

Without thinking, he steps into the center of the tunnel, casting himself in the subway train's oncoming light. It will be upon him in minutes, if not seconds. If he closes his eyes, he won't see its arrival. He'll feel nothing, except maybe the heat of the train's approach, and then it will all be over.

But the human will to live is perhaps the strongest impulse in creation, the drive that makes all other drives possible. And so when Jonas sees the outline of a steel door to his left, illuminated by the growing light from the advancing train, he recognizes it for what it is: a way out. A way to live. He bolts toward it as the tunnel gets brighter. He grips the handle, but it fights him.

The earthquake grows more forceful.

Jonas calculates that he has mere seconds until he's smeared against the very door he's trying to open.

The handle gives way with a *crunch* of rust, but more rust at the base of the door prevents Jonas from opening it farther than half an inch.

The tunnel grows brighter.

The train is almost on top of him.

With increasing urgency, he throws himself against the door, hammering it with his shoulder again and again and again. But apart from that initial half inch, the door remains as immoveable as a rampart.

The metallic wail that heralds the train's arrival is almost deafening now.

Jonas takes a few steps back from the door. He can see the train now. Two halogen lights scream toward him. Behind a wall of black glass, the driver reacts with panic and horror at the sight of him.

Then, a squeal erupts like the plaintive cry of a wounded animal, but it's the application of brakes on a doomed mission to slow an 85,200-pound steel missile going fifty-five miles per hour.

Jonas hurls himself at the recalcitrant door again. His head pushes past his shoulder and strikes the metal with a sickening thud. He is falling again, not down but forward. As he hits the concrete floor, a wall of hot wind pushed by the passing of the train floods over him. Whatever space he's entered trembles in its wake.

He doesn't bother to stand. He lacks the strength. He's at the base of a flight of metal stairs. The rest of the room is concrete. On one wall, there is signage marked with a cobalt blue logo, a circle with the letters **MTA** overlapped in white. *Metropolitan Transit Authority.*

The stairs loom before him. An invitation. But with safety comes the return of dolor, of desolation. The feeling of loss returns to overwhelm him, and he gets back to the business that was at hand before the subway interrupted him.

He cries.

But these tears aren't the same as the ones that gently fell from his eyes as he was holding Amanda for the final time, watching her breathe her last. Jonas cries with a violent urgency, forcibly expelling the tears from his body. Lying on the cold concrete, he wails. Each heave of his chest, each feral scream extracts a new volley of tears, like squeezing out water from a sponge. No one descends the stairs to intrude. Jonas is free to weep and howl and undulate on the floor for what feels to him like hours.

When he's finished, all he wants to do is sleep. He's never felt more tired but still wills himself to his feet. He recalls the time between Amanda's death and the realization that his work might provide a way of reuniting with her. In that interval, the intermediate stage between desolation and hope, Jonas learned that sometimes the hardest thing to do in life was just to live. It seemed impossible then. It feels impossible now. But having ruled out suicide, he has no other choice.

He shuffles to the stairs and begins to climb.

FIVE YEARS AGO

Jonas was lecturing to his class about quantum entanglement when it happened. "Philosophy tells us that two contradictory things cannot be true at the same time. Physics tells us that two different objects cannot occupy the same space at the same time. *Quantum physics*, though, contends the philosophers and the physics experts are wrong."

The lecture center was arranged like an amphitheater, with Jonas standing at the bottom, flanked by a flock of whiteboards and looking up at a sea of open laptops and an assortment of expressions that ranged from studiously interested to bordering on somnambulant. The room was three-quarters filled, seventy-five or so students—just enough to provide a crowd whose energy he could ride like a surfer cruising a wave. It was an energy exchange he'd come to understand over his years of teaching. He found the attentive listeners in the throng and gave his energy to them, which they would return, energizing him further. It was a flywheel, a virtuous cycle. And he would have been lying if he said he didn't love it.

"What we're talking about here is the phenomenon that occurs when two or more particles share a given space in such a way that the quantum state of each particle cannot be measured independently of the state of its peers. The two or more particles are said to be, at that point, 'entangled.'" Jonas's hands were flying, drawing the arc and relation of invisible particles in the space in front of him. "In fact, entanglement is the primary difference between classical physics and quantum physics.

It's a keystone idea, an idea which makes subsequent ideas possible. One of those ideas is that of quantum computing. Traditional computers are built on a *binary* architecture, ones and zeros. Each literal bit of data is either one or zero."

He had digressed—drifted out of his pedagogical lane—but he was on a roll, carried along by the momentum of his thoughts. Despite his detour, the energy exchange with his class remained potent. Even those who had been texting or daydreaming appeared focused. "But quantum entanglement recognizes a *third* possibility, that of the one and zero *coexisting*, being both true *and* false"—he paused for effect—"at the same time."

He crested so single mindedly on the wave of his rhetoric that he didn't even hear the snare drum roll. It wasn't until he heard Frank Sinatra's voice—*Why do I do just as you say?*—that he saw Amanda walking down the lecture hall's steps to meet him. It was fall, and she wore her hair down, her locks falling over a green cashmere sweater. She had a puckish glint in her eye and a Bluetooth speaker in her hand. "It Had to Be You" poured out of it.

The students smirked and tittered. Some flashed scattered looks of confusion, but they were in the minority. Amanda stood on the stairs that bisected the lecture hall, her hips swaying, as she lent her voice to Sinatra's.

Why must I just give you your way?

Jonas grimaced. "It seems my girlfriend is trying to make a point."

Then, to his surprise, a few of the students joined in. Their accompaniment felt more planned than spontaneous.

Why do I sigh, why don't I try to forget? It must have been that something lovers call fate.

"And"—he drew out the word, smiling through his teeth—"she's apparently drawn a few of you in as coconspirators."

As it turned out, it was more than a few. Soon, the entire class was singing along loud enough to drown out not only Amanda but the Chairman of the Board as well.

Kept me saying I have to wait, I saw them all, just couldn't fall, till we met.

Amanda raised her voice above the students and the speaker, her hair swaying as she bobbed and weaved in time with the melody. *It had to be you. It had to be you. I wandered around and I finally found the somebody who could make me be true . . .*

"I've always said you have a lovely voice," Jonas told her in mock protest. "I never debated that."

With her free hand, Amanda carved an elongated C shape in the air like an orchestra conductor, and the class stopped singing just in time for the next verse. Seventy-five faces lasered in on Jonas, each one daring him.

Jonas sighed his surrender. "And could make me be blue," he began to say instead of sing. But then the mood began to take hold of him. If his aversion to singing was steeped in embarrassment, well, Amanda had conspired to remove that element from the equation, hadn't she? *"And even be glad."* Music began to lace through his speech, his words buoyed by the melody. *"Just to be sad . . . thinking of you."* His stare found hers, and he felt an energy exchange of another kind. *"Some others I've seen might never be mean . . ."*

And then he let go, allowing his voice to soar, as he sang-yelled, *"Might never be cross or try to be boss, but they wouldn't do!"*

The class exploded in applause. As the song continued, Jonas surged past rows of seats to reach Amanda on the stairs. As Sinatra crooned about no one else giving him a thrill, Jonas took Amanda in his arms.

"I was never alive," he whispered in her ear. His voice cracked, and he fought off a swell of emotion, surprised by the tidal wave of sadness hitting him, driven by the realization that every minute he had spent without her was dim in comparison. Falling in love with Amanda, and Amanda's falling in love with him, was the equivalent of Dorothy's journey from Kansas to Oz, from black and white to Technicolor. "I was never alive until I met you."

Her lips found his. She dropped the speaker to embrace him fully. The undergraduates applauded and hollered as if they were at an actual concert. Sinatra played on.

NOW

At the top of the stairs, Jonas pounds against another steel door. This one is locked from the other side. He unloads his grief and fury in a futile assault on it until an MTA employee finally frees him from his confinement. Jonas tells the woman he is homeless, a claim his weathered expression and dirty, bruised face conspire to support. He tells her a story about stumbling off a platform and making his way to a maintenance door, and she buys it. No doubt it helps that the only thing people want out of an encounter with the downtrodden is for it to be as short as possible.

Now Jonas wanders another universe's Manhattan. He doesn't notice the various architectural differences. He doesn't hear the machine-gun patter of various dialects, none of which are spoken in his home universe. He doesn't register the chill that penetrates the thin layer of his all-cotton attire after the warm spring day, in another Manhattan, when Amanda had just been shot. The sky is slate gray. The air carries the sharp smell of cold, of smoldering charcoal.

He has no destination. He is hungry but has no desire to eat. He could find an American Express office and repeat the sad story of having been robbed, but he knows the claim is unlikely to withstand scrutiny in his home country. And that's assuming Jonas Cullen even exists in this universe.

Night is falling, and with it, the temperature. He knows he can't roam aimlessly forever, so he implores his mind to make a decision, to figure out someplace to go, but no thought will gain traction. His brain is an engine that refuses to turn over.

Stars try to poke through the gray curtain of sky overhead. The city's lights begin their nightly illumination against the gloaming. As beautiful as it is, it feels like Manhattan's way of telling him that time is running out.

The next thing he knows, he's standing on Riverside Drive, staring up at the brownstone he once called home, several universes ago. He drops to a knee. The sidewalk is identical to the one where Victor took Amanda's life but for the absence of her blood seeping onto the concrete. He feels the now-familiar tide of emotion welling up inside him. How long will he continue to feel like this? Will it ever stop?

He swallows hard and impels himself not to cry. Forces himself to his feet. *One step at a time,* he tells himself. *That's the way you'll get through this. Just one step at a time.*

He marches up the steps, consults the building directory, and finds the name he's searching for: **CULLEN, J.** He stabs the call button. No reply. He presses the button again. Nothing. Maybe his doppelgänger is out. Perhaps having dinner. Perhaps halfway across the world at some conference. Who knows how much he would travel as a bachelor?

But then the question—what if he's *not* single?—skulks into his thoughts. What if this universe's Jonas found someone who wasn't Amanda? The idea is an anathema, almost sacrilegious.

"Dr. Cullen's not home," says a voice from the foot of the stairs in a thick Guatemalan accent. Jonas turns to see Arturo, Mrs. Gomez's husband. He's heavyset, his breathing labored. "Hasn't been for a few days." He eyes Jonas carefully. "You look like him," he observes. "Are you related to Dr. Cullen?"

Jonas is struck by the irony of the question. "Jonas is my brother," he lies.

"I didn't even know Dr. Cullen *had* a brother."

"Our family situation is complicated like you wouldn't believe," Jonas replies, his tone bone dry.

Mr. Gomez offers up the sage nod of someone well traveled in complex family situations.

Jonas decides to take a chance. "Is Armando still the super?" he asks. "I'd like to get into my apart—" He pauses just in time. "My brother's apartment."

Mr. Gomez strokes his salt-and-pepper goatee, his brow furrowed in contemplation. "I've lived here twenty-six years. I don't remember a super named Armando. But Mr. Frank would probably be able to help you . . ."

Seconds later, Jonas is padding down the hall with Frank, the superintendent. The man is in his fifties and gaunt to the point of skeletal. He shuffles slightly off his left leg. His voice is a pit bull's growl, but a missing incisor lends some words an incongruous whistle.

"Kinda glad you dropped by," Frank says as he snaps the mother of all key rings from his belt. "I haven't seen your brother for a couple of days and need to talk to him about the smell."

"Smell?"

Frank selects a key from the menagerie and unlocks the apartment door. The stench that emerges is an assault. Pungent and fruity. A cantaloupe left out in the sun to fester.

"Been getting complaints from the other tenants," Frank grouses as he leads Jonas inside.

The layout of the apartment is the same as the one he had shared with Amanda. Some of the furniture and art is familiar. In the mess, Jonas detects a woman's touch, buried beneath a thick layer of recent bachelorhood. The thought brings a chill. Perhaps this reality's Jonas lost his Amanda as well.

"They're not happy. The tenants," Frank is saying.

Jonas scans the space. "Maybe a rat died in one of the walls," he posits.

Frank stiffens, wounded by the accusation. "My building," he bites, "don't got a rodent problem."

Jonas holds up an apologetic hand. *No offense.* "I'll take a look around. I'm sure I can address it."

"Where's your brother, anyway?"

"Hmm?" Jonas is distracted by the strangely familiar surroundings.

"Somebody said he might be out of town."

Jonas deadpans, "I guess that depends on your definition."

After the superintendent leaves, Jonas decides he'll wait a few hours to see if his counterpart returns. If he does, it will be the strangest reunion in history.

With nothing else to do, Jonas drifts through the apartment. The place is at once both familiar and foreign. It's the home he remembers, but a stranger lives here now. Books are scattered everywhere, covering almost every horizontal surface like mold. Furniture sits askance. A vase lies on its side with a dried bouquet spilling out of it. The apartment appears as though it was tossed by police hunting for evidence.

In the living room stands a shelving unit with framed photographs. Some are turned toward the wall. Some lie face down on the shelves. With a tentative hand, he reaches for one of the frames and rights it. Seeing the photo, he pulls it close. A gasp escapes his lips. The picture is of him and Amanda. A beach wedding. The sky behind them is aflame with the setting sun, lurid oranges and reds and yellows. The rapture on Amanda's face—on *both* their faces—is the stuff of songs and poems.

Hope is a double-edged sword. As sustaining as it can be, it has equal potential to be unimaginably cruel. It's this shadow of hope that slides into Jonas's thoughts like a knife.

What if Amanda is alive in this universe?

What if Thibault was wrong?

Jonas's heart swells and sprints. His mind constructs scenarios faster than he can cast them out. Amanda is alive. On vacation with his counterpart in this universe. They're together and happy and know nothing of the loss that has plagued him for two long years. The apartment's disorder was caused by a burglar who took advantage of their absence.

Still clutching the photo, he selects another, as if it might hold confirmation. Amanda in Central Park. The diamond ring glistering in the sun, taped inside a Frisbee. Hope continues to sing its siren song.

He returns the wedding photo to the shelf but holds on to the frame of Amanda in Central Park. He takes a deep breath and is instantly reminded of the apartment's reek. The nauseatingly piquant odor stirs him from his reverie. He considers the jumbled mess and abandoned decor. The reason that the apartment seems so familiar is because his own was in the same state. He'd stopped cleaning. He'd allowed clutter to fester. He'd banished pictures of happier times from his sight.

On the shelves in front of him, the down-turned and about-faced photo frames taunt him. They now banish hope, telling him he was a fool for even entertaining it. The truth is right in front of him: Thibault *wasn't* wrong. Amanda is gone from this universe.

And Jonas is just a trespasser in the home of a man who lost her too.

He ventures out of the living room to explore the rest of the apartment, still holding the framed photograph of Amanda in Central Park like a talisman. The hallways are lined with towers of books on physics and quantum mechanics. The kitchen is a war zone where a battle appears to have been fought by frozen food containers and bottles of liquor. The dining room, in contrast, remains pristine, suggesting that no one has used the space in months, if not years.

He leaves the bedroom for last. If any room were to remind him of his marriage, it would be that one. So perhaps it's a blessing that it's also the most altered room in the entire apartment. The bay windows are covered, but not by blinds or curtains. Closer inspection reveals the window coverings have been replaced with black trash bags. Their effect is to blot out even moonlight and the city's nighttime luminescence. He fumbles in the dark for the light switch, which he discovers is conveniently located on the same wall as in his universe.

The light reveals a room he does not recognize. The wallpaper has been painted over in white, every inch covered top to bottom with exotic formulae reminiscent of his tattoo but rendered in a madman's scrawl. Those patches of wall not covered with equations hold taped-up pages, articles and diagrams torn out of scientific journals and newspapers and magazines—an obscene collage.

The sight brings a queasy sensation. The arcane formulae with their ragged, urgent writing suggest a man who fell headfirst into a pit of grief and continued to plummet until he hit madness. The torn pages shriek with a wild desperation, a wretched search for theoretical ephemera.

On the nightstand, Jonas finds a sheaf of papers piled almost high enough to topple. Some instinct compels him to sit on the bed—its sheets unwashed—and pick up the stack. He shuffles through the papers, his fingers quivering. His stomach nose-dives at the sight of a laser-printed email confirming the payout on a life insurance policy. Jonas and his Amanda had taken out a similar one at the suggestion of some financial planner. He studies the email, and it confirms his dark instinct that this universe's Amanda is gone.

In this world, there is no Nobel, no heady night in Stockholm, no adoring crowd at the Aula Magna. Nor is there an ill-fated drive over the Centralbron. Yet Amanda is just as dead. Reams of paper from car-insurance companies and the New York Department of Transportation and the New York City Taxi and Limousine Commission tell the story: Jonas's Prius was struck by a taxi, which leaped a broken guardrail on the FDR Drive. Jonas reads conflicting denials of responsibility and varying offers of settlement. Polite entreaties for Jonas to refer the cab company's lawyers to his. Pleas for him to answer emails and other correspondence. Despite the players being different, the documents are eerily like those Jonas ignored in his home reality. Cards and printed emails of sympathy and condolence. He couldn't bring himself to read them before and feels no such compulsion to do so now. No words could console him, and he had no friends whose attempts at consolation he cared to endure. Without

Amanda, the world was empty, as bleak and stark as the moon. An ocean of sympathy couldn't quench the desert of his soul.

The papers and letters and emails form a fossil record that documents the months of grief he remembers enduring. But eventually he sees a break in the strata, a point where his doppelgänger's life begins to diverge from his own. Instead of going away quietly, the correspondence from friends and colleagues grows more worried. Their emails having gone unanswered, some take the trouble to write letters, each expressing mounting concern for the mental health of Jonas's counterpart.

In this reality, Victor made no claims of plagiarism. No review into jealous allegations was conducted. No tribunals were convened. This universe's Jonas held on to his position at Columbia University.

But then Amanda died. The bulk of the papers at the bedside is dedicated to a litany of complaints submitted to the physics department, revealing a tableau of wild outbursts in class on those rare instances when Other Jonas attended. There are reports from concerned students and teaching assistants who were watching their professor unravel.

In the pages, Dorothy Stanton volleys a series of requests that Jonas undergo a psychological evaluation. Over time, the requests morph into demands. The demands become reluctant threats. The coup de grâce is a letter terminating his employment. By this point in the epistolary narrative, it comes as a mercy.

All told, the papers tell a story of a grieving widower's coming undone, his eventual professional banishment and ostracism. Jonas sets them back down on the nightstand, feeling that he's committed an invasion of privacy, but then he's tempted by the bedroom closet, its door hanging open like an invitation.

Jonas pads inside. Shirts and slacks and pants hang over a floor littered with discarded items of clothing. Jonas considers his own wardrobe, dirty and probably smelling almost as bad as this apartment. Surely there are items with all-natural fibers here, and he's reasonably confident they'll be his size.

He flicks the closet light on and begins searching for a change of clothes. Out of habit, he scans for items that would reality-slip with him before realizing that he has no intention of leaving the universe he now occupies. Without hope of finding Amanda, he has nowhere else to go. In any universe. True, he *could* travel. The first pioneer of the multiverse. He could explore and document. He could publish in thousands of realities, collect Nobels in every universe. But what would be the point? Amanda would still be gone. An infinite collection of honors and laurels would not bring her back. Life would remain hollow. Colorless.

As he skulks through the closet, he feels something shift beneath his feet, just a slight give accompanied by a quiet creak. He nudges aside a small pile of laundry to excavate more of the floor and tests the floorboard with a tap of his shoe. It buckles slightly.

Jonas remembers the stench. He'd grown almost nose-blind to it, but it's more prominent in the closet. He descends to a knee and runs his fingers over the floorboard's edges. He pushes down with his other hand, and the wood seesaws up slightly, giving him more to grip. Lifting it out unleashes a new volley of fetid air, confirming his suspicion. He swallows hard against the impulse to gag and removes the other floorboards, exposing a narrow crawl space.

Jonas lowers himself down. His feet dangle, dropping inches before touching solid ground. *Concrete, maybe?* The channel is small and dank. Without enough room to stand, he crawls on his hands and knees. Cobwebs ensnare his face. A cockroach skitters near his hands. The stench is like a wall, and he forces himself to breathe only through his mouth. But this approach offers scant help, and he fights the urge to vomit.

Once his vision adjusts, he can make out a shape in the darkness ahead of him, black with a subtle sheen to it, evoking the image of an insect's carapace. A distorted lump is shoved into the maw of the crawl space, and closer inspection reveals that the patina catching the half light is some kind of plastic.

More garbage bags.

Beige masking tape coils around the bags, tightening around their contents and segmenting them into—

Jonas pales. Fear grips him.

What at first appeared misshapen now takes form. *A human form.*

Jonas's terror ratchets up, but it's overshadowed by a compelling need to confirm the bags' contents. He claws away at them with the urgency of a child opening presents on Christmas morning. The plastic stretches, frustrating his efforts. With growing exigency, he pulls and tears at the ebony cocoon, digging his nails into the plastic. Eventually it gives, and he's assaulted by the smell that emanates. He continues to peel away the plastic until even in the darkness he can see it.

A human corpse.

Jonas can just make out the face staring back at him with lifeless eyes. He knows it well. He's known it all his life.

It's his own.

NOW

Four hours, three drinks, and half a Xanax after shooting Amanda Cullen, Victor Kovacevic still can't stop his hand from shaking. Here in the palatial kitchen of his equally palatial Manhattan apartment, ten blocks and an entire universe away from the one in which Jonas is staring at a corpse with his own face, the gun rests on the bar top. Sitting on a stool, Victor stares at it. A Smith & Wesson M&P 9 Shield. Lying on the marble right next to his fourth glass of Macallan 18. The gun is a compact little thing, weighing just slightly over a pound, wrought of stainless steel, synthetic rubber, and a proprietary polymer. He bought it online for less than four hundred dollars.

The gun holds a total of eight bullets, and it's only been fired once. The Macon that Victor hired told him he didn't even have to practice. *Just point and squeeze,* the mercenary had said. *Most TV remotes are harder to operate.*

Macon would have been happy to do it himself, of course. The man had pulled triggers for far less than the twenty-five thousand dollars Victor was paying him. But Victor wanted to do the deed himself.

He picks it up and, not for the first time, marvels that the weapon has traveled to another reality and back. Jonas's method wouldn't permit it, but the transportation of nonorganic materials is just one of the many ways Victor has proved his skills to be superior to those of his nemesis.

But when he sees the ruddy fleck of Amanda's blood on his hand, he sets the gun down. He tries to scratch it off with a fingernail, but it persists. He thought he'd removed all the blood hours ago. He moves to the kitchen sink and washes, still unnerved by the sight of her spatter on his face in his bathroom mirror. Driven by the memory, he scrubs even harder now.

Out, damned spot; out, I say!

His right hand is still shaking, so with his left, he reaches out and drains the scotch. He has no idea why his hand should tremble, much less four hours after the deed. It was the right thing to do. The necessary thing. The thing he felt, in his bones, that the universe wanted him to do. And now it is done.

And his hand. Is. Still. Shaking.

He balls it into a fist, but still it quivers. Deciding that he needs to get his mind off Amanda, the image of her abdomen erupting with blood, Victor moves to the guest room, where the Cray XC30-AC supercomputer resides. Four towers, each the size of a refrigerator, dominate the room. Victor pours himself into the chair in front of his workstation and commands the computer out of its sleep cycle. It cost him $500,000, and Victor is once again thankful that Phaedra came from money.

His fingers fly along the keyboard. The usual commands cascade down the flat-screen monitor. The data reminds him of a waterfall. The Cray throws off a lot of heat in its labors, and Victor opens a window to let in the night air.

He questions why he's running the program again. The algorithm searches the multiverse for the quarks and neutrinos thrown off by Jonas's tether, like a magnet that pulls the needle from an unbounded number of haystacks.

But why? Amanda's dead. The scales of karma—of *justice*—are balanced.

It's over.

Yet he feels compelled to learn whether Jonas stayed behind. And if he did leave that reality, where did he travel next?

And why does it matter?

It's over.

The answer, of course, is the same reason his hand still shakes. The needs of the universe may be satisfied, but his—*his*—remain discontented. He was certain that Amanda's death would do it, but a flicker remains lit within him. *Hate.*

It occurs to Victor that if he can locate Jonas by his tether's emissions, it follows that he might be able to *manipulate* those emissions. Perhaps even disable the tether's operation entirely. And in so doing, Victor would sentence Jonas to a life of passing between universes— from reality to reality to reality—in a relentless purgatory.

Damned by the same invention Jonas had stolen from him.

The symmetry is too perfect to ignore. Once again, Victor hears the call of the universe. Charged, he returns to the workstation, opens a new window, and begins coding a new algorithm. He saves the file as KARMA2.0, and as he types away, he's hit by a realization.

His hand is no longer shaking.

FOUR YEARS AGO

The morning sun raked across their naked bodies, their limbs entwined like branches, basking together in their afterglow.

"Let's stay like this forever," Amanda said.

Jonas didn't argue and nuzzled his head against her chest. It was slick with sweat, and as his finger grazed a trail along her abdomen, he'd never known himself to be so content—a peace that fractured with an apocalyptic-sounding bang against the door of the apartment.

"It seems like someone has other ideas," Jonas deadpanned. Given the early hour on a Saturday, he assumed it was someone knocking on the door of the wrong apartment. That was fine. His mood was such that the apocalypse itself could come knocking and it wouldn't dampen his spirits. He pulled himself away—exulting in the feeling of his arms and legs rubbing against hers—and found his bathrobe. "Don't move," he said as he cinched it closed. "I'll be right back."

The banging continued, louder and more insistent. Jonas padded to the entryway as fast as he could.

"I'm coming. Just calm down . . ."

He moved to the door and opened it to find Victor standing on the other side. He was red faced, his nostrils flaring. His jaw was a coiled spring. "How could you?" he hissed. "How could you do this?"

"Victor?"

Victor shouldered his way past, letting himself inside. He was breathing heavy, his face ruddy and covered by a patina of sweat. "One of your TAs was talking about it," he fumed. "She said you were close to a breakthrough." He sounded as though he was still processing this, still straining to believe it. "That you were close to a mathematical proof of the existence of parallel worlds. *Parallel worlds.*" His tone was a mix of fury and accusation. "Tell me she's wrong," he demanded.

"Victor—"

"Tell me!" The room seemed to shake with the volume of his rage.

Jonas kept his tone level, locating a calm that surprised him under the circumstances. "I tried to show you my work a year ago," he said.

"Your work?" Victor thundered. "*Your* work?"

"Victor—"

"You mean *my* work!" His furor was volcanic. Saliva flew from his mouth. Jonas feared he might be beyond reason, that his fury was homicidal. He imagined Amanda in the bedroom, reaching for her phone, dialing nine one one.

"Victor," Jonas said, working to maintain his calm, "the idea of parallel universes—the Many Worlds Theory—that didn't originate with you."

"You knew I was working on a *proof.*" His finger jabbed at the air, barely missing Jonas's nose.

"Yes. Yes, I did." Jonas spread his hands wide, a gesture of conciliation and peace. "But you gave up on it." Jonas struggled not to sound accusatory. "You let it go, Victor. But I was inspired. I had hoped we could work on it together—that's why I showed you my calculations—but you rebuffed them, Victor. You were *adamant* about not revisiting a topic that had frustrated you. Which I completely understand," he added, coating his tone in reason and empathy.

Victor paced, stalking the apartment, ready to strike. He gave no indication that he'd listened to a word of what Jonas just said. To the contrary, he seemed to be in a world of his own, all vitriol and ire. Jonas couldn't believe it, but Victor had him genuinely afraid. In his mind, he willed for Amanda to call the police.

"I reviewed your equations," Victor hissed in disgust. "It's my work. Dressed up, but *my* work."

"Victor," Jonas started. His mind raced, desperate to find the right way of expressing himself. "I never *saw* your work. You *told* me about it, yes, but I never—whatever equations you reviewed, they were *mine*. And mine alone."

Amanda quietly emerged from the bedroom. She clutched her bathrobe tight around her. Afraid. Unaccustomed to witnessing such naked anger.

Victor remained focused on Jonas. "But you want all the glory for *yourself*," he accused.

"There is no glory," Jonas answered. "There is just me. Exploring an idea I couldn't get out of my head. I'm still a year away from publishing." The word "publishing" flew out of his mouth unbidden. Jonas felt his blood cool and his stomach clench. He had just waved a crimson flag in front of a bull.

But Victor seemed to calm. Jonas could feel him grow cold. If anything, it was more terrifying than Victor's wrath.

"Publishing?" Victor asked, making it sound like an atrocity. "By the time I'm done, you'll be lucky to get a job teaching eighth-grade physics."

It wasn't a threat. It wasn't even a promise. Victor had told him what was going to happen. A prediction.

"Victor—" Jonas said, convinced he could still find the words to calm his friend.

But Victor disappeared out the door.

Jonas stared at the open doorway and noticed he was sweating, even though he felt cold. He closed the door, and Amanda surged to him and wrapped her arms around him. "Are you okay?"

No, he wasn't. He didn't question whether Victor's accusations had been right. Despite the doubts and self-recriminations that would later follow, Jonas knew in his bones that he had committed no plagiarism, no theft of ideas. He knew his work was his own. But he dreaded Victor and what he knew the man was capable of. He shuddered, without realizing it or intending to, and he felt as if he had awoken the archetypal sleeping giant. And lost a friend. And, if Victor was to be believed, his career.

"Don't worry," he assured Amanda. "It's all going to be all right." It was the first time he had ever lied to her.

NOW

Jonas retches for what feels like days. Apparently spent, he remains on the cold tile, leaning against the porcelain toilet. He wipes away bile with the back of his hand and throws up again.

He decides he's not going to move until he is confident the vomiting has stopped. And until he can get his rubberized legs to obey his commands.

As he sits on the bathroom's hard tile, his mind races. Although he's in another reality, he can fathom only one person killing him: Victor Kovacevic.

He now believes Victor to be capable of anything. He's already demonstrated his capacity for murder twice, once with Eva by proxy and again by his own hand with Amanda. And that, Jonas reminds himself, is just the Victor he knows. There remains the possibility—if not the likelihood—that this reality has a Victor of its own.

The possibility of a Victor originating from this universe raises the question of why he would kill this reality's Jonas if Amanda was already dead here. Then again, what drives a man like Victor, in any reality, to homicidal madness?

Back in the bedroom, Jonas sets about the task of deciphering the impenetrable formulae that cover the walls. The cacophony of math appears impossible to untangle. But as Jonas pores over the jagged scrawl, it becomes ever clearer that his counterpart was working on multiverse theory. On one wall is a rudimentary version of the Many

Worlds Proof that won him the Nobel in his universe. From there, the equations reach out to embrace the theories and calculations that underlie the science behind untethering from one universe to travel to an infinite number of others.

The formulae are familiar, albeit with eccentric alterations, tiny rhetorical flourishes, like a song covered by another singer. The work of a mind almost identical to Jonas's own, yet changed in minute ways by a parallel existence, a shadow lifetime.

Then fireworks spark off in his head, and he feels a sharp pang at the base of his skull. He staggers forward and collides with the wall. He tries to pull back a curtain of pain to see clearly. He pivots around to face the attacker but is met with a man's fist. But Jonas refuses to recoil. He keeps his head low and leads with his shoulder and wills himself forward, bulldogging, throwing himself at the other man.

The impact sends them both spiraling to the floor. The man's fists fly up at Jonas, but Jonas is atop him. He has leverage and uses it, raining down a series of wild punches. He unleashes the blows without anger, only the desperate need to put the other man down and end the attack.

Jonas retracts a fist, ready to deliver another blow.

And stops.

The man beneath him isn't moving. He's still conscious, but the fight has gone out of him. He appears disoriented. And not, it seems, from Jonas's attack. He appears manic. Unhinged. His face is gaunt and unshaven.

But Jonas instantly recognizes it as his own.

He stares, straining to make sense of this.

Another doppelgänger.

He expects only one per universe. And this reality's Jonas Cullen is rotting away in a cramped crawl space.

In the interval it takes for Jonas's mind to reconcile what his eyes are seeing, the other Jonas recovers his senses and sends his fist hurling into the side of Jonas's head. Jonas rears back, holding a hand up against another volley as he staggers to his feet.

Other Jonas stands and assaults him again. Jonas falls back against the nightstand. He and the photograph of Amanda in Central Park crash to the floor as the doppelgänger surges forward, pressing his advantage.

Jonas struggles to stand, but his counterpart starts kicking him, causing Jonas to fold himself into the fetal position to protect his ribs and make himself as small a target as possible. Other Jonas keeps up the assault, alternating between kicking and stomping.

"I killed you!" Other Jonas is screaming, his voice disturbingly familiar. "I killed you! How can you be alive? *I killed you!*"

His foot sails again—this time toward Jonas's head—but Jonas catches it. Gripping the sole of Other Jonas's shoe with both hands, he twists hard to the left until he hears a faint *crack*.

Other Jonas wails in agony and falls back. Jonas staggers to his feet. His chest is on fire, but he doesn't think any ribs are broken. He chances turning his back to Other Jonas so he can lurch back toward the closet.

In seconds, Other Jonas is on the attack again with a guttural roar in Jonas's voice, but it is a sound Jonas could never envision himself making, even at the nadir of despair over Amanda's death. Other Jonas is almost atop him, but Jonas now has one of the closet's wayward floorboards in his hands. He swings it hard and is rewarded with the sickening sound of wood against skull.

Other Jonas drops to the floor at the outer edge of the closet. Out cold.

Jonas stares at this other man, studying him. Fingernails long, dirty. Clothes disheveled. Face gaunt. Familiar, but a stranger. A chilling funhouse mirror.

Jonas staggers toward the nightstand. He bends to retrieve the fallen picture of Amanda. But the glass is cracked, right across her face. He removes the photo from the fractured frame and runs a finger across Amanda's face.

Wishing it were the real thing.

Other Jonas lies unconscious on the floor. His head is bleeding from where Jonas struck him, but even if he were in pristine condition, he would still strike Jonas as pitiable. He is noticeably thinner, making him seem strangely older in appearance than Jonas. His skin is pale but for the smudge of unkempt stubble. His hair is wild and greasy.

Jonas studies this strange intruder. Maybe he isn't an intruder at all. Maybe this is *his* apartment. If so, who is the Jonas beneath the floorboards? What parallel reality does *he* hail from? Jonas's world cantilevers with questions as the most pressing one springs forth: *What will he do next?*

Jonas watches as Other Jonas stirs awake. At first, his movements are lolling, passive. A slow transit back to consciousness. Once awake, his eyes fly open. His head snaps forward. He jerks and discovers the torn bedsheets that have been repurposed to confine him.

Waking has done little to improve his appearance. He still resembles a shadow of Jonas, a desaturated version of himself. In the days following Amanda's death, Jonas imagines he might have appeared as pathetic. But only barely.

He sits opposite his twin. The two dining room chairs he's moved into the bedroom oppose each other like a reflection. The only difference is the men sitting in them. One is bound, the other is not. One has a bandage on his head, the other is uninjured, despite what the protestations inside his skull have to say on the matter.

Jonas is relieved to see that the mania has left his counterpart, leaving a detached confusion in its wake. Other Jonas lolls his head from side to side. Jonas lets him take as much time as he needs to orient himself. He needs his doppelgänger as lucid as possible, which, Jonas reminds himself, might be a heavy lift.

Eventually, Other Jonas focuses. He appears as unnerved by the sight of Jonas as Jonas was by the sight of him. Jonas has no idea what's going on behind those all-too-familiar eyes. The opaqueness of his twin's thoughts is disquieting.

Having gotten Other Jonas's attention, he begins with gallows humor. "Hi. Nice to meet me."

Other Jonas doesn't react. He's too busy staring at Jonas in disbelief. "I killed you," he says with utter conviction.

Between bandaging Other Jonas's head, moving in the chairs, stripping the bed, tearing the bedsheets, heaving Other Jonas onto one of the chairs, and tying him to it, Jonas had plenty of time to reflect on what may have happened. "You returned to the apartment," Jonas says, reconstructing the past hour. "You saw the floorboards. The crawl space. You saw me. And, what, you thought I was *him*?" He glances back in the direction of the closet, toward the final resting place of the third Jonas. "Somehow risen from the dead?"

"I haven't been at my most lucid recently, I'll admit."

Hearing his own voice respond, complete with his familiar syntax and inflections, is unnerving in the extreme. So is the fact that Victor *didn't* kill the Jonas lying beneath the floorboards. That Jonas was killed by the one he was staring at right now.

"Trying to murder yourself," Jonas says, "your *other* self, is a little more than just a lack of lucidity."

Other Jonas's head offers a shallow bob. A hint of a shrug. A half-hearted admission.

Then Jonas asks the question that is forefront in his mind. "Which one are you?" Other Jonas seems confused. "You or the other one. Which one is . . . ?" He stops, realizing he doesn't know quite how to put the question.

Other Jonas does. "You mean 'Jonas Prime?'" he asks, amused by the question. "The Jonas Cullen—the us—of this reality?" He cocks his head and gives a look of pity ordinarily reserved for funerals. "Does it matter?"

"Indulge me."

"Him. This is . . ." He stops and corrects himself. "This *was* his reality."

"Why'd you kill him?" Jonas asks.

Other Jonas chuckles. Everything is amusing to the mad. "Guess this world just wasn't big enough for the two of us." He laughs at his own joke.

"This isn't funny."

"Amanda always said I was my own worst enemy." Another joke. Like a borscht belt comic. *I've got a million of 'em, folks.* "It's like a riddle. When is killing yourself *not* suicide?"

"I think the better question is why do it in the first place?" Jonas feels the back of his neck beginning to warm and tastes bile in his mouth—he's starting to lose his patience.

Other Jonas eyes the closet, its doors still open, the crawl space still gaping. His familiar voice grows distant, his tone stripped of affect. "He was trying to stop me."

"Stop you from doing what?"

"From making the calculations. From finding Amanda." All evidence of humor vanishes, and Other Jonas becomes deadly serious, his voice laced with an echo of his earlier desperation. "I couldn't let him institutionalize me."

Jonas pushes down a pang of queasiness and asks, "Why was he trying to stop you?"

Other Jonas flashes confusion again. "Isn't it obvious?"

"Let's pretend it's not."

"He thought I'd 'break' the multiverse. He thought I was obsessive. I suppose I am." Other Jonas stares a hole into Jonas. "And before you start judging, it looks like *you* are too."

Jonas doesn't debate the point. "When she died . . . the *first time* she died . . . I couldn't leave here, this apartment. Could hardly get out of bed."

Other Jonas nods, sharing the same painful memory.

"I knew she'd want me to move on," Jonas says, "but I didn't know how. So I made a bargain with myself . . ."

"One hour at a time, one day at a time," Other Jonas says, knowing the mantra.

"Don't look back, just keep moving forward," Jonas responds.

Other Jonas stares at him like a curio mounted behind glass, an exotic specimen. "You said the 'first time' she died . . ."

Jonas adopts the tone of a penitent in a confessional. "I found her. The one universe where she's still alive. Or was," he corrects himself, his voice catching in his throat. "And I lost her again." The words come in barely a whisper.

"So why'd you come here?" Other Jonas asks. Jonas searches for a way to describe what he sees in his twin's face. Is it . . . sympathy?

"I had to go *somewhere*."

Other Jonas bobs his head at the simplicity of that. Perhaps he'd even made the same choice before insanity took him.

Jonas points to the equations running up and down the walls. "Are these yours or his?"

"Mine. He didn't want to have the first thing to do with finding her. All he wanted to do was die." He cocks his head to one side. "I guess you could say I accommodated him." He tries to laugh again, only to produce a croak reminiscent of someone choking. "But like I said, I couldn't let him stop me."

Something in the ephemera on the walls steals Jonas's attention. It's faint, like a road sign on the horizon, but it's there. Buried in the jumble of letters and symbols and numbers.

He rises and wanders to the east wall. He hadn't had the chance to finish reviewing his counterpart's work before. Slowly, the equations begin to take on meaning and substance, revealing a structure Jonas's mind can grasp. He follows the equations down, lowering himself to the floor. On the baseboard is a calculation he's never seen before. He works to make sense of the formulae, feeling Other Jonas watching him, slowly nodding encouragement. *Go on. You can do it . . .*

Jonas puts a hand to the baseboard. His fingers graze the equations there. He feels the same sensation he did two years ago, back in Stockholm, when he held a little piece of blue plastic marked by two blue lines that told him he was going to be a father.

He's staring at a miracle.

"Thibault was wrong," he exhales. Astonishment and relief. "He was *wrong*. There's a *second* universe. *Another* universe where she's still alive." The words, the sound of hope, echo in his mind. *She's still alive.* Jonas turns back to the equations. "And you found it."

"Yes. And before you ask, that's the last one."

"Why didn't you go there?" Jonas asks.

Other Jonas shrugs. "I'm trapped here." He strains against the bedsheets holding him in place. "Even before you tied me to a chair."

"I don't understand."

Other Jonas lets an exasperated sigh escape him. Then, as though to an obstinate student: "CERN's Large Hadron Collider unanchored you, right? Like cutting away ballast, it allowed you to slip realities." Jonas nods. "I did the same. The problem is, the effect wears off eventually. The quantum energies dissipate over time."

Jonas had forgotten. He struggles for breath. The world becomes liquid.

"That's what happened to me," Other Jonas says. "I found out where Amanda is, where I needed to go, but not before I lost the ability to go there." However long he's been marooned in this reality hasn't been long enough to erase the bitterness of this development.

"You have to be feeling it by now," Other Jonas continues. "The sensation. The pain in your body. Each time you jump universes. You feel that *tingling*, don't you?"

Jonas does. He had convinced himself that the pain was the result of all the abuse he had taken recently, a residual effect of his reality-slips, but he can't deny that his body's protestations emanate from a deeper place, in his very marrow. An unusual, inexplicable pain. The kind of pain reserved for disease instead of injury.

Other Jonas regards him. "You've been feeling the loss of the quantum effect."

"What happens when it's gone?" The words come out clipped.

"You'll be trapped. Same as me."

"How much time do I have?" Jonas asks, feeling like a condemned prisoner.

"Untie me, and we can find out." Jonas returns a skeptical stare. "You know I can't do that kind of math in my head. *We* can't," Other Jonas corrects. "I promise I won't try to kill you."

Jonas considers this and concludes that he has no choice but to take the risk. As he unties Other Jonas, he admonishes, "Try anything, and I'll lay you out again. Apparently, in my reality, I work out more."

"Cute," Other Jonas says as he stands. "First, I'm going to need to examine your anchor."

"What?"

Other Jonas points to Jonas's tether. "That. Your anchor."

"I call it a tether.'"

"*Potay-to, potah-to.*" Other Jonas shrugs as he moves toward the closet. The stench is much worse with the floorboards displaced, but it doesn't seem to bother Other Jonas. He emerges with a thick object the size of a serving platter. An assembly of naked circuit boards, transistors, and microchips cluster atop it. Other Jonas rests it on the soiled bed and snakes out a fluorescent-orange power cord from the device, which he plugs into a nearby socket. "I need to see your anchor—your tether," he corrects.

"I can't take it off for long."

"Tell me something I don't know. But maybe you could be a touch more patronizing while you're at it." He points to a space in the center of the device, roughly the size of a hand. "Just rest your whole hand here."

Jonas leans down to do as instructed, watching Other Jonas manipulate a series of microswitches affixed to the neat row of circuit boards. Jonas feels a slight tingle as electricity courses through him.

"How long will this take?" Jonas asks.

"As long as it takes."

A small LCD screen comes to life in the corner of the rectangular device. A series of decimal numbers, like IP addresses, flash across the display. Jonas watches his doppelgänger study them.

"Give me a second," Other Jonas says as he moves to the nightstand. "You can take your hand back." He rifles through the papers piled atop the nightstand, turning over sheet after sheet until he spots one that's clear of writing. From the drawer, he produces a pen and sets to work running the numbers he memorized from the LCD's readout through a gauntlet of equations.

"Although your *tether* is designed to regulate the quantum radiation in your body, it also absorbed it at the same level and is leaking it in similar fashion. Which means the rate of energy dissipation can be measured."

"You can figure out how many more times I can reality-slip," Jonas says.

"Yes, but that's only part of the problem."

"What's the other part?"

"I thought I was smarter than this," Other Jonas sighs. "It's very disappointing, I don't mind telling you."

"Don't play games with me," Jonas snaps.

"Actually, I'm playing games with *me*."

Other Jonas taps his calculations with his pen. "If my math is right—which it is—you can untether yourself only two more times before you're permanently stranded in whatever universe you end up in."

"Only two more times," Jonas breathes.

"And then you lose the ability to slip realities. Permanently."

"Why? Why only two times?" Jonas demands.

"I told you: Your tether is leaking quantum radiation. It's like a battery." Other Jonas shrugs. "Batteries wear out."

Jonas forces himself to accept the reality of this. "You said that was only part of the problem . . ."

"Yes. Before you lose the ability to reality-slip, you have to make sure that whichever reality you end up in has a particle collider."

"Why?"

Other Jonas heaves a heavy sigh, as though explaining this to a child. "Because by that point you'll only have one reality-slip left. Two minus one is one, right? You'll be down to one last untethering, and you're not going to want to waste it." Jonas shoots him a look. *Elaborate.* "Right now, every cell in your body is working to expel the quantum radiation you've loaded them up with. Moving between realities speeds up that process. Remember the battery? You can't replace it, but you can give it one last—brief—jolt by topping it off."

"With a particle collider."

Other Jonas applauds and points to another corner of the wall, jabbing his finger in the direction of more equations. "And to risk butchering this analogy, you're going to want to be very specific about the type of electricity you use for the top-off."

Jonas turns to the equations, the theoretical physics memorialized there. "You're saying I need to recalibrate what remains of the quantum energy in my cells with radiation of the correct wavelength to send me to the reality where Amanda is."

"The last time you reality-slip, yes," Other Jonas confirms. "But I think my battery analogy is more elegant." He swats the idea away. "Point is, you need a battery charger in the form of a particle collider."

Jonas points back to the baseboard with Other Jonas's formula for the third universe. "And to calibrate the collider based on those calculations."

"He finally gets it," Other Jonas notes, fatigued.

"Not entirely. Why can't I just save myself a reality-slip? Why not just use a particle collider in *this* universe?"

Other Jonas gives a chuckle that sounds like radio static. He works his way over to a section of the wall where a newspaper article is taped. He takes it down and hands it to Jonas.

Jonas scans the article. Another gut punch. "They shut down CERN," he gasps. "What about—"

"*Other* accelerators? Keep reading."

Jonas does. In this universe, the Large Hadron Collider was the last particle collider to be decommissioned. In this universe, an accident at New York's Brookhaven National Laboratory killed thousands, leading to global protests—most fueled by the religious notion that smashing protons together was the exclusive province of the divine—which ultimately resulted in shutting down the world's thirty thousand particle colliders.

"That's madness," Jonas hisses.

"What, there are no moral panics in the universe where you come from?" Other Jonas cannot keep the disgust from his voice. "This universe positively exults in them. The point is, you have two choices: break into one of the decommissioned accelerators and try to start it back up—which, having tried it, I really wouldn't recommend—or reality-slip again and hope for a more scientifically tolerant universe."

Hope. Jonas's thoughts lurch once again in its direction. With renewed urgency, he snatches the paper and pen from his counterpart's hands and returns to the baseboard, scribbling formulae with a fury. Anticipation wells up within him with each stroke. Perhaps his doppelgänger's mania is contagious.

As Jonas writes, he hears Other Jonas cautioning, "All that being said . . . and I say this knowing what you promised yourself—what *we* promised ourselves—you should consider the fact that the energy dissipation, the ticking clock, the fact that every collider has been mothballed in this reality . . ."

"Means what?"

"That you can't swim against the tide of the universe."

The pen nearly breaks under Jonas's hand. Once again he feels the sensation of someone stepping on his grave. "What?"

"I said, 'You can't swim against the tide of the universe.'"

"I knew a woman who said that exact same thing to me once."

"Eva Stamper." Jonas reacts, surprised to hear that name. "I guess we've both met her in our travels," Other Jonas muses. "Interesting."

"'The universe favors certain outcomes.'"

Now it's Other Jonas who regards his twin with pity. "Reality-slip yourself home," he implores. "Before the quantum energy leaves your body forever. And if you can't find home, find somewhere livable, and do what I never could."

"And what's that?"

"Move on."

Jonas shakes his head. His other self may as well have suggested that he learn to fly. "You know us both better than that."

Other Jonas, his face full of condolence, pads over to the nightstand and places a reverent hand on the stack of papers chronicling the slow destruction of Jonas Prime's life. "The only thing I know anymore is what we do once hope is lost."

"That's why I don't lose hope," Jonas says. His voice is iron. He folds the paper and slips it into his pocket. The sensation of it against his leg brings comfort. "I'm sorry I can't stay to—" He searches for the right words. "To help you."

With that, he turns away. It's hard to leave him in this squalor, flirting with madness, a dead body rotting away beneath his feet. But Jonas doesn't have a choice. His crusade requires complete devotion. He's almost out the door when he feels Other Jonas's grip on his shoulder.

"And what do you do if you can't find Amanda? What do you do when the effect wears off and you're trapped in a reality without her?"

"Then I kill myself and be with her that way." But both men know that's not how true love works. That Jonas is giving voice to his grief, not his soul, which knows better, which knows he needs help. That part of him—crying for aid—slips from his counterpart's grip and out of the apartment. He hears the door close behind him and wills himself forward with the same admonishment he's repeated countless times over the past two years.

Don't look back.

NOW

Only in the mind of a scientist, Victor reflects, could curiosity eclipse vengeance. The thought of sabotaging Jonas's tether remains warm, a comfort. But he set it aside once the Cray reported that Jonas had returned to his Riverside Drive apartment. By his count, that would make at least three separate universes where Jonas had chosen to call the brownstone home.

Victor had been so singularly focused on revenge that he hadn't taken the time to consider a multiverse's worth of Jonases. He knew they existed, of course. But his hatred for "his" Jonas was so lasered that the notion of doppelgängers was an unwelcome distraction. Now, though, the thought of Jonas finding a twin—meeting him, talking to him, and, God forbid, gaining assistance from him—can't be ignored.

And so Victor stands in a living room, which stirs a memory of visits he'd made to the same home in another universe. But now the place reeks and is in disarray. He finds an arrangement of photographs, all turned down or backward. The Jonas who resides in this universe knew Amanda and lost her. The thought brings a smile.

He stands there for longer than he should. At some point, Jonas— this universe's version or the one Victor knows—will either come home or hear him walking about. Victor should be concerned, afraid of a confrontation, but he isn't. That's what the M&P 9 Shield at the small of his back is for.

A voice comes from the apartment's recesses, slurred and laced with humor, but the voice is unmistakably Jonas's. "Came back, huh? Nice to see you come to your senses." An amused snort. "Always knew I was smart."

Victor follows the familiar voice and enters the bedroom. The smell is significantly worse in here. Black garbage bags hang over the windows. The only furniture is a ladder, a chair, the bed, and a nightstand burdened with stacks of papers. The once-white bedsheets are a grayish yellow and swirled in a torrent. Equations, sketchy and desperate, flow across every wall. Erratic though they might be, Victor sees in them the calculations of multiversal destinations.

And then he sees him. Standing near the bed. Bloodshot eyes. Sallow skin painted with a thin layer of stubble. A mop of hair as unruly as those bedsheets. But still recognizable as Jonas. At least, *a* Jonas. He sways on his feet. A bottle of bourbon, with maybe a mouthful left in it, dangles from his fingers.

"Who the hell are you?" this Other Jonas says, his tongue languid. Whatever fear he might have of an intruder in his home has evidently been muted by the bourbon.

Interesting, Victor observes, *apparently I don't exist here.*

He returns his gaze to the equations on the wall. That this universe's Jonas managed to develop the Many Worlds Proof without a Victor Kovacevic to crib from should be vexing. But Victor's narcissism stands against the thought like a wall, preventing him from entertaining the notion that any version of Jonas is capable of discovering the secrets of the multiverse without drafting off Victor's brilliance.

"Who *are* you?" this Jonas barks, louder and more insistent than before.

Ignoring him, Victor continues to study the manic formulae carpeting the walls. He pushes through the scattershot mania of the equations, working to excavate the math, the thinking, that lies beneath.

"Hey!" Other Jonas is shouting now. "Get the hell out of here before I—"

"Before you what?" Victor cuts him off. "You can barely stand up, Jonas."

"How do you know my name?"

Victor waves at the walls. "Where did you get these calculations? Are they yours?" His voice adopts the tone of accusation. "Are they his?"

"Okay, that's it. I'm calling the police," Other Jonas threatens, despite the dead body beneath the closet. He begins to hunt for his phone, but the search appears hampered by his inebriated state. Victor slams him up against one of the annotated walls.

"Where," Victor repeats, his voice clipped with impatience, "did you get these calculations?"

Other Jonas stares back, trying to fight his way through a fog of liquored confusion. "I . . . they're mine."

"I doubt that very much." Indeed, this Jonas appears as though he can barely calculate the tip at a restaurant.

"It was—it was a while ago. Before . . ." He glances down at the bottle hanging limply in his hand.

Victor recognizes the look in his eyes as shame. "He came here, didn't he? The other you."

Other Jonas tries and fails to fight through the haze of booze, stammering for an answer. But Victor has no interest in waiting. He resumes reviewing the equations. The formulae are rendered in an erratic hand, but he recognizes the math.

"Your doppelgänger," he says, "the Jonas Cullen of another universe, a parallel world. He came here, didn't he?"

"Who are you?" Other Jonas asks again, now seeming more frightened than confused.

Victor turns and lasers in on Other Jonas. "He was here."

"He's gone now," Jonas responds.

"Where did he go?"

Other Jonas shakes his head. "I don't know."

Victor's forearm pistons out and pins him to the wall with enough force to sway the lamp overhead. "But you know *something*."

Victor watches Other Jonas's expression change. Slowly, fear and confusion transmute to anger at this stranger who has invaded his home. Victor watches as defiance wells up in the man. "I told him where to go."

At first, it sounds to Victor as though Other Jonas is claiming he told his doppelgänger to go to hell. But then Other Jonas repeats himself. "I told him where to go." This time, the words come out less defiant. Simple. Almost plaintive. *I told him where to go.*

Keeping the man fixed to the wall, Victor glances back at the equations. A terrible epiphany begins to take shape. "You found another one," Victor says. "You found another universe where she's still alive." The words spill out with reverence and awe. Somehow, this addled drunk has found something Victor had deemed impossible.

Victor looks back at the math on the walls. He scans the equations, eyes flying across the formulae, trying to pluck the universe's location from the numbers and symbols on display.

"It's not there," Other Jonas says. "The location of that universe. That's what you're looking for, isn't it?" Victor doesn't answer. "I wrote it in a notebook. The other me took it."

Victor returns his focus to Other Jonas. "Why didn't *you* use it?" he asks through gritted teeth. "Why are you even here, in this universe? Why aren't you with her right now?"

Other Jonas explains his predicament. The news that Victor will eventually lose his ability to slip realities chills him. He feels himself blanch. A smug grin takes shape on Other Jonas's face. "You're slipping realities too," he says, his voice laden with realization. "Another explorer. Well, *explorer*, the concept that your cells might eventually lose their ability to travel the multiverse is something you *might* want to concern yourself with," he taunts. "Wouldn't want to find yourself trapped in a universe that's not your own."

Victor shrugs off the jeer, relinquishing his grip on Other Jonas. Victor's fingers run across the surface of his tether bracelet, manipulating the capacitance sensors built into its housing. "You look quite miserable here," he tells Other Jonas. "I'm glad."

The bracelet glows, lambent with power. Space folds in on itself, and a second explorer of the multiverse blinks from Other Jonas's apartment.

NOW

Jonas throws himself into the city, plunging into an ocean of light and steel, glass and neon. A multitude of humanity swells around him. He flows into the current and walks, swimming in a sea of anonymity.

It dawns that he should have asked Other Jonas for money before he left. But he could no longer resist the compulsion to get away from his doppelgänger. He had no longer been able to face himself. Literally.

And so he walks. And walks. And walks. The night air is bracing. He tells himself it will bring him the focus he needs to think and figure out his next move, but the truth is he's just cold. So he walks faster. And thinks. And thinks.

He reaches into his pocket and feels the paper folded inside. His doppelgänger's work. The quintessential answers to the test. His salvation. If he can leave this universe and travel to another that has a CERN. If he can gain access to its Large Hadron Collider or an equivalent machine. If Other Jonas's math holds and he's properly calculated the universe where the third and final Amanda is still alive. If. If. If. And all without help or money.

A neon sign across the street winks in the darkness. A tattoo parlor. Another coil of neon announces **ATM INSIDE**. It's a burning bush, a sign from on high. A plan takes shape in his mind.

He drifts across the street and into the shop. Every surface is either ebony or glass. It smells of incense and cheap pizza. His arrival draws curious stares.

Jonas pushes toward the counter, where the cash register is manned by a guy in his late twenties. His face and arms are given over to a tapestry of dragons whose forms undulate over each muscle. Fire issues forth from fanged jaws, flames dive-bomb toward his wrists. If he has a patch of skin on his body not covered in ink, it must be under his clothes.

"Help you with something?" the man behind the counter asks. He makes no effort to hide the annoyance in his voice. He looks like he's getting ready to tell Jonas that the restrooms are for paying customers only.

Jonas pulls the calculations from his pocket and lays the paper down on the glass counter. "I need this done."

Dragon Man picks up the paper and smirks. "Well, this is new. Ain't nobody asked me to ink 'em up with *math* before."

"But you can do it." Jonas doesn't ask so much as assert, willing the answer he wants.

Dragon Man considers, his attention never leaving the equations. "Quite a bit here. You'll be more comfortable if we spread this out over a few sessions."

"I need it all done tonight."

Behind Dragon Man the wall is covered with artwork and designs. Fodder for potential tattoos. A menagerie of religious symbols and superheroes and a variety of flowers to rival any nursery.

Jonas points to one. "That one too," he says.

He pulls up his sleeve to expose his un-inked forearm as Dragon Man reaches behind to pull down Jonas's selected design.

A snake eating its own tail, twisted into an infinity symbol.

The floor of the tattoo parlor is linoleum, but it's as sticky as flypaper as Jonas stands from the chair. The skin of his inner right forearm burns with hours' worth of inscriptions. Not for the first time, the tattoo artist remarks on Jonas's stamina, his threshold for pain. "Never seen anything like it, brah. And definitely not in, well, a guy like you. Someone who comes off as, y'know, academic. No offense."

"None taken. Thank you." Jonas considers his new tattoo. The lines of equations glow with crimson halos on his skin. The artist is right to comment on Jonas's tolerance. He had moments when he would have allowed himself to pass out but for the embarrassment and the possibility that the artist would stop. "You did very good work," he offers.

"It's no problem," the man says. "But it is five hundred."

Five hundred dollars that Jonas doesn't have. "Where's your cash machine?" he asks as casually as possible.

"In the back. On your left."

Jonas nods his thanks and walks toward the rear of the parlor, where he finds a long hallway. He walks straight past the mobile ATM and into a unisex restroom. He locks the door behind him. The room is as small as a walk-in closet—smaller, in fact, than the one where he discovered his twin's corpse. It smells just as bad. A fluorescent bar flickers overhead.

The mirror is scratched with crude hieroglyphs of male genitalia. Jonas catches his reflection beneath the graffiti. The face staring back at him reminds him more of Other Jonas than of himself. The stubbled face. The unkempt hair. The fatigued eyes that nevertheless burn with desperation. And the menagerie of bruises he's accumulated in the past several hours. They mottle his skin beneath the eye and on the side of his jaw. He didn't realize he looked so bad. It's a miracle the tattoo artist didn't comment on it or, worse, turn him away.

Jonas runs the tap and stoops to splash water on his face, as if that will improve his appearance. The water has a fetid smell. It runs down the sides of his face like tears.

He breathes deep, mentally preparing himself to risk his life by traversing the multiverse for the penultimate time. Once again, he pulls the tether off his finger. Once again, he unmoors himself from the universe and surfs the multiverse.

His entire body tingles. Electricity courses through him. The pangs in the core of his limbs return. The sensation of the quantum energies leaving his cells is a reminder that he has only one of these interuniversal trips left.

Reality begins to slide all around him. He thinks he should be used to it by now—the human brain becomes accustomed to anything over time—but he can't imagine ever becoming inured to the world, the *universe*, changing all around him. The walls of the bathroom disintegrate, revealing a desolate cityscape with broken skyscrapers looming like the skeletons of giants.

A Manhattan he recognizes flashes in front of him before being replaced by a more upscale restroom. In a blink, the room transforms into a broom closet. Another blink and the closet is covered in drywall and wiring and piping, the conduits all lancing Jonas for a single agonizing millisecond before snapping away, revealing a congested city street.

A crush of humanity flows toward him. The people wear gas masks. Rubber tubes snake from the masks to tanks slung over their backs like humps. Jonas takes an instinctive breath and is punished with an acrid smell that sears his lungs. He coughs uncontrollably, then the reality blinks away, and he's deposited yet in another universe.

The sound of sirens pummel his ears. People run past him in every direction, buffeting him and knocking him about. He hears the crackle of fire and the whine of a missile. Figures on gurneys, burned to the point where they resemble zombies, are shuttled past. Screams ring out. Desperate wails compete with the bleating Klaxons. In the center of the tumult, an ashen-faced toddler sobs alone.

Jonas laces the tether back onto his finger, and the shifting of the universes instantly ceases, like slamming into a wall. He looks around and sees that he's back in familiar environs. A mirror. A sink. A towel dispenser. A toilet. *You can travel across the multitude of realities,* he thinks, *but you still end up in a bathroom.*

Fortunately, this one is much nicer than the one he departed. He smells the prominent aroma of bleach. The mirror is unmarred, except for a business card wedged into its bevels that advertises "Tantric Sexual Healing & Orthodontics."

If Other Jonas is right, and Jonas has no reason to believe he isn't, this is the second to last time he'll be able to take such a trip. He feels the downward pressure of his quest, the multiverse's odds stacking against him, but he pushes those doubts aside. *One step at a time.*

The first step takes him out of the restroom. He's met with the same long corridor and bad lighting. Another caustic smell, but of a new variety. He walks out into a space draped in neon and filled with mannequins standing at attention, dressed in black leather studded with metal ornamentations. The room is devoid of tattoo chairs, but the glass case in front of the cash register remains the same. Behind it is a woman who must be at least sixty. Her hair is cut back to a silver mohawk. Light glints off the steel piercings that dot her cheeks, nose, eyebrows, and ears.

"Help you with something?" she asks, eyeing him with suspicion after his abrupt arrival from the rear of the shop.

Jonas shakes his head and heads for the door. He can feel the lady's gaze tracking him as he goes.

Out on the street, he is surprised by daylight. It had been evening when he'd entered the previous reality's tattoo parlor, and he apparently spent the entire night and into the morning getting his new tattoos.

People walk past him, their heads down, hands shoved into their pockets, their backs hunched. The sun shines, yet the sky remains slate gray. The effect extends to buildings and clothing and even street signs, like the color has been bled from the world. A desaturated Earth.

The traffic on the streets cries with the labors of overtaxed engines. Tailpipes belch black clouds. Vehicles lumber past with little variation in style and even less in color. Utilitarian, nondescript. What little aesthetics they possess seem frozen in the 1960s.

Looking around, Jonas thinks that this Manhattan feels more reminiscent of eastern Europe than the New York City he knows. The metropolis seems old beyond its years, an aging barfly hunched over his drink on the stool he's kept for decades. The architecture is brutalist and bland, evoking the feeling of Soviet-era Russia.

He approaches a corner and sees a soldier in ebony body armor stationed there, assault rifle at the ready. His face is hidden beneath a helmet, goggles, and balaclava, all black with a matte finish, offering no reflection, no hint of light. The man's biceps is wrapped with an armband displaying a black iron cross on a white field.

The soldier—though "storm trooper" would be more accurate— turns in Jonas's direction. Jonas pivots and walks as fast as he can across the street without giving the appearance that anything is out of the ordinary. As he goes, a large armored truck slips past, as lumbering as the storm trooper and as black as the man's gear, an iron cross stenciled on its side.

Another storm trooper awaits on the sidewalk. He stands next to a street vendor, who has a landscape of T-shirts and baseball caps laid out on a listing card table. All the items are festooned with an American flag, but these, too, are different. The red has been leached to a lifeless maroon, the color of a scab. The blue has been traded for black. And the field of fifty stars is gone, replaced with that same iron cross.

Unease washes over Jonas as the vendor catches him staring at his wares. "You want to buy one? Maybe two?" Jonas can discern no New York accent. He thinks he might be mistaken, but he believes he can detect a trace of German.

The storm trooper glances his way. Despite being faceless, his body language suggests suspicion.

"Just browsing," Jonas manages to croak back to the vendor. "Thank you."

He moves off. The storm trooper's eyes follow, so Jonas quickens his pace, faster but not too fast, falling into step with a passel of citizens, camouflaging himself in the anonymity of the city.

He walks for blocks and blocks. Once-familiar street names reveal themselves to have German analogues. The normal soundtrack of the city—the honking and jackhammering, the yelling and cursing, the music playing out of open windows—is absent here, replaced by an eerie shuffling silence.

As he weaves himself through Midtown, he senses a presence. Something, someone, following him. He tries to catch a glimpse of this hunter in the reflections of shop windows, in the side-view mirrors of parked cars, but each time, the man slips away, disappearing, but not before offering the hint of a glimpse. Jonas's first thought is that he's being pursued by Victor or maybe an incarnation of Macon. But those reflected glimpses, almost subliminal, suggest otherwise.

Jonas stops abruptly, spinning to look behind him. There, at the end of the block, hidden behind a curtain of passing pedestrians, is . . . himself. Another doppelgänger.

Jonas steps toward the man, drawn like a magnet, as people pass between them. As he pushes through the throng, he loses sight of the man. The doppelgänger now has his back to Jonas, receding down the block, hiding himself in the crowd.

Jonas starts shoving people aside, desperate not to let this latest twin get away. Some bark, "Hey!" or "Watch it!" He ignores them all. His quarry is almost at the end of the block when Jonas grabs him by the shoulder and pulls the man around toward him.

The face he sees is a stranger's.

"Excuse me," the man says, politely perturbed.

There's enough of a resemblance to cause Jonas to question whether the doppelgänger he saw was a mirage.

"I'm sorry," Jonas says, relinquishing his grip. "I thought you were someone else."

Eager to disengage, Jonas spins away without looking and almost collides with a baby carriage. The mother pushing it hisses at him for his clumsiness. The incident draws the notice of another storm trooper.

Jonas pinwheels away from the mother and child only to catch his own reflection in the window of an electronics store, his face super-imposed over a crush of computers and tablets and heavy monitors burdened by cathode ray tubes. He begins to turn away when an idea seizes him. *Maybe, just maybe . . .*

He heads inside. The interior of the store is narrow. On the left is a wall dotted with sun-bleached fliers and posters advertising various technologies that strike Jonas as decades old. The right half of the store is taken up by a long glass display case that doubles as a service counter. Inside the case is a menagerie of electronics. A man with a paunch and a receding hairline is the store's only employee. Behind him, small items hang from hooks on a wall of pegboard. Mobile phones in clamshell packaging dangle. The magic words **PREPAID MOBILE** wink out at Jonas from behind the plastic. Hope springs for a moment, until he notices that none of the phones have keyboards or displays larger than a matchbook and, therefore, are ill suited for the purpose he has in mind.

"Excuse me," he asks the clerk, "but do you have any smartphones?"

The clerk just stares back at him. "Excuse me?"

"You know, with internet access."

The clerk regards Jonas as if he's an idiot. "An internet phone."

"Yeah. Exactly."

The man jerks a thumb over his right shoulder. "I keep 'em in the back. Do you got a license?"

"A license?"

"You know . . . a permit," the clerk says, his patience fraying. "You need to be permitted for internet access." He says this as though he's explaining that a car has to stop at a red light.

"Yes, of course," Jonas rallies. "I have a permit." He doubles down. "Government issued." This earns him a curt nod, and Jonas presses his luck further. "Do you have one I could demo?"

"Demo?"

"Yes. You know, try it out?"

The clerk brightens with understanding. "Demo. Never heard that before." He disappears into the back. When he returns, it's with a simple slab of charcoal-colored glass. "Here you go."

Jonas activates the phone. A staircase of reception bars appears in the upper left corner of the screen. This may be a demonstration model, but it has cellular service or whatever passes for the equivalent in this reality.

"Must be some kinda big shot if you got a permit to access the net," the clerk observes. "You work for the State Directorate or something?"

"Yeah," Jonas says as he brings up the phone's web browser. "I'm in . . . science."

Even though Jonas knows she's not here, he still has to search for Amanda. Other Jonas could have been just as wrong as Thibault. He searches Amanda's maiden and married names but finds nothing, as expected. His own name is next. Again, no luck.

"You wanna buy that?" the clerk asks, making no attempt to hide his annoyance.

"Do you have any other models? So I can comparison shop?"

The clerk glowers back at Jonas, emits a grunt, and returns to the back room.

The moment he's gone, Jonas bolts for the door with the demo phone gripped tight in his hand. He spills out onto the street with his heart jackhammering. Nothing in this universe suggests that law enforcement goes easy on thieves. He walks as fast as he can without appearing to hurry. The next corner can't come fast enough, and he rounds it hastily and buries himself inside the nearest cluster of people.

He visibly startles when a sharp clanging rings out, the rapid chiming of a bell. From its distance and direction, Jonas knows it's the electronics store's alarm. It takes enormous effort to resist the urge to turn toward it, but he forces his feet to keep walking, his legs to keep pumping. He wills his eyes to remain forward yet cast slightly down. He adopts the posture of the other citizenry, hands buried in his pockets, back rolled forward. *Be small. Be invisible.*

But then the cry of a Klaxon punches his gut. A jet-black police car barrels directly toward him, iron crosses on its flanks, flashing red lights on its roof. He feels the blood rush from his face as two storm troopers stride directly toward him. He grips the phone and calculates whether it's possible to drop it. Better yet, can he slip it into a passerby's purse or pocket?

The police car careens past, close enough that its siren's wail hurts his ears. It whips from view, but the storm troopers are on top of him. One collides with Jonas's shoulder, bodychecking him. "Out of the way," he grunts as he moves past.

People on the street crane their necks to trace the storm troopers' path. Jonas can't decide whether to go along with the crowd, so he settles on a noncommittal head bob. The storm troopers recede from view, and Jonas finally notices he's been holding his breath.

With each block he clears, those breaths come a little easier. After ten or so, his heart is no longer trying to punch its way out of his chest. But the ill-gotten phone still feels like a weight in his pocket, an albatross. He's convinced the people he passes can sense it, that it marks him. He assures himself again and again that the fear is just his imagination.

Hours pass. Jonas's legs burn with the exertion of walking the length of the city. Even when he wants to stop, is desperate to stop, he doesn't know where it is safe. All of Manhattan—or whatever it's called here—feels as if it's under occupation. He staggers, the muscles in his legs no longer cooperating with the madness he's demanded of them.

The sun hangs low as he meanders into what he knows as Stuyvesant Square park, though a sign reads SCHRECK SQUARE PARK. The greenery is pockmarked with benches, and the desire to sit, if for only a moment, is overwhelming.

Then, a flash of panic. It occurs to Jonas that the store clerk might be able to trace the purloined phone. Jonas berates himself for his failure to consider every possibility. But the concern is reason enough for him finally to chance a look at the stolen phone. If it *is* being used to track him, he has to make quick use of it and then dispose of it as fast as possible.

He brings the browser back up and searches Henri Thibault's name. As the phone makes its wireless connections, Jonas risks a glance at the people milling about the park, watching for any sign of anyone watching him.

The search produces a waterfall of results. Jonas reviews them with desperate interest. Thibault is not only alive in this reality, but he's also a scientist of the same renown. Jonas feels a swell of hope as he reads about Thibault's receipt of the Nobel Prize in Physics six years ago. He lives in Prague, not Switzerland, but Jonas reminds himself that Europe is where he must go in any case, assuming that this universe *has* a CERN in Europe.

He is already working out ways he might be able to get across the Atlantic when he reads about the arrest. He scans the article with growing concern. It's worse than an arrest. Thibault was tried and convicted. And is now serving a life term for "crimes against the state."

Jonas fights despair. This universe's Thibault could have arranged for access to a particle collider. It seems that the reward for clearing one hurdle is just another hurdle to clear. No, a series of hurdles, stretching into infinity. But he tells himself to shake off that feeling. *One step at a time.*

Following that edict, he types another name into the search field. *Please. I can't do it alone. I need someone to help me through this world. Please.* He taps Enter.

A hit. A series of hits. Jonas breathes out his relief. He pours over the web page and is rewarded with the stunning discovery that Eva Stamper not only exists in this reality but is living and teaching right here in Manhattan. His body sags with relief.

"You." The word comes down to him from on high. Jonas looks up to see a storm trooper towering over him. His pulse quickens. The storm trooper's crotch is at eye level, and one strike to the balls could buy Jonas precious seconds to make a run for it.

"What are you still doing out?" the man demands.

Confusion buffets Jonas. The phone shakes in his hand. He commands his fingers to still and forces himself to speak. "Excuse me?" The words come out in a croak.

The storm trooper shifts on his boot heels. Impatient. He cocks his head in the direction of the rest of the park, which is disquietingly empty. "It's almost curfew."

Jonas's terror quickly transmutes into relief. He can't help but imagine that he looks like an idiot to the jackboot.

"Get yourself home," the storm trooper says, agitated. "And do it fast."

Jonas stands, nodding his compliance. "Yes, sir. Sorry, sir." He shuffles off as fast as he can.

With no money for a taxi or public transportation, Jonas treks uptown to Columbia University, which in this reality is called Von Braun University. Fortunately, the rest of the city is also racing the curfew, and he's once again able to cloak himself in the bustle. Less fortunately, the sun outruns him, and he's forced to continue past curfew.

As darkness drapes the city, Jonas traverses each block, deliberate but cautious. Storm troopers are everywhere. Armored trucks festooned with iron crosses rumble past, their roof-mounted spotlights dancing over sidewalks and skulking up the sides of buildings. Any group of two or more people is accosted, but Jonas doesn't slow down enough to see if the same is true for loners like himself.

He breathes a sigh of relief when he sees that the university's open campus hasn't changed. He doesn't see any gates or guards or fences, and he's able to stride onto the quad just as he had back when he was a professor in another universe.

The academic building off West 120th Street, where Eva Stamper has her office, is a redbrick affair fronted by an entrance of tinted glass and black steel. In Jonas's universe, the building is known as Pupin Hall, after Michael Idvorsky Pupin, inventor of the overload coil that made long-distance telephone calls possible. Here the building is named for Werner Heisenberg, a more apt dedication for a physics building, given that Heisenberg is—at least, in Jonas's home universe—one of the pioneers of quantum mechanics.

Just as he did back at the Université de Lausanne, Jonas spies a heating vent to sleep on. He curls up, feeling the temperate air, imagining that he's never felt quite as tired. He doesn't remember falling asleep, but he dreams, as he always does, of Amanda. Every night, she tells him the same thing, as regular as the tide: *I know you'll find me. You won't let anything stand in your way. Not even the universe. I know what people tell you, what you sometimes tell yourself, that it's impossible. But I know—I know—it's not impossible.* Her entire body vibrates with the force of her convictions. *It's not impossible because* you're *doing it. You believe in the existence of a multiverse, but I believe in* you.

And he sleeps, deeply, nuzzled in the warm embrace of that faith.

FOUR YEARS AGO

In 1939, Enrico Fermi, Leo Szilard, and a group of other physicists began work on inventing a self-sustaining neutron chain reaction. They worked in the basement of Pupin Hall at Columbia University. When the Japanese attack on Pearl Harbor prompted a relocation of this work away from the coast—to the University of Chicago—the endeavor retained the name of its city of origin: the Manhattan Project.

The cradle of nuclear warfare loomed over Amanda's head. Eleven floors of red brick, topped with the copper dome of the Rutherford Observatory, stretched up to the winter sky, a black sheet with pinpricks of light piercing it.

Amanda paced in front of the building as her breath birthed tiny clouds in the air. She felt her gut begin to give back what little dinner she had been able to get down. She balled her hands into fists to keep them from trembling.

She turned back toward the building, with its neat grid of windows and its copper roofline, and wondered what was happening inside, but the stalwart, storied edifice held no answers.

As worry rose within her, it occurred to her that this was as concerned as she'd ever been for another human being. It didn't matter that they weren't married. Her life was now entwined with Jonas's, and his with hers. Marriage, she understood in that moment, was a bureaucratic distinction, the legal amalgamation of two bank accounts, the public acknowledgment of the more meaningful union that preceded it—the joining of two souls. This was what it meant to share a life, to take on another's hopes and dreams as your own, and for them to do the same with yours. She felt fear for Jonas and his career, his personal and professional reputations, as viscerally as he did.

The only difference was that he was in the building while she was exiled to the outside, forbidden to enter the place where everything was being decided. She had no voice. She had no means to affect the verdict of the disciplinary hearing that Victor had wielded his influence to convene. She was not invited to give her account of how he'd shown up at Jonas's apartment—*their* apartment—abusive and belligerent and paranoid. She couldn't tell the Columbia faculty and administrators that she believed Victor Kovacevic to be unhinged. No, that wasn't quite right. Beliefs were subjective. Victor's rage-filled, borderline violent affect that morning wasn't a product of her imagination. She'd witnessed it. As dispassionate an observation as recognizing that cobalt was blue. Indeed, her entire career, her life, was centered around what she took in with her own two eyes, and that power had never failed her. She knew in her bones the kind of man Victor was, what he was capable of.

And she was terrified.

She knew Victor had not only the ability to destroy the man she loved but also possessed the means to do so. It was a frightening combination. She had tried consoling herself with platitudes like "the truth always prevails," but even at thirty-four, she was old enough to know what a fiction that was. The world worked the way men like Victor wanted it to, and they learned how to manipulate it to their own advantage.

After what seemed an eternity, the building's double doors swung open, and Jonas spilled out. She looked at him and felt her heart plunge. He was a husk, his expression vacant. The brilliance she'd become so accustomed to, had fallen in love with, was gone from his gaze. In its place, she saw only confusion, as if he'd just learned that water wasn't wet or the sky wasn't blue. She didn't ask him what had happened. She didn't need to. She knew the verdict he had just received was dire.

She watched him stagger to a nearby bench and fall into it. She lowered herself to his side and took his hand in both of hers. She waited until he could find the words, until he was ready to speak. She would wait forever if she had to.

When he finally spoke, it wasn't what she expected. "They cleared me of the plagiarism," he breathed. He sounded neither despondent nor triumphant. He didn't even sound relieved. He sounded spent, beyond the point of exhaustion.

She exhaled without even being aware that she had been holding her breath. But although the news was good, the best that either of them could hope for, she knew better than to celebrate and resisted the urge to embrace him. She just kept his hand clasped and waited to hear the reason he looked so lost.

"But Victor is department chair," Jonas finally said.

"What does that mean?" she asked, dreading the answer.

"That the board couldn't stop him from firing me." He delivered the news with as much dispassion as he would a weather report, but Amanda's world instantly constricted to that little bench. She felt the same despondency and fear and anger that Jonas must have been feeling in that moment but evidently couldn't express. She wanted to shoot to her feet and storm off into that building, to find Victor and rage at him. She wanted to thunder at the administrators, the bureaucrats, the petty little people who had been either so stupid as to believe Victor or too spineless to defy his wishes. She wanted to burn the entire building to embers and felt like she could do so merely with the force of the fury she felt.

Jonas leaned forward and rested his arms on his legs. He stared out into nothingness. He spoke, but Amanda couldn't make out what he was saying.

"What, honey?" she asked, her voice a whisper.

"What if he's right?" Jonas repeated. "If not for him, I never would have started work on parallel universes. I never would have tried to formulate a proof for their existence."

"And I never would have taken up painting," she replied, "if my parents hadn't taken me to see a David Hockney exhibit when I was six." She turned Jonas's face toward hers. "Inspiration isn't imitation, Jonas. Artists and scientists both build on the work of those who came before them." He looked away, seeming unconvinced. "If you had really stolen from Victor, stolen anything," she said, "the board would have said so."

"I wish it were that simple," he answered.

"Tell me how it's not."

"He showed me his work," Jonas confessed. "Over the years, as he was wrestling with the project, Victor would occasionally ask me to look over his equations."

"So?"

"So . . . how do I know some of his ideas didn't influence my own? Even on a subliminal level."

"You don't," she responded simply. "But you told me you tried to get him to look at *your* work, didn't you?"

"That's right," Jonas answered, with no idea of what point Amanda was trying to make.

"And why'd you do that?"

"Because I'd hoped he'd want to work on it with me. Together."

Amanda's hand swept the air. "Exactly."

"What's your point?" Jonas's fatigue was almost all-consuming.

"My point is . . . these aren't the actions of a thief. If your intention really was to *plagiarize*"—she leaned hard on the word—"you wouldn't have invited Victor to join in."

Jonas acknowledged the truth of that with a halfhearted shrug.

"Trust me," she implored him. "No one understands plagiarism as well as an artist. I might not be able to appreciate the nuances of parallel worlds or quantum theory, but I'm pretty confident in my ability to recognize theft." Jonas flashed her a skeptical look. "And I know the man I fell in love with. I know his soul." She reached out and touched the center of his chest.

Jonas took her hand in his. "In any case, I'm out of a job."

"Any university would be lucky to have you," Amanda said. New thoughts ignited her. "We'll move. There's no law that says I can only paint Manhattan. We can go anywhere—" She was already imagining new places, new opportunities, new homes, but she found herself stopping short. Jonas had a look she'd never seen before, and it frightened her. Sickened her. She could feel the blood drain from her face. "What?"

"No one is going to hire me," he answered. As before, there was no emotion behind his words. He might as well have been back in the lab, reading off the measurements taken by some instrument or coldly reporting the result of a calculation.

"I don't . . . I don't understand," she heard herself stammer. Her fear was transforming into dread.

"He's already salted the earth," Jonas said with an impotent shrug. "His word against mine. Paper covers rock."

"I still don't understand, Jonas."

"He can keep people from hiring me. It's like he said back at our apartment, he can keep me from ever getting another job." He shook his head, emotion finally seeping into his voice. It wasn't anger or sadness but disbelief. "He was in there . . . *bragging* about it." Jonas's face contorted. "It's all over for me."

Amanda shook her head in defiance. "No." She bit at the air, the word manifesting as a puff of white. "Your research . . ."

"I haven't even finished it." He let out half a laugh, a mixture of incredulity and bitterness. "The TA who told Victor what I'm working on . . . she made it sound like I was close to finishing. But I'm not. Not really. Not even close."

"So get close."

"What?"

"Finish. Now you've got the time."

"But not the reason," he answered, his voice laced with despair. "I don't really see the point of going forward."

"Why not? Something compelled you to start down this path. I think you were inspired. It's really no different than when I begin a painting."

Jonas grimaced and wagged his fingers. "Not exactly. You have a dealer. You have a gallery. There's an outlet for your paintings."

"That hasn't always been true."

"My point is that an academic paper is meaningless—literally meaningless—if other scientists don't read it." He sighed. "And no one will publish me."

"They will." Amanda's voice was steel. "Because you *are* going to finish. Because you're *compelled* to. You're going to finish, and it will be brilliant. Because *you're* brilliant. That's not—look at me. That's not anything anyone can take away from you. Not ever."

His lips bent to a thin smile. She knew him well enough to know that he was considering it, working the problem. "I'm unemployable, with no savings to speak of. To be honest, I'm pretty close to broke."

"I'm an artist. Broke is our default." She punctuated this with her best wink.

He looked at her with disbelief. "Anyone else would run away."

Amanda gripped the sides of his head and drilled her eyes into his. "I'm not going anywhere." It felt like the most important thing she'd ever said to the most important person in her life at the most important moment in her life. "I'm not going *anywhere*," she reiterated.

She waited for his reaction, and it was worth it. Slowly, at the speed of a sunrise, Jonas began to smile. Starlight bounced off the edges of his eyes, slick with tears. Their lives really were entwined, and she would never let him give up on his gifts.

They sat together on the bench, their fingers woven. Overhead, the stars blinked down on them in silence.

NOW

Eva Stamper's office at Von Braun University is a thirty-five-minute commute from her flat on a good day. On a bad day, when the city's overtaxed subway system strains under the burden of its outdated infrastructure, it's a fifty-five-minute trek. Nearly an hour. Today is a bad day. And so Eva is in a mood. She could have used that time to work on her presentation this morning. She would have awakened earlier but for the fact she'd been working on that same presentation until three in the morning.

She stomps toward Heisenberg Hall, wishing she hadn't tried to save a few minutes by foregoing her morning coffee. The building is locked. She's the first one at work. Typical. As she works to fish her keys from her purse, she notices a homeless man curled up atop the heating vent. A rare occurrence but not unheard of.

"This isn't a hotel," she admonishes. "If the University Guard sees you, they'll throw you in prison."

The bum stirs and turns over, revealing a face marked by bruises and coated with stubble. His clothes look like they've been through a war, and his hair is a rat's nest. As he stands, he appears astonished.

"Eva," he breathes.

To hear her name from this stranger's lips is unnerving. Eva feels herself pale. "Do I know you?"

"I suppose that would all depend on your definition of 'know.'" She stares back, not knowing what to say. "I'm sorry," he apologizes. "Inside joke." She's unnerved by the way he stares at her as though they're friends. But the man is a stranger. "Would you give me five minutes of your time?" he asks.

"And why would I do that?" She says it like a dare.

The man answers by pulling up his left sleeve to expose a line of equations running down his inner forearm. "These formulae," he ventures. "I'm willing to bet you've seen a piece of this somewhere before. *In college.*"

Eva feels a flush of panic. *Who is this stranger? How does he know what she learned in college?*

"You studied physics," he says with surprising urgency. "You thought about changing disciplines. To psychology. But here, in this world, you didn't. Here, you became a physicist."

Eva brightens. Suddenly, it all makes sense. She understands what's happening here, and she's relieved. "Roberta put you up to this, didn't she? Tell her that her sense of humor still needs adjustment."

She turns to unlock the door, but the man won't be deterred. "This equation here," he says, jabbing at his skin and leaving tiny white circles on the formulae, "this is a Schrödinger equation. What do you know about the Many Worlds Theory?"

Eva doesn't have time for games. "Only what I learned in Introduction to Quantum Mechanics," she tosses off.

"You got an A, though."

Eva looks back at him, utterly flustered. It's not that he knows her college transcript—anyone could uncover that—it's that he knows exactly what she was about to say, and the way she was going to say it. She pales. Her stomach performs a barrel roll, and she stares at him with frightened eyes.

"Invite me inside, Dr. Stamper," the man says. "We have a lot to talk about."

∞

One of the corollaries of the principle that all universes share certain qualities is that people's reactions demonstrate a relatively predictable consistency. Although hardened by coming of age in a fascist society, this reality's Eva retains her inquisitive spark, the same curiosity that drew "his" Eva to Jonas, that opened her mind to the incredible. Jonas can't help but find the quality alluring.

Eva spends twenty minutes sweeping her modest faculty office for listening devices. After pronouncing the room clean, she explains, "I admit it's more than a little paranoid, but I've heard stories of the State Directorate conducting surveillance on academics. Ideas are the most dangerous things in the world. And I have a feeling *your* ideas, Mr. Cullen, are among the most hazardous."

This observation proves to be a profound understatement as Jonas shares his story, beginning with the night in Stockholm, the Nobel, the crash. He tells her about his tether and the quantum energy slowly leaking from his body. He explains that he knows what she's thinking because of his encounter with her doppelgänger. He leaves out Victor and Amanda's second death. He omits the other Eva's demise.

Eva appears to take it all in with the same calm as her twin. "If I understand the Many Worlds Theory properly, there's a world where you and your wife are both alive, where perhaps the accident never even happened."

Jonas has to admire the parallel. "Yes. There's already a world where I'm happy," he says, remembering the words of her doppelgänger. He watches her startle slightly, knowing that's what she was going to say next. It's like a form of telepathy. "But I—*this* me, myself—*I* can't be happy without her. I can't be anything without her. I might as well be dead."

He feels her staring, and he lets her. He can only imagine the multitude of thoughts that must be racing through her mind as she works her way from skepticism to acceptance. On some level, he admits that he wants the turn to be quick, to get back to the same easy rapport they had once enjoyed.

From the new vantage offered by this alternate reality, he notices qualities her twin had possessed but which he hadn't allowed himself to notice. The way the left corner of her mouth curls up ever so slightly in a subtle perpetual smirk as though she sees through you but is amused by what she observes. How the lilt of her voice betrays a reassuring kindness. Despite the omnipresent dread of this universe, she has a vibrancy to her even her counterpart didn't possess.

For a breath, they share a gaze like a cable pulling taut between them. That this all unfolds instinctively, in a matter of seconds, doesn't shield the moment from feeling like a betrayal. He watches her move to a state-issued computer and begin typing away.

"What are you doing?" Jonas asks.

"Searching the internet for information about your wife in this reality."

"I already did. I stole a smartphone, or whatever it is you call it here. She doesn't exist in this universe."

"You ran a search on a commercial phone using public internet, the information on which is *heavily* redacted by government censors." She types away, eventually stopping with the final stab of a key. "You said your wife—"

"Amanda."

"You said Amanda died in a car crash?"

"Yes."

Eva points to her computer monitor. "In this reality, she died in a plane crash."

Jonas fights to keep the image from his mind. He'd have better luck holding back the tide.

"A car crash," Eva is saying, "a plane crash. Have you considered the possibility . . ."

"That the universe *wants* my wife dead?"

"The universe doesn't 'want' anything, and I was going to put it a bit more delicately than that. But generally . . . yes."

"I'm definitely aware that variations in the multiverse are limited by what we call 'fate.'" His eyes wander her desk—the top of which is carpeted with an academic's organized chaos—and sees a framed photograph of a man in military uniform. "Your husband?" he asks.

Eva darkens slightly, the affect of a widow. "Yes. He—"

"Died in action," Jonas says, completing the thought. "Afghanistan?"

Eva shakes her head. "Israel." Jonas knows her faraway look well. "I suppose the universe wants Brian dead too." She looks to Jonas, and her tone is empathetic but firm. "But you don't see me breaking the laws of the universe to be with him. Why do you get a second chance when the rest of us don't? What makes you so special?"

Eva's doppelgänger had asked the same question. So had Victor aboard the airliner. Each time, Jonas evaded answering.

"What makes *you* so special?" Eva repeats.

"Because I'm the one who can do it," Jonas says. "Don't tell me that if you had the means to be with your husband again—"

"Don't," Eva warns. Again, Jonas is reminded that they're not friends in this reality.

"—that you wouldn't make everything of that opportunity," Jonas continues. "And if you *had* that chance and didn't take it? Wouldn't that be a kind of murder?"

"That's offensive."

"But not wrong. My life's work has been about seeing the world as it is. Not how we want it to be or wish it to be, but how it really *is*. The rules that comprise our reality." Bottom line: "I can't pretend I don't have the ability to find her. And with that ability comes a *responsibility*, don't you think?"

Eva rubs her forehead as though trying to push an idea into it. Her jaw pulses with gritted teeth. "I thought you *didn't* know which universe your wife is in."

Jonas pulls up his sleeve. Other Jonas's equations run up his arm. "These calculations were worked up by a doppelgänger of mine, a version of myself from another reality."

Eva pulls on a pair of wire-rimmed glasses and examines the formulae with a practiced eye. "Don't take this personally, but from the look of these equations, I think this other you might just be a bit smarter."

"And a bit crazier. Either way, he had a breakthrough." Jonas taps the new tattoo with his free hand. "He calculated the correct reality. The one—the only one left—where she is still alive."

Eva studies the equations. Encountering an Eva who pursued physics instead of branching off into psychiatry is a lucky turn. "If I'm reading this right, you're going to need energy to untether yourself again and make the jump to the proper reality. *A lot* of energy."

"I know. I've done it before."

For the first time, Eva appears incredulous. She scoffs, "Where could you possibly get your hands on that much quantum energy?"

"I broke into CERN."

Eva blinks. "What's a CERN?"

Jonas deflates, his spirits dashed by the fecklessness of parallel realities. "There's no Large Hadron Collider in this reality?"

"I don't know what that is." Regret passes over her face.

"It's a particle accelerator. Without one . . ." He can't complete the thought. Can't summon the energy to say the words aloud for fear that doing so would make the hopelessness of his situation real. The thought of chancing another reality-slip, of squandering what little quantum energy his cells contain on another ill-fated attempt, is crushing.

Then, a lifeline. Eva posits, "There's the Superconducting Linear Accelerator in Hiroshima."

Jonas sparks back to life. "What?"

"I'm not sure if the specs are the same, but I can find out for you."

Jonas's head ratchets up and down, nodding as though to will the idea into being. "Thank you," he breathes.

Eva flashes him a look. *Not so fast.* "Even if it's what you're looking for, it's not an easy facility to gain access to."

"Neither was CERN."

"So how'd you get in?"

"I hired a group of mercenaries," Jonas answers, immediately understanding how ridiculous that sounds. "Really."

"Maybe we can find a better way," she deadpans.

"That would be optimal."

"I know someone at Hiroshima. Maybe he can help."

"Thank you, Eva."

She gives him a polite nod. "You said we met before. Where? I mean, I know it was another universe, but where in the world?"

"Switzerland."

A blank stare. "Never heard of it."

"It's in Europe." Another blank stare. "In other realities."

Eva thinks on that for a moment. "So in at least one other reality, I live in Europe. But you managed to find me in this universe on the other side of the world."

"Convenient for me," he admits.

"Considerably," she says. "Particularly since I seem to be the rare theoretical physicist just reckless enough not to have you committed."

"Just open minded enough," Jonas corrects her.

"Either way," she says, "there's clearly some force that"—she grasps for the right word—"keeps drawing you to me. And, I suppose, me to you."

She smiles. And he's reminded of Amanda. The two women share the same spirit, the same warmth.

"I thought you said that the universe doesn't 'want' anything," he challenges.

"I'm still figuring out the universe."

"Aren't we all?" They share a moment of connection. Like when they had almost the same exchange back in Switzerland. He pushes it aside as irrelevant. *Focus on the task at hand. One step at a time.* "We're going to need to get me a passport."

"If it were only a passport," she says and turns back to indicate her computer. "I searched on your name too. There's no Jonas Cullen in this reality. You don't exist." She turns back to face him. "We're going to need to somehow get you a whole *identity*."

It takes Eva two weeks to arrange a new alias for Jonas. He spends that time as a virtual prisoner in her flat, sleeping on her couch as he did in Switzerland. Eva is fortunate enough to have a computer in her home, and Jonas whiles away his time alternating between triple-checking Other Jonas's calculations and researching the history of this reality's Earth. At first it appeared as if Germany had won the Second World War, but that's not how events unfolded at all. In fact, humanity didn't even experience a Second World War in the sense that Jonas understands it.

After World War I, fascism arose in Germany, but it built to a global conflict that more closely resembled the Cold War. Adolf Hitler came to power but had the restraint not to overplay his hand. In the United States, more than twenty thousand people still attended the Nazi rally at Madison Square Garden in New York City before it changed its name to New Berlin. Nazism passed over the globe like a pandemic rather than a juggernaut. Citizens of democratic countries voluntarily chose the reassuring certainty of authoritarianism, and Hitler became führer of the world almost without firing a shot. An international day of mourning was declared when old age claimed him at ninety-two. Every continent on earth is dotted with monuments to his memory.

In this branch of history, Jonas's parents never met. It's disconcerting to exist in a world where one has never existed before. Amanda still became an artist, though, and Jonas finds her works in the annals of Eva's enhanced internet. They are as beautiful as he remembers, but they lack the inspiration of the paintings he knows. This is a diminished world, and Amanda's art reflects that.

She married a lawyer, a tax attorney. Her husband wasn't with her on the Deutsche Lufthansa flight from her mother's house in Westmunich (California) when it crashed. It seems that this universe took its pound of flesh, too, as had so many before.

After fifteen days, Eva secures them tickets to Maryland. Jonas doesn't ask why certain states retained their original, non-German names. His focus is on the numerous checkpoints he will have to navigate on their odyssey. Eva has transit passes for them, but at any one of the checkpoints, Jonas could be instructed to produce individual identification. That Jonas would need identification to go obtain identification is a bitter bureaucratic irony.

They take a train that runs the same route Jonas remembers from various Amtrak excursions between New York and Washington, DC. However, bucolic suburbs have been replaced with large apartment buildings, featureless slabs of concrete. Rolling fields and wetlands and forests have been cleared to make way for factories. Smokestacks cough black smoke into already gray skies.

In the privacy of her apartment—after the regular sweep for listening devices—Jonas asked Eva why the world chose oppression over freedom, dictatorship over democracy. She looked at him, apparently struck by his guilelessness. "Freedom," she said, "is hard for some people. I suppose it's hard for *most* people. Life is easier when there's someone above you telling you what to do."

"There's nothing easier about living in constant fear that you'll be informed upon by your neighbor," Jonas contested, "or imprisoned or worse for saying the wrong thing."

Eva just wagged her head the way one does when a child asks where the water in the tap comes from. *Your innocence, your naivete, is adorable.* "No one is afraid," she said. "Because no one ever thinks it's going to be them."

Not that Eva approves of her world, and she's not alone. She explained to Jonas that a group—they call themselves "Partisans"—works quietly behind the scenes to resist global fascism. Knowing even a single member of the group is dangerous, carrying with it the threat of life imprisonment or worse, but Eva knows a Partisan cell in Baltimore. It took two weeks of dead-dropped messages, transported by couriers risking their lives, to arrange the meeting.

After the train lets them off, Jonas and Eva walk for five miles to the agreed-upon rendezvous point. On the way, Jonas poses the question he's been putting off for two weeks. "Why would your friends help me?"

"They're not my friends," she corrects him. "I share my internet with one of the Manhattan cells. But it's the Baltimore cell that can fabricate documents."

"Which brings me back to why would they help me?"

"They're helping *me*," she counters. "They owe me more than a few favors." She doesn't elaborate, and Jonas judges that it would be bad form to press the point.

They arrive at a small intersection of bisecting streets in the shadow of a looming power plant. Shoots of green strain to rise through the cracked asphalt. Jonas can't help but think of them as a metaphor.

They stand in place for almost an hour. Jonas feels as if he's being watched. He tries to indicate as much to Eva with a look, and she answers only with a sober nod. They very well may be under surveillance.

"They're not coming," Jonas finally concedes, as much to himself as to Eva.

Her response is to point to the road ahead, where a black Cadillac makes its way toward them. Its windows are tinted, and its headlights shine against the day's oppressive gloom as it pulls up and stops in front of Jonas and Eva.

"Don't speak unless spoken to," she advises. "And do whatever they instruct. Don't ask questions."

A woman alights from the rear of the car. She wears a putty-colored pantsuit and no jewelry. Her haircut is utilitarian. She seems to be no more than thirty but has an air of experience about her. "Spread your arms," she says. Eva does as she's told, and Jonas follows suit. The woman pats them down, a thorough and professional job. "Wait here," she instructs. She moves to the Cadillac's trunk, which dutifully pops open, and she pulls out a few items and slams it closed. She returns to Jonas and Eva, handing them each a pair of noise-canceling headphones. "Put these on."

They do.

"And these." She tosses two black bags cinched with cord. Jonas and Eva pull them over their heads as instructed, and the woman pulls the cords tight around their necks.

Jonas hears a second car door opening accompanied by another set of footsteps. This second person guides them, blind and partially deaf, into the rear of the Cadillac, making no effort to be gentle.

They drive for what feels like another hour, but Jonas can't really be sure. The car navigates several turns, and he asks himself how much of the trip is theater, whether they're really driving all that far. Eventually, the car begins to slope downward, and Jonas has the sensation that they're descending some kind of ramp.

The Cadillac stops. Through the headphones' noise cancellation, Jonas hears the faint *ka-thunk* of the transmission being thrown into park. The door next to him opens, and hands fish him out. They rip off the black bag and headphones. Jonas blinks and sees that they're in an underground garage. The idling Cadillac and a lime-green van, paint chipped and dirt covered, are the only vehicles present.

"Who's your favorite singer?" asks a man in his twenties. He wears jeans, a crew neck shirt, and a leather jacket. He's the only other person in the garage.

Jonas has no favorite singer, but he answers "Frank Sinatra" just the same, having no idea whether Frank Sinatra exists in this reality.

"Call me Frank," the man instructs. Everything about him is perfunctory. *Let's get this done as fast as possible.* Jonas glances behind him, back toward the Cadillac and Eva. "She's fine," Frank says.

He moves to the van and swings open its rear doors. Inside is a table and some equipment, including what Jonas recognizes as a laser printer and lamination machine. On the inside of one of the doors, a white screen hangs off a roller.

Frank points to it. "Stand in front."

Jonas takes his place as instructed. "Thank you for doing this."

"Look at the camera," Frank says. "Don't smile." He produces this universe's equivalent of a Polaroid camera and snaps a photo. As it rolls out of the camera's mouth, he hands Jonas an ink pad and an index card. "I need both thumbprints."

Frank climbs in the van, a makeshift counterfeiting studio, and sets to work as Jonas stamps each of his thumbs onto the index card. As he hands it over to Frank, he considers how much Eva has shared about his circumstances. It's a safe bet, he thinks, that she declined to mention he needs a new form of identification because he's from a parallel universe.

"I need five minutes," Frank says as he works.

Jonas notices that neither the van nor the Cadillac have license plates. The garage displays no signage. He has no idea where he is, and no one else would, either, his body having previously been cleared of any GPS trackers or the like by Eva. They're in an underground chamber invisible to any orbiting satellites. The Partisans are thorough.

After three minutes, Frank hands Jonas his new passport. It's black, with **PASSPORT** embossed across the cover in silver letters. Below them, an iron cross. And beneath that, the words FEDERATED STATES OF AMERICA in a sans serif font.

"Thank you," Jonas says. "I know how dangerous this is for you, and I appreciate it."

Frank retrieves the headphones and black bag. "Put these back on," he orders, without a hint of warmth.

∞

Two days later, Jonas presents his new passport to the Deutsche Lufthansa attendant at Himmler International Airport. She returns it to him, along with his one-way ticket to Hiroshima, Japan. Eva has a ticket of her own, which includes a return to New Berlin.

"Last chance to pull out," Jonas offers.

"I'm pretty sure there'll be other chances along the way. But I'm good."

"You sure?"

"Assuming I'm not institutionalized, I'll get a paper out of this like you wouldn't believe."

They both smile, the kind of moment of connection that has been happening between the two of them with greater and greater frequency. Jonas has had to draw from the depths of his memory— to the years before he knew Amanda—to understand why they feel so familiar. They are moments of chemistry, harbingers of attraction and the promise of something more. But again, he buries the thought.

"Speaking of your career," he ventures, "are you sure you can take this time away?"

"Fortunately for you, it's not considered 'time away.' I can easily claim a visit to the Spire as a part of my job."

"The Spire?"

Eva lowers her voice in the din of the airport. "This universe's equivalent of your CERN."

Jonas realizes how far he has come without knowing the specifics of Eva's plan, a testament to how much he has come to trust her.

"My access to the Spire seems like yet another coincidence to keep us in each other's orbits," she says.

"I prefer to think of it as the universe's way of paying back a little bit of what it owes me," Jonas retorts.

The remark earns him a warm look. The air between them crackles, and Jonas remembers that the last Eva died unrequited in her love for him. In those rare moments when he was honest with himself about her, Jonas could admit, in the most private reaches of his mind, that the attraction was mutual. The same could be true with this universe's Eva, if he were to allow it, but he won't. He can't. Even if he is no longer married to Amanda, he remains betrothed to the idea of her.

In awkward silence, they make their way through the terminal, which is far less congested than Jonas expects. Most of the travelers are men in business suits and military uniforms of various stripes. Eva is one of only a handful of women. There are no tourists.

Thinking on this, Jonas asks, "Was it difficult to get a travel visa?"

"Just the ordinary bureaucracy. Which means the ordinary bribe."

"All this money you're spending," he says, "how much are you cutting into your savings?"

"Don't worry about it."

"I do."

"I receive a bereavement stipend from the government," Eva says, her voice slightly distant. During their nearly three weeks together, Jonas has intuited that the subject of her husband is off limits. This is no more apparent than when they board the plane. Once in their coach-class seats, Jonas spies Eva staring at a soldier across the aisle from her. He resembles the man from the photograph in Eva's office. She wipes away a tear.

The flight attendant makes announcements in English and German. The passengers are lectured on how to fasten a seat belt. Jonas doesn't see any children aboard, and the hush of the cabin is disquieting. Then the plane's engines whir, and the floor beneath him vibrates. They taxi almost immediately—no interminable wait on the tarmac, no endless queue of jets awaiting clearance for takeoff.

Their flight path takes them over the island of Manhattan. From his window, Jonas can see Ellis Island, or whatever it's known as here, but the Statue of Liberty does not stand watch in front of it. In its place is a towering iron statue of a figure with its arm and hand outstretched, fingers straight as a ruler. It's too far away for Jonas to get a proper look, but he's confident that the figure is Adolf Hitler.

THREE YEARS AGO

The first week in March had always been Amanda's favorite, when New York City shrugs off the shackles of winter, and gray skies yield to blue. She enjoyed watching the city reawaken, the world wrapped in sunlight, the air smelling of new beginnings. Spring in Manhattan felt like a second chance.

She and Jonas walked hand in hand through Central Park. The sun felt warm and seemed to make the whole world glow. They both wore shorts and T-shirts. His read MAY THE $F=ma$ BE WITH YOU. Amanda's ponytail was threaded through her Mets cap. They didn't speak as they strode across the slab of green carved into the heart of Manhattan. They didn't need to. The feeling of their fingers intertwined, their bodies close together, moving in time with each other's steps, was enough.

She heard Jonas's phone buzz in his pocket. She weaved a finger through her ponytail, a nervous habit, as she watched Jonas pull out his phone and blanch at the screen.

"It's her," he said. His voice was laden with uncertainty.

Amanda didn't need to be told. She knew from his reaction, and the instinct was confirmed with a twinge in her stomach. The call was from the managing editor of the *Journal of Applied & Computational Mathematics*, and she felt her heart begin to canter. This was one of those moments when their life together could change. She nodded encouragement. "Answer it."

"If they don't—" He stopped, unable to give voice to the thought, lest it become true. "If they don't publish it, I'm out of options."

It had been a year since his dismissal from Columbia. A year of watching as Jonas's friends and colleagues peeled off and abandoned him one by one. It wasn't that they believed the allegation of plagiarism, they insisted, with varying degrees of sincerity. What went unsaid was that they were more afraid of Victor than loyal to Jonas. Amanda fumed to herself and her girlfriends and raged on Jonas's behalf, but he weathered each defection and betrayal with stoic composure. Amanda had watched as he threw himself into his work, devoting countless hours to his Many Worlds Proof, diving deep into theoretical minutiae that she thought she had no hope of grasping.

He had tried to explain his work to her. He had a knack for conveying quantum physics in terms she could understand, but invariably he descended into a tangent and left her behind. She recognized the words he was using as English, but their arrangement made no sense. What mattered, though, was the way he lit up like Times Square when he talked. She didn't understand "relative state formulation" or a "wave function collapse," but it was of no consequence. The spark in him—the spark she'd fallen in love with—was all that mattered.

She didn't know whether he would be able to complete his work, though she had faith in him. If he completed it, some scientific journal would publish it, she hoped, and for a year she had been sustained by the absence of the hopelessness Jonas had felt that night on the bench at the Columbia campus. She lived in dread of seeing that look on his face again, knowing that to see him so broken would break her in turn.

To keep that thought at bay, Amanda stepped in front of Jonas, looked him in the eye, and reminded him, "I'm not going anywhere." She had repeated the assertion countless times in the previous year, and with no less sincerity.

Jonas thumbed his phone to answer the call. "Yes," he managed, his voice tentative. "This is Dr. Cullen."

Amanda studied his expression, his body language, anything, to glean a hint of what was being said on the other end of the call. Her heart galloped.

"I see," Jonas said. He offered no sign of whether the news was good or bad. "Yes."

Amanda searched his face for a hint, any clue she could decipher, and saw nothing. The tension was unbearable.

"Thank you," Jonas said, his voice as level as the horizon.

She watched him tap the phone to end the call. He stared at it while she stared at him, searching for any sign of hope, resisting the urge to ask, willing herself to wait for the verdict.

After an eternity, Jonas finally said, "They're going to publish it." He sounded stunned. The thought escaped him in a breath.

Amanda let out a scream. She clutched Jonas tightly and yelled her joy in his ear. Still embracing him, she jumped up and down. In her heart, she knew she was feeling relief and elation in equal measure, but she didn't care. This news was a year in the coming and well worth the wait, and she felt unburdened immediately.

Then, strangely, something struck her in the back. She pulled her arms from around Jonas. Whatever had hit her flopped to the ground. Her first instinct was that a bird had flown into her, but looking down, she saw it was a fluorescent-pink disk. A Frisbee.

A goateed hipster with a stud in his nose ran up. "Sorry!" he yelled. "My bad."

Amanda shook her head, recalling her first time meeting Jonas two years before. Life had an ironic way of repeating itself. She looked to Jonas and mock-chided, "Did you pay him to do that?"

Jonas didn't answer. Instead, he turned to face her and got down on one knee. Something disconnected in Amanda's brain. Was what she thought was happening actually happening?

Jonas shrugged. "So what if I did?"

The world stopped. Everything seemed brighter, louder, more real. Amanda's mind oriented itself to record each second, full with the knowledge that this was one of life's most important moments. Her fingertips tingled. She couldn't feel her legs. The entire world shrank to the patch of grass where she was standing.

Jonas handed her the Frisbee. There was a spot beneath its surface, like the anticyclonic storm on Jupiter that Jonas had shown her at the Hayden Planetarium. She flipped the disk over to get a better look and gasped. Taped to the underside was a diamond ring. Her breath caught in her throat, but she managed to remark, "You certainly timed the hell out of this."

"Yeah, that was a lucky accident," Jonas admitted. "But it's like I've been telling you, the universe—"

"Favors certain outcomes," she breathed. She held the Frisbee in her hands and stared at the ring. It held a single diamond, its facets catching the sunlight and reflecting it back through the tape. The hipster snapped a photo with his phone. She looked at Jonas, who was still kneeling. "You know you can get up now, right?" She wanted to kiss him, to tell him she was desperate to marry him, though in her heart, they were already committed beyond marriage, and she didn't care if that made any sense at all.

"Not yet," Jonas said. A puckish grin formed on his face, and Amanda wondered what was next. His smirk grew a little wider, and then he asked, "Why do I do just as you say? Why must I just give you your way?" It was like when he described his work to her; she recognized the words as English, but they made little sense.

Then recognition dawned. Her eyes widened. "No," she whispered through teeth bared in a wide grin. "You're not actually going to . . ."

Yes. He started to sing.

Amanda beamed and laughed. She could never remember being as happy, and her joy was so potent, she didn't even feel the tears gushing from her eyes.

"Why do I sigh, why don't I try to forget? It must have been that something lovers call fate . . ."

"I love you too much," Amanda cried. In that moment, it was all she knew and ever wanted to know.

"*Kept me saying I have to wait,*" Jonas bellowed, shooting to his feet. His hands waved. People started gathering to stare in slack-jawed astonishment, but Jonas didn't seem to care. He was scream-singing, fueled by joy and abandonment, with no regard for who was watching. "*I saw them all, just couldn't fall, till we met!*" He drew out "met" to at least four syllables. His voice cracked. He was leagues away from being on pitch. "*It had to be you! It had to be you!*"

Amanda was suddenly aware of the Frisbee still dangling from her hand. She turned it over, peeled the ring away, and slipped it on her finger. She felt her tears at last. One day, she would look back and examine why she had given herself over to such emotion. Why would a ring and a promise mean anything when she'd already given herself to this man and committed her life to his? She reminded herself that her tears and her joy weren't the products of the promise of marriage but rather her appreciation of Jonas, a man who had gone from thinking that singing was "silly" to doing it as loud as his lungs permitted in front of anyone around to witness it.

It was the most perfect moment her mind could conjure, and Amanda had never known such joy.

NOW

Hiroshima, like Japan itself, has thrived in a world without a Fat Man or Little Boy, without bombs, without a pair of nuclear holocausts. Here, 150,000 souls never died by fire in the time it takes a bird to flap its wings. Japan never entered the Axis alliance, sidestepping the descent into authoritarianism made by many of its sister nations.

Nevertheless, the city retains many of the same qualities Jonas remembers from his lone visit, six years and several universes ago. The streets remain clean enough to eat off. The people are buoyant and polite. The food is exquisite. Everything is done properly or not at all. It is a country populated by proud citizens who have every right to their national esteem.

The skyline is largely unchanged but for one notable exception, a massive tower that erupts out of the ground to claw at the sky. Jonas estimates that it's even taller than the Burj Khalifa in Dubai. It is sleek and bright, a shard of silver planted in the middle of the city as if by God. Little wonder why they call it "Za Supaya"—the Spire.

Two days after his arrival in Hiroshima, Jonas walks, carrying two plastic bags laden with new purchases. He's relieved to have left an electronics store without having stolen anything. The apartment he's renting with Eva is a five-minute walk from the Spire, a prefurnished lodging of the kind favored by businessmen on long trips. The apartment has only one bedroom, but Jonas takes comfort in the routine of sleeping on the couch.

He enters and finds Eva working on her laptop. He pulls a charger from one of the bags. "Will this do?"

"Perfect," Eva says, reaching for it gratefully. "Can't believe I forgot to pack mine."

"Well, we left in a hurry."

"What about you? Did the store have everything you need?"

Jonas begins emptying the bags. He spreads a coterie of electronic items out on the coffee table, including circuit boards, copper wiring, and an AC adapter. "Mostly. There are a few precision tools I'll need to find at a jewelry store or something. I'm not worried, though. If I can't find them in Japan, they can't be found." He could have made his purchases in New Berlin, of course, but that would have meant trying to get them through security at Himmler International, and the risk just wasn't worth it.

"This is all for your tether?" Eva asks.

Jonas gestures to his work. "I don't know how it will react to the recalibration of the particle collider. Seems like a sensible precaution just to overhaul it entirely. Of course, I'll need to replace the lithium-ion battery."

"Of course," Eva says dryly. "But I thought if you take the tether off"—her fingers flutter like a flock of birds—"you'll leave this universe."

"That's what makes it tricky. I'll have to work with one hand while the other maintains contact with the capacitance sensors on the inner circumference." Eva greets this news with a blank stare, and Jonas just waves the notion away. "At any rate, I hope it's all moot. The idea is to leave this reality for my final destination. Either way, I won't need the tether anymore."

"You know," Eva says, "for some reason, I find it mildly offensive that you keep referring to *my* reality as 'this' reality." Her tone is playful.

"I apologize." Jonas bows his head in mock penitence. "I need to make sure *your* reality's Linear Accelerator will do the same job as *my* reality's Large Hadron Collider." He looks down at the formulae on his arms. "I only have one more shot at this," he continues. "Speaking of which, have you received any word from your friend?"

Eva hesitates for a fraction of a second longer than Jonas expects. "He says he's still working on it." Her voice sounds far away.

"Are you okay?" he asks.

"Fine." Something in her voice still sounds less than convincing. "I made us reservations at Sushitei Hikarimachi tonight. Hope you like omakase." She forces a smile and carries her laptop and new charger off into the bedroom.

As Jonas watches her go, he wonders what's bothering her. For someone so warm and inviting, she has moments of inscrutability.

Dropping the thought, Jonas turns back to the parts he's collected. He has a lot of work to do.

∞

Victor's Cray has lost the scent.

After encountering Jonas's pathetic doppelgänger—a low-resolution copy of Victor's nemesis—Victor tasked his computer to scour the multiverse for signs of the quarks and neutrinos thrown off by Jonas's tether, but those signs went inexplicably dark. Of course, Victor has no way of knowing that the phenomenon was an unintended consequence of Jonas's "overhaul." And so Victor continues to search, pushing his machine to its limits. He weaves new algorithms and releases them into his computer models like hounds on the hunt. He codes and recodes and codes again. His computer peers into universe after universe, but each time, his hounds return breathless and empty handed. The multiverse contains a near-infinite number of realities, yet all are quiet.

Victor considers the possibilities. That Jonas could be dead is the first that comes to mind, but in that case, his tether would still be working, casting off telltale neutrinos. Or maybe Jonas and his tether reality-slipped and found themselves underground, their molecules coalescing with that of soil and silt, rocks and pebbles. Such a mishap would likely damage the tether beyond operation, accounting for the lack of detectable neutrinos. The thought of Jonas tortured by dirt in his bones and rocks in his blood brings a smile.

Victor rolls the idea around in his head, envisioning all the myriad ways Jonas could be consumed by the earth. Each vision is more grotesque than the last, but in every one, Jonas's mouth is agape, caught in the act of a final, silent wail of indescribable agony.

As satisfying as this ending would be, as exquisite a justice as Victor could contrive—Jonas ultimately killed by his own attempts to defy the will of the universe—he knows it's not the explanation. True, it's just an instinct, but that same intuition has guided Victor throughout his whole life. It won him Phaedra. It brought him to the zenith of his profession. The fact that that very same instinct lost him both is an inconvenient point he chooses to ignore.

He *knows* that Jonas is still alive. It's just that his tether has ceased to function. But that doesn't mean Victor cannot find him.

Jonas resides in a world not his own. A dog in a manger. An interloper. In whatever reality he has landed in, his presence is unnatural, an anomaly. As a matter of science, such peculiarities should be easy to detect. The multiverse may possess a near-infinite assortment of realities, but it is only a matter of time until Victor locates his nemesis.

And then they'll finish this.

∞

Though modest in appearance, Sushitei Hikarimachi is considered one of the best restaurants in Hiroshima. White lamps dangle, casting a sheen on the laminated menus, which seem out of place in such a high-end eatery. Jonas and Eva share a table along the wall, where they are served slices of fish so delicate, they're almost translucent. Sashimi in assorted shades of pink and ivory. Sushi that rises to the level of art.

"Can I ask you a question?" Eva says.

"Of course," Jonas answers. "Anything."

"I've been avoiding it . . ."

"Why?"

She waves at the air with her chopsticks as though trying to catch the right words with them. "I don't know. It feels selfish. Or weird. Or something."

Jonas smiles warmly, trying to recapture some of the camaraderie and lightness that he has enjoyed with Eva in both her incarnations. "Why don't you just ask and let me be the judge?"

Eva reaches for her sake and drains the small glass. "You told me how you met me before. Well, not before. Elsewhere. Not elsewhere . . ." She shakes her head and furrows her brow. "There's really no good word for it, is there?"

Jonas shrugs. "Scientific breakthroughs often require new words to describe them." He studies her and is reminded of her beauty, a quality he's studiously ignored since meeting her counterpart several universes ago. Why? He casts the thought away. "You want to know what you were like," he observes, reading her. "If you were different."

She nods, a hint of embarrassment in her expression.

"You weren't different," he assures her truthfully. "You were pretty much exactly the same, right down to the way you picked at your right thumb."

Eva had been digging at the skin of her thumb with the nail of her index finger, but she stops, instantly self-conscious. But then another emotion replaces it. Jonas has had enough experience with feeling like someone was stepping on his grave to recognize it in someone else, and he knows that he's just made a serious mistake.

"Why are you using the past tense?" Eva asks.

Jonas's blood cools, but he plasters a smile over his face. "Because I *met* you, past tense. I'm not still meeting you."

Eva leans forward, steepling her fingers. "Do you know what I've discovered?" She bears down on him with a polygraph stare. "We're both horrendous liars."

Jonas swallows hard. He had led them both into a thicket by mistake. "Do you want to know . . ." He gestures an invitation with his hand, but the offer is clear in its insincerity.

"No." Eva darkens. A coldness emanates from her. The distance Jonas had begun to feel between them now seems like a chasm. "I think I've learned more than I want to."

She waves for another glass of sake and returns to her meal, her chopsticks pecking away at the fish like the beak of a pelican.

They finish the rest of the meal in silence.

THREE YEARS AGO

Thirty-five Hudson Yards was also referred to as "Tower E," a hybrid hotel and residential building on Manhattan's West Side. Although shaped like a prism, the sheets of glass that covered it reflected light rather than refracted it. Jonas wondered if the architects were aware of the irony.

He stepped out onto the roof, which soared over a thousand feet into the air. It was a beautiful spring day, and from this vantage he could see all the way across the Hudson River to Weehawken, New Jersey. Dappled sunlight danced along the surface of the water, looking almost electric.

He remembered a time when looking out from such a height would have unnerved him. Amanda had cured him of that, as she had cured him of so many things. Loving her made him want to be a better person, and all the things that once frightened him now seemed insignificant.

He saw her near the roofline. Her back was to him, and she was gazing out toward Hell's Kitchen. Her hair waved almost imperceptibly in the gentle breeze. Next to her was a massive canvas, a huge five-foot square resting on a pair of easels. The canvas was coated in intersecting streaks of graphite. Lines plunged toward vanishing points. Although it was still rudimentary, Jonas could make out enough detail to suggest falling rather than flying. It was an unexpected departure for Amanda, whose prior works had always conveyed the idea of soaring.

He took a moment to admire her, the way she leaned on her right leg, cocking her hip almost imperceptibly to the side. The sun drew highlights in her brunette hair. The wind wafted at her T-shirt, making it flutter.

Amanda rarely painted this late into the day. As the afternoon waned, she said the shadows grew too long for her to work. The darkness cast by the city's skyscrapers were, to her eye, like claws tearing through Manhattan. She preferred to work when the sun was high, and the light was sublime.

But now the sun was going down, and Amanda was flawlessly backlit by it. The sky looked as if it were aflame. Amanda's burgeoning project was set ironically against what itself looked like a painting. Jonas took out his phone and snapped a photo. It captured her silhouette perfectly, and her inchoate project peeked in just enough to tease what it could become, what she would make it.

Jonas put his phone back in his pocket. "Hey, baby." She didn't turn around at first. He assumed she was focused on some detail, so he approached and took it in. Amanda worked in a way such that to see her art up close was to reveal an entirely different perspective, art within art, a painting within a painting. "This one's coming along," he commented. "It's different, though. The vanishing points are lower." He gestured toward the bottom of the canvas. "See? I pay attention when you explain stuff to me." His tone was playful.

Amanda still didn't respond, which was odd.

Jonas looked at her, and in an instant, his worry spiked. Her eyes were red. A tear had carved a line down the dust on her cheek. He felt cold. "Amanda?"

"I'm fine," she said unconvincingly as she turned to face him. She looked leaden, pinned under some weight.

"What's wrong?" He felt an urge to take her in his arms but sensed she didn't want to be held in this moment.

Amanda bit her lower lip, as she often did when she was upset. He could see her straining not to cry. "I saw Dr. Gilberg today." Jonas's veins turned to ribbons of ice. He must have looked terrified because Amanda immediately added, "I'm fine. I'm not dying or sick or anything."

But Jonas felt no relief, *could* feel no relief. Not until he knew what was wrong. He watched as she bit her lip harder. Her head gave a little shake as her tears started to swell. Her jaw jutted forward, trying to keep sorrow at bay with anger.

"There's a growth on one of my ovaries," she managed.

Jonas couldn't resist any longer. He took her in his arms. He felt her body tremble against his, his shoulder damp beneath where Amanda rested her head. He stroked the back of it. "It's going to be okay." He hoped he sounded more convincing than he felt.

Amanda shook her head vigorously. "They have to operate." She was sobbing hard now. Her tears drenched his shirt as she gripped him tighter. "I hate—" she began. "I hate—" She couldn't get the words. Tears were getting in the way.

"Hate what, honey?"

"I hate that I'm scared." The words came in a rush, laced with defiant resentment.

"It's okay to be scared. *I'm* scared. But we're going to take this one step at a time, all right?" He pulled back slightly so she could see his face. "It's going to be okay," he promised. "It's going to be okay." He paused before venturing, "Is there anything I can do for you right now?"

She stopped crying but didn't let him go. "Just hold me."

And he did. Until the sun disappeared behind the skyline, and the stars began to wink down on them. Jonas hid his fear from view, the expression on his face that asked, *What are we going to do now?*

NOW

Another week passes. Jonas moves in a trio of whiteboards and fills them up with equations that test Other Jonas's calculations, continuing the work begun in New Berlin. All the while, Eva keeps her distance, literally and figuratively. With increasing inventiveness, she manufactures reasons to avoid him. She must run an errand. She must buy more groceries. She must keep up with her own work and, for reasons she can't or won't articulate, can only do so at the Hiroshima City Central Library. She takes up running with the zeal of a religious convert. But Jonas can't shake the feeling that she's running less for exercise than to get away from him.

He thinks about pressing the issue. Since the meal at Sushitei Hikarimachi, he's come close several times, only to retreat, afraid to broach any topic that could lead to a discussion of what happened to Eva's doppelgänger on the Seidenstrasse, which would lead to a discussion of how it happened, which would lead to his disclosing the threat of Victor's crusade against him. And then he would be forced to explain why he never told her about it.

Jonas asks himself now why he didn't. What impulse drove him to conceal the full truth of his circumstances? He's asked so much of her, and she's given it without hesitation or reservation. But she's done so from behind a veil of ignorance, unaware that, somewhere in the multiverse, a man is trying to stop him. And that effort has already led to Eva's death once before. Jonas tells himself that the act of concealment is protective—to safeguard Eva against some threat he can't articulate—and he is shocked by the ease with which he lies to himself.

To explain Victor's vendetta would be to expose the reason for it, the allegations of theft and plagiarism. And although Jonas is secure in the belief that he committed no such crimes, he's forced to admit to himself that he's concerned Eva might think otherwise. That she might lose some measure of respect for him, see him as lesser. But what would it matter if her estimation of him shrank a little? The answer lies in those fleeting moments of connection, the chemistry they've been sharing with increasing frequency.

Feeling guilty and ashamed, Jonas tries to wrap himself in the familiar cloak of belief in the purity of his endeavor. Getting back to Amanda requires singular focus. And he's come too far to alter his course now.

Besides, he reassures himself, Victor likely declared victory the moment Amanda crumpled to the sidewalk two universes ago. Victor doesn't know—can't know—about the other Amanda, the one discovered by Other Jonas. Victor must think that Jonas's mission, and thus his own, is now over. Victor must have moved on, resumed whatever life he had left after being consumed by envy and bitterness and hate.

Eva must be safe.

So why not tell her? Jonas finally resolves to do exactly that, to tell her everything. And to apologize for keeping secrets from her. He's going to promise never to do it again.

Eva emerges from the bedroom on her way out of the apartment. "I'm going to head over to the Spire, see if the personal touch can work something."

"Your friend still hasn't returned your calls?" It's been eleven days.

Eva grimaces. "No," she says. Her expression is part disappointment, part apology. And yet, it comes off as slightly insincere for a reason Jonas can't pin down. "I guess Dr. Kobayashi isn't as good a friend as I thought."

Stress claws its way up Jonas's back, a creeping feeling he's been trying to keep at bay since they arrived in Japan. Back in New Berlin, he explained Other Jonas's theory that the initial burst of quantum energy he'd taken back at CERN had unmoored him from the multiverse and afforded him the ability to slip realities. But as Other Jonas said, the effect is temporary. Whatever energy he might absorb from the Spire's Superconducting Linear Accelerator is purely for a one-way trip.

He looks to the trio of whiteboards, each covered in a rainbow of formulae and equations. Two of the three are dedicated to confirming Other Jonas's calculations. The third represents an inchoate attempt at calculating the rate at which his body is leaching quantum energy, how much time he has left as an interuniversal traveler. He points to it. "I don't know how much longer I have left before I'm marooned here, unable to reality-slip no matter what. But I don't think it's much."

"It'll all work out," Eva says after a few seconds' hesitation. Her optimism is saccharine, sweet but false. She punctuates it with a smile for good measure. "I'm going to go see if Dr. Kobayashi will meet with me. I'll be back soon." And she goes.

After the door shuts behind her, Jonas tries to return to his work. But he can't focus. A doubt nags at him. He reaches for the prepaid cell phone he purchased upon arriving in Japan and dials zero one three zero for information.

"*Moshi moshi. Anata wa eigo hanashimasu ka?*" he asks, exhausting almost all the Japanese he's learned in the past eleven days. *Hello. Do you speak English?*

"Yes, sir. How can I help you?"

"I need the number for a Dr. Kobayashi. I don't know his first name, but he works at the Spire."

Evening has fallen. Eva returns home. It's strange to think of this rented apartment with its furnishings as anything but a glorified hotel, much less "home." She is bone tired after spending her day meandering around Hiroshima. It wasn't her first time taking in the city, but the experience never grows old. To weave herself through a place—wandering without purpose, without concern for being stopped, without fear of being asked to present proof of her residency or commanded to "state her business"— is a freedom as pure and marvelous as fresh air. She looked at every face she passed, drank in every feature, every idiosyncratic nuance of individual appearance. *Do they even know,* she asked herself, *how blessed they are?* The truest freedom, she realized, is not to be aware of how free one is.

In the darkness, the living room is a minefield, a shrouded obstacle course. She navigates it with care, taking pains not to upset the wires and electronics and other technological ephemera littering their temporary home. Her concern is less about waking Jonas than about what waking him would mean. For eleven days, she's labored to avoid any conversation with the potential to be real, anything that could wander into the forbidden territory of their feelings for one another. *Her* feelings for *him,* she corrects herself, a secret she keeps with the rigor of an unfaithful spouse. But the connection between them is undeniable, she believes. As unyielding as granite.

She's inches away from the short hallway that leads to her bedroom when a light comes on. The illumination startles her. She whips around and sees Jonas sitting in a chair. Wide awake.

He's been waiting for her.

For as long as she's known him, which isn't long in literal terms but feels as though it's been all her life, he's worn his emotions on his sleeve. Now she sees that figurative sleeve covered in anger and betrayal and disappointment.

"What the—" She startles. "What the hell are you doing there?"

"Waiting for you."

"In the dark?"

"I was thinking."

Eva watches him rise from the chair. Slowly. Coiled. She can feel the anger radiating off him. Her heart races. Whatever he has to say to her, she dreads it. Too much has gone unsaid between them for too long, but she's kept her own counsel for a reason, and she's not ready to deviate now.

"I called the Spire," he says.

She's not surprised. A part of her knew it the moment he turned on the light and revealed himself. "I can explain—" The words are out of her mouth before she's even aware. An uncontrollable impulse, a survival instinct. *I can explain.* Could she be any more of a cliché?

"I spoke with Daisuke Kobayashi," Jonas says. His voice is so distant it might as well be coming from another country. He sounds pained, and that breaks Eva's heart in turn. "He said he never heard from you. No calls. Not even an email." He shakes his head as if straining to believe it. "This whole time," he says, "you've been . . . pretending, feigning helping me when you weren't. Why?"

Eva feels a single tear and instantly hates herself for what she considers a failure of strength. She wipes it from her cheek as though smudging out a mistake.

"You've been different," Jonas says. "I thought I knew the reason, but . . ." His hands spread apart as if trying physically to grasp the problem between them. "But I think I was wrong. I just—" He sighs. "I just need to know what's going on. You know I'm working on borrowed time. I just—" He stops. Eva thinks he might cry. She sees him willing himself not to. "I just need to know why this is happening."

And "this," she knows, is her betrayal. She's been biding time, waiting out the days until the quantum energy in his body is finally exhausted, and he is unable to leave.

"You know why," she says. Her voice is barely a whisper.

"What I mean," he says, choosing his words carefully, "is that I don't understand why you pretended you were trying to get me into the Spire?" Pain coats his voice. "Why were you burning off time you know I don't have?"

Eva's first reaction is to feel amazed. How could he not know? "You know why," she says, feeling the words emerging from her depths. When she finally says it, it's like a dam bursting. Like falling, surrendering to gravity. "I love you," she gasps.

She closes the distance between them until she's close enough to feel the heat of his body near hers. Close enough to kiss. He doesn't recoil.

"I know how much you miss her," Eva says. "I know what it's like to live with loss. To wish that fate had dealt a different hand. But a life spent wishing things were different . . . isn't a life."

The expression on Jonas's face breaks her heart. It's a knowing look, an admission that she isn't telling him anything he doesn't already know.

Finally he says, "I'm not just wishing things were different. I can *do* something. I *am* doing something."

She freezes him with a look. "What happened to the other me?" she asks. She watches him go pale. "What happened to the me you met before?"

"It's not important—"

"If that were true, you would have told me already," she counters. "If that were true, you wouldn't look the way you do right now. Like you want to be anywhere but here." She stands her ground, immoveable. "Tell me the truth."

Jonas swallows hard. She watches his throat piston up and down. A long silence stretches between them as he tries to find the words. Eva waits. She has all the time in the world. Finally, he says, "There is a man. Another scientist. He's trying to stop me. He hired a mercenary."

"And?"

Jonas swallows again. His voice cracks. "The mercenary tried to kill me. But you died instead."

Eva reacts as though stung. Is it possible to be shocked by the answer she was, on some level, already expecting? Yes, she decides, it's absolutely possible.

"I'm sorry I didn't tell you," Jonas says. "I should have. Or maybe I shouldn't have. I don't know." His head shakes with his remorse. "I don't know," he repeats. "But I'm sorry."

Sympathy wells up within Eva. The kind of sympathy that can only be fueled by love. She's standing on a precipice, weighing whether to take the single step that will plummet her into the abyss. "Am I the only person he killed?"

"The mercenary, yes. He was trying to kill me. You were . . ."

"Collateral damage," she croaks.

"It was an accident. It was—" Jonas's voice trails off. He seems gaunt and physically pained. "But the scientist—his name is Victor—he . . ." His breathing is ragged, as rough as sandpaper. A tear blossoms. "He killed Amanda. Another Amanda. One I had found in another universe. He shot her dead, right in front of me. He didn't want me to be with her. Any her. In any universe."

Eva's heart breaks for him, and it catches her by surprise. She didn't think she had any sympathy left to offer. She thinks of the mercenary and the scientist and the thought of Jonas's final salvation lying lifeless in front of him. "You've said the universe favors certain outcomes."

"Yes."

"And this mercenary . . . this scientist . . . your wife dying yet again . . ." She lets the thought die stillborn. It feels like an act of cruelty to speak it aloud.

"What's your point?"

Eva feels tears pooling in her own eyes now. Are they for Jonas's pain or her own? She has no idea. The only thing she knows for sure is that this is the most difficult conversation she's had in her life. "My point," she says, her voice tremulous, "is your point. That the universe wants things to turn out a specific way."

"Or ways, yes. So?" Impatience creeps into Jonas's voice.

But Eva presses on. "So have you considered the possibility that this mercenary, this scientist . . . your wife dying again . . . have you considered that they're all the universe's way of trying to get you to stop? The universe is *begging* you to stop."

Jonas stares at her, looking betrayed again.

This, she tells herself, *is an intervention.* "You said you found my doppelgänger in Switzerland. But in *this* universe, I live in New Berlin. Where you just happened to be."

"What's your point?"

Eva throws him a look to suggest that he should already know the answer. "The universe wanted me to meet you. The universe wants this." She gestures between the two of them. "*I* want this." Her eyes widen with the realization that she hasn't truly stepped off the precipice. Not yet. Not really. But now she does. "*You* want this."

∞

You want this. The words echo in his mind. *You want this.* Her and him. Together. Lovers and maybe more. *You want this.* Three words, but they feel like an assault.

Because they're true.

He's felt the connection between them. The pull. He felt it back in the Switzerland of an entirely different reality. He felt it in New Berlin, standing at the door to her faculty building. He felt it over the past several weeks in every conversation tinged with attraction, every stolen glance. He feels it now, finding himself cursing her for being so bluntly honest yet loving her for that same honesty.

Loving her.

It feels like a betrayal. And not just of his wife. Of his very soul. Of everything he's been living for, everything he's ever held true. Shame consumes him. In all his life, he has never felt so weak or so lost. Words escape his lips but at such a low volume that even he can't be sure he's actually spoken them.

"What?" Eva asks.

He swallows. As much to choke down tears as anything else. Then, louder, he says, "You're right."

He watches her brighten. Hope is the cruelest mistress, and he watches it fill her. His heart breaks to squelch it, and doing so requires all the conviction he can muster.

"I care about you, Eva," he says. "And, yes, I might even love you. Either way, I feel a connection to you that goes beyond friendship that I know could become so much more if I let it."

"If you let it?" Her voice trembles with uncertainty.

He pushes the question aside. "And you're right when you say that the universe wants us to be together."

"But?"

"But don't you see?"

She shakes her head. Tears fall down her face. She makes no effort to wipe them away.

"The universe," Jonas stammers, "doesn't want me to find Amanda. I don't know why. All I know is that it's thrown up every possible obstacle. Victor is one. Victor's mercenary is another. And another . . ." He stops. Breathes deep. He doesn't want to say it, but he has to. Because he knows it's true. "And another is you."

The slap catches him unawares, but he knows he deserves it. Eva is sobbing now, tears falling over the betrayal and heartbreak evidenced on her face.

"I'm sorry," Jonas says, meaning it. "I shouldn't have said that."

"Why not?" she asks, anger filtering into her voice. "You believe it." She stares at him with disdain, all traces of sympathy or even pity gone. "You'll believe anything to keep on believing you can still be with her. *Should* still be with her."

Jonas doesn't argue the point. No one has ever told him anything more right.

Eva looks at him, her eyes pleading, and speaks with the urgency of someone trying to prevent someone else from committing murder. "But you can't be with her, Jonas. You have to know that. The whole universe is resisting you. You can't fight fate."

Is there any greater temptation than truth? If so, Jonas has never felt it. Not the way he feels it now.

"But you *can* be with me," she says. "You have a choice. You can choose to live. You can choose to be happy."

"But I don't want to." The words fly from his mouth unbidden. Visceral. "I don't want to," he says again, if only to prove that the first time wasn't a fluke. "I care for you, Eva. I might even love you. I might be *in love* with you. But—" He stops, inwardly testing his convictions and finding them to be as solid as steel. "But if it's a choice between being with someone who's not Amanda and being alone, then I—*I'll be alone*." He reaches down deep and pulls up the most truthful thing he can say. "I'm sorry, Eva. I'm so very sorry."

He waits for her to speak, buttressing himself against the most hateful thing she could say. But Eva just presses her palms into her face and smudges away her tears. She walks out of the room, trailing heartbreak, leaving Jonas alone. As alone, he thinks, as anyone has ever felt.

THREE YEARS AGO

In the wake of Amanda's diagnosis and the looming specter of her surgery, Jonas abandoned his work on the Many Worlds Proof and devoted himself completely to her. He wanted to be fully present, the way she had been for him. If he could have gone under the knife in her place, he would have done so without hesitation. Unfortunately, round-the-clock attention wasn't what Amanda needed as the date of the operation advanced like an invading army. She told him she had to throw herself into her work, to plunge deeply into it, to feel the same sensation of nose-diving that she was trying to convey in the piece she was working on. She spent every possible hour working away on the rooftop of Tower E. It felt to Jonas as though she was trying to outrun the shadow of surgery and illness, to bury her fears beneath her art.

Jonas tried to distract her with plans for their wedding. Almost immediately, they had settled on a beach wedding at sunset out on Long Island's Montauk Point. But Amanda refused to let herself get seduced. Apart from her art, she said, her entire life was on pause, everything frozen in amber until the surgery, until the growth was excised and someone from hospital pathology pronounced it benign or malignant. Until she knew whether she had a future and understood its shape. Jonas imagined that this is what it must feel like to await sentencing for a crime one hasn't committed.

The morning of the operation, they walked uptown to Mount Sinai Hospital. Amanda wanted to see and smell and feel the city.

Jonas recalled how, a year prior, to sustain his imperiled career, she had suggested moving away from New York. But Jonas knew that was impossible. For Amanda to be removed from Manhattan would be tantamount to being removed from one of her limbs. Her art wasn't merely an expression of her love for the city but the manifestation of her profound, almost biological connection to it. They both knew this hospital visit might end with a diagnosis that could change her life— and thus *their lives*—forever, and Amanda wanted to drink in the city one more time before that happened. Before they might be forced to become different people.

In the waiting room, Jonas cracked his knuckles and read magazines that chronicled current events from two years prior. He stared at the television, tuned to a silent CNN broadcast with closed captioning, mounted on the wall. He tried to convince himself he was hungry enough to buy something from the vending machine. It wouldn't be a long procedure, he was told, but every minute seemed to stretch to hours.

Eventually a nurse materialized, a matronly woman in floral-patterned scrubs. She told him the procedure was over and that he could see Amanda. When he stood up, the world spun, and he feared he might pass out. The nurse led him out of the waiting room and down a corridor. His legs felt heavy and recalcitrant. He asked after Amanda, but the answers seemed to come from far away. He teased out little fragments—"got it all," "clean margins"—but he understood nothing beyond the need to get to Amanda, to see for himself that she was okay.

The nurse deposited him in Amanda's room and closed the door. Amanda lay on her side, her back to him. The vertical blinds were half-closed, and shadows raked across the room. Jonas dragged a chair to the edge of the bed and collapsed into it. "Hey, baby." He whispered but didn't know why.

Amanda rolled over, and Jonas nearly gasped. Her face was pallid but for the dark rings under her eyes. Wires of hair hung down across her forehead. He forced himself to smile and reached out to take her hand.

"The nurse says they got it all," he said, without a full understanding of what that meant. Like how he would pretend to understand football by repeating the last comment he'd heard on television. He knew the team he was rooting for but grasped none of the specifics of the game being played.

"It's benign," Amanda said. "The growth."

Jonas felt a cataract of relief. He exhaled and gripped her hand tighter. The room seemed to brighten, despite the blinds. "Oh thank God," he breathed. "That's great. That's—that's the best news ever." He felt giddy. Lightheaded.

But then, just as quickly, he paled. He assumed Amanda was tired, her sallow appearance the result of postoperative fatigue or anesthesia or both. But he was struck with the realization that her pallid look was due to neither of these things. He felt his stomach bottom out. Something was still tragically wrong.

Amanda swallowed hard. She started to cry. "Because of the surgery," she began, speaking with a slow tentativeness, "Dr. Gilberg . . . she says . . ."

Jonas held his breath. He felt little pieces of himself die in each of her silent pauses.

"She says that it's very unlikely . . ." Amanda clamped her mouth shut against the sobs trying to escape from it.

Jonas put another hand over hers. "Whatever it is, it's okay," he assured her, meaning every word. "It'll be okay. *You're* okay. That's all that matters." He had never believed anything more.

But Amanda shook her head in defiance, rejecting Jonas's assertion that she was okay. "She doesn't think I'll be able to get pregnant."

Jonas was instantly hyperaware of his surroundings. The monitoring devices Amanda was wired up to, which had previously seemed as quiet as a whisper, seemed to thrum loudly. The blinds hung over the window like garish teeth. Beyond them, a siren warbled past. Outside, behind the window's divide, life spun on, ignorant of the hopes and dreams evaporating within the hospital room, unaware that futures barely imagined were being erased.

"We never talked about having kids," Amanda said. "But I always assumed . . ."

"Me too."

Jonas didn't know what else to say. In the hours and days that followed, though, he wished that he had. He weighed how he could be so heartbroken over a possibility he had never really thought about before, let alone discussed with the woman he was to share his life with. How had they never talked about whether the contours of that life included children? Had they both been too focused on their work? Or did this omission, shocking in hindsight, speak to a larger issue?

Jonas was seized by a horrible and profound fear. Was this the beginning of their end? He tried to push the thought away. But it was too late.

NOW

In the aftermath of his conversation with Eva, sleep eludes Jonas. He wakes in the middle of the night and tries to work, but he cannot focus. All he can think of is her—the first "her" that isn't Amanda in as long as he can remember. She's there, sleeping in the next room, this other woman whom, in the solitude, in the quiet hours of the evening, he can admit that he loves. He can even confess to himself that he might feel the potential of a love to rival what he feels for Amanda.

Eva's twenty, thirty steps away. She might even be waiting for him, as unable to sleep as he is. She could be sitting up in her bed or staring up at the ceiling, waiting in her bedroom for him to enter, offering everything he needs in his soul. Love and companionship and sex, yes. But also closure. She's tempting him with peace, the end of his long, difficult struggle.

When he closes his eyes, he sees Amanda. *Go to her,* she tells him. *Move on from me. Move on with your life.*

He wants to cry, but the tears won't come. He wants to scream, but Eva would hear. He is so very tired, but sleep refuses him, and so fatigue just pulls at him like a weight.

Thinking that fresh air is what he needs, he escapes out into the night. His joints moan in protest as he walks. Other Jonas had told him this is a sign of his body losing its ability to reality-slip. Is it possible that he's lost it already? That he's waited too long and is now confined to this universe? If so, he's rejected Eva in the name of a woman he will never be with. He's marooned in the desert and just refused an oasis.

He walks for hours. Stars glister overhead. Eventually, the horizon glows, and the rising sun renders the sky a brilliant orange. As the world brightens, Jonas wanders the paths of Hijiyama Park. The cherry blossoms are in bloom, tiny explosions of color dangling from branches. He finds a bench and watches the park fill with joggers and dog walkers. As they pass, Jonas thinks of each of their unique lives multiplied by an infinite number of universes. He imagines an endless tapestry woven from threads of such variety that they form a sea of color, rainbows on rainbows.

He pulls a five-hundred-yen coin from his pocket. Flips it. Catches it. Flips it again. Flip. Catch. Flip. Catch. After a minute, it takes on the quality of silent meditation. Flip. Catch. Flip. Catch. Flip. The morning sunlight glints off the coin's golden circumference as it tumbles in the air. Its motion reminds him of the limousine careening off the Centralbron, gravity causing it to pinwheel like the coin. Flip. Flip. Flip. With the exception of only two realities, the limousine's fatal roll—in a multiverse of uncountable universes—ends with Amanda's body broken on impact. *Tails, you lose.*

Jonas loses himself in the repetition. The light playing across the coin. The faint harmonic *ting* it makes when launched by his thumb. The percussive thwack as he snatches it from the air. Flip. Catch. Flip. Catch. Flip. The runners and trotting dogs on leashes give way to morning commuters who give way to tourists and bird-watchers. And still he sits. Flip. Catch. Flip. Catch. Flip.

"What are you doing?"

Jonas catches the coin and looks up. It's Eva. Her eyes are red from crying. He doesn't think to ask how she found him, and she doesn't offer. He flips the coin again.

"Birthing universes," he says. A new one with each flip. Schrödinger's yen.

"I thought you said it didn't work that way."

"I don't know anything anymore," Jonas answers. His voice is distant. Unmoored. A moment of silence passes. Another to add to the pile of such moments that by now rises as tall as a mountain. Finally, he rises to his feet. "I'm sorry," he says, and means it.

"This would be easier," Eva replies, "if you didn't apologize." Her voice remains even, her jaw tight.

"What would be easier?"

"Are you finished?"

Jonas doesn't understand. "Finished with what?"

"Your calculations. Whatever you need to do with your tether. Are you ready to go?"

"Yes." In truth, he finished only the previous night, while sleep eluded him like a fugitive.

"I called Dr. Kobayashi this morning," she says. "He's expecting us."

Suddenly, the world seems clearer, brighter. The birdsong wafting through the park takes on a cheery timbre. Jonas looks at Eva, this incredible woman. This woman who can think of him even after he's broken her heart. This woman who chooses him even though he rejected her.

"What did you tell him?" he asks.

"I told him a colleague of mine needs a favor, but the request has to be in person."

"Probably safer than the truth."

"Probably."

Her heartbreak seems all the more gut wrenching for the will she's summoning to overcome it. "Eva . . . ," he says, unsure of what words will follow.

"Loving you means helping you," she says, answering the question held in his thoughts but not formed. "I don't like it, but that's how it is. Because if you don't find her . . . then it was all for nothing."

Jonas marvels at the enormity of the gift she's given him, greater than anything he can conceive of. He's panged by the guilt of knowing that loving him as she does means letting him go to be with another woman in another universe. The idea is so big that he couldn't embrace it even if his arms were the diameter of the world.

Eva looks away. It seems as though she might cry, but no tears come. Instead, a curious smile forms on her lips. Her voice carries the slightest lilt of hopefulness when she says, "Somewhere . . . there's another me. And there's another you. And that you . . ."—her voice pitches upward—"*that* you chooses to stay."

She turns toward him, her eyes still lit with the spark that envisions a reality where the two of them are together and that may have been one of the hundreds of universes Jonas might have just created by flipping a coin.

It takes a little over an hour for Jonas to return to the apartment, calibrate his tether with its new battery, and change into his all-natural "traveling clothes." The living room turned workshop is a muddle of whiteboards, stray dry-erase markers, and tangles of wire. It's as if science itself exploded in the modest room.

He moves to gather up the mess, but Eva stops him. "You don't have that kind of time."

"I don't even know *if* I still have time," he admits.

"Only one way to find out." She draws a halting breath. "Come on."

They get into the Honda Civic that Jonas rented solely for the purpose of traveling to the Spire. He drives. He's never been to the Spire before but doesn't bother with GPS. All he has to do is drive toward the giant needle piercing the earth. But as they pass over the Enko River, the Civic slows to a crawl. The street is choked off by traffic.

Jonas hits the brake and throws the car into reverse. He yanks the wheel to spin them around just as another tidal wave of traffic surges to meet them.

"It's too early for rush hour," Eva points out.

"You're right," Jonas says. An instinct about what is happening begins to rise in him, turning his stomach. He jerks the wheel hard and guns the accelerator. The car rides up on the curve, two-wheeling the sidewalk. Pedestrians scatter.

"What are you doing?" Eva almost screams.

"We have to get there." He's white-knuckling the wheel, leaning forward, jaw set. Complete determination. Total focus.

"It'll be okay, Jonas," she reassures him. "You'll get there. You'll be able to reality-slip. But not if you get us into an accident."

"It's not that simple." Cars honk in protest. People volley epithets, which he doesn't need to speak Japanese to understand, at Jonas. "Dammit!" he screams and punches the steering wheel, his frustration boiling over.

"Just calm down," Eva implores. Despite the circumstances, her voice is as soothing as a cold breeze.

"You don't understand—"

"Then explain it to me."

Jonas swerves the car off the curb and around a corner. He keeps the Spire in his peripheral vision. The tower appears to erupt out of the horizon itself. They manage to get half a mile when the car unexpectedly drops to the ground.

"What happened?" Eva asks in a panic.

What happened was that all four tires just exploded in unison. The odds of this are incalculable. Inertia carries the hobbled Civic forward, its steel undercarriage scraping the pavement, birthing sparks. When it stops, Jonas bursts out of the car. Eva is close behind. She stares at the quartet of ruptured tires, which have been reduced to shards of rubber.

"This is impossible," she says.

"It's the universe." Jonas sets his jaw, speaking with deep conviction. "The universe is trying to stop me."

He watches as a battle between what Eva knows and what she's just observed rages inside her. He grabs her by the wrist, and they sprint toward the Spire. It's closer now but still too far for comfort.

"This doesn't make any sense," Eva says between heaving breaths. "Why is the universe trying to stop you *now*?"

"Because I've never been this close before," Jonas theorizes. "Newton's third law: 'For every action, there is an equal and opposite reaction.' The closer I get to my goal, the more the universe is going to fight me."

They turn another corner, and Eva stops abruptly. "There. It'll be faster." She points to a subway entrance, but Jonas stops her.

"No. We'll be trapped underground."

She looks back toward him, her face etched with infinite patience. "You're trying to outgame the *universe*. You realize how ridiculous that sounds, right?"

"C'mon," he says with a smirk, "you've gotta be getting used to it by now."

Eva smiles that little wry smile he's come to love. But it passes quickly when the ground begins to shake. The tempo of the vibrations rises. The ground rolls, undulating. All around, people struggle to keep their footing. Some fail. Storefront windows shatter outward, spraying glass. Off in the distance, sirens bleat and echo.

Eva stumbles, but Jonas catches her. "Okay, maybe it's not so ridiculous," she deadpans.

"C'mon." Jonas takes her hand, and they run as well as they can with the ground quivering under their feet. They pass people being rag-dolled by the tremors, but Jonas's drive is singular. And Eva won't let herself lose him. They dodge toppling lampposts and hurdle cars beached up on sidewalks. They avoid the geyser of a ruptured water main. The world tips ninety degrees.

"If the universe won't even let you get there, how is this going to work?" Eva asks, doubt infecting her voice.

"We're getting there," he insists, willing it to happen.

Sure enough, they do. Day turns to night as they enter the massive shadow cast by the Spire's enormity.

"My point is," Eva insists, "security could stop us, the equipment could fail. A million other things could go wrong."

"One step at a time." It's all Jonas has to guide him in this moment. Three PhDs and a Nobel, and this is all he knows. *One step at a time.*

The thought has barely taken form when a car attacks him, jumping up from the street toward the sidewalk. He hears Eva scream his name, her voice laced with panic, as he clocks its approach, instantly filled with an overwhelming urge to jump—a primal survival instinct—though he barely manages to leave the ground before the car barrels into him.

Jonas has only jumped eight inches, maybe a foot, but it's enough to save his life. Rather than being rooted in place when the front end strikes him, he's just barely airborne, and the impact causes him to tumble like a gymnast.

When he falls, the sharp crack is the loudest sound he's ever heard. Louder than the metallic cries of the limousine launched off the Centralbron. Louder than the gunshots sparking off the steel railings at CERN. Louder even than the single shot that sent Amanda crumpling to the sidewalk.

His first thought is that it's the crack of his bones. His ribs, most likely. But then he realizes it's the sound of the car's windshield spiderwebbing against his form as it charges into him. The collision hurls Jonas skyward again. He pinballs off the car's roof before careening off the rear and smashing to the street. Behind him, the car clambers through a store window.

The sidewalk's concrete claws at Jonas as he lands. Pain rockets through him. He has no idea if this is the aggravation of old injuries, a symptom of the quantum energies leaving his body, or merely the result of this newest series of assaults. It's all he can do to keep from passing out. He wills himself to breathe. Something akin to sleep starts to grip him, and he commands himself to stay awake.

Then, hands are on him, trying to pull him up, but he's too heavy. He regains communication with his legs and discovers they still work. He eases himself up, guided by what he assumes are Eva's hands.

"Oh my God, are you okay?" she asks. He was just hit by a car, but the question doesn't strike either of them as stupid.

Jonas tries to speak but can't, so he just nods his head.

"Is anything broken?" Eva asks.

He shakes his head, though in truth, he has no idea. It feels like every bone in his body is broken.

The ground is still shaking. The city has become an ocean, and they're being buffeted by the undulating street. Everything is swaying, and Jonas feels like a tiny figure in a snow globe being shaken vigorously by a child.

Pain is only a signal, he reminds himself, *just neurons communicating with themselves.* He reaches for Eva's hand and pulls her behind him. They don't run so much as fall in the Spire's direction.

"It's a matter of will," he says.

"Are you talking to yourself or the universe?"

Jonas truly doesn't know. "Is one more sane than the other?"

"Good point."

The earth moves and shifts and rumbles, protesting Jonas's defiance. If this truly is a battle of wills, then it's simply a matter of refusing to surrender. The tremors become so violent that Jonas and Eva can no longer run. It's all they can do to keep their balance, to keep moving forward, each step an act of cosmic rebellion.

With chaos blooming all around them, they press on, swimming against the tide of people flowing from the Spire in a chorus of frightened screams. Jonas pushes them aside, Eva following in his wake, until they land in a plaza of steel and greenery. Water that normally jets up from carefully designed fountains now erupts in errant, wayward volleys that smack against the polished concrete.

Overhead, the Spire looms and sways. Jonas knows that its frame is threaded with massive springs designed to buttress the huge structure against such assaults from the earth. He looks up and can barely see its summit.

They are so close. *So close.*

He grips Eva's hand tighter and pulls them both inside. And the moment—the exact second—they spill into the granite and travertine lobby, a marvel of bleeding edge architecture and design, the earthquake ceases. It happens so fast, it's as if a switch has been thrown.

"This doesn't make any kind of scientific sense," Eva says, disbelieving.

"That's what every scientist says," Jonas answers her. "Right before it *does*."

Eva looks over to the reception desk, where a guard dutifully remains at his post. He barks at them in urgent Japanese.

"I'll deal with him," Jonas tells Eva. "Find Kobayashi."

"You're assuming he didn't evacuate with the others," she cautions.

"More like *hoping like hell*," Jonas corrects as he makes for the reception desk.

Minutes later, Jonas and Eva ride an elevator in solitude. The tower's technology makes the ascent whisper quiet and conveys the feeling that they are ascending to heaven itself. While CERN's Large Hadron Collider had been constructed horizontally and spanned two countries, the Spire's Linear Accelerator has been built vertically, running down the core of the massive tower and deep into the earth.

"Lucky the elevator is working," Eva remarks.

"It's not luck," Jonas says. "It's seventy thousand yen." Eva stares at him quizzically. "I bribed the guard to turn the elevators back on."

Eva appears impressed by his forethought. She reaches into her purse, pulls out a small box tied with a red ribbon, and hands it to him.

Jonas studies the box, turning it over in his hands. "What's this?"

Eva stares at it in mock fascination. "Hmm. It appears to be a gift of some kind."

The echo of his distant past gnaws at him. He wills himself to ignore it, unties the ribbon, and opens the box. He pulls out a hand-knit patch of some kind. Its stitching, as delicate as air, forms the shape of an infinity symbol formed by a snake eating its own tail. An Ouroboros. Just like—

"Just like your tattoo," Eva says. "It's all cotton. Natural fibers. It should . . . make the trip with you."

Jonas looks up at her, moved beyond words. This woman he loves. This woman he rejected in the hope of another.

"I wanted you to have something that reminds you of me," Eva explains.

Jonas looks down at the Ouroboros, then back up at her. "I don't need a reminder," he says, meaning every word. His eyes tell her what words feel inadequate to express: *I'll never forget you.*

Guilt wells within him. Of all the things he's done to get back to Amanda, he regrets nothing more than the pain he's caused this woman whose love he doesn't deem himself worthy of. He opens his mouth to say as much. And that's when the elevator stops with a jolt.

"The universe?" Eva asks.

"Or just bad luck. The universe might just snap the cable and send us plummeting."

"That's not funny."

Jonas shrugs—*it's a little funny*—and reaches for the doors. He hopes he can pry them open with his hands and is rewarded for his wish. They're stuck between floors, and he can see the outer doors. He sets to work opening those.

"How do you know how to do that?" Eva asks.

"I watched someone do this kind of thing back in Switzerland, several universes ago," Jonas says, stretching to reach the outer doors, which ultimately give with an echoing *shunk.* Jonas holds them open and looks to Eva. "Ladies first."

"I see they also have sexism in your home universe."

"Yes," Jonas retorts, "but there they call it 'chivalry.'"

Eva chuckles and heaves herself up and out of the elevator. Jonas follows her, extricating himself from the moribund elevator car. A sign tells them they're on the ninety-ninth floor.

"Seventy-five floors to go," Eva says, pointing to the stairwell. "Guess the universe wants you to get your exercise."

The stairs recede beneath their feet as they trudge upward. Eva takes the lead, and Jonas watches from behind as her legs piston up and down. They're barely three floors into their ascent when his lungs start to burn in protest, but Eva's stride keeps its regular rhythm.

"Have you thought about what happens after you find her?" she asks.

Jonas has to catch his breath. Speaking is harder than he expected. "What . . . do you mean?"

"If the universe really is trying to stop you, what makes you think *it* will stop once you find Amanda?"

The thought had never occurred to Jonas. It brings a chill. "I told you, I'm still trying to figure out the universe," he deflects.

"I'm serious." The ease with which she's talking as they climb feels like a taunt. "Your reward for making it to Amanda could just be a lifetime of—I don't know how to put it—universal mischief."

It's hard not for Jonas to feel some irritation that Eva is bringing this up now. Is this some final attempt to dissuade him? Does she expect him to abandon his crusade right at the point when he's so close to its end? "I don't know, Eva," he snaps, gasping.

"I'm sorry if I—"

"My hope is," he explains, forcing softness back into his tone, "that after the waveform collapse that results from my being reunited with Amanda occurs, the universe will return to homeostasis."

"Are you just throwing science at me now?"

Yes. But he doesn't say that. Instead, he admits, "The truth is I don't know what's going to happen. This whole"—he searches for the right word—"phenomenon was unexpected. But maybe my understanding about universal destiny was too simplistic. Perhaps the universe isn't always consistent about the results it favors. After all, this is the same universe that compelled me to work on the Many Worlds Proof in the first place."

"That sounds a bit like rationalization."

"Because it is," he concedes. "But if destiny is real, then I have to believe that *hope* is too."

THREE YEARS AGO

Jonas's paper, "The Many Worlds Proof: Mathematical Evidence of the Existence of Parallel Universes," had been selected for publication in the *Journal of Applied & Computational Mathematics*. Although regularly listed among the world's top ten quantum mechanics journals, its editor had been the last to consider Jonas's work and the only one to commit to publishing it.

Victor's reach within the academic community was wide, touching every journal of renown, and the shadow he cast was long, dimming any and all prospects for publication. Worse, Victor dangled the threat of bitter and protracted litigation, and few editors had the stomach for the kind of trench warfare they knew he was capable of.

In the end, though, it only required one courageous editor and the power of Jonas's idea, which proved too compelling to ignore. Proof of the existence of a multiverse had the power to alter humanity's perception of its own existence, a shift in perspective no less radical than when Nicolaus Copernicus proposed heliocentrism and ousted Earth from the center of the universe.

The ramifications of Jonas's work were just as seismic, the equivalent of proving the existence of gravity. The practical applications were endless, and the moral dilemmas were boundless. Chief among both was the feasibility of travel to one of these sister universes. It was an axiom as old as humanity that once a destination is discovered, there immediately follows the desire to reach it. Would it be possible to visit these alternate realities? *Should* it be possible? Jonas knew he had opened Pandora's box. But he knew with equal conviction that that is what scientists do, trusting that humanity is prepared to weather the aftermath.

In the weeks leading up to publication, Jonas spent hours ensconced in the New York Public Library, copyediting and fact-checking and pressure testing every word, equation, and idea. The hours flew by while Jonas was cocooned in the main reading room, pecking away on his MacBook. He returned home every night to the new apartment, a co-op on the Upper West Side that he and Amanda had bought.

The place had been Jonas's idea, a gambit to get Amanda's mind off their setback. "Setback" was the word they'd tacitly agreed to use during the increasingly rare circumstances when they talked about the difficulty Amanda would have getting pregnant. "Difficulty" was another term they agreed upon. The word maintained a patina of hope, the possibility of possibility, better than "unlikelihood" or "inability." Unfortunately, the apartment felt more like a consolation prize than a home. Worse, and Jonas had only come to grasp this in hindsight, their home had only one bedroom, and the absence of a second served as a sad reminder that they wouldn't need one.

Jonas had wanted children. He wanted a family. He wanted to share the love he felt for Amanda with one or more children. So he'd proposed adoption. Amanda admitted that the idea had crossed her mind, too, but she wasn't ready to go there yet. Thinking about it would make their "setback," their "difficulty," a reality. She had scant hope of victory but wasn't yet prepared to surrender.

Whenever they were together, Jonas would stare at her, his gaze turning more diagnostic as he carefully examined every aspect of her mood, wary of hairline cracks or fissures in her affect. He could see it weighed on her but was unable to stop. He fought against the fear that he was losing her and consoled himself with platitudes. *This is all in your head. Time heals all wounds. Stop worrying, and take things one step at a time.* Was it possible that after two years of telling Amanda he loved her too much, it was actually true? That there was a limit to how much one person can love another without smothering the other?

Apparently. Because when Jonas returned home one night, he found the envelope. It was cherry colored and nearly square, propped on the kitchen counter with his name written in Amanda's angular print, sharp and precise. He could feel paper inside, folded in quarters, and something else. Small and round and untethered. It slid around inside the envelope, and Jonas felt his heart clutch.

Dread rose within him as he tore the envelope open. Amanda's engagement ring slid into his hand. He heard himself make a sound like a wounded animal. It wasn't the noise he imagined whenever he'd pictured the world ending.

NOW

Victor's Cray has been on the hunt for days, scouring the multiverse for signs of Jonas's tether and its signature neutrino emissions. With each processing cycle that passes without success, Victor's belief that Jonas is marooned or dead grows. As the Cray combs through universe after universe, reality after reality, without finding its quarry, Victor works to convince himself that his holy war against Jonas might really be over.

His mind—always prodigious, always active—begins to meander. He has the reconstruction of his life to consider, the rebuilding of his career. He could continue to live off his divorce settlement, but he knows he's not built for the life of a dilettante. Eventually, the thought of a Nobel Prize beckons. Surely, the scales of cosmic justice cannot be balanced until Victor receives the same accolades that have been bestowed upon Jonas. And why not? Jonas stole his work, and that theft drove Victor to improve upon it. Jonas won the Nobel for a series of equations that proved the existence of parallel worlds, but Victor has invented the means not only to map them, as his Cray is doing this very minute, but also to travel to them, and with great precision. This achievement overshadows what the Nobel Committee lauded Jonas for by several orders of magnitude. Jonas may have proved the theoretical existence of fire, but Victor *invented* it, a discovery with no less potential to change the world.

Soon he's filling notebooks with ideas for applications. Historians will pack libraries with books about alternate histories. A cure for cancer could be discovered in the infinite multitude Victor will open the door to. He'll bring fusion—sustainable, clean energy to change the world—from a parallel Earth where it's been perfected. Whole new technologies will be made possible from the curation of inventions from other universes. "Crowdsourcing" will be replaced by "reality sourcing." Victor will give the world the means to become a utopia. Eventually, the Nobel Prize feels too small an ambition.

As Victor writes and thinks and writes some more, as the notebooks—crammed with new ideas—begin to pile up, Jonas becomes a distant memory. Victor once heard that "hate is a nutritious emotion; one can live off it for years." And that's been true for him. But with the idea that Jonas is dead, and Victor's future is incandescent with possibility, hate and its sibling, vengeance, leave his heart. He feels lighter. Younger. He toys with the thought of restarting his life. He thinks of calling Phaedra.

Then the Cray awakens, and everything changes.

The algorithm was one of the first Victor wrote for the supercomputer. For years, it's been buried beneath strata of newer code. He wrote it as a baseline for the detection of different universes, a way of drawing a signal from the noise of the cosmos. Universes, he discovered, have their own quantum signatures, each as unique as a snowflake. Such signatures are more complex than a billion strands of DNA, but then, that's what he had the Cray for.

And today, the Cray reports an anomaly unlike anything Victor has ever seen. Data floods the computer display in the arcane language he himself invented, but it makes no sense. He tries to draw meaning from what he's seeing, but he might as well be blind. The reason, he discerns, is that the Cray itself doesn't know what to make of what it's detecting. It's trying to apply Victor's algorithm to a phenomenon it wasn't built to understand, like trying to talk to a dog by barking at it.

At first, Victor worries this is somehow his doing, that a version of himself in some neighboring reality attempted to put one of his ideas into practice and, in so doing, broke the world or tore the fabric of spacetime. The thought that he might not have his own doppelgänger—his own counterpart who found the same keys to unlock the secrets of the multiverse—was the purest form of narcissism. Of course there's another Victor out there with the ability to slip realities, and of course he's done something horrible.

A coldness clutches Victor's chest as he dives deeper and deeper into the data the Cray is throwing back at him. If he can't determine what exactly is happening, he has no hope of fixing the multiverse he fears his twin has broken. He writes hundreds of lines of code, fashioning newer and newer algorithms, trying to bring the problem into focus. He's a Copernicus, working to craft a more accurate vision of the universe, but he fears that the "telescope" he is constructing isn't equal to the task.

He works feverishly, without food or drink or sleep. A kind of madness overtakes him. At least, he begins to fear it might be madness. How else can he explain the data his new algorithms have conjured? Even in his own mind, the thought sounds irrational: *The universe he is studying appears to be in an act of open rebellion.* The idea doesn't even make sense. How does a universe rebel? And against what? But the closer Victor examines the event—a cascade of events, really—the more solid, the more accurate that interpretation feels. The universe is reacting to some unnatural stimuli. He envisions a stone thrown into a pond.

And then it hits him.

The anomaly isn't him. No version of himself caused what he's witnessing. The stone in the pond *doesn't belong.* The universe is reacting to a foreign incursion, the way an infected organism spikes a fever in reaction to a virus.

Victor has no doubt what the virus is. *Who.*

He hears the siren song of the Nobel Prize and tries to return himself to thoughts of research, of reconstruction and reconciliation. He tries to put Jonas Cullen out of his mind. The man isn't worth the obsession, Victor reminds himself. Jonas has stolen too many years as it is. *Let it go,* some voice inside him beseeches. The voice sounds like Phaedra. *It's over. Or it can be if you want it to be. All you need is to move on.* She makes it sound so easy. Like lying down. Surrendering to gravity.

And he knows it would be easy. More than easy. He wants to let go. He is tired of his crusade. Pursuing a vendetta is exhausting business. Vengeance takes its toll on the vengeful.

He turns again to the Cray and thinks of unplugging the beast. Letting go would be that easy. He'll turn it off and call Phaedra. He'll do it right now. The late hour doesn't matter. He'll wake her up if he must.

The Cray's power cord runs to an industrial outlet Victor had to have specially installed, snaking past the desk where his keyboard and monitor lay, where he has logged countless hours in pursuit of his blood feud with Jonas. En route to the outlet, he catches a glimpse of his reflection in the monitor. He doesn't recognize the man staring back at him. And if his own reflection is a stranger, there's only one reason why, one person responsible.

Beneath the reflection, data waterfalls, tempting Victor with the location of his nemesis. Before he's even aware, he's sitting down at the workstation, translating the information the Cray has surfaced into a specific reality, a universe where he can find Jonas and end this. He's close. It's almost over, he tells himself. Why would he abandon his crusade now, when he is so close to its end? This will be done by the end of the week, he tells himself, bargaining like an alcoholic weighing whether to enter a liquor store. The end of the week. Then he'll call Phaedra. But first he has work to do.

NOW

Jonas and Eva spill out of the stairwell onto the Spire's 174th floor. The landing is mostly white with accents of silver and pale maple. The sky outside is framed by a window of curtain wall glass, offering a view of pure blue beyond. They are more than half a mile up.

A man waiting by the elevator turns, surprised to see anyone emerging from the stairwell, which is rarely utilized and was only included in the building's design to comply with the local fire code.

The man is in his fifties. Japanese, with gray flecking his hair and a goatee. His affect, the way his eyes soak in detail and exude intelligence, identifies him as a fellow academic. A Spire identification card, laminated with his picture, hangs from a lanyard around his neck. It reads **KOBAYASHI, DAISUKE.**

"Dr. Kobayashi," Eva says, extending her hand. "Thank you so much for seeing us."

Kobayashi looks to the stairwell door, mouth agape. "How many stairs did you just walk up?"

"Too many," Eva says. She's still short of breath.

"Due to the earthquake?"

"In a manner of speaking," Jonas deadpans.

Eva gestures to him. "This is my friend, Dr. Cullen."

Jonas shakes Kobayashi's hand. "Thank you for your help, Doctor. And for not evacuating with the rest of the personnel."

"I had to stay to satisfy my curiosity," Kobayashi says, studying Jonas. "Dr. Stamper asserts that you're quite accomplished in the field of quantum theory. But the only Dr. Cullen I was able to find on the internet is a seventy-three-year-old ob-gyn in Prague." Jonas can't tell whether he's suspicious or curious or, perhaps, both.

He offers an innocent shrug. "You know what the situation is like back in . . ." He nearly says "America." "Back in my country. It helps to stay off the internet as much as is practicable," Jonas says, employing the cover story he'd rehearsed with Eva.

"Under better circumstances, Dr. Cullen would be considered a renowned physicist," Eva chimes in, playing her part.

"In a parallel universe, maybe," Jonas ad-libs.

Kobayashi obligingly chuckles. "In any case, I have a colleague who has a colleague who owes Dr. Stamper a favor, so . . ." He spreads his hands. *Here we are.* "She said you wanted to see the SLA?"

"SLA?"

"Superconducting Linear Accelerator," Kobayashi explains patiently, albeit with a hint of surprise that Jonas isn't familiar with the term.

"Yes, exactly. Didn't know the acronym," Jonas covers.

Kobayashi gestures down the hall. "This way," he says, leading them out to a massive circular steel walkway that runs inside the circumference of the entire building. "We call this the 'Upper Outer Ring,'" Kobayashi says, playing tour guide. "It's used mainly as an observation deck."

"I can see why," Eva says. "This is incredible." Her voice echoes slightly in the massive cavern.

Kobayashi points to a steel tube that wraps around the inside of the Outer Ring, coiling around and down the SLA like a snake around a caduceus. "And that's the *Inner* Ring. It's how the SLA itself is accessed."

Plunging through the center of the Inner Ring is a vertical channel of steel. Veins of cable run along its surface. The complexity of the technology is enormous, but overall, it appears similar to CERN's Large Hadron Collider. The main difference, Jonas notes, is that whereas the

LHC is arranged in an underground loop, the SLA thrusts straight down through the Spire's core 130 miles or more, he suspects. If he's correct, the construction alone would be a remarkable achievement, surpassing his own universe's record for underground digging by more than 99 percent.

"It's breathtaking," Eva observes.

"You picked an interesting day to visit," Kobayashi says as he leads them around the Outer Ring. "We haven't had an earthquake here in over a year. Then it stopped, as if someone just snapped their fingers." He illustrates this by snapping his own. "No warning. No aftershocks. Remarkable."

"Was any damage done to the SLA?" Jonas asks, his interest more than academic.

"No. It runs over one hundred miles below ground, so it's extremely well anchored. Essentially, the building just shakes around it."

"I'm surprised there's not more security," Jonas notes. "Metal detectors, that sort of thing."

Kobayashi chuckles. "It wouldn't do much good to stage a robbery here. The lightest component of the SLA weighs seven thousand tons. No, the only things here to steal, I'm afraid, are ideas."

"What about security cameras?"

Kobayashi wrinkles his brow. "We had to take them out. The electronics were wreaking all manner of havoc with the equipment." Then suspicion worms its way back into his tone. "Why so many questions about our security?"

Jonas's hand lashes out, and Eva holds Kobayashi steady as Jonas presses the cloth to the scientist's mouth. Kobayashi's eyes roll back to white courtesy of the chloroform Jonas cooked up in the kitchen of his rental apartment. He slumps, and they ease him down to the steel floor.

"No reason," Jonas answers.

Two minutes later, Jonas and Eva are heading along the catwalk toward the Upper Inner Ring. The tunnel is fronted by an enclosed structure that looks to be the size of a small room. Jonas fears its door is locked and hopes the key ring he lifted off the unconscious Dr. Kobayashi contains the requisite key.

"How long will he be out?" Eva asks.

"Ten minutes, assuming the universe doesn't have any more surprises for me. You'll have some explaining to do once I'm gone."

"Oh, I've got that covered," she says, her voice light. "I was your hostage."

Jonas nods at the simplicity of that and asks himself why he hadn't thought of it. They arrive at the Inner Ring's entrance, and it's unlocked. Kobayashi hadn't been kidding about the Spire's lax security. Jonas heaves open the steel door and heads inside.

He's moving with such urgency that he doesn't see the men standing there, side by side. Reflections. Twins. Their faces identical in every respect, save that one's beard is trimmed back to a goatee. One wears khaki combat fatigues, the other black wool and Kevlar. Both wear tether bracelets.

Both look like Macon.

Jonas feels his stomach bottom out with the horrible understanding that Victor has sent them, each from a different universe. The energy required, the sheer effort, is almost beyond calculation. Such is the intensity of Victor's vendetta.

Jonas commands his body to move—turn, lock the door behind them, figure out another way into the SLA—but his feet are rooted. Every artery crackles with adrenaline, but he's frozen. Vulnerable. Trapped.

"Dr. Cullen," one says.

Jonas feels Eva tense behind him. A short gasp escapes her lips.

"We're here with a message," the other Macon intones. "Turn around. Leave. Never come back. Do that, and he'll let you live."

Jonas stands his ground.

"He's avoided killing you up until now," the first Macon says. "This is about karma for him. His version of it, at least. And he hasn't wanted to put your death on his ledger."

How considerate, Jonas thinks, wholly uninterested in the moral calculations of a malignant narcissist.

"But he will," the second Macon adds. "If that's what it takes to stop you. So . . . leave. Final warning."

Jonas opens his mouth to speak, but he has to strain to keep fear from seeping into his voice. "This isn't your concern. I know Victor is paying you, and probably paying you well. But this is between him and me. Now . . . *step aside.*"

The two Macons don't confer. They don't glance toward each other or engage in any other form of silent communication. They just charge toward Jonas in unison, their faces expressionless, betraying no anger or affect of any kind. *This is just a job to them,* Jonas notes. Killing him will produce no more emotion than taking out the trash.

Without warning, a thunderclap echoes in the chamber. The Macon in Kevlar staggers back as the one in khakis surges toward Jonas . . . and past him. Jonas spins toward him just in time to see the man's head snap back in a grotesque replay of Macon's demise back in Switzerland. This time, though, the entire base of his skull explodes and pulls Macon backward like a string.

Then Jonas notices Eva with a gun in her hand. It's a Glock, just like the one the original Macon once gave him. She holds it in a two-handed grip, her stance wide. She's had training—that much is clear. Her expression holds a steely-eyed confidence as she pulls the trigger again, and Jonas watches the top of the Glock trombone back and forth as it spits out a shell casing, which pinwheels away.

The next shot strikes the other Macon in the center of his forehead. He collapses next to his doppelgänger, instantly dead. The two Macons share the same vacant stare.

Eva lowers the gun. "Are you okay?"

Eva shoulders past him toward the entrance of the Inner Ring. "C'mon," she says. "Someone might have heard those shots. We have to keep moving."

As he follows her into the Inner Ring, his power of speech returns. "You brought a gun?"

"I *bought* a gun," she corrects him, "after you told me about the mad scientist—literally, a very *mad* scientist—and his mercenary. It wasn't easy, but I figured it'd be worth the trouble."

"Wasn't easy? Japan's gun laws are among the most stringent in the world."

"*Your* world maybe."

Jonas looks back at the pair of Macons. "You killed those men—"

"From what you've told me, there are millions of others where those two came from."

"What I mean is . . . where'd you learn to shoot a gun?"

"My husband taught me. He wanted me to be safe." Her voice grows distant. "I don't really want to talk about him right now."

They walk in silence, following the curve of the tunnel, skulking in haste for what seems like half a mile before the tunnel's curve reveals the presence of two security guards. Both men in their early thirties. Both armed.

Jonas's adrenaline spikes. One of the guards reaches for his sidearm while the other keys his walkie-talkie's shoulder microphone.

"*Roku-Gōki kara chūō e. Sekushon san-hachi ni shin'nyū-sha ni-mei. Otome,*" he reports in rapid-fire Japanese.

Eva throws Jonas a panicked look. *What do we do?* Shooting the Macons was one thing, but the cold-blooded murder of two security guards doing their duty is quite another. Before Jonas can answer, the guard with the sidearm points it straight at Eva.

"*Anata no buki o otose,*" he orders.

Eva doesn't seem to understand whether he wants her to put her hands up, get down on the floor, put her gun down, or some combination of the three.

"*Anata no buki o otose,*" he repeats, only louder. As if lack of volume is the only reason she can't understand him. He takes a mighty step forward and slaps the gun out of her hand. It clatters to the floor, and he kicks it down the length of the tunnel, back in the direction where Jonas and Eva came from.

Meanwhile, his partner spins Jonas around, pressing him against the tunnel wall. The armed guard does the same with Eva.

"Wait. I can explain," Jonas says, but the protestation sounds pathetic.

"Ashi o hiroge. Buki o motte imasu ka?"

The guard with the walkie-talkie begins frisking Jonas. His partner confiscates Eva's purse. Both maneuvers are executed with more violence than seems necessary.

The armed guard tears through the contents of Eva's purse, producing a small black Moleskine notebook. He rifles through the pages, finding them all covered in Jonas's baroque equations and crude schematic drawings of the tether's inner workings. *"Kore wa nan da,"* he demands. *Tell me what this is.*

Jonas asked Eva to bring the notebook "just in case," a stopgap to buttress the formulae inked on his arms. *Belt and suspenders.* Now, though, the calculations and sketches look like the ramblings of a madman, the plans of a would-be bomber.

His mind churns, working the problem, trying to think of a way out of this mess. Dozens of excuses and explanations and apologies flood his consciousness, but he doesn't even know if these men speak English. He contemplates overpowering them, using surprise to his advantage, but the guard's grip is too strong.

Three gunshots ring out, echoing in the tunnel, made louder by its confines. Jonas's heart jumps. *Did the other guard shoot Eva?* He looks over, panicked, but she's okay. His relief is quickly pushed aside by confusion. If the guards didn't fire, then who did?

The man pressing Jonas against the wall uses his free hand to trigger his shoulder mic. *"Chūō, are wa nanideshita ka? Jūsei ga kikoemashita . . . ,"* he says with a frightened urgency, apparently as unnerved by the gunfire as Jonas is.

The only reply is a fourth gunshot, this one filtered through the radio, and the sharp crackle of static. The man shoots a worried look at his partner. Jonas can see that they're both scared. The Spire is a scientific facility. Their presence is for insurance purposes only. Their guns are for show. They would see more action guarding a cathedral.

With the guard distracted, Jonas throws his head backward, the back of his skull striking the guard in the face. He staggers back, dazed, and Jonas headbutts him again. A pinwheel of tiny fireflies crosses his vision, but he stays conscious. The guard does not.

As the man drops, his partner bulldogs toward Jonas, instantly forgetting Eva and, apparently, the fact that he has a gun. Eva is screaming at Jonas—*"What are you doing?"*—but his focus is on the guard hurling himself at him. Macon prepared him for this, taught him to turn an opponent's inertia against him, to use his environment as a weapon. Jonas grabs the guard by his uniform and uses the man's momentum to send him careening into the wall. He might as well have hit the guard with the tunnel. The man falls, unconscious, inches from his partner.

"Oh my God," Eva repeats over and over.

Klaxons begin bellowing, and the overhead lighting unexpectedly changes, instantly bathing the entire tunnel in red.

"We have to move," Jonas says.

But Eva seems rooted in fear and confusion.

"Eva," he reiterates, "we have to go."

She turns to retrieve her gun, but Jonas stops her. "There's no time."

Almost on cue, more gunshots ring out. Louder this time, which means closer. Jonas darkens. Fear challenges him. He wills himself to avoid its grip.

"How many Macons could he bring here?" Eva asks.

"I don't know," Jonas says. "As many as he could construct tethers for, I suppose." He grabs Eva's wrist. "It doesn't matter. We have to keep moving." As he pulls her, he sees one of the guards clambering to his feet.

Jonas virtually drags Eva down the long corridor, hearing the guard's footfalls—the machine-gun steps of a man in better shape—closing in. As they run, the tunnel begins to slope away, the path corkscrewing downward. Gravity is a wind at their backs, pushing them on.

Then a door appears to their right. Steel, with a metal push bar. Jonas throws himself into it, hoping it's not locked. It isn't. *Thank heaven for small favors.* It swings open, and he explodes out onto a narrow steel catwalk, one of several that spiral out from the towering SLA to connect with the Inner Ring's corkscrew, like spokes on a bicycle wheel.

A low frequency thrum greets them. It's not generated by the power surging through the SLA but by the air flowing through the massive cavern more than two thousand feet above ground. The catwalk feels as slender as a tightrope, and the shaft beneath them appears bottomless. With a drop greater than one hundred miles, it might as well be.

The view reminds Jonas of those precious hours spent on rooftops with Amanda, tempting fate, embracing vertigo. Without that experience, he'd be gripped by nerves and nausea right now, frozen by panic. He offers up a silent prayer of gratitude to his wife.

With Eva right beside him and, he imagines, the guard not far behind, Jonas surges forward, faster than is sensible, given the altitude. His footfalls tap out a cadence as he flies down the catwalk.

Then his momentum stalls at a pair of shoes in front of him. He follows them up and sees the gun. The same one that shot Amanda. The sight of it resurrects the memory and conjures anger. His gaze continues to rise, but the face he sees doesn't belong to a Macon.

It's Victor.

Whatever humanity his nemesis once possessed has vanished like a mirage. In its place, Jonas sees nothing but acid. Hate. A man devoid of mercy and thriving on vengeance. A man not only capable of committing murder, but hell bent on it.

THREE YEARS AGO

The note from Amanda was one page in her precise handwriting marching down the paper. Blue ballpoint ink dug little divots through to the opposite side, which Jonas could feel beneath his fingers as he held the instrument of his heartbreak.

There were details, of course, but they seemed insignificant. Amanda had been feeling every emotion that he was. The mystery of why they had never discussed children before. The riddle of why the topic should be so important now. Jonas's penetrative staring and Amanda's remorse for being bothered by it. The feeling that the train of their relationship had been derailed. Amanda articulated his own emotions with greater precision than he had been able to. How ironic, Jonas thought, that they would remain in sync even as they grew apart.

The letter ended with Amanda informing him that she was moving out. It didn't disclose where she would be staying.

About a week before, Jonas's editor had begun tempting fate. The name "Nobel" kept coming up in their exchanges. If the magnitude of Jonas's work held up under scrutiny, she said, a Nobel Prize in Physics was inevitable. Jonas remembered shuddering on the phone when she said the word. *Inevitable.* It was a unique kind of torture that as his professional life rose, phoenixlike, from the ashes of Victor's smear campaign, his relationship with Amanda would rupture. But maybe, he thought, that was how life was, that there was an equilibrium to its highs and lows. The universe favors certain outcomes. Who's to say the corollary isn't that the universe imposes homeostasis on one's fortunes?

But Jonas refused to accept the will of the universe. He violently rejected the idea that he could only be "so happy," that fate set limits on it. He railed against the thought that he had to choose between a Nobel Prize and Amanda. Even if he did, he would choose her without hesitation. The Nobel was just a slab of metal without her. The existence of a multiverse was a hollow discovery without a world in which they were together.

NOW

"Hyōketsu!" The scream comes from behind Jonas. He glances back to see the guard advancing, his service revolver held in a tenuous two-handed grip that reeks of training. *"Hyōketsu!"* the guard repeats before resorting to English. "Freeze!"

It's unclear which of the other three people on the catwalk he's addressing, but Victor is the one who brings up his gun. He fires twice. Jonas feels the bullets blur past. He turns sharply around, fearing one or both might strike Eva, and he's punished for the quick movement by a reassertion of vertigo. The world sways.

The metal door sparks, and the guard flies back, his gun tumbling out of his hands. The dead man and his gun hit the catwalk at almost the same time, producing a metallic clank and a muscular thud, a perverse call and response. The gun dances on the steel pathway as the guard rolls off the catwalk and plummets in silence. Jonas hears the wet sound of the body ricocheting off one of the lower catwalks and then . . . nothing.

He swivels his head to Eva, needing to reassure himself that she's safe. Apparently intuiting this, she bobs her head slowly, keeping a cautious watch on Victor.

Jonas turns back to him. His entire body feels tight. Cables under tension. Every muscle taut. Every cell screaming. He wishes he hadn't stopped Eva from going back for her gun.

"This isn't personal," Victor says with a pathological failure to appreciate that his vendetta is nothing *but* personal. His voice barely rises above a whisper, and Jonas almost can't hear him in the din of the massive chamber. Victor's tone is distant. His body is here, but he sounds as if he's speaking from millions of miles away.

Jonas thinks to speak, to reason with his former friend. But all he can think of is the gun in Victor's grip. All he can see in front of him is Amanda bleeding onto the sidewalk, her eyes filled with tears and a sad confusion about what was happening to her. Jonas swallows, and he tastes metal. Anger. Adrenaline.

"I told you to accept the judgment of the universe," Victor says. "I told you that, remember?" He sounds plaintive, almost wounded.

Jonas measures the distance between himself and Victor, calculating whether he can close it before Victor can raise and fire his gun. His own wrath, his need for vengeance and justice for Amanda, eclipses any survival instinct, and he would throw himself at Victor right now but for the chance that an errant shot might strike Eva.

"I told you to accept the judgment of the universe," Victor repeats. He sounds disappointed, as though this is for Jonas's own good. And then his voice grows cold and hard, with a terrifying ferocity. "But then I realized . . . *I* am that judgment."

Jonas watches, transfixed, as Victor raises the gun, his finger coiling around the trigger. The barrel levels straight at Jonas's heart. From someplace far away, some distant country, a part of Jonas rages and commands him to do something, anything. It can't end this way. Not like this. He reminds himself—his mind bellowing a primal scream—that Amanda is waiting for him in another reality.

Without thinking, Jonas drives headlong at Victor. Victor's finger is squeezing the trigger, but Jonas wills himself to believe that he can get to Victor faster than Victor can fire.

He can.

Jonas collides with Victor, angling so that his shoulder, bone under a thin canopy of muscle, drives into Victor's sternum. On impact, he hears the air rush from Victor's lungs. The sharp *crack* of the gun stings Jonas's ears—Victor's managed to get a shot off—and at this range, it's as loud as the end of the world.

Pressing his advantage, Jonas pushes all his weight down on Victor, forcing them both down to the catwalk. They land hard, but Victor gets the worst of it, the catwalk slamming into his back, punctuated by Jonas falling atop him.

Victor lets out a scream of either agony or rage. Jonas can't tell which. The gun, still in Victor's grip, arcs up toward Jonas's head. Jonas catches Victor's wrist with both hands and jerks it back as hard as he can. Once. Twice. Three times. He scratches at Victor's wrist hard enough to draw blood, but Victor does not relinquish his hold.

Jonas jerks his body slightly so that the next time he yanks Victor's arm, Victor's hand is positioned to strike the catwalk's steel edge.

Victor wails in pain. Jonas is sure he hears the crack of bone. But all that matters is that Victor *let go of the damn gun*, so Jonas drives his arm down again. And again, the bones in Victor's hand snap, sounding like popcorn popping. Victor howls once more, and this time the gun falls from his shattered hand and plunges down the shaft.

Victor moans in a paroxysm of agony. Jonas pushes himself off and tries to stand. His head feels light. His chest heaves and falls, and he realizes he's hyperventilating. He commands himself to slow his breathing, but his lungs rebuff him. Too much adrenaline. Too much rage.

He watches Victor roll on the catwalk, his good hand cradling the broken one, undone by a level of physical anguish he's had no experience with, the novelty almost more debilitating than the pain.

"Jonas."

The cavern's thrum is so loud and Jonas's breathing so rapid that at first he doesn't hear his name.

"Jonas."

It's Eva.

Jonas pivots. He knows he shouldn't turn his back to Victor, but the way Eva spoke his name contained an unsettling amalgam of fear and weakness. A disquieting echo of the past.

And stranger still, Eva isn't where she should be. Panic leaks in as Jonas's eyes dart down to find Eva lying on the catwalk. Her fingers are laced across her midsection, blood snaking through them. Her breathing is rapid and shallow. She looks afraid.

The world spins. Jonas's breath won't catch. He's lightheaded. He wants to vomit. He wants to scream. He wants to cry.

"No." The word is barely audible, the moan of a dying animal. He drops to his knees beside Eva. "Just—try not to talk, Eva," he says. "Just breathe. Just breathe."

As Eva does her best to comply, Jonas considers her abdomen. The gunshot wound glistens, spurting blood with each beat of her panicked heart. His hands work to stanch the bleeding, but he feels Eva's warmth flowing between his fingers.

"Jonas," she says, each syllable a labor, "I feel cold."

He starts ripping away at his shirt, tearing strips for a makeshift bandage, but she stops him, raising her hand to his. She looks toward the massive spear of the SLA. "You have to go."

"I'm not leaving you." *Again.* If Jonas knows anything, he knows this.

"*I'm* leaving," she whispers.

The words, a reverberation of the past, are a kidney punch, a confirmation that Jonas is witnessing another Eva's death.

"Don't be sad," she says. A smile blooms on her face, an expression of contentment. "There are other realities where I'm alive."

Jonas tries to blink back tears, but they race down his face.

"And in one of them," she says, "I'm with . . ." She doesn't finish the thought. *Can't* finish it. But the idea has left her with the hint of a smile, even though she's gone.

Gone *again.*

Jonas stays with her, kneeling as though in prayer. His face wet with tears. Her blood on his hands, literally and figuratively. Another death in his personal ledger.

But it was all for nothing, he reminds himself, if he stays. He has to go. He has to leave. Right now. *One step at a time.*

As he rises, he hears the scream. A single rage-filled, animalistic syllable. Jonas is barely to his feet when Victor tackles him back down to the catwalk. He rains punches down on Jonas with his one good hand, screaming and cursing, an emeritus professor reduced to a rabid dog.

Jonas pours all his anger and rage and hate—plus his grief for both Amandas and both Evas—into his two hands. He balls them into fists and hurls them at Victor. In the distance, the Klaxon still blares, providing a perverse soundtrack to the brawl. Even Victor's splintered hand gets in on the action, oblivious to the broken bones, his own rage as potent as Novocain. Jonas withers under the assault. Each punch drives the back of his head against the steel catwalk. He throws his hands up, trying to block Victor's onslaught. He begins to pass out.

And then he sees a tincture of black. A small slab of metal resting on the catwalk above his head. Distant, possibly out of reach. As Victor pounds away with his fists, Jonas keeps one arm over his head as a shield while his other hand reaches for it. It's far. Too far.

Jonas stretches. Pain isn't a factor anymore. His fingertips graze and swipe at the object, causing it to pivot farther out of reach. His fingers splay and flail. *Please,* his mind screams. *Please.*

Maybe a silent plea is all it takes because suddenly the object is in Jonas's hand, his fingers curling around it, feeling its solid form.

The security guard's gun.

Jonas brings it around, startling Victor, who is still atop him but no longer in control. Jonas's finger pulls against the trigger. He thinks of Eva. He thinks of Amanda, bleeding to death in his arms on a patch of Manhattan concrete.

"You won't," Victor says with more confidence than Jonas expects.

"Macon taught me how," Jonas reminds him.

"I mean you won't *do it*."

Jonas tastes bile, his anger fueled by Victor's arrogance.

"You're many things," Victor says. "A thief. A plagiarist." Venom in his voice. He shakes his head, lips curled in disgust. "But not a killer."

"You're right," Jonas says, wondering if it's true, before he smashes the gun across Victor's head, knocking him over and rendering him unconscious, his arms hanging over the edge of the catwalk. "But I needed the gun to knock you out with."

Rising to his feet, Jonas is tempted to enjoy the sight of Victor lying on the catwalk, bruised and out cold. But then he hears boots striking metal, alerting him that reinforcements from Hiroshima's National Police Agency are on their way.

He moves fast, dragging the deceased security guard's bulk toward the door. Rigor mortis hasn't set in yet, and the corpse's pliability makes it difficult to maneuver. Not for nothing do they call it "dead weight." The sounds of the police's approach grow louder. Jonas tells himself that the echo of the tunnel is magnifying the clatter, that he has time yet. He marshals his strength and heaves the guard up so that the corpse is propped against the door, turning the man into a macabre makeshift doorstop.

Jonas leapfrogs over Victor and races down the length of the catwalk toward the Linear Accelerator. His nerves, already humming like a metropolis's power grid, begin to redline. This is the most perilous moment in his entire plan. His original incursion into CERN was aided by the fact that he had been there multiple times. But the Spire isn't just foreign to him. Despite the scant details he pulled off this universe's internet, it might as well be an alien landscape.

Then he sees a small alphanumeric keypad, camouflaged by a tangle of cables and a cluster of circuit boards. He consults his newest tattoo based on Other Jonas's calculations and compels his fingers to march along the keypad. There is no screen, no monitor, no way of knowing whether he's entering the right data in the right order.

He punches in what he thinks is the last sequence in a series of necessary commands. He spots a green button in the lower right corner of the pad and whispers a single-word prayer. "Please."

He pushes the button.

For five heavy breaths and who-knows-how-many beats of his racing heart, nothing happens. Hopelessness reasserts itself, taunting him with the truth that he was always destined to fail. What hubris could have compelled him to think he could swim against the tide of the universe?

The Linear Accelerator answers with an earthshaking drone so loud and visceral that it feels sprung from the Old Testament. The catwalk vibrates. Jonas is gripped by a feeling of majesty.

Behind him, he hears the martial drumbeat of boots on steel, the metallic ballet of automatic weapons chambering new rounds of ammunition. Jonas doesn't have to turn around to know it's Tokushu Kyūshū Butai, a Special Assault Team, Japan's version of a SWAT unit.

"*Mashin kara hanarete kudasai! Watashitachi ni wa buryoku kōshi ga mitome rarete iru . . .*" the leader commands. When Jonas doesn't comply, the man switches to English. "Get down. We are authorized to use force."

Jonas ignores him. If he's done his job properly, he's shunted the SLA's output to the patch he opened through the access panel, creating a "leak" of quantum energy. But if he moves more than six inches from the spot where he's standing, his body won't be close enough to absorb the Linear Accelerator's output.

"*Kare no atama o neratte. Watashi no meirei ni shitagatte happō suru junbi o shite . . . ,*" the SAT leader says, ordering his men to aim at Jonas's head and await the command to fire.

The cacophony of the SLA is now close to deafening, a low bass that Jonas feels in the center of his chest, almost loud enough to cover the sound of six military-grade assault rifles disengaging their safeties.

Jonas closes his eyes. He calculates that he has three more seconds until the Linear Accelerator unleashes its full potential. Hopefully, it will take the police longer than that to shoot him through the head. The interior of the access panel and its metal casing are suddenly dotted with tiny red lights, which briefly dance before disappearing into the shadow that Jonas casts against the SLA. *Laser sights taking aim at his head and back.*

Jonas remains calm. In three seconds—less—this will all be over. He will either be dead in this universe or alive in another, reunited with Amanda.

"Wait for me," he whispers. "I'm on my way."

The Linear Accelerator generates an earth-shattering thrum that eclipses a blaze of fire as the police unleash their rifles' fury. For a millisecond, Jonas feels his body burn. A bright flash blossoms out from the center of the Linear Accelerator, and for a split second, Jonas thinks it's the most beautiful thing he's ever witnessed.

Then he's flying, hurled back from the SLA. He feels himself slam into the SAT officers, the muzzles of their weapons, hot from their recent discharge, digging into him like tiny brands, before he falls again. The catwalk rises to swat at him, and Jonas feels the impact flip him over. He thrashes, his hands flying in search of the catwalk's edge, but he grasps only air.

And he falls.

THREE YEARS AGO

The Parker New York was an unremarkable hotel on West Fifty-Sixth Street, the kind frequented by business travelers, where every room came equipped with a coffee machine that brewed cups from little plastic pods. Jonas rode the elevator to the seventh floor, padded down the carpeted corridor to room 712, and knocked without hesitation.

He saw a shadow pass over the fish-eye lens embedded in the door. A pregnant pause. He envisioned Amanda on the other side, weighing whether to unlock the dead bolt. She waited long enough that Jonas thought of knocking again, but then the door swung open, and she stood there, framed in the doorway.

"How'd you find me?" She sounded half-amused, more impressed than perturbed.

Jonas shrugged. "I've found you in Manhattan before," he reminded her. "But this time was easier." He held up his iPhone, displaying the Find My Phone app. A small circle with a photo of Amanda floated over the Parker on a map of New York City. "Getting your room number out of the person at the front desk was a little more challenging, though." He pulled out a Verizon phone bill, still in its windowed envelope with her name and their address. "But apparently you *really* wanted 'your assistant' to give this to you." He held up her engagement ring. A tiny star, cast by the overhead lighting, sat atop the diamond. "And this."

Amanda looked at it and glowered slightly. "I can't take that," she said.

Jonas continued to hold it out. "Then take it in trade. For an explanation."

"I wrote everything in my note."

"A *conversation*, then. You owe me that much. You owe *us* that much." Jonas's eyes pleaded with her.

After a moment's consideration, Amanda retreated inside. Jonas stepped in and let the door close behind him. The room was a typical affair, with decor by committee, sweatshop artwork, and a bedspread that looked like patterned vomit. It hurt Jonas that she had chosen to spend time here rather than with him.

Amanda sat on the bed. Jonas remained on his feet. They each waited for the other to talk. Finally, Jonas said, "Everything you wrote, I've felt. Everything."

"Then why do we need this conversation?"

"Because we're wrong. Because all those feelings are temporary. They'll pass."

"They won't."

"They will. We're good together. Maybe we didn't talk about starting a family because there are *a lot* of things we don't talk about. Because we don't *need* to."

She stared down at the carpet. "Do you want the truth?"

Jonas didn't hesitate. "Yes. Of course."

"You want children." The way she said it carried a glimmer of accusation.

"What?"

"On our third date, you talked about your friend Peter. About how you met his baby daughter." Jonas stared back, confused. "The way you talked about holding her . . . your eyes came alive. And I knew in that moment that you desperately wanted to be a father. Even if you didn't know it yourself."

Jonas shook his head. "I *don't* know. I *think* I do. And if you want kids, too, we can have that discussion. We can talk about adopting. But the only thing I know, the *only* thing," he repeated, "is that I want to spend the rest of my life with you."

Tears began to glisten in Amanda's eyes. "I love you too much . . . ," she began.

"I love you more," said Jonas, completing their catechism.

"No." She shook her head. "What I mean is, I love you too much to see you make any compromises. I want you to be with someone who can give you everything you want."

Jonas dropped to one knee to be face to face with her. "*You're* everything I want." He felt like he was begging for his life. He was.

She shook her head again. "You're not being rational."

"No, I'm not. You cured me of that. You cured me of everything. I love you."

She leaned forward to clasp his hands. In her touch, he found the same electricity as when he first saw her on the Columbia University quad. "And I love *you*," she said. "That's why I want more for you than I can hope to give."

"Except you don't get to make that decision," he asserted. "Not alone." Conviction flowed into his voice like molten steel, building in hardness and strength with each passing second. "I'm here. I'm *right here*. Right now. Telling you that all I want—the *only* thing—is to spend the rest of my life with you." He rose slowly. "You want to talk about what I 'deserve?' I'll settle for being taken at my word."

She stood up to meet his gaze. "And what happens when you see another friend's baby? Or a child playing in the park? And you wake up the next morning with regret?"

"The only way I wake up with regret," he said, "is if I wake up and you're not there next to me." He gripped her hands and moved close enough to kiss her. The small channel of air between them felt charged, heavy with emotion and sorrow and attraction. "I love you. And I'm not going anywhere." For months, she'd repeated those words—*I'm not going anywhere*—and this was the moment to return that vow. "I'm. Not. Going. Anywhere."

Her chin rose as she looked up toward him. Her lips parted, and her eyes held an unspoken entreaty. "Then don't go," she whispered before she kissed him.

NOW

Jonas shoots up and is rewarded with a throbbing in his skull. Settling back down, he realizes he's lying on a bed. He inspects his surroundings, expecting to see his makeshift bedroom in the apartment he shares with Eva. But the room is painted white. No wallpaper. No mass-market furniture or symptoms of a long-term rental. Venetian blinds front the windows instead of curtains. A thin white sheet covers him. A tube snakes into his arm, trailing back toward what he assumes is an IV stand.

He's in a hospital.

A new worry strikes him like lightning. He throws off the sheet to find his hand. It's there. The tether. He exhales his relief.

Relaxing back down into the bed, he takes a quick inventory. He survived the onslaught of six assault rifles unleashed at him. He survived a fall from the highest constructed perch in the world. The odds of all this are almost too infinitesimal to contemplate.

He is still absorbing these revelations when the doctor enters. She appears to be in her late thirties and wears a white lab coat over medical scrubs. A stethoscope is draped over her neck. A name is embroidered over her right breast, but it's in kanji.

"*Kon'nichiwa. Anata wa totemo kōun'na hitodesu,*" she says.

"Do you speak English?"

"Of course," the doctor says. "Are you American?" Jonas nods. "Interesting story about you," she continues, her voice warm and friendly. "Spire security found you unconscious."

"Spire security . . . ," Jonas echoes, his voice ragged. His spirits dive-bomb. Hope withers.

He hasn't gone anywhere.

The doctor nods. "They had no record of you having even entered the facility. Nothing in their logs. Nothing on the security cameras."

Jonas sits up. A tiny green shoot of hope springs within him. Kobayashi said the Spire didn't *have* security cameras.

The doctor continues. "Until you just popped up on them. Out of the clear blue. Two different feeds. 'Popped up,' that was their term. You just *appeared* on one of the catwalks. Like you came out of nowhere."

Jonas feels a swell of elation, suddenly buoyant with reverie.

"You were unconscious," the doctor continues, "so they brought you here." She indicates the equations on Jonas's arms, left bare by the hospital gown. "Those are very unusual tattoos."

"There's a long story behind them," he demurs. Thoughts are flying faster than he can catch them. He dares to allow himself to feel giddy.

"I'd imagine."

He feels the doctor assessing him, scanning for signs of madness. He sees a phone on the wall and catapults himself—still tethered to the IV stand—toward it, as eager for a change of subject as for the phone. "I need this," he says and removes the receiver. There's no touch pad underneath it. "How do I use this?" He tries without success to keep the desperation from his voice.

The doctor stares blankly at him. "You should get back in bed," she says.

Jonas grips the receiver tight. "I need to call someone," he says. "I need to call someone right now. Please. *Please.*" He imagines he must seem out of his mind. He doesn't care.

The doctor regards him with pity. "It's a hospital phone. There's no outside line."

Jonas sags. He must cut a pathetic figure because the doctor reaches into her lab coat and produces a phone protected by a case dotted with a floral pattern. She enters a four-digit code to unlock it and then hands it to him as if it were a five-dollar bill and he were a beggar. "Here," she says, her voice sympathetic.

Jonas grabs the phone and punches in the number for the apartment he shared with Amanda, hoping she lives there, hoping the number hasn't changed, hoping and hoping and hoping.

One step at a time.

He listens to the synthetic beeps designed to approximate a ringing phone but which just sound like the trill of birds. His palms are sweating. The phone feels slick and heavy in his hand.

Finally, a woman answers. "Hello?" She sounds exhausted.

Jonas does a quick calculation: it's currently 3:00 a.m. in New York. "Amanda. Amanda?" he blurts, practically screaming.

"No," the woman answers.

Jonas's stomach drops along with his hopes. The voice on the other end doesn't belong to his wife.

"This is Emily," the stranger says.

Jonas looks down at the tattoos on his forearms—the formulae, the calculations, the work of two Jonases, the sacrifice of two Evas—and weighs how they could have betrayed him. It doesn't seem possible. He is speechless. He doesn't know what he looks like in this moment, but the doctor is staring at him with grave concern. He leans against the wall. He can't feel his legs.

The doctor observes him with concern and pity, apparently questioning whether she did the right thing by letting him make a call. Jonas ignores her. His heart is crumbling.

"I'm house-sitting for Amanda while she's out of town," Emily says.

Jonas's head lurches forward. His mouth springs open.

"Is there something I can help you with?" Emily asks.

But Jonas can't answer. Words won't breach the wall of sobs he's coughing out, unable to draw breath. Tears plume. Snot escaping from his nose. A primordial release of fear and tension.

Somewhere, the doctor is asking him something.

"She's okay," Jonas manages to say. Not a question. "She's okay," he repeats, astonished.

"Who? Amanda?" Emily asks. "Amanda's fine. She's—" Jonas feels her suspicion rise. "Who is this?"

Jonas ends the call. He's learned everything he needs.

Spent, he lets his legs go limp. His back slides down the wall until he's sitting on the floor, the phone in its cute floral case clutched tight in his hand. His face is slick with tears.

I'm house-sitting for Amanda while she's out of town. He rolls the phrase around in his head, examining it from all sides, all vantages. *I'm house-sitting for Amanda.* Amanda. His Amanda. Who has an apartment. Which requires someone to watch over it. While she's out of town. *Because* she's out of town. Because she's here. In this reality. *Alive.*

Tears that were so hard to surface in grief now flow unrestrained from joy. Jonas's heart feels so big it might burst, and even if it did, he still could not imagine himself more content.

"Are you okay?" the doctor asks.

It's all Jonas can do to nod. He slowly rises to his feet, his face contorted in a grin so wide it hurts. He thinks about calling Emily back and asking whether she might get a message to Amanda, but every scenario he can envision strains credibility to the breaking point. Another search on the doctor's phone confirms that this reality's Jonas Cullen, Nobel laureate, died two years ago. Whoever Emily is, she isn't equipped to tell Amanda that her husband has returned from the dead.

Another search yields the location of an American Express office, a thirty-minute walk from the hospital. He's already rehearsing a story in his mind when the doctor asks him again if he's okay, assessing whether Jonas presents a danger to himself or others.

"I'm fine," he says. "I just want to go home." This is the absolute truth.

"And home would be . . ."

"New York. Manhattan."

"Well, you certainly are a long way from home, Mister . . ."

"Monroe," Jonas says, using Amanda's maiden name. "Evan Monroe." He could do without the good doctor researching "Jonas Cullen" and discovering a dead man was walking around her hospital.

"Mr. Monroe, your body has suffered a trauma. I think you should get back in bed and rest. There are a number of tests I'd like to run."

"I feel fine."

"Be that as it may," the doctor rebuts, "you showed up at a highly advanced and highly secure scientific facility with nothing in your pockets but a cloth patch embroidered with the number eight. I'm sure the police are going to want a word with you."

"Excuse me?"

"The police—"

"No," Jonas shakes his head, suddenly desperate. "The patch. Do you have it?"

The doctor reaches into the pocket of her lab coat and produces the Ouroboros patch that Eva gave Jonas. He takes it from her and fights off a spate of emotion.

"I just want to go home," Jonas says, wiping away an errant tear. He holds up the phone. "There's an American Express office nearby. They can give me a new card. I can use it to get home."

"I'm not sure about that," the doctor shrugs.

"Don't worry," Jonas says with confidence. "I've done it before."

"That's wonderful," the doctor says, "but like I said, the police are going to want to speak with you."

"Have I broken any laws?"

"I'm not an attorney. But I suppose there's an argument to be made that you were trespassing in the Spire."

"Are they pressing charges?"

"Not that I'm aware of."

"And I'm not injured, right? There's no medical reason to keep me here."

"No medical reason," she says, leaning on "medical."

"In that case—"

"But a few *psychiatric* reasons are springing to mind."

Jonas hands the phone back to the doctor. "You're right," he says. "This situation is unusual."

Caught off guard by Jonas's sudden cooperation, the doctor considers the phone in her hand, weighing her next move. "I'm going to order a CAT scan," she says. "Let's just confirm there's no physical damage before we . . ."

"Move along to the 'psychiatric reasons'?"

"One step at a time," the doctor says.

"Words to live by," Jonas deadpans. He climbs back into bed, the paragon of reasonable comity.

She shoots him another look full of the skepticism born of his sudden acquiescence, but it transmutes into a friendly smile, and she heads off.

When the door closes behind her, Jonas leaps from the bed and dresses as fast as he can. He needs to leave before an orderly comes back to retrieve him for the CAT scan. Like a criminal, he skulks out of the room and into the hallway. As he passes patients and personnel, he works to affect the confidence of someone who's where he belongs. An elevator takes him down to the lobby. It feels as though everyone is watching him. Looking. Assessing. Judging. When he finally escapes into the open air, he rewards himself with a deep breath.

He thinks he has the directions to American Express memorized, but the streets quickly become a tangle. He gets as far from the hospital as he can before he risks asking passersby if they speak English and can point him in the direction of the American Express office. Most speak English, but no one knows where American Express can be found.

Finally, a woman in her sixties breaks out her phone and sets Jonas off in the right direction.

When he arrives, he recites the story that had worked for him before. This time, he doesn't have to wait. The officer doesn't retreat from view, spiking his concern that police are being called. This time Jonas's replacement card is produced promptly, accompanied by a sincere apology for his fictional ordeal. As before, the card offers a new lease on life. Jonas's emotions are the stuff of television commercials. *With this card, all things are possible.*

His next step is to get to the American embassy in Tokyo. It's a one-hour flight, but he doesn't have the requisite ID. He has no alternative but to hitchhike, a process that ends up taking thirteen hours. By the time he's finally standing in front of the nondescript office building that serves as the United States' diplomatic presence in Tokyo, it's the middle of the night.

Making a mental note of the embassy's location, Jonas wanders. He takes in the looming skyscrapers, a crush of architecture awash in bright lights. To walk the city is to be inside an electronic billboard. He has no idea what month it is, but the air is crisp. He should be cold, but he isn't. He should be hungry, but he passes restaurant after restaurant. He should be exhausted, but he has no desire to sleep. His footsteps feel light. Everything he sees is sharper. This, he now knows, is what it's like to live past grief. The only thing standing between him and Amanda is geography. Halfway around the globe may as well be a walk around the block for someone who has traversed universes.

Nine hours later, the embassy's consular officer, a Japanese woman in her thirties, is peering at Jonas over black-rimmed glasses with thick lenses. Her expression drips with incredulity as he repeats his now-familiar story.

"What a nightmare," Jonas exclaims. "The bastard took my wallet, my passport, even my damn health insurance card . . . I thought Japan was supposed to be safe, y'know?" He holds up his American Express card. "I'm just lucky I kept this in a separate pocket." He feigns astonishment at his purported good fortune.

The officer takes the credit card and types some information into her computer. She considers her display and sours. Jonas knows what's coming but tries to act surprised when she says, "I'm sorry, Mr. Cullen. But our records show you as deceased." Her expression is impenetrable.

Jonas shrugs with as much charm as he can muster. "I feel a little tired, but I'm *pretty sure* I'm not dead." He adds a smile for disarming effect. "You know, I happened to read an article in *Wired* about how hackers are altering public records like that," he says, hoping *Wired* exists in this universe, or at least that it doesn't rouse suspicion. "I guess it makes identity theft easier somehow."

"Sounds right," the officer replies, but coming off as disingenuous. "If you could just wait here for one moment . . ." She stands and moves off with Jonas's credit card in hand.

Jonas cranes his head, trying not to draw attention, and sees the officer talking to a marine embassy guard. Although he can't make out what she's saying, she speaks urgently, stabbing at the air with Jonas's card.

This is wrong.

The thought arrives unbidden, and Jonas is gripped by a powerful instinct to leave. If it's a choice between that and waiting to retrieve his card—and getting arrested and detained for questioning—there's really no choice at all. He's free from the fear of being deprived of his tether, but he's terrified of any development that could keep him separated from Amanda for even a minute longer than necessary.

He slowly rises from his seat and begins to pad toward the lobby, hoping the officer will remain focused on her conversation with the marine long enough for Jonas to slip out of the building. It takes him three minutes to reach the outdoor gate that surrounds the embassy. Two more marines stand guard. The gate is maybe eighteen feet away.

"*Sumimasen. Tomate, kudasai,*" a voice calls from behind him. He ignores it, but then the man switches to English. "Excuse me, sir. Could you please wait a second?" The voice carries enough steel to leave no doubt that it isn't a request.

Jonas keeps walking toward the gate, fourteen feet away, pretending the marine isn't addressing him. Footsteps sound behind him. The marine has summoned reinforcements. Jonas feels nauseated.

"*Teishi,*" the marine says. "Stop right there."

Jonas starts to slow. He feels the marine drawing close. He looks ahead to the gate.

And he bolts.

The marine and his cohorts are yelling now, barking commands to stop. Up ahead, the gate begins to close. Sprinting, Jonas collides with a woman but doesn't break stride. She spills to the ground in his wake. He feels the stares of everyone witnessing the commotion, but his focus is on the gate, slowly closing like a maw.

As he races toward it, a guard moves to grab him, but Jonas slips the man's grip. He throws himself through the gate, barely threading the gap as it closes. It bites at his shirt. For a second of panic, Jonas's sleeve is pinched in the gate, but he yanks his arm, tearing the fabric, and shoots out into the street. A chorus of the pursuing marines tells the ones at the gate to "Open it up! Open it back up!"

Jonas darts down a narrow street, dodging cars and mopeds. He chances a glance back and sees the marines in pursuit. He fights the tide of traffic, parrying against the current, and comes face to face with a huge bus. It bears down on him, thirty thousand pounds of metal, just like the one in New York. This time, though, he surges across the street, drawing an arc around the front of the bus such that it flies past him, forming a makeshift bulwark between him and the pursuing marines. It takes only seconds for the bus to clear, but that's all Jonas needs to slip into the closest store. A mannequin provides cover as he watches the marines fan out and disappear into the crowd.

NOW

Eager to put as much distance between himself and the marines as possible, Jonas heads out of the city. He finds a man willing to trade a peacoat for his shirt. It does little against the creeping chill, but it's better than nothing.

The escape from Tokyo brings the problem of getting to America without a passport. He doesn't even have a change of clothes. The soles of his shoes feel threadbare, as though they're sucking up cold from the ground and channeling it straight into his feet.

In a bookstore, he finds a guidebook for Japan. A plan begins to take shape. It will require luck, for certain things to break his way, giving the universe more opportunities to thwart him.

Using a map torn from the guidebook's pages, Jonas walks along the shoulder of a highway, traveling west. His thumb remains poised toward the road, but no one stops. At night, cars whip past. The halogen headlights of oncoming trucks envelope him in brightness before thundering on.

Exhausted beyond description, Jonas eventually stumbles. His legs refuse to take another step. On the side of the highway, a sign straddles a culvert, where he takes refuge. He is cold and hungry and thinks he has never been so tired. He doesn't fall asleep so much as pass into it as if crossing a border, awake one moment and unconscious the next. A deep slumber without dreams.

In what seems like only a minute, the rising sun and roar of traffic snap him awake, and his odyssey continues. He keeps his thumb out, despite the fact that his hand weighs a hundred pounds and his shoulder burns with the effort of holding his fist aloft. He tries walking backward to change arms, but he's too fatigued to summon the coordination required.

It would take five days of walking nonstop to get from Tokyo to Osaka. Despondency grows with each car and truck and van that ignores his offered thumb. It is as though they are doing the will of a disapproving universe.

But then, a respite. An eighteen-wheeler rolls past, bathing Jonas in light before pulling off to the shoulder. The driver, a man in his sixties with a face of leather, knows just enough English to convey that he, too, is en route to Jonas's ultimate destination of Hyōgo. Jonas exhales, not quite believing his luck. Even more fortunate—the man has mochi to spare. As he eats, Jonas remembers that the last time he ate anything was before he and Eva left for the Spire. He inhales the rice cakes.

The driver deposits Jonas in Hyōgo Ward, a quaint portside town. Still ravenous, he finds a street vendor and, when the man is preoccupied with a customer, pockets a single plum. He waits until he's far away, well inside the Port of Kobe, before risking his first bite. The pop as his teeth puncture the skin is visceral. Juice floods his mouth, and the soft meat of the fruit is springtime itself. He's convinced it's the most delicious thing he's ever tasted.

The port is more than two miles long. Massive merchant ships sit in thirty-four berths running the length of the shore. The dense plants and generators and factories of the Hanshin Industrial Region provide a backdrop of omnipresent gray. Cranes swing cargo containers overhead. Trucks and forklifts skim over the asphalt, belching out diesel fumes and coughing up black clouds.

Jonas moves from ship to ship, giant floating cities with names like *Golden Nori* and *Guanabara* and *Heroic Ace*. He looks for vessels bound for America and captains who speak English and might be looking to take on another hand. He talks to crews as they work. He sees a lot of shaking heads.

Eventually he finds a captain who doesn't hire him so much as takes pity on him. "This is hard work," the captain says. "Tough labor. Men are the lightest thing on this boat."

"I don't mind hard work," Jonas assures him.

Seeming to find this humorous, the captain grabs one of Jonas's hands in his. The man's skin feels as coarse as rope. He offers up a dry chuckle and tells Jonas his hands might as well belong to a child. He doubts Jonas has seen a hard day's work in his life. "But we'll change that," he promises, flashing a grin that's missing two teeth.

The ship is the *Tōya Maru*. The chief mate gives Jonas some clothing from the laundry's lost and found, and that night, he enjoys his first proper meal in days. Two hours later, his stomach, unaccustomed to being full and traveling by sea, throws it all overboard.

The days are long but filled with tasks that make the hours pass swiftly. Jonas is assigned to replace chipped paint, to grease the fittings on hatches, grease the fittings on tackle, grease wire. Everything on the ship seems to require lubrication. One day, one of the ABs—able-bodied seamen, Jonas learns—spies the equations on his arms and starts asking questions. After several ill-fated attempts to put the man off, Jonas confesses to being a scientist. This leads him to getting assigned technical work. He's put with the ship's chief engineer and ends up hanging off the bow, making repairs to the bow-tank level sensor as the ocean gallops beneath him.

He lets a beard carpet his face and grows tan from working in the sun. His darkening skin begins to obscure his tattoos, but it doesn't matter. Whether he reunites with Amanda or not, he knows this is the reality he'll die in. Surely the quantum energies have left his body by now.

One night, the ship is buffeted by a terrible storm. Waves as high as buildings crest over the bow and assault the deck, swarming the ship. The ABs chatter and gossip about a "sudden cold front" or the ship's radar failing to spot the oncoming hurricane, but Jonas holds a different fear, a concern that this universe might be waking to his presence, forming designs on stopping him from reaching Amanda. He tries to console himself with the argument that such worries are a ridiculous way for a scientist to think, but he knows better. He's *witnessed* it.

Two more storms break out. Power failures plague the ship. Mechanical failures. Every day, the vessel develops new ailments. The crew openly begins to consider the possibility that the voyage is damned. In every conversation, Jonas keeps his own counsel. He focuses on his share of the repairs.

Despite the universe's best efforts, the *Tōya Maru* makes port in Seattle, Washington. In the dead of night, the massive vessel slips into a berth. Even though it's three o'clock in the morning and the night is as black as pitch, the men begin the work of off-loading their cargo. Amid the hoisting and winching, in the shadow of swinging cranes, Jonas slips away into the predawn darkness.

His salary from the ship pays for a Greyhound bus ticket to New York. But in Montana, the bus breaks down on the side of I-90 East. The passengers disembark to stretch their legs while the driver works to repair it. Rather than waiting for the man to undo the universe's mischief, Jonas hitchhikes and ends up bouncing around in the rear of a dented pickup truck he estimates is at least twenty years old. Of course, the pickup also develops trouble.

Jonas transfers to a train, which manages to get as far as North Dakota before the universe stops it. Another bus takes him through Minnesota and then Wisconsin. The universe throws traffic and unseasonable snow at it. The journey is labored.

In defiance of the universe, Jonas passes through Pennsylvania and then New Jersey. With Manhattan in sight, he begins walking. It's the middle of the night when he arrives at Van Brunt Street. The city that never sleeps rises from the horizon like a waking giant. Apart from a handful of minor changes—a street with a different name, a building with a different facade, the Mets with an extra World Series championship to their name—it's the New York he remembers. It's the New York that's home.

He quickens his pace with each step that brings him closer to the Upper West Side. He should be exhausted, spent beyond belief or description, but his strides grow quicker. He fears another storm or earthquake. Or the universe could conjure some new mischief to delay him. But he's so close now that he knows nothing can truly *stop* him.

His spirits begin to lift. In short order, he is running, sprinting down streets just coming to life with the dawn. He races past garbage trucks and newspaper deliveries and storefronts opening for the day. He outpaces early morning joggers. His arms piston and his legs burn, but he doesn't care. He's close. *So close.*

He rounds a corner, and then he sees it. The brownstone seems no different from the one where Amanda was shot, where Other Jonas lived, where *he* lived with Amanda in what feels like three lifetimes ago. He bounds up the stairs, his lungs heaving. A finger trembling with anticipation moves down the buttons of the building directory before settling on her name—**CULLEN, AMANDA**—on a sun-bleached label beneath a cloudy film of plastic. A metal button dusted with fingerprints next to it. Jonas's finger hovers over it for the briefest of seconds. He imagines what he'll tell her. How he'll explain the impossible. How he'll implore her to listen to his voice, to trust her memory of it. *To believe him.* He's here. He's back, and he's alive, and he can't wait to tell her all the details of his incredible story, but first he just needs to hold her in his arms and tell her that he loves her.

He pushes the button.

And waits.

He presses again. He's shaking as though experiencing withdrawal. His ears are warm. His palms are sweating. He pushes the button a third time.

Behind him the door swings open, and a young boy, no more than ten, bounds out, a *Dragon Ball Z* backpack slung over his shoulder and a childlike spring in his step.

"She's not home," he offers before bounding down the steps.

The boy looks like Mr. and Mrs. Gomez. A nephew or grandson, maybe? Jonas springs after him. "Excuse me. What do you mean she's not home?"

The boy stops. He glances skyward, looking toward the brownstone. "Mrs. Cullen. You were buzzing her, right?" Jonas nods. "She's not home. She's been painting in the mornings lately."

It's all Jonas can do to keep himself from hugging the boy. The wave of relief that hits him must unnerve the kid, because he says, "Are you okay?" The question comes out the way so many children's questions do, without a sense that the answer is important.

"I'm fine. Do you know where she is? Do you know where she is right now?" Jonas can hardly keep the desperation out of his voice.

"I don't know," the boy answers.

Jonas's mind wheels. He's searched for Amanda in a multiverse of near-infinite realities only to have lost her in a city of over eight million people. Then an idea takes shape. "Do you have a phone I can borrow?" he blurts.

The boy hesitates. His parents have probably taught him not to share his phone with strangers. Nevertheless, he digs into his pocket and produces a five-year-old phone in a *Power Rangers* case. "I have to get to school."

"Thank you," Jonas says. "This'll just take a second." He searches for Amanda's gallery. A few seconds of eternity pass before the phone confirms that Amanda is associated with the same gallery in this reality. He taps to get the phone to dial the number. It's just past eight o'clock in the morning, before business hours, but Jonas is feeling lucky. Hope, that feckless stranger, is visiting him once more.

"Logan Gallery," a male voice answers.

"Mitchell—" Jonas blurts, leaping at the voice.

"No, this is Vincent. Can I help you?"

Jonas breathes deep. *Now comes the hard part.* "This is Officer Stamper with the NYPD," he says. "I need to locate Amanda Cullen."

He endures a pause on the other end of the line. "She may be going by Amanda Monroe."

Another pause. "What's this regarding?" Vincent asks.

"I can't disclose that," Jonas vamps. "She's not in any trouble, but I need to speak with her immediately. In person." He looks down to see the Gomez boy shifting on his feet, impatiently waiting for the return of his phone. "My understanding is that she's out painting right now. Would you happen to know where?"

Another pause. Jonas holds his breath. Then, finally, Vincent responds. "At this time of day, she's usually working. She likes the light."

Jonas forces calm into his voice. "Do you have an address?"

Vincent does. It's only six blocks away. Jonas is already plotting a course in his mind as he says, "Thank you."

"She's not in trouble, right?"

"No. No trouble at all."

"She'll be on the roof."

"I know."

"Wait. How would you kn—"

Jonas kills the line and returns the phone to the boy. "Thank you."

"I didn't know you were a cop," the boy says. "Why don't you have your own phone?"

"That . . . is a very, *very* long story," Jonas says. "Thanks again." With that, he takes off running.

Streets and avenues fall behind him as he runs, surrendering to his passage. For a blissful moment, it seems the universe has run out of tricks. But this time it doesn't throw storms or earthquakes at him. It throws a *parade*. Entire city blocks are sectioned off by wooden blue sawhorses and police on horseback. Jonas darts through, ignoring shouted police commands and even weaving through a marching band.

He makes it another half block when he's tossed into the air by a hand made of fire. Gravity smashes him back onto the sidewalk. He hears screams and astonished reactions. Still lying on the ground, he turns to see shattered concrete and traces of blue flame. Some kind of gas main explosion.

A passel of Good Samaritans is lifting him to a chorus of "Are you all right, buddy" and "Holy shit." Jonas shrugs them off, muttering, "Thank you. I'm fine." He hears incoming sirens. Someone tells him he should wait for an ambulance, but he takes off again.

His body protests as he sprints. But the pain is meaningless. He feels hope aborning. The universe may have been plotting his defeat, but it's a fickle beast. It may have set Eva in his path to distract him, to stop him, to pull him off his pursuit, but Eva also *helped* him. The universe may be driven by fate but not with a singular mind. Jonas has faith. He has himself. He has the *will* to get to Amanda, to hold her in his arms again and never let her go.

He shoots across the street and once again finds himself airborne. In seconds, he's landing atop the windshield of a taxi. As the glass spiderwebs beneath his weight, he thinks of how often he's been hit by cars lately. The trick, he's learned, is to go limp, relax the muscles, and let the impact absorb the kinetic energy. He ricochets off the taxi and lands in the street. The pain is intense, as usual, but it's dampened under a cloud of adrenaline. Jonas throws himself to his feet and keeps running as the taxi driver unleashes a string of expletives such as can only be found in New York City.

Another gas main explodes nearby, but Jonas doesn't even break stride.

Two more blocks.

I'm almost there, Amanda. I'm almost there.

NOW

At this time of year, Amanda's favorite part of the day is when the morning sun hits just right. Its light plays over the city with the faintest tincture of yellow, imbuing it with a warmth that should conflict with the cold hues of concrete and steel but nevertheless makes the silvers and grays and blacks of Manhattan gleam with a special shine.

The sky is an incandescent blue mottled by thin veins of white. It looks like a painting, a cliché that always makes Amanda grimace, amused by the irony that her calling should be to render that which looks like a painting into an actual painting. But here, in the sky, 1,550 feet in the air, what is ironic also feels holy. She does her work among the clouds akin to an angel. Pigeons turn circles above her, a silent reminder that Amanda is treading on their turf.

It took six months and a troop of lawyers to get the requisite permits and approvals, a panoply of bureaucratic sign-offs, to work here on the roof of 225 West Fifty-Seventh Street, what the developers dubbed "Central Park Tower," the tallest residential building in the world. Standing at the roofline, with the city laid out before her bathed in immaculate light, Amanda is surprisingly at peace.

After Switzerland, after the accident, she thought she might never pick up a pencil or paintbrush again. Her paintings came from her subjects—God's-eye views of her favorite city in the world—but her *art* came from within, from the images she formed in her imagination. But when she closed her eyes, all she could see was Jonas, his own eyes staring back at her, lacking the spark of life but nevertheless conveying confusion, a deep shock that he should find himself hanging lifeless amid broken and twisted steel and plastic and shattered glass. For more than a year, those eyes haunted her—the last thing she thought of when she tried to sleep, the first thing she envisioned upon waking, and the subject of every dream in between.

Friends were concerned. Colleagues were worried. Family members tortured themselves trying to devise new ways to prompt her to rejoin the world. She slept intermittently. She ate rarely and drank far too much for anyone's comfort. Eventually she withdrew into her apartment, rarely leaving.

In all her life, she had never known such despair. A therapist, whom she reluctantly started seeing at the urging of a friend, liked to talk about the five stages of grief. But Amanda knew only the fourth, depression. And it did not feel like a "stage." A stage is an interval you pass through, a time that eventually ends. She felt only depression, like a new, permanent destination. Jonas had won the Nobel Prize for proving the existence of a nearly infinite number of realities, but for Amanda there was only *one*, a universe where the man who had been her entire world was gone.

For a time, she tried to motivate herself with the notion that the cloistered life she was living wasn't what Jonas would have wanted for her. She berated and chastised herself, trying to transmute her grief into self-loathing, punishing herself with the idea that her despondency was a kind of betrayal of her husband's memory. But even that didn't work. Her sorrow was a biological imperative, a compulsion she could neither ignore nor deny any more than she could resist breathing.

Eventually, the idea of joining him took root in her mind like a disease. She imagined going to a rooftop, taking in the view of the city one final time, and diving off into another world, another universe, where she and Jonas would be reunited. In that new, imagined reality, she was no longer barren. She would be the mother she'd always hoped to be and give Jonas all the children he deserved, all the children she so desperately wanted. They would have his brilliance and her gifts, and she would love them with every cell in her being.

Amanda recognized the malignancy of this fantasy. But she was in pain—legitimate, understandable, *rational* pain. She knew she should grasp at one of the many lifelines—therapy, treatment, counseling— that her friends and family threw to her, yet she resisted them despite her best efforts. With each passing day, the idea of reuniting with Jonas took on more shape and substance in her mind.

In time, it also took on specificity. She chose One World Trade Center, the tallest building in Manhattan. The building's official height is a deliberate 1,776 feet, but the roof height is "only" 1,368 feet. At that altitude, she'd been told at some point, a person falling off is likely to pass out before their body explodes into mist on the ground.

Getting access to the roof wasn't difficult, not for an artist who plies her trade on rooftops all over Manhattan. In fact, she'd already painted from the top of One World Trade Center. But once she got onto the roof and positioned herself at the northwest corner, she was struck by a profound flood of emotion that swept over her like a tsunami. The city-scape she saw before her was as familiar as her own reflection. She had captured it perfectly in the painting she had titled *Pinnacle*, the painting Jonas had been taken by in her gallery the second time she ever saw him. She remembered the look on his face, the amazement and disbelief that she had so movingly captured the majesty of the city on canvas, con-jured with her paints and her brushes. Amanda had never been able to shake the feeling that when Jonas learned that she was the artist behind *Pinnacle*, that was the moment he had fallen in love with her.

She had no memory of falling to her knees. She had no recollection of when she'd started to cry. She had cried after the accident, of course, and at the funeral, and after the funeral. In fact, she'd cried every morn-ing and nearly every night since. After two years, she thought she had no more tears left to shed. But in that moment on the roof, the grief rose inside her and flew out in a torrent of tears. Kneeling, her body heaved uncontrollably as she keened and wailed, feeling as though she were performing an exorcism on herself. Even now she is amazed no one heard her cries. Her only audience were the birds wheeling overhead.

She still had difficult days and troublesome nights, but eventually the time between them grew. She no longer declined dinner invitations. She didn't drink as much. Her friends started to comment that she was "looking better" and "putting some weight back on." She could not claim to be happy, but at least she was no longer depressed. She existed in an emotional purgatory, a liminal space between all-consuming grief and a future without Jonas that she couldn't yet see.

She spent her days walking the city, pummeling herself with a singular, tortured question: *What will I do now?* The idea of moving sprang to mind, but New York is home to her, and the thought of leaving it is anathema. Her agent fielded calls and emails proposing commissions. Her gallery made repeated inquiries with varying degrees of politeness. Whatever artistic urge that once drove her seemed to have died with Jonas. But unlike Jonas, she did not mourn its passing.

Then one day, on one of her walks, she found herself in the shadow of a looming tower, one of the many new constructions that had sprouted up amid her despair. She charmed the doorman into showing her the rooftop and was awed by what she saw up there. Staring out at the city, she started editing the image in her mind, imagining it beaming in the morning light.

And she knew she would paint again.

She's worked at the top of the Central Park Tower for three weeks now. Sketches. Studies. Experimenting with angles. Finding the light. Trying to recapture that spark of inspiration she felt eight years earlier when she first stepped out onto a roof and saw the city the way birds do. It has been slow going, but she finally feels like she's there. Two days ago, she felt confident enough to bring her bespoke canvas, five feet by five feet, up through the freight elevator. Her hand now feels free again, the pencil as light as air between her fingertips as it glides along the canvas, leaving beauty in its wake.

Amanda is so consumed by her work, so deep in the zone, mesmerized by the cityscape slowly pouring out from the tip of her pencil, that at first, she doesn't hear him. And when she does, it sounds like a memory, a trick of the mind.

"Amanda."

The voice is tremulous and tentative but unmistakably his.

"Amanda," it comes again, a little louder now. A little surer.

Amanda feels a compulsion to turn around, but she ignores it until she feels a presence behind her and the sound of footfalls on the asphalt. *This is ridiculous.* The inchoate thought blazes through her mind as she turns around.

And sees him.

Backlit by the sun, shimmering like a mirage. An illusion. But with details no hallucination could account for. He's thinner, his clean-shaven face slightly gaunt, his cheekbones more pronounced. And older, his hair salted with wisps of gray. His clothes are threadbare and appear as if he's been wearing them for days.

He walks toward her, slowly, his footsteps labored. He has a look of awe on his face like a penitent staring into the eye of God.

Amanda opens her mouth to speak, but no words come. Her mind screams at her that this isn't real, can't be real.

But then he's taking her in his arms, and his embrace feels like the most real thing she's ever known. She surrenders to the moment. If this is what her losing her mind is like, she doesn't want to be sane.

They're both crying now, a chorus of joyous sobs in the light rush of the wind.

Eventually, Amanda manages, "How?"—the single syllable carrying all the astonishment and amazement of divinity.

"It's a long story," Jonas says. "I know that sounds horribly cliché, but it's true. It's really true."

"And this is real?"

"It's real."

Suddenly aware that her eyes have been closed, she opens them to take in Jonas's face. She reaches to confirm he's real. Light plays off a tear running down his cheek, throwing a tiny sparkle. Her whole adult life has been spent replicating the world as she sees it, and she knows that no mirage could ever be so detailed.

As she wipes away the tear, another man steps into view behind Jonas. Another ghost. Another impossible resurrection. But after this remarkable reunion, she can no longer deny the evidence looming in front of her. Somehow Victor Kovacevic, eighteen months dead from pancreatic cancer, is here on the rooftop with them.

"Victor?" she whispers.

Jonas turns and sees him, too, one mirage recognizing another. "How—"

"Jonas, what's going on? What is this?"

"I'll explain everything," he reassures her. He looks at Victor. "How can you be here?"

Victor smiles, a serpent's grin. "Don't be so dense, Jonas. You're smarter than that."

Amanda watches confusion play across Jonas's face. Her mind is churning, trying to make sense of what she's witnessing. She hears a sudden crack of thunder, and her heart leaps in her chest. The morning sky abruptly darkens. Overhead, cumulonimbus clouds appear without warning. Sheets of rain begin to fall. Lightning strikes inches from where Jonas is standing. Any wonder or confusion Amanda has been feeling is replaced with a primal sense of fear.

"What's happening?" she yells over the din of the storm, her voice laced with terror.

"It's the universe," Victor answers. "It doesn't want this." Then, with an eerie calm, he reaches into his coat and pulls out a handgun. "It wants *this*," he says, leveling it toward her.

Amanda has never seen a gun outside of television and film, and the sight of one causes her to gasp. All around her Mother Nature rages, hurling rain and lightning down on them. Behind Amanda, raindrops drum away at her embryonic painting. If she turned from the gun and looked, she'd see a weeping canvas with grayish streaks crying down its surface.

Jonas is surging forward, trying to reason with Victor—*Can it really be him?*—while rain and lightning lash about them. "Victor . . . you don't want to do this. Just—just put the gun down. Put the gun away and we'll talk. Whatever the problem is, we can talk this out."

Victor raises the gun another inch. "I've already talked it out. This is what the universe wants."

Amanda watches his finger curl around the trigger. Everything moves in slow motion, taking on the quality of a dream. *That's what this is,* she thinks. Of course, it has to be a dream. With that epiphany, all that is happening—the preternatural storm, the two dead men resurrected, Victor's mania—snaps into focus and makes sense.

When Victor fires the gun, Amanda first mistakes the report for another thunderclap. But then she sees Jonas drop to his knees. Her mind reconstructs the previous second: Victor shot at her, and Jonas threw himself in front of the bullet. She watches, slack jawed, as crimson mists into the puddle beneath Jonas's crumpled form.

She drops to her knees, instinctively cradling him in her arms. His form sags ominously in her grip. Everything blurs as her eyes fill with tears and rainwater. She clears them with the back of her hand and sees a bloody chasm where Jonas's heart should be. Her hand rockets forward to stanch the bleeding, but his blood geysers between her fingers. She thinks to move for her phone, back near the roofline with her forgotten canvas. She could call for help, but that would mean leaving Jonas, and she fears he's too far gone already.

Jonas's fingers tremor toward her face. Blood peeks from between his teeth. "I did it," he breathes. "I made it back to you."

Amanda shushes him with a soothing whisper. "Don't talk. Save your strength. I'm going to get my phone." She decides she has to chance it. She has no other choice. "It's right over there. I'll be right back." She moves to set him down, but he grabs her shoulder, shaking his head. His eyes are devoid of hope, lids fluttering, on the verge of surrender. Amanda doesn't have to be a doctor to know that he is fading fast.

"I love you," he rasps. Amanda can't fathom the burden, the difficulty of uttering those three simple syllables. She watches him swallow hard and set his jaw and steel himself for the exertion of uttering two more. "Too much."

"I love you . . . ," she says, her voice breaking. "I love you more."

And then he's gone. His chest no longer rises and falls in jagged spasms. Blood no longer gushes between her fingers with each beat of his heart. His face is frozen in what perversely looks like awe, the beatific expression of someone en route to the afterlife.

Amanda feels sick. She has no idea how or why, but she has just relived the worst moment of her life. That it should come so shortly after she had just begun to put her life back together feels like the lowest form of cruelty. She expects to feel the return of grief, for it to come roaring back, but another emotion rises in its place.

Fury.

Her body warms against the chill of the raging storm. It starts in her heart and radiates outward, building with an intensity so great it almost frightens her. Her body tenses as she reverently lowers Jonas's body to the rooftop. She cradles his head and sets it down gently. Slowly, she feels herself rising to stand.

Victor remains in the very spot where he raised the gun with the intention of killing her. It's still clutched in his hand, but she no longer cares. It's already taken everything from her that she cares about.

"What have you done?" she says, less a question than an accusation. She's surprised she's not screaming.

"I balanced the universe," comes the reply. His voice is as level, as clenched as her own. He looks at her through a veil of driving rain, consumed with a fire—a mania—that Amanda has never seen before and cannot begin to comprehend. Were she not so enraged, she would be terrified.

"What does that mean?" she demands, desperation infecting her voice. She stares a hole through Victor, this man who should be dead, this stranger aflame with hate, and she knows in an instant that there's no explanation that would make sense, or that would even matter anymore.

The man she loves is dead. Again.

NOW

The elevator tops out one flight below the building's roof. He explodes out of it and into the nearest stairwell. He pounds up the steps two at a time. Compared to his endless ascent of the Spire, this is as easy as a walk around the block. Thunder echoes above, and he isn't ashamed to think the storm is meant for him. In one universe, an earthquake; in this one, a parade and a taxi and two gas main explosions. Just the impertinent flailing of the universe. Obstacles to overcome. Unimportant.

He throws himself up the stairs, through the door at the top, and out onto the roof. Wind and rain slap at him. Electric static from the whipcrack of lightning tenses his hair and beard. He stops short as thunder rolls above. Through a curtain of rain, he sees the shapes of three people. His stomach knots. His heart feels as though someone is clutching it. Everything slows and becomes dreamlike. A waking nightmare.

One of the figures is Amanda, but any joy he might feel at seeing her is eclipsed by the sight of the man she's talking to. Victor has a gun in his hand, the same gun that claimed Amanda and Eva. Even in the heat of this horrible moment, Jonas has the presence of mind to scold himself. He could have killed Victor back at the Spire. He could have shot him. He could have hurled his unconscious body off the catwalk. Instead, he showed the mercy Victor would have denied him. What had seemed an act of decency is now revealed to be one of reckless negligence. If Victor kills Amanda now, it will be like Jonas pulling the trigger himself.

The third person lies lifeless in a pool of water and blood. Between the rain and the angle of the body, Jonas can barely make him out. But he doesn't need to see much to recognize his own face. Clean shaven and wearing different but similar clothes to his own. Another doppelgänger. Another Jonas in pursuit of Amanda. Stopped tragically short of reaching his goal.

Jonas's mind flashes back to the fascistic iteration of Manhattan and remembers the feeling of someone lurking behind him, perhaps even following him. Even now, in this most pregnant of moments, a part of him marvels at the immaculate order of the multiverse. Of all the Jonases in the multiverse, it stands to reason that he wouldn't be the only one with the means and drive and tenacity to scour the multiverse for the woman he lost. One such Jonas now lies dead at Amanda's feet.

She turns from Victor and sees Jonas. He watches her straining to make sense of what she is seeing. In turn, Victor reacts to her reaction, and Jonas's stomach twists.

"Jonas?" she whispers.

He doesn't hear. He's racing across the rooftop—his footfalls producing tiny geysers of splashing water—running with a desperate urgency. Lightning fires down in front of him, but he does not stop. He cannot stop. Through the downpour, he pictures Victor raising the gun. He imagines Victor aiming at Amanda, his finger closing around the trigger. Fear speeds his steps. Fear and terrible fury.

"Get away from her!" Jonas thunders. Thunder roars a reply.

A gunshot sounds, and Jonas hopes it's lightning as he feels himself collide with Victor, driven by a preternatural need to get him as far away from Amanda as possible. He hears a clatter, a mechanical thunking, and hopes it's the sound of Victor's gun dropping to the roof. Still tangled in a kind of macabre dance, the two men assault the rooftop's balustrade before it disappears. Inertia carries them over the side. Jonas might have heard Amanda scream, but between the driving rain and the rushing wind and the thundering of his own heart, it's impossible to know for sure.

He and Victor remained tangled as they fall. Synchronicity strikes again, he thinks, reminded of the balletic free fall of his limousine as it leaped the bonds of the Centralbron. He and Amanda tossed around like dice in a tumbler. The floors of the Central Park Tower strobe past. Jonas and Victor fall, racing the raindrops.

Gunmetal flashes in front of Jonas, a glimpse of steel wrapped around Victor's wrist. His tether bracelet. Jonas's fingers splay toward it as they drop. A fall from this height will kill them both, but before he goes, Jonas is consumed with a singular thought, a pure, naked instinct: *I'm going to die destroying Victor's work.*

Victor appears to sense what Jonas intends. Both men are geniuses in their own ways. Victor retracts his hand, but Jonas is faster, clawing at Victor's tether. Feeling its metal frame beneath his hand, Jonas rakes his fingernails against Victor's skin. He hears his nemesis scream and knows it's more in rage than real pain. His fingers close around it, grabbing skin and steel, not letting go.

Like Jonas's, Victor's tether is a delicate piece of technology. It practically falls apart in Jonas's grip. Tiny pieces spiral off. A nearby flash of lightning illuminates their tiny edges. Victor bellows, but the roar of the wind drowns out his rage. Jonas is about to surrender to his imminent death, to rest at last, when the storm blinks from existence.

As he falls, reality changes all around him. Rain is replaced with sunlight. Sunlight gives way to nighttime. The Central Park Tower disappears, only to be reborn as another structure entirely. The city winks in and out, its skyline rising and falling as though filmed in time lapse.

Jonas knows this shouldn't be possible. Other Jonas told him that the reality-slip from the Spire would be a one-way trip. Jonas checked and double-checked his doppelgänger's math, and it was sound. But the shifting kaleidoscope of universes now suggests otherwise. Or maybe the "top-off" he received back at the Spire operated differently than predicted. Or proximity to the destruction of Victor's tether is to blame.

Either way, Jonas thinks—as he witnesses a cornucopia of reality shifts, each one a different die roll of Creation—it's an appropriate way for him and Victor to meet their ends, tumbling through universes.

He thinks of Amanda, hoping the gunshot he heard was either errant or lightning. His only wish is that she live on. He's never wanted anything more, and now, in his final moments, he understands that he wanted so much—he has wasted his life on wanting.

When the ground finally rises to meet him, it's a mercy.

But Jonas doesn't die. This should be impossible, but he's in too much agony for it to be otherwise. Despite all the tortures his body has suffered since leaving his room at NH Genève Aéroport, he's never felt like this. His head throbs. Each beat of his heart brings a new volley of pain. His chest is on fire. He moves a hand to palpate the offending area, but it gives way, sinking beneath his touch. He feels two ribs swinging free, and the ensuing pain clouds his vision with black spots.

Every breath is an effort, and his only reward for each is a new spasm of suffering. And yet he manages to get to his feet, where he sees why he's not a smear on the pavement. He's not on pavement at all. He's on an elevated pathway—a kind of footbridge—that stretches between skyscrapers, part of what he now sees is a latticework of pathways connecting the city's buildings, each one offered up by the multiverse to break his fall.

Jonas is about to take this as an Eva-like sign that perhaps the universe isn't working entirely against him when he's thrown back down to the footbridge's laminated metal. He knows who the attacker is, the moment reminiscent of their fight back at the Spire, two men atop a thin expanse. But this time, Victor is fueled by the memory of his earlier defeat. He refuses to let up, to cease, to stop his fists from hurling down.

The only saving grace is that Victor appears focused on Jonas's head, mercifully avoiding his shattered ribs. If anyone is on the footbridge to witness this attack, they're not interceding. Victor releases another punch, and Jonas feels his nose collapse. His mouth feels wet and tastes of copper.

His hands preoccupied with defending his head, Jonas brings his knee up—as hard as he can, grateful it's not as broken as the rest of him—and connects with Victor's groin. Victor howls in pain and redoubles his efforts. He swings a fist against Jonas's flank, and Jonas feels one of the wayward ribs stab his lung. Now it's his turn to scream, but he can't catch enough oxygen.

Sensing his advantage, Victor grasps at Jonas's throat. Jonas reaches up to pry Victor's fingers away, but Victor maintains his grip, his knuckles as firm and white as ice. He stares down at Jonas with a cold intensity. Jonas feels a hunger, a primal drive, to plead for his life, but the words won't come. There's nothing in his chest but fire and blood and two jagged talons tearing him apart from the inside.

His flailing thoughts grasp for hope and seize on the idea that maybe there are more versions of himself out in the multiverse. That maybe at least one more exists and can find his way back to Amanda. That in a multiverse with as many realities as grains of sand on a single earth, there could still be one—*just one*—where he and Amanda are together. And happy. Maybe even with a child.

The thought brings him peace, which warms his soul as his body begins to grow cold. His eyes slowly close, and he stops struggling against Victor's grip. He's ready to rest now. He's ready to go.

But then he's falling again, the footbridge having disappeared out from under him. Gravity tugs, pulling him down, while Victor, still atop him, hands still wrapped around his neck, pushes down.

Reality changes around them again. Snow scratches at them for a heartbeat. In the next, they plunge through fire. The sky runs from gray to black to blue to an incandescent orange.

Deep within himself, Jonas summons the strength to struggle one final time. He writhes and wriggles, and still Victor's hands remain clasped around his throat. He manages to shift his weight, and then he's rolling over, atop Victor. And Victor, in turn, rolls over him. They're tumbling end over end, like Amanda's and Jonas's ill-fated limousine, like the five-hundred-yen coin Jonas flipped in Hijiyama Park.

Jonas or Amanda.
Heads or tails.
Each fifty-fifty flip with the potential to birth a new reality.
Victor or Jonas.
One will break the other's fall.
The universe favors certain outcomes.

TWO YEARS AGO

They married beneath an azure and coral sky on a beach at the eastern end of Long Island. Waves kissed the shore behind them as a small group of guests sat on white folding chairs arranged in an arc. The wind gusted gently off the water, and the air smelled of salt and charcoal.

Amanda's agent, a woman in her seventies with a voice like it was aged in an oak barrel, officiated. She was, by turns, touching and moving and funny. She spoke about how Jonas and Amanda were both only children who had lost their parents. She confided that she'd always harbored a maternal love for Amanda and now felt the same for Jonas. She thanked God for allowing the two of them to meet in the multitude of New York City.

Jonas wore a tuxedo that his friend Peter helped him pick out. Amanda had on a crepe-white Vera Wang dress with a high neck halter. Her hair was trimmed into a short bob for the occasion, and the cut made her eyes sparkle. Or maybe it was just the occasion.

They wrote their own vows.

Jonas spoke from memory. "Amanda, I'm not going to talk about destiny or how the universe favors certain outcomes. You've already had to endure endless lectures from me about both. But each time, you've hung on every word, endured every tangent, followed me into each intellectual cul-de-sac. And you do it with patience, yes, but more importantly, curiosity. I love how you see the world, which is evident not just in your incredible paintings, but in your heart. You live life with a mindfulness and a presence that others—including, *especially*, myself—can only hope to emulate. You're radiant and kind and loving. You make me want to be a better person." He paused to fend off a tear. He wanted to soak in the moment, as he knew Amanda would, too, to engrave an image of it on the wall of his mind, perfect and vivid and permanent. "I love you in ways I don't know how to express. But I promise to spend every day, for the rest of our life together, trying." He smiled at her. "I love you too much."

"I love you more," she replied earnestly. She glanced down at the notes she had prepared. "I'm an artist. You're a scientist. I don't think anyone could find two people less alike. But that's just the outward appearance. The truth, like most truths, is found on the inside." She looked again at her notes, sheets of heavy stock covered with her precise scrawl. But then she folded up the paper and spoke from the heart. "What we have in common completely eclipses our differences. We think the same way. We feel the same way. We both look at the universe and find the beauty in it. I look in your eyes, in your heart, and I find the same beauty. You're a brushstroke. You're an equation. You're the whole universe. You're *my* whole universe. And I love you far, far too much."

He gave his head a little shake. "I love you more."

The usual pageant of formalities followed. Rings were exchanged. A pronouncement was made. They kissed as the sun descended to the horizon. Phone cameras captured the moment from every conceivable angle.

They held the reception outside, at a small resort on the shore called Gurney's. A live band played, and they both danced with abandon. Jonas remembered once telling Amanda that he could never discern the purpose of dancing, but that felt like a lifetime ago. In many ways, in all the ways that mattered, it was. That version of himself felt so distant that it was like a separate, parallel universe. He had learned that dancing was one way to convey the feelings that he lacked the words to express.

Jonas thought of his Many Worlds Proof and imagined the other Jonases of the multiverse. Did they have an Amanda? He felt pity for the ones who didn't. Theirs was a world without music—bland, desaturated, muted. Jonas decided he would rather die than surrender to that kind of existence.

He searched the dance floor for Amanda. Guests swayed in front of him, obscuring his line of sight, but eventually he found her through the sea of people. She moved in time with the music, shaking her hips, one hand raised to the sky, the other corralling the wayward sway of her dress, pulling it up just far enough to reveal that she was barefoot. He stared at her, drinking in the image, so taken with his new wife that he didn't realize that he had stopped dancing. Bodies twirled around him, oblivious.

Amanda looked resplendent, and Jonas envisioned dozens, hundreds, thousands of such tiny moments in the decades to come. Each one a chance to relive that instant when he first saw her. Each one its own little miracle.

He had no way of knowing that in less than two years, she would be dead.

NOW

Victor's hands are around Jonas's throat. In his entire life, he's never felt such rage. He imagines Jonas's windpipe cracking beneath his thumbs. He knows they're falling. He knows that realities are spinning like a cosmic roulette wheel around them. He knows he's falling to his death, and he doesn't care. He's consumed in a mad race against time, driven by the desperate need to kill Jonas before the inevitable impact kills them both. On some level, he knows it's irrational. What's important is that it feels imperative, the culmination of his life's work. Or the eclipsing of it. It doesn't matter. Nothing matters in this gossamer-thin moment except that Jonas die at his hand.

But Victor dies never knowing whether he succeeded.

His final act is to collapse beneath Jonas's weight, cushioning his rival's fall. In the end, Professor Emeritus Victor Kovacevic ends his life as the equivalent of a human airbag.

Jonas lies in a puddle of sinew and bone and blood. Every nerve ending in his body cries out in distress. He has two broken ribs and a punctured lung. His skull and left tibia are fractured. He would think he's dead but for the pain.

He rolls off Victor's prone form and immediately discovers what real pain means. He should feel elation or relief, but every emotion is eclipsed by agony. He tries to draw breath and ends up coughing, which produces a jet of blood and nearly causes him to pass out. He fears he's going to drown in his own gore.

There are no sirens, he notices. No ambulances rushing to save him. No one is coming to his rescue. There is no hope. The universe is daring him to take solace in the fact that he outlived Victor. And there is some consolation in that, he must admit. He's never thought of himself as a killer but finds joy in the fact that Victor is dead, and he is not. Even if that will last only a few moments. And the joy shames him.

A part of him will always blame himself for Victor's vendetta, suspicious of the possibility that Victor was right, that his own achievements were the result of Victor's brilliance. "If I have seen further," Isaac Newton wrote, "it is by standing on the shoulders of giants." The thought plagues Jonas. Had he stood on Victor's shoulders? And if so, was there anything so wrong in that? Shouldn't what was good enough for Newton be good enough for Cullen?

Jonas has no answer, despite years of asking himself the question. Lying on the cold, hard ground—his lungs bleeding, his bones broken, each breath a labor—he starts to believe that this is what he deserves. The world grows dark, and the basic act of keeping his eyes open begins to feel impossible.

Voices begin to leak into his reverie, but they sound distant, walled up.

"You okay, buddy?"

"Don't move, okay?"

"Help's on the way."

"I'm done, Amanda," Jonas mutters. "Wherever you are . . . I'm done. And I'm sorry."

"Don't talk," one of the voices says. "Save your breath."

"I'm sorry. You—" Jonas's voice catches. He feels a tear escape. A memory tortures him. "You can't swim against the tide of the universe."

He feels no electricity, no pinpricks beneath his skin. Whatever quantum phenomenon that has made his recent trips possible is now spent. This universe, this reality, is finally—*finally*—the last one he will ever know.

And the thought that Amanda is still alive, that she will now mourn a trio of Jonases, is more painful than anything his body has endured.

So Jonas lets go. If there's an afterlife, there's an Amanda there waiting for him. He goes to her.

NOW

Somewhere far away, a child is crying. Jonas is barely cognizant of it and completely unaware that it's really the wail of a siren. He is deaf to the murmur of the crowd, to the commotion of the paramedics as they strap a blood pressure cuff on him and check his airway.

Questions and commands are barked at him. "Sir, can you hear me?"

"Can you look at me, sir?"

"Can you feel that?"

"Can you squeeze my hand?"

The answer to every question is no.

His body moves in response to each of the paramedics' manipulations as though dead. They poke and prod him, needles are produced, veins are punctured, but nothing changes.

Jonas hears someone calling his name from a million miles away. No, not calling—screaming. A woman's desperate voice. Amanda's voice.

If he could open his eyes, Jonas would see her pushing through the throng of onlookers, tears streaming down her face, which is pale with terror. One of the paramedics turns from Jonas to hold her back, but she keeps screaming his name.

One of the cruelties of death is its capacity for delusion, for creating hallucinations of divine perfection as one slips the bonds of life. This, Jonas is convinced, is the reason he's hearing Amanda's cries. "I'm coming, my love," he gasps. "Don't worry. I'm coming."

"I'm here," she replies, and for the first time, it doesn't sound distant. For the first time, he feels hands on his face, sliding over his sweat and tears. "I'm here," the voice repeats with an urgency he can't make sense of.

His mind, always his most reliable asset, fights through a fog of pain, laboring despite lack of oxygen. If the voice belongs to Amanda, if the voice isn't from whichever plane exists after death, if what he's hearing is real, it would mean that of all the universes he fell through, he somehow landed back in the one where Amanda is alive. The odds of such a thing are beyond even Jonas's ability to calculate. The only explanation is that, deprived of blood and oxygen, he's hallucinating, a predeath psychosis.

But her lips feel so real on his. The tears falling from her eyes and onto his face are beyond his capacity to imagine. Her pleas, her desperate cries for him to open his eyes are . . . beyond his ability to ignore.

It feels impossible, the hardest thing he's ever done, but Jonas opens his eyes. And the image he sees is watery, a photograph slowly coming into focus. But he can't deny it. He's looking up at her. Amanda. Crying and smiling. Terrified and relieved. Grieving and joyous. All at the same time.

"I knew you'd find me," she says through tears.

Jonas tries to speak, but the words don't come. It's all he can do to keep breathing, to keep looking at her. To feel the grip of her hand. To see her face. To know that, somehow, he's home.

The crowd is chattering as the paramedics work, and suddenly an entire city reasserts itself. But as Jonas stares up at the woman he loves more than his own life, the two of them are the only two people who exist in the entire world.

In the entire *multiverse*.

TWO DAYS LATER

After the paramedics wheel Jonas into the emergency room, after the doctors mend him as well as they can, after the x-rays and CT scan, and once he is comfortably stoned on painkillers, the inevitable questions come. *How did a dead Nobel laureate wind up in their hospital?* Jonas's first instinct is to answer truthfully. After all, a basic Google search would reveal the work he'd won the Nobel for. If the world was ready for a mathematical proof of the existence of parallel worlds, why not flesh-and-blood proof? The truth would also have the virtue of explaining his eccentric tattoos.

In the end, though, he decides that whatever the world may or may not be ready for, *he* isn't ready to become the focus of its attention. He isn't ready for the avalanche of questions, the assault of media scrutiny, the hurricane of notoriety. He's not willing to succumb to anything that might pull his focus from Amanda.

And so he lies.

He takes care not to embroider the story with too many details. When the limousine capsized, he was thrown from the wreck. He had amnesia. He lived among the homeless. No one thought to look for a Nobel laureate among Switzerland's lost and discarded. In time, he recovered his memories. In time, he made it back home.

He has no explanation for the corpse that was recovered from the wreck, but it's fortunate that this reality's Jonas was cremated. Of course, in time, someone will assemble all the pieces and conclude that they don't fit. Perhaps that someone will review Jonas's Many Worlds Proof and draw the inevitable conclusion. But that is a problem for another day. Maybe it will be a sign that Jonas is finally meant to reveal what he achieved to the world.

In time, he assures himself, he'll think about what to do with his life's work, if anything. The formulae on his arms serve as an ever-present reminder of the enormity of what he invented and brought forth into existence. He didn't set out to change the world, he tells himself, just to repair his own. But having devised the means to travel to nearly infinite worlds, he knows that what he has created could be used to alter the course of humanity, and not just in this reality, but in countless others. The vastness of that possibility, the magnitude of the responsibility, makes his head swim.

As they exit Mount Sinai Hospital, Jonas looks to Amanda, taking comfort in the knowledge that none of these decisions will be his to bear alone.

"What is it?" she asks.

"Nothing." But Amanda indicts that response with a look. She has always seen through him, seen him better than he can see himself. "Well, not nothing," he admits. "But now's not the right time for it. There will be plenty of time later."

"Whatever it is," she says, weighing him with a glance, "it's on your mind."

He sees no point in denying it. "But not in a bad way. Not in the slightest."

"Well, there's something on *my* mind," she says. "I haven't really known how to bring it up."

"That's easy," Jonas shrugs. "Just bring it up."

"It's about Victor," she says.

This reality's Victor died of pancreatic cancer a year and a half ago. The presence of his corpse on West Fifty-Seventh Street presented yet another conundrum. When the doctors pronounced Jonas well enough to answer questions, he told the police he had no idea whom he had landed on. When they asked how he came to fall from such an apparently great height, Jonas claimed short-term memory loss, transient global amnesia, rather than theorize how passing through multiple universes slowed their descent enough to make survival possible.

With Jonas proving either uncooperative or unreliable—the police couldn't be sure which—the NYPD ran Victor's fingerprints without success. A DNA match would be attempted, but it was unlikely to produce results for the same reason that the fingerprint search returned no records. Victor's biometrics weren't in any database; he had never been arrested or otherwise associated with law enforcement in this reality. Eventually, a review of his dental records might produce some perplexing questions but only if Victor's doppelgänger's dental work matched his own. In any case, Jonas has time to consider his responses in the event that the police return to ask him more questions. He sets the odds of that at fifty-fifty. A coin flip.

"What about Victor?" he asks Amanda. In the hospital, he gave Amanda a truncated version of events: he and Victor both devised the means to travel to parallel universes, and Victor, motivated by a perverse sense of cosmic justice, was trying to stop Jonas from reuniting with her. He left out any mention of the demise of her own doppelgänger.

"Well," she ventures, "if there was more than one *you* trying to get back to me . . ." Her voice trails off. During their conversations at Mount Sinai, Amanda understandably struggled to come up with the right words to articulate this strange conundrum. "If there was more than one Jonas trying to reach me, wouldn't it stand to reason that there would be more than one Victor trying to stop him? I mean, you?"

"I don't know," Jonas answers. Apart from the omission of Amanda's ill-fated counterpart, he would never lie to her. "I don't know if there are other Victors out there." He stops walking and takes her hands in his. Not since they exchanged their wedding vows has he spoken to her with such conviction. "What I *do* know is that I found you again. And no one—in any universe—is ever going to take you away from me."

A smile blossoms across Amanda's face. "I can live with that," she says.

"So can I."

"But what about other *you*?" she asks. "There was already one."

In the hospital, Jonas had given a lot of thought to a potential legion of Jonases, each one as set on finding Amanda as he had been. The possibility will always exist. That, after all, was the beauty of the multiverse: its penchant for endless possibility.

"Well, *if* another me were to show up," he says, thinking of what Eva said to him when they discussed the same question, "then it would certainly make for the world's most interesting love triangle."

The thought of Eva surfaces a memory. Jonas digs into his pocket, only now noticing that he happens to be wearing the same pants he wore back at the Spire. He pulls out the Ouroboros patch that Eva sewed for him, cradling it in his fingers, thinking of her. How she risked everything to help him. The feelings she engendered in him. The grief brought on by her dying—twice. The guilt of feeling responsible both times.

"What's this?" Amanda asks, taking the patch. "It looks like my tattoo. And yours, too, I guess."

"A friend of mine made this for me," he says, his voice cracking.

Some instinct pulls his gaze across the street. The sidewalk is choked with tourists and New Yorkers. The steady pulse of Manhattan. Among the throng, Jonas can make out a couple walking arm in arm. A man and a woman. The man wears United States Army Ranger fatigues. Jonas recognizes him from a photograph in a faculty office at Von Braun University. As he walks, the woman rests her head on his shoulder, laughing at whatever it is he just said.

Eva looks happy.

"Is everything okay?" Amanda asks.

"Yes," Jonas says, staring as Eva and the man she loves disappear into the crowd. "Everything is exactly as it should be."

Amanda takes his hand and leads him on. "Let's get you home."

"Sounds good. It's been a while."

As they walk, Jonas looks to the night sky and considers the stars in their multitude. Their light—hundreds, thousands of years old—winks down on him. For each one, he imagines a universe populated with an almost countless congregation of souls. He thinks of their lives and their deaths, their hopes and dreams, their crushing losses and disappointments. Some will die without ever having made a mark upon their world. Others will conjure breathtaking works of art—plays, songs, paintings, poems, symphonies—from nothing. Like Jonas, a select few will give birth to insights that will challenge their very perception of reality. All will experience the exquisite torture, the brutal blessing, of what it means to be human. Each of these lives is its own universe.

Tonight, Jonas and Amanda will return home and try to make another.

ACKNOWLEDGMENTS

Some stories want to be told.

My initial notes for what has evolved to become this novel are dated February 26, 2013. The journey has been a long one, and I've been blessed with the help of many fellow travelers along the way.

Meyash Prabhu was the first to dig into my pile of work, extricate this story, and find it worth pursuing.

Amanda would have been largely absent from the narrative but for the wise counsel of Palak Patel, Elishia Holmes, and Mike DeLuca.

As they have for well over a decade, Cliff Roberts and Wendy Kirk served as both traveling companions and guides, helping me navigate challenging terrain despite the wide variety of accidents and storms and earthquakes the universe threw at me.

My longtime, long-suffering assistant C. M. Landrus—a wonderful and wonderfully talented writer in her own right—was the first reader I imposed on. Her sharp-eyed observations and insights were as invaluable as a simile or metaphor. (Inside joke.)

My former book agent, Erin Malone at WME, also provided much appreciated feedback and encouragement. Anthony Mattero at CAA took up the baton without costing us even a millisecond in the race. (With apologies to C. M. for the metaphor.)

The remarkable Season Kent graciously donated her time and plied her trade as one of the best music supervisors in film and television—and now prose. She's one of the best people I know, and I desperately miss working with her.

∞

Some stories want to be told.

But not all stories want to be published. Finding the right home for this one was challenging and at times seemed impossible. It was during one of those moments when it seemed that this story might not see the light of day that novelist Alex Segura volunteered his advice and assistance. Alex and I are familiar with each other from our respective work in the comic book industry, but his help was practically the equivalent of coming to the aid of a complete stranger. The greatest mitzvahs are those done for people one barely knows, with no potential for reciprocation. Through his generosity of spirit, Alex introduced me to Chantelle Aimée Osman at Lake Union. Chantelle was the first editor to recognize what this book was and, more importantly, what it could be. She is, as she said on our very first phone call, this book's first fan. The gift of her support and encouragement is one I can never adequately repay.

Among the many things Chantelle brought to this project, perhaps the greatest is the involvement of its editor, Jason Kirk. His notes, insights, and line edits elevated every page. He even served as my de facto science adviser. Pairing me with an editor who happens to have more than an armchair understanding of the cosmos is just one example of Chantelle's prodigious brilliance.

Chantelle and Jason, along with eagle-eyed and OCD-in-the-best-possible-of-ways copy editor Megan Westberg and proofreader Jenna Justice, and our sensitivity reader Mary Ruth Govindavari, have all guided me through the unfamiliar waters of prose with patience and grace. If this novel reads as such—and not like the media with which I am more comfortable—it is entirely due to their efforts. I will be forever grateful for everything they've taught me.

In addition, production manager Angela Elson indulged me with similar patience and counsel and, I suspect, was instrumental with Chantelle in affording me a deadline extension when I really needed one.

Finally, *domo arigato gozaimasu* to my friend Kiomyi Fisher, who gamely jumped in at the proverbial last minute to clean up my *osoroshii*—horrendous—Japanese. Any mistakes contained herein are wholly mine.

∞

Some stories want to be told.

The easiest part of telling this one was writing about Jonas's feelings for Amanda. All I had to do was think of my wife, Tara. If Jonas and Amanda's child turns out to be half the person our daughters Lily and Sara are, then Jonas and Amanda are truly blessed indeed. I love the three of you far, far too much. You've made me the luckiest husband and father in any lifetime.

Best,
Marc Guggenheim
Encino, California
August 2023

ABOUT THE AUTHOR

Photo © 2023 Greg Pak

Marc Guggenheim grew up on Long Island, New York, and earned his law degree from Boston University. After over four years in practice, he left law to pursue a career in television.

Today, Guggenheim is an Emmy Award–winning writer who writes for multiple mediums including television, film, video games, comic books, and new media. His work includes projects for such popular franchises as *Percy Jackson*, *Star Wars*, *Call of Duty*, *Star Trek*, and *Planet of the Apes*.

Guggenheim currently lives in Encino, California, with his wife, two daughters, and a small menagerie of pets. Keep up to date on his latest projects with *LegalDispatch*, a weekly newsletter where he shares news and notes about writing, comics, and the entertainment industry, at https://marcguggenheim.substack.com.